THE RED SCARF

Roy Nichols needs to
from losing his motel. The new highway was supposed
to go through, providing plenty of business, but now
it's been delayed. The bank refuses to help, and his
brother turns him down. Desperate and on the way
back home, he catches a ride with a bickering couple
named Vivian and Teece. They start drinking, then
Teece gets spooked, and crashes the car. That's when
Nichols discovers that his travelling companions have
been carrying a briefcase full of cash. Teece appears to
be dead, and Vivian confesses that they have robbed
the mob, and begs him to help her escape. But to do
that, Nichols will have to lie to his wife Bess...to the
cops...and ultimately, to a very dangerous man named
Radan.

A KILLER IS LOOSE

Ex-cop Steve Logan is down on his luck. With a baby
on the way, Logan decides to pawn his last pistol to a
bartender friend. On his way, he rescues a stranger,
Ralph Angers, from being hit by an oncoming bus.
Angers is an eye surgeon and a Korean War vet, and he
has plans to build a hospital in town. Unfortunately, he
is also prepared to kill anyone and everyone who gets
in the way of his plans. So when Angers manages to get
a hold of Logan's Luger, he also drags his rescuer into a
nightmare of murder and insanity. Logan becomes a
hostage to Angers' plans, and there will be no mercy to
anyone who gets in his way.

The Red Scarf
A Killer is Loose

BY GIL BREWER

INTRODUCTION BY PAUL BISHOP

STARK
HOUSE

Stark House Press • Eureka California

THE RED SCARF / A KILLER IS LOOSE

Published by Stark House Press
1315 H Street
Eureka, CA 95501
griffinskye3@sbcglobal.net
www.starkhousepress.com

ISBN-13: 978-1-944520-55-7

Text layout and design by Mark Shepard, SHEPGRAPHICS.COM
Cover design by Jeff Vorzimmer, ¡caliente! design, Austin, Texas
Cover illustration by Ernest Chiriacka.

First Stark House Press Edition: October 2018

GIL BREWER—
THE DARK INVADER
By Paul Bishop

In 1969, I was fifteen-years-old and obsessed with collecting paperback tie-in novels based on my favorite spy and detective shows. Carefully read (so not to crease the spines) tie-in editions of *The Man From U.N.C.L.E.*, *I Spy*, *Mission Impossible*, *The Mod Squad*, *The Rat Patrol*, *Mannix*, *Get Smart*, and others still sit on my bookshelves fifty years later—touchstones from my teen years.

These franchise tie-ins were traditionally written on a *work for hire* basis, which provided a one-time fee to the authors. The writers were often picked for their ability to deliver a quick manuscript turnaround (sometimes in as little as a week), prior tie-in experience, or those in desperate need of a quick payday. They received no royalties for their work—even when a book sold over a million copies, which was not unusual.

Many tie-in novels bore little resemblance to the shows on which they were based as they were frequently contracted to be written prior to the show's television debut—sometimes even before final casting for the characters was decided. The writer might only be given the first draft of a pilot script to work from—a document which would invariably change significantly before the show went into production.

There was a trio of paperback tie-in novels connected to one of my favorite TV shows—*It Takes A Thief* (*The Devil in Davos*, *Mediterranean Caper*, *Appointment in Cairo*). For three seasons on ABC, Robert Wagner starred as Alexander Mundy, a world class cat burglar and jewel thief blackmailed into using his skills for the United States government in order to stay out of prison. As with most tie-in novels, the three *It Takes A Thief* paperbacks were designed with eye-catching glossy covers displaying publicity photos associated with the show.

I will admit these covers were my biggest motivation for collecting TV tie-ins. I was not sufficiently knowledgeable at the time to care who wrote the books. It wouldn't have mattered in the slightest. The only thing I was interested in was collecting the new books and stories connected to my favorite shows. As a result, the importance and history of the author behind the three *It Takes A Thief* tie-ins completely escaped me.

Ten years later, I had transferred my obsession for TV tie-ins to the dark world of noir. While devouring Cain, Woolrich, Goodis, and Thompson, I stumbled across *The Red Scarf*, a noir novel by some guy named Gil Brewer...

Wait...Why was that name familiar?

I perused my bookshelves and there they were—the *It Takes A Thief* tie-in novels all three written by none other than Gil Brewer. I would later understand they were not examples of Brewer at his best—more rough first drafts than finely crafted finished products. They were written between 1968 and 1969. This timing was the most likely reason for their lesser quality, as it was after Brewer had suffered a mental breakdown and while he was in the middle of a slow decline into alcoholism. Brewer continue to ghostwrite novels and churn out salacious hack work (of even more suspect quality) under pseudonyms until the mid-seventies, but the *It Takes A Thief* tie-ins were the last books published under his own name.

While the attributes of Brewer's *It Takes A Thief* ventures were questionable, I quickly found something different in the pages of his novel, *The Red Scarf*. It was something dark, raw, and utterly brilliant. Brewer infused it with anguished prose as terse as Hemingway's as he thrust his protagonists into a twisted plot where the only choices available were bad, worse, and wretched. This was noir at its finest—comparable to any exploration of human darkness before or since.

Brewer's father had written stories for the early air action themed pulp magazines. While Brewer was heir to his father's skills for popular fiction, he was also heir to his father's penchant for the bottle. A high school dropout, Brewer had a checkered history of employment before he enlisted in the Army during WWII. After the war, he settled in with his parents in Florida, where they had relocated from upstate New York.

Florida would provide strong literary fodder for Brewer. The heat, the oppressive, humidity, and the swampy atmosphere made it the perfect setting for stories inhabited by slatternly women and men living on the ragged edges of society.

His parents finally grew tired of his literary affectations (ponderous manuscripts with pretentious titles such as *House of the Potato*), his drinking, and his seduction of a neighbor's wife (whom he would later marry). When his mother tossed him out, Brewer found himself desperate for money. Having no skills and no desire to work in any other occupation, he was compelled to set aside his desire for critical acclaim and write for—*gasp*—money.

He would always perceive this situation as an injustice. In the depths of alcohol soaked delusions, he would fall into deep depression over the failure to achieve his rightful place in the pantheon of *important* writers. Depression led to more drinking, which led to more depression, and the deadly spiral continued. In reality, Brewer was blind to the cold truth. He *was* an exceptional talent. He *was* an important writer. However, his talent and his importance did not lie with the glitterati, but with the common man who devoured popular fiction, and whom he understood on a base level.

In the face of pressing need, Brewer aimed his typewriter at the voracious and well paying market for paperback originals—fast, entertaining reads for the working Joe who wanted a little spice (or what passed for spice in the 1950s) with his fiction. With the help of agent and former *Black Mask* editor Joseph T. Shaw, Brewer sold *Satan Is A Woman* to Gold Medal, seeing it published in 1951. Gold Medal was a genre paperback line created by Fawcett Publications, and the noir address of some of the most revered genre masters of a generation.

He sold two more novels to Gold Medal—*So Rich, So Dead* and *13 French Street*—in quick succession. It was between the covers of these Gold Medal paperback originals where Brewer found the true home for his stripped down, biting prose—one hundred and forty pages of short, uncluttered sentences, featuring sharp dialogue and a blend of equal parts despair, lust, and bad decisions. If Dante had envisioned an eighth level of Hell, it would be populated with characters and situations created by Brewer.

Over the next fifteen years, Brewer wrote thirty-three novels under his own name. Almost all were variations on the theme of an ordinary man led into wanton corruption and to his ultimate destruction by the type of women for whom wolf whistles were invented. Brewer took this base theme and overlaid it with a patina of erotic sleaze, banking on his stated belief that "sex…is the big element we deal with in life every day—the push and pull of human nature."

His third book for Gold Medal, *13 French Street*, gave credence to this assertation. With raw lust fueling the book's squalid sexual focus, it sold over a million copies. While this sales achievement should have been reason for celebration, not everyone was please by the perceived immoral content of the book. Shaw, his agent, asked him not to rely so much on *flesh* and *sex angles*, and his editor—concerned about rumblings from censors and the morals police—insisted Brewer tone down his narratives.

However, despite their editorial disapproval over the subject matter of *13 French Street*, Gold Medal gladly relied on the book's salacious reputation to pimp new titles by Brewer. Even Brewer's last novel for Gold Medal, *Backwoods Teaser*, published in 1960, bore the banner, *By the Author of 13 French Street*.

13 French Street would go into eight printings and numerous *overruns*.

With this burgeoning success, Brewer refused to listen to the voices of caution. After reading the blatant promiscuity Brewer described in the opening to his follow-up novel, *Shadow on the Dust*, Shaw implored him to build the narrative more slowly, so readers would have a chance to develop some sympathy for the nominal hero. Again ignoring the advice, Brewer kept pouring on the sexual heat, only to find the completed manuscript rejected by Gold Medal due to it's plot being *entirely reliant on sex*.

This was a bucket of cold water, which should have shocked Brewer into compliance, but still didn't (or couldn't) get the message. He was obsessed by the demons faced by all noir authors—words, alcohol, and lust. While other writers had the ability to show some restraint, Brewer—in spite of his anguished, paranoid, distributing of blame when inebriated—willingly embraced his demons.

Gold Medal tried to keep a tight hold on Brewer's fiction, but he continued his fixation on sexual enthrallment in titles such as *Hell's Our Destination, 77 Rue Paradis*, and *A Killer Is Loose*. Instead of rejecting the novels based on their supposed contempt of the subject matter, Gold Medal was hypocritically happy to pad their bottom line with the profits from Brewer's lewd take on the human condition.

Chasing cash, Brewer was also slinging words at the short fiction market. It was here, in 4,000 to 10,000 words, where he turned loose sexual themes too indecent (by the morals of the times) for the 60,000 to 70,000 word paperback market. Unlike Gold Medal, the short story crime magazines had no scruples over what they published as long as it sold copies.

Apparently a taste of sin in a short story was acceptable, but a full meal in a novel caused indigestion. However, these stories of window peepers, panty sniffers, gropers, and other sexual fetishes—even short ones—still incensed the official moral censors. Criminal charges of pornography and *sending obscene, lewd, lascivious, filthy, or indecent matter* through the U.S. Mail hellfired down on the editors of cheap digest-sized magazines—such as *Accused, Guilty, Pursuit*, and *Manhunt*—all targeting those types of stories that were Brewer's best work.

His addictions, unsteady work habits, and continued preoccupation with fetish-based stories eventually led to him being dropped by Gold Medal (although he did make it back in to their ranks for a single novel a few years later). His novels spiraled down from the publishing high-rises (Fawcett Gold Medal) to the sidewalk (Crest, Lancer, Berkley) and then the gutter (Monarch, Banner). His short stories only occasionally found favor in *Alfred Hitchcock Mystery Magazine* or *Ellery Queen Mystery Magazine*. More often they found minimal paying homes in *Hustler, Adam*, and even lower scale men's magazines—which were almost always slow to pay what was owed.

Unfortunately, things got worse. A move to California with his wife Valerie left him without access to peer support of any kind. His struggles with alcohol took him away from the typewriter. His mental state was deteriorating. His inability to get the brilliance in his head onto the page resulted in confused and rambling book proposals destined for rejection.

When a serious traffic accident landed him in the hospital, he was not only physically injured, but virtually off the rails mentally. With professional help, he hauled himself back to the lip of the pit. He began writing solid prose again, but during his time away from the typewriter, the market for his stock in trade tales of dark sexuality had virtually dried up. He had traded Valium for alcohol, but the resulting addiction was even worse. He fought his way off the Valium, but took up with alcohol again—his need for addiction never defeated.

Moving back to Florida did not change the situation. With no choices left to him, Brewer gnashed and wailed, but was forced to turn to the lowest forms of hack work to establish any kind of cash flow.

He wrote sex books under a variety of house names, spicy stories for the lesser men's magazines, and gothic tales under the name Elaine Evans. Writing pal Marv Albert paved the way for Brewer to write two entries in the men's adventure series *Soldato*, which were published under Albert's Al Conroy pseudonym. He ghosted tales for Ellery Queen, Hal Ellison, and five novels of the Israeli-Arab war, which bore the name of Harry Arvay, an Israeli soldier. An opportunity to join the ranks of ghosts writing the Executioner series was promising, but fizzled when his work didn't match creator Don Pendleton's vision of the series.

And he wrote the three *It Takes A Thief* novelizations, which still grace my bookshelves.

The alcohol took it inevitable price as even the hack work he desperately needed to survive became scarce. Brewer and Valerie agreed to separate, even though she would continue to support him emotionally and financially. In January 1983, Valerie found him dead in his apartment. It was an ignominious end to the career of a writer whose talent deserved so much more.

The irony, of course, is that within a relatively short time following his death, Brewer's best work began to be recognized. It started with the French, who have always known a good noir when they see it. A French production company bought the rights to *A Killer Is Loose* for a five figure advance, releasing a film version in 1987. *The Red Scarf* was reprinted in both England and France finding a hungry audience. Brewer's short stories were suddenly in demand for prestigious anthologies, which further fueled interest in his work and distinctive style.

The two stories that started the Brewer revival, *The Red Scarf* and *A*

Killer Is Loose, are perfect examples of Brewer's ability to create nerve-wracking hell rides of classic proportions. The sheer frenetic energy of their prose and their pervading sense of impending terror make their selection for this collection a natural pairing.

Originally rejected by Gold Medal and other paperback houses, the hardcover rights for *The Red Scarf* were purchased by a small lending-library imprint for a paltry $300 advance. Perversely, Fawcett, Gold Medal's parent company, overturned the original rejection, buying the paperback reprint rights on the cheap for their Crest imprint, which had a much lower reputation than Gold Medal.

The Red Scarf, however, is the perfect noir, making its odd publishing history unimportant. It was my first true taste of Brewer—*It Takes A Thief* tie-in novels aside—and I devoured it.

Small business owner Roy Nichols and his wife are caught between the razor and the strap. Faced with financial ruin after his brother reneges on a loan, Roy is loath to tell Bess, his sweet wife, they are going to loose the roadside motel into which they have sunk all their cash and dreams.

Desolately hitchhiking home, Roy is the perfect sap. When sexually charged slattern Vivian Rise and her shady boyfriend, Noel Teece, give him a ride, complications—as they say—ensue. Those complications involve a briefcase of illicit cash, a drunken car crash, a gambling syndicate who want their money back, a mob enforcer, and police both corrupt and straight.

As each startling twist unfurls, the cogs and gears of the story interlock smoothly. As the darkness of inevitability presses down, one bad decision follows another, and Roy is dragged deeper and deeper into the quicksand of despair and fear. We want him to save himself and Bess, as we cringe with each rachet of suspense.

Brewer manipulates his plot masterfully. His characterizations of all involved is irreproachable, his prose sharp and controlled, his dialogue as terse and as dry as a twig in the Sahara. You can't stop reading even though you find you have stopped breathing.

Comparatively, *A Killer is Loose* was Brewer's sixth novel. His specialty of trapping his protagonist in a web of terror, paranoia, and dread and empathetically transmitting those feelings to his readers had been honed to the sharpness of a killer's stiletto.

Written in less than two weeks through a haze of cigarettes, coffee, and booze, *A Killer Is Loose* is raw first draft with resultant awkward flashes. However, the sheer immediacy of the narrative connects readers not only to the characters, but unexpectedly attaches them directly to the writer himself. The thin veil between Brewer and those devouring the story is remarkable. It verges on breaking the fourth wall, yet maintains its structure due to the rapid-fire unfolding of events.

With damaged eyesight, a baby literally on the way into the world, a backlog of unpaid bills, and the threat of high hospital fees on the dark horizon, ex-cop Steve Logan is forced to make a hard decision. He elects to pawn his prize Luger to a bartender who handles those types of transactions. On the way, his life goes from tough to terrifying as noirish coincidences and complications descend on him like a fever.

Reactively saving the life of Ralph Angers, a stranger getting off an incoming bus, is the first good intention paving the road to hell. Ralph is quickly revealed to be an eye surgeon living in a world of dangerous delusions. He has no compunction toward killing anyone he perceives as trying to stop him from his fantasy of building a hospital. To prove his point, he snatches Steve's Lugar and wastes no time killing the bartender with the pawnshop sideline.

Here, Brewer excels at his craft as he creates a nightmare of paranoiac proportions—a desperate man and a former stripper (this is a noir after all) caught in unrelenting suspense by a calm, but brutal maniac.

Don't expect to sleep well after reading these splendid tales, which display the power of Gil Brewer—a man out of step with himself in a world too slow to recognize noir genius before the curse of self-destruction took its toll.

—May 2018
North of Los Angeles

A nationally recognized interrogator and expert in deception detection, Paul Bishop spent 35 years with the Los Angeles Police Department where he was twice honored as Detective of the Year. A novelist, screenwriter, and television personality, his fifteen novels include five in his LAPD Homicide Detective Fey Croaker series. His latest novel, *Lie Catchers*, begins a new series featuring top LAPD interrogators Ray Pagan and Calamity Jane Randall...
WWW.PAULBISHOPBOOKS.COM

The Red Scarf
GIL BREWER

ONE

About eight-thirty that night, the driver of the big trailer truck let me out in the middle of nowhere. I had stacked in with a load of furniture all the way from Chicago and I should have slept, too. I couldn't even close my eyes. Brother Albert had turned me down on the loan, and all I could think of was Bess holding the fort in St. Pete, and us standing to lose the motel. How could I tell her my own brother backed down on me? The dream. So the driver said if I could make it to Valdosta, then Route 19, the rest down through Florida would be pie. He gave me what was left of the lunch he'd bought in Macon. I stood there under a beardy-looking oak tree and watched him rumble off, backfiring.

It was raining and snowing at the same time; you know, just hard enough to make it real nasty. The road was rutted with slush, and the wind was like cold hands poking through my topcoat. I had to hang onto my hat. I ate the half piece of chocolate cake he'd left, and the bacon and cheese sandwich. I saved the apple.

A couple of cars roared by, fanning the road slop clear up to my knees. I didn't even have a cigarette. I figured this was as broke and lowdown as I'd ever be.

My feet were already soaked, so I started walking. I came around a sharp curve in the road and crossed a short wooden bridge. Then I saw the sign.

ALF'S BAR-B-Q
Drinks
Sandwiches

The sign was done in blue lights and it kind of hung like a ghost there in the dripping trees. It swung and you could hear it creak. Just the sign, nothing else.

I kept walking, feeling the change in my pocket, thinking about a cup of hot coffee and some smokes and maybe it would stop raining. Or maybe I could hit somebody for a ride.

Then I saw how I wasn't going to hit anybody for any ride. Not here. Not at Alf's. If a car stopped at this place, they'd either be crazy, or worse off than I was. There was this bent-looking shed with a drunken gas pump standing out front in a mess of mud, and Alf's place itself was a sick wreck of an old one-room house, with the front porch ripped off. You could still see the outline of the porch in the dim light from the fly-freckled bulb hanging over the door. Tin and cardboard signs were plastered all over the front of the place.

I went inside, and it was like being hit across the face with the mixed-up smells of all the food Alf's place had served for the past ten years.

"Ho, ho, ho!" a guy said. He was a big, red-faced drunk, parked on an upturned apple crate beside a small potbellied stove. He looked at me, then at the thin man behind the counter. "Ho, ho, ho!"

"You best git on along home." the man behind the counter said to the laughing one. "Come on, Jo-Jo—you got enough of a one on to hold you the rest of this week and half of next."

"Ho, ho, ho!" Jo-Jo said.

I brushed some crumbs off one of the wooden stools by the counter and sat down. Alf's place was a compact fermentation of all the bad wayside lunchrooms on the Eastern seaboard. With some additions. He had a coffee urn, a battered jukebox, two sticky-looking booths, a chipped marble counter, and a greasy stove. The ceiling was low; the stove was hot.

"What'll it be?" the counterman said. "I'm Alf. We got some fine barbecue." His hair was pink and sparse across a freckled skull. He wore a very clean white shirt and freshly ironed white duck trousers.

"Cup of coffee, I guess."

"No barbecue?"

"Nope."

Alf shook his head. I turned and glanced at Jo-Jo. He was wearing overalls with shoulder straps. He was a young, rough, country lush. His eyes had that slitted hard-boiled egg look, his mouth broad and loose and his black hair straight and dank, down over his ears. Combed, it would be one of these duck cuts. He was a really big guy.

I heard a car draw up outside. Jo-Jo took a fifth of whiskey from his back pocket, uncapped it, drank squinting, and put it away. He stood up, stretched, touching his hands to the ceiling, reeled a little and sat down again. "Son of a gun." he said. "Dirty son of a gun."

Alf put the thick mug of coffee on the counter. "Cigarettes?" I said. "Any kind."

He flipped me a pack of Camels. I heard a man and woman arguing outside, their voices rising above the sound of a car's engine. A door slammed. The engine gunned, then shut off.

"Damn it!" a man said outside.

The door opened and this girl walked in. She hesitated a moment, watching Jo-Jo, then she grinned and stepped over toward the counter, letting the door slap.

"Ho, ho, *ho!*" Jo-Jo said. Then he whistled. The girl didn't pay any attention. Jo-Jo looked her up and down, grinning loosely, his eyes like rivets. Then the door opened again and a man came in. He stood staring at the girl's back.

"Viv." he said. "Please, come on, for cripe's sake."

She didn't say anything. She was a long-legged one, all right, with lots of shape, wearing a tight blue flannel dress with bunches of white lace at the throat and cuffs. She was something to see. There were sparkles of rain like diamonds on the dress and in her thick dark hair. She half-sat on the stool next to me, and looked at me sideways with one big brown eye.

"You hear me, Viv?" the man said.

"I'm going to eat something, Noel. That's all there is to it. I'm starved."

"Ho, ho, ho." Jo-Jo said. I heard him uncap the bottle and drink noisily. He coughed, cleared his throat and said, "I reckon your woman wants some barbecue, mister."

The guy breathed heavily, stepped over behind the girl, and just stood there. He was a big-shouldered guy, wearing a double-breasted dark-blue suit, with a zigzag pin stripe. His white shirt was starched. He wore a gray homburg tilted to the left and slightly down on the forehead.

"Come on, Viv." he said. He laid one hand on her right arm. "Please come on, will you?"

"Nuts. I'm hungry, I told you."

She haunched around on the stool and smiled at Alf. "I'll try the barbecue. And some coffee."

"Sure." Alf said. "You won't be sorry."

The guy sighed and sat down on a stool beside her. Alf looked at him, and the guy shook his head.

"You better eat something." the girl said.

The guy looked at her. She turned front again. I could smell whiskey, but it wasn't from Jo-Jo. They'd both been drinking and driving for quite a while. They had that unstretched, half-eyed look that comes from miles and miles on the highway.

I sat there with my coffee and a cigarette, nursing the coffee, waiting. They were headed in the same direction as I was. I'd heard them come in.

After Alf served her a plate of barbecue, with some bread and coffee, the guy spoke up. He'd been sitting there, fuming. "You got gas in that pump outside?"

"Sure." Alf said. "Absolutely we got gas."

"How's about filling her up?"

Alf started around the counter, nodding.

"Now, aren't you glad we stopped?" the girl said. "We won't have to stop later on."

"Just hurry it up." the guy said without looking at her. "Feed your face."

Alf was at the door. "You'll have to drive your car over to the pump." he said.

I looked at him. The guy started toward the door. Jo-Jo was trying to get up off the apple crate. He was grinning like crazy, staring straight at the girl. I looked and she had her skirt up a little over her knees, banging her knees together. You could hear it, like clapping your hands softly.

Neither Alf nor the guy noticed. They went on outside and the door slapped shut. I could feel it; as if everything was getting a little tight. The girl felt it, too, because she paused in her eating and Jo-Jo made it off the apple crate and started across the room.

"Say!" Jo-Jo said. "You're pretty as a pitcher."

She took the mouthful of barbecue and began to chew. Jo-Jo sprawled over against the counter, with his hair hanging down one side of his face, and that bottle sticking out, and he was grinning that way. "Gee!" Jo-Jo said. "Cripes in the foothills!"

I got off my stool and walked around to him. "Come on." I said. "Go back and sit down. You're kind of tight."

He looked at me and gave me a hard shove. I went back across the room and slammed against the wall.

"You?" Jo-Jo said to the girl. He held up two fingers and wrapped them around each other. He had fingers like midget bananas. "Me?" he said.

The girl went on eating. She pulled her skirt down over her knees and chewed.

He reached over and took hold of her arm and pulled her half off the stool toward him, like she was a rag doll.

"Girly." he said. "I could make your soul sing."

I nearly burst out laughing. But it wasn't funny. He was all jammed up.

"You wanna drink?" he asked her.

She was struggling. He got up close to her and started trying to paw her. She had a mouthful of barbecue and he started to kiss her and she let him have it, spraying the barbecue all over his face. He grabbed her off the stool and went to work.

She wasn't doing anything but grunt. He got hold of her skirt and tried to rip it. I was there by then, and I got one hand on his shoulder and turned him and aimed for his chin. It was all in slow motion, and my fist connected. He windmilled back against the counter.

"That dirty ape!" the girl said.

The barbecue was still on his face. When he hit against the counter, the bottle broke. He stood there watching me, with this funny expression on his face and the whiskey running down his leg and puddling on the floor. Then he charged, head down, his hair flopping.

I grabbed his head as he came in, brought it down as I brought my knee up. It made a thick sound. I let him go. He sat down on the floor, came out straight and lay there.

"They grow all kinds, I guess." the girl said. "I sure thank you." she said. "Thanks a lot."

"Forget it."

She kept looking at me. She kind of grinned and lifted one hand and looked at the door. Then she turned and went over to the stool and sat down with her barbecue again.

"What's door opened, and the guy came in. He saw Jo-Jo. What's this?"

"A little trouble." I told him. "It's all right now."

Alf came in and closed the door. He saw Jo-Jo. His face got red. "What happened?"

I told them. The girl was eating again. Then I noticed she stopped and just sat there, staring at her plate. She turned on the stool and looked at the guy. "Pay the man." she said. "Let's get out of here."

I looked at her, then at the guy. I had to nick them for a ride. I had to.

"I'm awfully sorry, miss." Alf said. "He don't really mean no harm. It's just his way."

Nobody said anything. This guy pulled out his wallet and looked at Alf.

"The gas was six, even." Alf said, "The barbecue's a dollar. That's seven. Even."

The guy counted out a five and two ones. He handed the bills to Alf and Alf took them and stood there with them hanging limply from his hand. Jo-Jo moved and groaned on the floor.

"Come on." the guy said to the girl.

"Listen." I said to him. "How's chances for a lift? I'm going the same way you are. South. There's no—"

"No dice. Come on, Viv."

I looked at her. She looked at me. "Oh, let's give him a lift." she said. "It's all right, Noel."

He gave her a real bad look. "No."

She bent a little at the waist and brushed at some crumbs. She looked at the guy again. Then she looked at me and winked. "Come on." she said to me. "We'll take you as far as we can."

"Thanks." I said. "I really—"

"You heard me, Viv." the guy said. "I told you, no!"

I figured, the hell. If I could get the ride, that's all I cared about. I didn't care about what the guy wanted. Then I saw the way his face was.

"He helped me out." she said. "You heard him say what happened, Noel. That dirty ape would have done anything. Suppose this man hadn't been here? What would I have done?"

"Ho, ho, ho." Jo-Jo said. He was lying flat out on his back, staring at the ceiling.

I looked at the guy and he looked at me.

"All right." he said. "Damn it."
The girl took my arm and we moved toward the door.

It was a Lincoln sedan. The guy, Noel, walked ahead of us, his feet splatting in the mud. He got in under the wheel and slammed his door.
"Don't pay any attention." the girl said. "We maybe can't take you far. But it'll help, anyway. In this weather."
"Anything'll help, believe me."
She opened the door before I could reach it. She climbed in. I closed the door and opened the rear door.
"Get in front." the guy said.
She pushed the front door open and I slammed the rear door and got in. She jigged over a little and I slammed the front door and we were off like a bull at a flag.
We struck the highway, slid a little, straightened out. "Noel." the girl said. "Stop the car again."
I looked at her. She sure was a pip.
"What?"
"I said, 'stop the car.' So he can take off his hat and coat. He's all wet."
The car slowed and came to a stop. The windows were closed, heater on, and you could smell the stale cigarette smoke. I remembered my cigarettes back there on the counter at Alf's.
"Throw 'em in back." she said. "Okay?"
I opened the door and stepped out into the night and took them off and tossed them in back, beside a couple of suitcases and a brief case on the seat. Then I got in and this time she didn't shove away. In fact, she looked at me and smiled and snuggled down comfortable.
"Is it all right now?" the guy said, real evil. She didn't say anything.
He popped it to the floor and we roared off.
I sat there without saying anything for about a mile. Just waiting. It wasn't just the cigarette smoke in this car, or the hot air from the heater, either. You could taste the trouble that had been going on between these two.
"I hope you're happy now, Noel."
"That's enough."
"Just remember what I said."
"I told you, Vivian!" He let it come out between his teeth. Not loud; just hard. "That's enough. You hear?"
She sniffed. "Just remember."
He tromped and he tromped. The car bucked and leveled off at eighty-three. We were flying. There wasn't much wind, but you could see that rain and snow whipping up out there.
"Thanks for the lift." I said. "It's a rotten night. Not many'd stop on the

highway tonight. Any night."

"One good turn deserves another." she said, grinning.

You could almost hear him grit his teeth. He was really hanging onto that wheel. I turned and looked at her, putting one arm across the back of the seat. She tipped her head, freeing a good lot of the thick dark hair where my arm squeezed. In the dash lights, there was a sheen on her long slim legs. She looked at me then, with one big brown eye. Then she began watching the road.

You could smell the whiskey in the car. It seemed to have impregnated the upholstery.

"Going far?" the man said.

"Down the coast. St. Pete."

He breathed heavily, hulked over the steering wheel. I couldn't watch him very well without stretching. He made me nervous.

She laid one hand on my knee. "Honey. You got a cigarette?"

"There's a carton in the back seat, Vivian. You know that."

She patted my knee. "You know? I'm glad you're with us. Least, Noel's not cursing."

"I'll curse."

She hitched up and turned and got on her knees on the seat, pawing back there. The dash lights were bright. I looked away.

"On the floor, stupid."

She came up with the carton and a bottle, turned and sat on my lap, slid off onto the seat and smiled at me again with that one big brown eye. "Bet you haven't got a cigarette?"

I told her she was right.

She ripped open the carton and handed me a pack. "Care for a drink?"

"Damn it, Vivian."

She parked the fifth on my knee. I took it.

"All right." the guy said. "All right."

We drove along for a while, swapping the bottle. I was hitting it hard. She took enough, too. The guy, Noel, was just touching it now and then.

The whiskey got to me good. But I sat there, propped up, smoking cigarettes and letting the night stretch out. Thinking about Bess. She was a good wife, a wonderful girl. And my brother Albert was a twenty-four carat stinker.

Everything was sour inside me. He knew he would have got the money back, if he made the loan. I never welched yet. Knowing Albert, I should never have tried going clear to Chicago to ask him, figuring a personal talk might be better than a long-distance call.

"Roy." he says. "You must learn to hoe your own row. I'd gladly help you if I thought it would really be helping you. But you seem to have forgotten that I warned you not to attempt this foolish motel business."

And Bess down home, maybe even praying. Because if the highway didn't come through by our place, as planned, we were sunk.

And that guy, Potter, at the bank. Hovering behind his desk in a kind of fat gray security. And the way his glasses glinted when he looked at me, "We're sorry, Mister Nichols, but there's nothing we can do. We've given you one extension, and you're behind again. Another extension would only make matters worse for you in the long run. And as far as another loan of any kind is concerned, you must see the impossibility of that. You've got to make the effort to clear up your debt and meet future payments. The government stands behind you only so far, Nichols. You must do your share."

"You don't understand, Mister Potter. Everything we own is in that motel!"

"We understand perfectly. We handled your government loan. But remember, when you went into this motel business, we all were assured the new highway would come past your place of business. It seemed a safe risk. Now it's all changed. They've suspended construction, pending the settlement on a new route. And that." he shook his head, glasses glinting, "put us all in a bad spot, indeed."

"But you—"

"We have no choice, Nichols. Place yourself in our position. You're extended far beyond your means now. Either you settle to the date, or we'll be forced to—well, foreclose, to put it plainly. If I were you, I'd make every effort, Mister Nichols—every effort."

"But the highway may still come through."

"But when? *When?* And we can't take that risk, don't you see? Suppose you're granted a year's extension? And suppose it *doesn't* come through? What then?" The gentle pause, the clasped hands, the dull gleam of a fat gold ring. "Surely, you must comprehend. See, here—if we make a loan to you, and you can't pay it—and there's every indication you won't be able to—what then? You'd be worse off than you are now. You'd lose your business, your investment—not only that, you'd have our personal loan to pay. And no way *to* pay. Of course, we could never make that loan. Never. I'm sorry, Mister Nichols. Very sorry, indeed."

"My name's Vivian. Vivian Rise. This is Noel—"

"Enough, Viv. Snow's letting up. Just rain, now."

"Teece. That's his last name. Isn't that a real sparkler?"

I told her my name. "Pleased to meet you."

"We're going South."

"A good time for it. How far you going?"

I glanced down and he had his hand gripped on her thigh, giving her a
hell of a horse bite. She tried to stand it. But he kept right on till you could
see tears in her eyes, and she was panting with the pain....

"Have some more." he said sarcastically. "There's another bottle back
there."

"Sure."

I was floating. I sat there, riding up and down with the bumps, with my
eyes half-closed. Trying not to remember Bess, waiting there, running up
to me when I got home, her eyes all bright, saying, "Did you get it? Did
you get it?"

I held the bottle up and let it trickle down, warm.

"It's hard drinking it like that. We should have some chasers. Noel, why
not stop and let us get some chasers?"

"Crazy? We've wasted time already."

"I mean it, Noel. Noel—!"

Then he said, "My God!"

"What's the matter, Noel?"

We were on the outskirts of Valdosta, passing a brightly lighted
restaurant. A gray Cadillac was parked outside, and a man leaned against
the trunk, watching the road. As we passed, he straightened up and ran
around the car.

Teece didn't answer the girl. He just stomped on the gas and we lit out.
Nobody said anything. It was still raining, but not much snow. The road
leaped around in the headlights.

We came through Valdosta kind of like an aimless, runaway horse. I
caught on how he was watching the rearview mirror. He wheeled the
Lincoln around onto 31, and I could feel how tense she was.

"Noel—this isn't the right road."

"It's the right road now."

The whiskey was deep down in me. My head just didn't care. It was
warm and she was warm and I had a cigarette. I knew something was
wrong. These two weren't just tourists. *They* were wrong, but it didn't
matter, because I was lucky to have the ride. Just Bess, waiting, with me
coming toward her like a kind of crazy bumble bee.

"God, Viv!"

"Maybe we were wrong. It's probably nothing."

I let my head buzz against the window, feeling the speed, watching it out
there, streaming by the window, black and gleaming and wet.

They were whispering. "He's back there."

"Well, lose him then."

"Damn it, Viv. It's your fault *he's* with us."

"Anything the matter?" I said.

I cramped up on the edge of the seat, the way we were flying now. The needle was past a hundred.

He was hunched up over the wheel, breathing hard. I was still fastened onto the bottle. They weren't paying any attention to me now.

"I've lost him. Now to keep him lost till we can get on another road."

"Noel. Do you really think—?"

"Think? I *know*."

We came around this curve. The road was humped to begin with. There were a lot of trees out there and it wasn't raining hard. Just misting.

We hit the curve and it was a blind one. It turned inside out. He spun the wheel this way and that, riding the brakes. We just kept going, as easy as you please, right off the road, over treetops, and down. Nobody said a word. We hit and flew like a bad landing and started to roll. Up and over, up and over.

Glass shattered. Steel crunched and grated.

We really went.

TWO

Water splashed and gurgled somewhere. There was an odor of fresh earth and grass and wet leaves.

"Noel?" I heard her say that. Then it was still again. I knew I was on the ground and half of me was in running water. I couldn't move.

"Noel?"

Then a long silence. I went away for a time, then slowly came back again.

"No-o-*eeeel!*"

Somebody was thrashing around. It sounded like a giant with boots on, wading in a crisp brush pile. The rain had stopped. There was a moon now, shedding white on pale trees and hillside as I opened my eyes. I tried to see the road. It was hidden. I didn't dare move. We were in some sort of a gully. I lifted an arm. I turned my head. It hurt.

Something stabbed cruelly into my back. I turned, rolling away from the icy water. I was soaked. I was lying on a car door. There was no sign of the car, the girl, or the man.

Only her voice, some distance away. "Noel."

Shivering, I closed my eyes tight, remembering Bess like a kind of sob. Remembering all of it. And then this crazy ride with these two crazy people. Fear washed through me, and I lay there, listening, scared to stand up and look.

Finally I got to my knees. I seemed to be all right. My neck hurt, and my right arm. I glanced at my hand, and saw the blood. I flexed my fingers.

They worked.

I moved my shoulders. They hurt, too. When I put weight on my right knee, something stabbed me in the ankle. In the moonlight, I saw the big sliver of glass sticking into my ankle, through the sock. It was like a knife blade, only much broader.

I yanked it out. It hurt and the blood was warm, running into my shoe. I moved my foot and it was all right. It hadn't cut anything that counted. It would have to stop bleeding by itself. My teeth were all there and I could see and hear and move everything.

Except the little finger on my left hand. That was broken and if I touched it, it was bad.

"Mister Nichols?"

I didn't say anything. I got on my knees again, looking around, trying to find the car. Her voice had come from some distance away. Somebody kept thrashing in the brush.

A suitcase and what looked like my topcoat were lying near the door. I looked at the door and it had been torn neatly from the body. Then I saw the other suitcase and I started to get up and saw the brief case.

I kept on looking at that. The clasp was torn open and some kind of wispy scarf was tied to the handle. Only that wasn't what made me look.

It was the neatly bound packets of unmistakable money. I touched them, picked one up and saw the thousand-dollar bill, and put it down.

It was like being hit over the head.

"Mister Nichols?"

I started laughing. Maybe it was the whiskey. I needed money; not a whole lot, compared to this. But plenty for me. And right here was all the money in the world.

"Are you hurt bad?" I asked.

"No. Only my knee. See?"

"Where'd all the blood come from?"

"I don't know. My hand's cut—look at my dress. It's ripped to pieces." She began to look kind of funny.

"Are you all right?"

"What'll we do?" She started away. I caught her and held her. She fought for a minute, then stopped.

"Now, for gosh sakes. You're all right."

She turned and ran in the other direction. Her dress sure was a mess. She stumbled in circles all around between the trees. I got it then. She was looking for that brief case. She ran into the open by the stream where I had been. She splashed into the water and out and jumped over the car door.

I went on over there and held her again. "You're all right. Now, where is he?"

"Down there. Over the edge. He's dead. I saw him.… No. Don't go down there."

She ripped away from me. She had seen the brief case. She went to it, landing on her knees, kind of looking back at me over her shoulder, her hair flopping around.

She shoveled that money back in. The clasp wouldn't work. She got the scarf off the handle and wrapped the scarf around the case and tied it tight.

I went over and dragged her up. She held the brief case, pulling away from me.

"Where is he?"

She pointed in the direction of a bent pine sapling. I turned and walked over there, the blood squashing in my shoe. I came past the pine tree and saw skid marks.

I stopped at the abrupt edge just in time. The car was down there. Not too far, about fifteen feet, lying crumpled on its side, smashed to junk, in a rocky glen with the water splashing and sparkling in the moonlight.

The guy was spread out on the rocks, his feet jammed in the car by the steering wheel. The bright moonlight showed blood all over his face and his suitcoat was gone and his left arm had two elbows. He was more than just dead. He was a mess.

"We'd better get an ambulance."

She hurried over by me and I got a good look at her face. I never saw anybody so scared in all my life. "He's dead. What good would an ambulance do? Come on—we've got to get out of here."

I looked at her and I thought about that money and I knew she was working something; trying to. She turned and walked away from me toward the wooded hill and the road.

A car went by up there and for an instant she was silhouetted against the headlights' glare through the trees. She looked back at me, then slipped and sat down.

I went over to her. She'd lost her shoes and her stockinged feet were muddy. She looked bad. "Don't you see?" she said. "We've got to get out of here."

She tried to get up. I put my hand on top of her head and held her down. "Whose money?"

"Mine. It's my money."

"Awful lot of money for one woman to have. What about *him?*"

"Never mind about him. It's my money, and we've got to get out of here before they find us."

"Thought you said that money was yours."

"It is."

I held her down with my hand on top of her head. She was so mad, and scared too, you could feel it busting right up out of the top of her skull.

These crazy people. All that money. And Bess and me only needing a little. I wanted to crunch her head like a melon.

I was still bleary from the whiskey and my head was beginning to ache bad. But there was something else in my head besides the ache. I kept trying to ignore it.

"It's taken two and a half years to get that money. We've got to get away from here. Nichols, whatever your name is, you've got to help me."

"We'll have to get the police."

She tugged her head away from my hand and stood up. She was still hanging onto that brief case. She grabbed my arm with her other hand. There was a streak of blood down the side of her cheek.

"It's stolen money, isn't it?"

"No. And we can't go to the police." She began to rock back and forth, trying to rock me with her, trying to make me understand something. Only she didn't want to tell me about it. "We're up the creek, Nichols."

I kept trying to figure her. It looked like she was in a real mess.

I tried not to want any part of this. I started away from her. She came after me.

"Please—listen!"

"You're not telling me a damned thing. Look, you two picked me up and fed me whiskey. I shouldn't have taken it. But I got my troubles, too. They're big troubles to me. So now look what's happened. I'm still drunk and I don't even know you. And back there. Your boy friend's dead. How about that? I'm getting out of here."

"Don't you see? If you hadn't seen the money—then you'd have helped me."

"We'd go to the police. Like anybody else. You got to report an accident like this. There's a dead man down there. Don't you realize that?"

"He doesn't matter."

"Somebody was following you, weren't they? We saw somebody in Valdosta and you'd just turned off the main southern route, too. Only you turned back, and we were followed. That's why this happened."

She looked as if she might cry. Well, why didn't I call the police then? Why didn't I do what I should have?

"They'll be back."

"You stole that money."

"You're wrong, Nichols. You've got to believe me." She stood perfectly still and got her voice very calm and steady. "It won't hurt you to help me. If you knew who Noel was, you'd understand that it doesn't matter about him being dead."

There was one thing: Her fear was real.

"We'll take the suitcases and get out of here. Down the road somewhere. Change clothes. His clothes'll fit you."

"Oh, no."

"But you can't go any place the way you are. Look at you. Mud—blood. Neither can I. We'll clean up and get dressed. Then we'll find the nearest town and you can help me get a hotel room."

"Lady, you're nuts."

She dropped the brief case then, and faced me. She put both hands on my arms and looked me in the eye. Straight.

"Nichols." she said, "there's absolutely no other way. He'd dead down there and I'm all alone. I'll bet you can use some money. I've got plenty and I'll pay you well. If you don't help me, they'll find me."

"Let them. This is too much for me."

And I wanted it to be too much. But the sight of that money was like catching cold and knowing it would turn into pneumonia. If only that guy had lived, then I'd have an excuse.

We stood there and the moonlight was bright on her face. Her dress was all torn, her hair mussed up, and there was this streak of blood on her cheek. There was something about it. It got me a little. She looked so damned alone and afraid, her eyes big and pleading. And there she stood, hanging onto that brief case, like that.

THREE

Well, near the edge of the town, there was this big billboard beside the concrete. It was at the bottom of a shallow slope, across a small creek. We were walking tenderly, me with the blood drying in my sock. And Vivian in her stocking feet, on tiptoe. A car passed us, but by that time we were behind the billboard out of sight.

She took off her dress. "Turn your back, Nichols." she said, "and get some clothes out of his suitcase. We've got to get away from here. Hurry!"

I was afraid if I sat down I'd never get up. I staggered around, having trouble with the one sock. Finally when I yanked at it, it peeled like adhesive, but was stiff as cardboard. There was quite a hole where the glass had stuck in, and it was bleeding again. The hell with it. Only that was the whiskey still talking.

After she got through, I scrubbed off the blood and mud. My ankle kept bleeding. I fumbled in the suitcase and found a handkerchief and tied it around my ankle.

I kept glancing over there at that brief case. "I'll help you find a room.

That much."

Still trying to convince myself. I got dressed in his clothes, transferred my wallet and stuff and put my coat and hat on again.

She bundled the old clothes together and walked away into the trees. When she came back, she didn't have them. Her movements were still jerky. You could tell by the way she moved and looked that she was living in a pool of fright.

"No kidding, where'd you get that money?"

"It's mine."

We closed the suitcases.

She picked up the brief case and started out around the billboard. Then she glanced back. The moonlight was on her—fur jacket, long black hair, high heels and scared.

"All right." I grabbed the two suitcases, forgetting about my pinky. It hurt like hell. I went on after her, dressed in a dead man's clothes.

I kept trying hard not to think of what Bess would think of this business. It wasn't much good. Then I looked at that brief case in Vivian's hand again. "You'll have to take one of these suitcases."

"Why?"

"Because my finger's busted, that's why. I can't handle the both of them."

She took hers and went on. I didn't want all that money. Just a part of it. Her heels rapped real loud on the asphalt. She had a long stride and she walked with her chin up.

On the road we kind of half-ran, half-walked. She kept looking behind us, and trying to see ahead. She had me as nervous as herself.

She was taking some kind of big chance.

So was I. But she knew what it was, what the odds were. I was playing it blind.

There was more to the town than I'd figured, but it still wasn't much. All the houses were asleep and her heels made terrific echoes in the still cold.

A car came down the main drag and she gave me a shove into a store front. I listened to her breathe, with her face pressed right up to mine. It was kids in the car, with the radio blaring.

"Off the main street, Nichols."

We turned away from the car tracks. There was a hotel down there with a rusty-looking marquee and white bulbs saying: *Hotel Ambassador.* Three bulbs in the "D" were smashed. She stopped under the marquee and faced me. "You can't just leave me."

"Why can't I?"

"You've come this far. It's not going to hurt you."

I looked at her, saying nothing.

"Is it, Nichols? How could it?"

The wind blew down the street, dusting along the curb, blowing newspapers and small trash past the hotel. "Look, Nichols. You can't imagine the jam I'm in."

"That's any reason why I should be in it with you?"

"I'm not asking that."

I looked down at the brief case, then remembered what she'd said about paying me. "I was just on my way home." I said.

"I know that. St. Pete, wasn't it? Well, you can't start home now, anyway, Nichols. You're tired. I'm not asking a whole lot. I can't do it myself. You'll have to help me. I've got to get out of the country."

"Honest to God, you sound crazy."

"That's the way it is. I'll pay for it. I'm not asking you to do it for nothing."

"I've already—"

"That's what I mean. Listen, I'm so scared that it's all I can do to walk. If I told you, you'd understand."

"I don't want to know."

"But I've got to tell you."

We stood there, and the accident and the dead guy sat there in the back of my mind. I'd already come this far, and it was a long way.

Her knuckles were white, she was holding the brief case that tight. The wind started to blow in her hair. She set her suitcase down and lifted her hand and brushed some hair off her cheek. She was an absolute knockout.

"Well?"

FOUR

It had to be one room. When I said something about getting separate rooms, you could see the fear bubbling up inside her like acid. She wouldn't leave me for a second.

I felt pretty bad. I needed a drink and I was sick. Only there wasn't any chance of getting a drink, and I kept thinking more and more all of a sudden, about that dead guy back there in the gully, bloody and broken.

"I'll pay you well, Nichols."

"Get off it, will you?"

So we were Mr. and Mrs. Ed Latimer on the register. I couldn't see as it mattered much. The clerk yawned and blinked and tossed me the keys and said, "Two-oh-two."

But when we went up the stairs, I glanced back and he was watching her legs from under his hand.

It sure was a dingy place.

She sat on the bed and said, "Cripes!"

I didn't say anything. There was the bed, a straight-backed chair, a paint-peeling, battle-scarred bureau with an empty water pitcher, and a pencil on the bare top. There were brown curtains on the window, and the walls were painted blue. There was one lamp by the bed with a frothy pink shade, and the bathroom looked older than the hotel.

She sat there on the bed and I stood by the closed door and it was cold. Finally she got up and went over and peeked out the window, around the shade, and turned with her hands clasped together like she was praying.

"They won't find me here. Not only one night." She looked at me, then she took off her fur jacket and hung it in the closet. She opened her suitcase and said, "Here." She had a bottle. "It didn't break." she said. "Noel always had a lot of bottles."

"Get off him."

"He might even have another in his bag, there."

Something came up in me. It was like fighting, and you get in a good punch. This punch was aimed at that something inside me. I hadn't been able to level off. But now I had a flash of that old white logic.

I turned and went over to the door and opened it. "The hell with this. I'm taking off."

I walked out and closed the door and started down the hall. The door opened and her heels rattled down the hall after me. "Nichols!"

"No."

She grabbed my arm. I dragged her a couple of steps and stopped.

"It's my money. I'm afraid."

"You're lying like hell. You expect me to believe something like that?"

"Make it business, then—let's say I hired you."

"Let go."

We were standing next to a door. The door opened and a guy stuck his head out and stared at us. "Will you two please shut up?"

We went back into the room and I stood by the door, holding it open, and looked at that brief case leaning against the night table. She had the bottle. The scarf she'd tied around the brief case was red, bright red.

She began to look as if she'd fall to pieces. It was all jammed up inside her and she didn't know what to do. Then she set the bottle on the bureau. There was a woolen blanket folded at the foot of the bed. She took it out and spread it and opened the bed.

"I'm freezing, Nichols."

I went and sat in the chair and looked at the bottle. Then I took it and opened it and had a long drink.

I looked at her and she was standing there in the middle of the room, staring at the wall. She had her hands together like that. She kept staring, lost.

The color of the dress she'd put on was taffy. Some sort of soft material. It stuck to her. She had a lot of chin, too, and a broad soft mouth and these great big frightened eyes.

"You're going to tell me, lady. Who was it following us? What's it all about?"

"I'd better have some of that, Nichols."

She took a sip out of the bottle, and I went over and closed the door and took off my coat and hat. She sat down on the edge of the bed and stared at the floor. I could see her getting ready to lie again. Then she crossed her legs and leaned back on her elbows. She cleared her throat, and I looked at that brief case again.

"So Noel was my boy friend. You can call it that. I've known him for three years. He took money down this way every two months."

"Why?"

"The people—the people he worked for."

"Yeah. But who?"

"Well." She folded her fingers together and bent her hands back and swallowed. I took a drink, watching her. As she watched me, her eyes kind of hazed over with thinking, Can I get away with a lie? And then her eyes cleared, and she wasn't going to lie. You could see that little bit of relief in her, too. And I couldn't get that money out of my mind. She cleared her throat again. "Well." she said, "Noel, he worked for the syndicate. He was a courier." She paused. "My God." she said, "the things that can happen!"

"Go on."

"I don't care. Anyway, they had him making runs through the South. The syndicate runs gambling places in the South, see? It's a very carefully controlled business. For instance, there's a place in Baltimore, and Atlanta, too. Well, every two months it was Noel's job to make the run with working capital. He carried cancelled checks, papers, notifications of change, stuff like that. Sometimes he'd pick up a part of the take, sometimes not. He never really knew what would happen till he reached each place."

I watched her, listening, and not liking it.

She said, "So I thought of how Noel and I could get this money. He would carry quite a pile on these trips, only they always watched him, tailed him. He never knew where, either. Listen, I was never mixed up in it. I just wanted to get him clear of them."

"Sure."

"It's nobody's money that'll do any hurt. I mean, it's not stealing. Not like—" She stopped.

I took another drink. She was tight. I don't mean drunk, I mean scared, all tied up inside; frozen. You could feel it and she kept swallowing as she talked. The whiskey was reaching me, though.

I kept feeling lower all the time. I kept remembering Bess, and her wondering where I was. This was five days now. Tomorrow would be six. Damn that Albert!

She began to tremble. "Noel said he'd maybe try it. All right. So when they got so they trusted him, then we'd take the money and leave the country together. So every trip, he'd watch how they kept track of him. And we wanted a trip where he skipped the Baltimore and Atlanta places, see? One straight through. And this was it, this one. Only they must have caught on—there in Valdosta. We were going to New Orleans, along the coast and Noel made the wrong turn and one of them was waiting for that. Noel turned back, all right, but it was too late and he knew it. You couldn't explain it, see? And with you in the car, too? And then, he made the run, and that was the worst, when Noel panicked. So that's who was following us.

"Listen, they won't stop at anything now. You can't just give them back the money. It's too late for that. It's too late for the stop at Tampa. That's where he was supposed to go, and me with him. I wasn't supposed to be with him. It's too late for anything, but getting away." She paused, looking at me, bent over a little, her eyes wide and bright. "I've got to get away." She shook her head. "You can't possibly understand. But right this minute, they're hunting. It's a lot of money. It was always in cash, see? It had to be that way for them, and Noel was a trusted courier. God, maybe they've missed the car, the wreck. So that'll slow them down. But they're hunting. And they know how to hunt. They'll kill me."

Maybe some of it was lies. But basically it was the truth, because you could see it all through her.

"Noel wanted to back out, but I kept at him. It's my fault. We'd been arguing in the car when we stopped at that place. That's half why he let you come along, I think, to—to shut me up. We were going right on to New Orleans."

She didn't say anything for a time. I took another long one from the bottle and glanced at the brief case.

"A lot of money?"

"A terrible lot. But they've got crazy ethics. A thing like this is unpardonable. It's like any business—except you know what they do to somebody who crosses them? You know what they do to a woman who crosses them?" She looked away, her face pale and expressionless. Then she looked at me again. "But I've got that money and I'm keeping it. It took two and a half years to get this far."

"Not very damned far, huh?"

She put both hands against her face and turned around.

I looked at her back and I knew just why I was sticking here. It was the money, all the way. I'd seen it, and I couldn't get it out of my head. Bess and I needed money so damned bad, and there it was right by my foot, leaning against the night table.

It was crazy, maybe. She was crazy to think she could get away with it. And telling me all this, but she had nobody to turn to. In the back of my mind I began to know I was going to help her. It didn't really matter where she got that money.

I got up and went into the bathroom and found a glass. I washed the glass and filled it with water and came back and sat down in the chair again. I was drunk. I drank some of the water. It tasted like dust.

"If you're lying—I'll quit on you."

She just looked at me.

"I been a bum. Before I met Bess. She's my wife."

She didn't move. She was thinking.

"That's right. I was in the Merchant Marine, and the war. I been around enough to know. You think I don't read you?"

"You can get a car in the morning. I'll give you the money, so you can buy a car."

"I met Bess in New Mexico, where her folks lived. A little town. We had that thing and we got married without a cent. I worked in a gas station and we bought a trailer, and I got hold of some dough and we bought a house. We sold the trailer. Then I couldn't make it again, so we sold the house and bought a car and came to Florida. I worked the shrimpers. We saved a lot. Then I heard of this thing."

I was drunk and running off at the mouth. I couldn't stop. I felt sad. I was trying to convince myself out loud that this was the thing to do. It was crazy, all right. But it was happening.

"So finally I got a line on this place, a motel. Somebody'd built it in the wrong place and went broke. Then news got around they were going to put a new highway through. It's coming right through in front of the motel. Twenty apartments. Bedroom, living room, kitchen and bath. Real nice.

"So I'd never used my G.I. loan, see? So it was tough, but I got that and right along in there Bess's old man died. He left her quite a bit. We used it all. I went into hock all around. We managed to get this place. We met the down payment. It's nice. We're happy. No money, but happy. Then payments begin to come due."

"Mmm."

"We just manage, sweating out the highway. They began work, see? Then we don't manage and I had to start stalling. I got an extension from the bank, all right. But then that time went. I tried to get a job. I couldn't find one that would pay enough." I took a long drink. "So they suspended work on the highway." I told her about the bank refusing a personal loan; how it was.

"Why are you telling me all this?"

"Just want you to know."

"You don't know what trouble is, Nichols.... Well, go ahead. Finish."

"Well." I said, "this highway will sure be something, if it does come through. We're right on it. We'll get the business. From the North, straight through to Miami. They started work, sure. Only the 'dozers sit out there and the tar vats, and nobody's working. Nothing happens, because that damned commissioner wants a different route. Meantime, if I don't have the money, we lose the place. We lose the place—I'm done."

She leaned over and pushed her plump lips to my ear and said, "Nichols."

"So I went up to Chicago." I told her about Albert.

"Tomorrow I'll give you enough for the car. We'll drive on down. Then you can see about plane tickets. Or a boat, or something so I can get out. I'll pay you well, Nichols."

The bottle was empty. I dropped it on the floor.

She reached over and put her palm against my face and turned my head. We looked at each other.

I slumped back in the chair and watched her.

She took her suitcase and went into the bathroom and when she came out I was still sitting there. She set her suitcase down and opened the other one. She was wearing a red polka-dot negligee. She found the bottle she'd mentioned and set it on the night stand and turned the light off. Then she moved by me to the window and raised the shade and opened the window. A cold wind yawned into the room. She went back and got into the bed. The sign from the hotel outside lit up the room.

I got up and took the bottle and returned to the chair. I opened it and had a drink. Then I got the glass of water and drank some and set it on the bureau. I sat in the chair with the bottle and watched her.

"You'll freeze."

"You wouldn't understand."

"The bed's warm."

I took a drink and set the bottle on the bureau and fell off the chair. I got up on the chair again and watched her.

"Nichols?"

"What?"

"You can't sit there all night!"

"Shut up."

Then she was standing by me, pulling at my arm. I stood up and fell flat on my face. The floor was grimy and there was no rug....

In the morning I was hung over bad, and plenty sick. She gave me the money and I went out and found a car. I wasn't thinking yet. I couldn't think.

It was a good car. It was a Ford sedan and it hadn't taken more than a half-hour to get the papers changed. The used-car dealer took them to the courthouse himself, while I waited on the lot.

He came back, smiling through the flaps of his jacket collar, turned up against the cold. He was a tall guy with bloodshot eyes and he was happy over the sale.

"You've got a good car." he said. "A good car."

"Thanks."

"Boy!" he said. "Everybody's running out to the other end of town this morning. Big wreck out there. Police are going out there now, I reckon. Maybe I'll run out there. Somebody spotted a smashed-up Lincoln out there. Sailed right over the damned pine trees."

"Oh. Anybody—? They find anybody?"

"I don't know. I'm going to run out there."

So I looked at him, and it was like something clicked inside my head. Maybe it was just the cold morning. But I suddenly didn't want any part of this. It scared the hell out of me, just standing there. I'd gone too far, and I wanted to get home to Bess. Money or no money.

I took the papers he'd given me and put them in the glove compartment of the car. Then I turned to him again.

"Look," I said. "Do me a favor?"

"Sure."

"You got an envelope?"

He went into the little office and came out with an envelope, frowning. I turned away and took what money there was left and put it in there and sealed it and handed it to him.

"Do me a favor." I said. "Take this, and the car. Drive the car over to the Ambassador Hotel, all right? Leave the envelope at the desk for Mrs. Ed Latimer. Got that?"

"Yes. Sure, but—"

"Better yet. Take it up to room two-oh-two, see? The envelope, of course, with the car keys and papers. She'll tip you. Tell her you brought the car over. All right?"

"But, I don't understand."

"You don't have to. All right?" I repeated the names. "Take your time. There's no hurry. Wait an hour or so."

We looked at each other. I turned away and started walking fast down through the town toward the main southern route.

I wasn't on the corner under the stop light more than three minutes, when this convertible came along with an old guy and his wife. They were headed for Key West. Sure, they'd be glad to take me to St. Pete. I got in and sat quiet.

It wasn't till we were way down in Florida that I remembered I'd bought that Ford in my name. So the rest of the way, I sat there sweating with that, trying not to think about it. Then trying to think what to do about it. Nothing.

It wasn't much good, I'll tell you. The old guy and his wife knew I was sick. Getting to St. Pete didn't help, either.

FIVE

They let me out on Lakeview. They were headed for the Sunshine Skyway bridge, and if it hadn't been for Bess, I'd have stayed with them. "We'd be glad to take you wherever you live." the woman said.

"Thanks. It's all right."

The old guy wanted to move on. His wife wanted to talk. I grinned at them and started across the street. They started off toward their happy, unworried vacation.

I crossed to the sidewalk and began walking down Lakeview. It was off schedule for the bus, so I'd probably have to walk all the way home. It was afternoon. The sun slanted across a stately row of royal palms along the street and the air was warm. Two girls in shorts went riding by on bicycles, jabbering at each other. Cars hissed past on the asphalt. Over there between patches of green jungle, beyond cool-looking homes, you could see Lake Maggiore, pale blue and shadowed in the sun.

I moved along, trying not to think. I'd have to face Bess with this, and with the rest of it in the back of my mind. Vivian and that damned money. I'd been that close to a solution, and then turned away from it. Maybe it was wrong. I felt bad and I wanted to feel good. I'd done the right thing, it had to be. But did it matter? *What was I going to tell her?*

How do you tell them you've failed them at the last ditch? Especially when they depend on you; when they're sure of the way you do things—banking on you, like they do.

I remembered that guy, Teece, lying twisted in the wreck, and I began to feel better. I needed something to fasten my mind to. I was well clear from them both and that had to be right.

Crossing another block, it was plenty warm. I paused under a young banyan and started peeling my coat. I turned and glanced back there along Lakeview to see if a bus might be along.

A Ford sedan slid into the curb, tires scraping, steam frothing white and hot from under the fenders and hood. Vivian looked at me, pale-faced, and beeped the horn.

I looked away, shrugged back into my coat, and started walking. It wouldn't do any good. There was no place to run, and anyway, you don't run. There were about fifteen more hot blocks to my place. I heard the cars peel by through the shadows and the sunlight.

"Nichols—"

The car door slammed and I heard her running lightly across the grass and down the sidewalk after me, her heels snicking. A young guy and his girl came strolling out of a nearby house. They stopped, whispering, watching. The guy grinned behind his shoulder.

She caught up with me, grabbed my arm.

"Go away, will you?"

"You ran out on me before. You can't run out on me now."

I kept staring down the street. In the back of my mind, I knew nothing was going to work. She'd found me, just like that—and it was only natural she would come on down here. I looked at her and she was plenty worried. Worse than before, even.

She began to laugh. It was a kind of strained, muted, hysterical laughter. "Nichols. Come back to the car!"

"What d'you want with me?"

"You know what I want."

I figured I should have had sense enough not to try and get away from this one.

"Come on." she said. "Will you?" She stood there watching me with her eyes all shot full of worry and waiting. "The minute that man from the car lot drove up to the hotel, I knew." she said. "I knew even before that. I got one of those feelings."

We went back to the car and she climbed under the wheel and sat there. You could hear the steam hissing, and the engine creaked a lot.

"I'm going to stay right at your place, Nichols."

I turned and looked at her. She didn't bother looking at me. "Like hell." I told her.

"It's got to be that way. I've got to be able to get to you." Then she turned to me and her voice had that dead seriousness she was able to get. "How could you run out on me like that? After all I've told you?" She turned away and laid her head down against the steering wheel. She was going through plenty. Vivian kept her head pressed against the wheel.

"You can't stay at my place." I heard myself say. "What about my wife?"

"God, I thought I'd lost you. I got to thinking, suppose he lied to me. Suppose he doesn't live down here at all. There was no way of telling.

Nichols, I'm about dead from driving. I didn't know what I was going to do. I had to find you."

"What about my wife?"

"She doesn't have to know."

"You're damn right. She isn't going to know. Hear?"

"Don't worry. I'm going to pay you. That's all you want—money."

I'd made up my mind, now. "That's for sure." Well, all right. I'd let her stay at the motel. She'd be a customer. Somehow. A guest. Some guest. Then I told her about how they'd spotted the wreck.

She came around in the seat like a shot. "Why didn't you tell me?"

I didn't say anything. She started the car. It took some starting, it was that hot. Finally she got her going and you could feel the fear in her and the dead tiredness.

"Where's your place, Nichols?"

She was sitting up on the edge of the seat, staring at the windshield as if she were hypnotized. It was hard to figure her as a woman who would play it this tight. She was nice looking; more than that.

She sure had fouled me up.

I had her park the car on a side street, three blocks from the motel. The car was still steaming. I told her to get some water and she didn't say a word. I got out and leaned in the window and looked at her.

"You wait a while, then just drive up front. Give me enough time. It's the Southern Comfort Motel."

"All right. Some name, Nichols?"

We watched each other. She had her hands clenched tight on the wheel.

I turned and took off my hat and coat and started down the block toward home. It hadn't turned out the way I'd wanted. You get caught in something like this and you get in deeper and deeper, and you begin to accept it.

Traffic had been rerouted off the main street past our place. The bricks were torn up and there was a tractor sitting silent across the way.

I walked along, alone and beat and kind of lost. Everything was cockeyed, but there was that money. I kept thinking about that. It had to work, now.

My head ached and I needed a shave and I was in a dead man's clothes. It's real great, the things that happen to you. You don't even have to look for it hard.

Southern Comfort
Motel
Vacancy

I could see it down there.

"*Vacancy.*" That was a hot one. We'd never once used the "*No Vacancy*" sign. But it did look good down there. The lawn would have to be mowed. I'd have to get at it right away. And some fronds on two of the plumosas needed trimming.

Walking along, I began to feel a little better. Sanctuary down there. And it was Bess who made it that way, made me feel good.

It took up a whole block. Boy! Nichols, the land baron.

Why didn't they put that highway through? I wasn't the only one, there were other motel owners going through the same thing. But most of them had been in business for quite a while. They had a nest egg.

You *could* limp along the way the road was before. But with it shut off and the detour, you had nothing.

The hedges needed trimming, too. I hadn't noticed that before I left. Then I saw the hedge that ran along the side nearest me had been trimmed about halfway.

Bess again. I'd told her never to do that. I started walking faster, unconsciously.

It was good to be home.

So then it all rushed back into my mind, maybe worse than before, like it does sometimes. Her, in the Ford, waiting back there. The wreck. The brief case with all that money. And Teece—Noel Teece, lying there dead with his two elbows on one arm.

Bess was sitting on the steps by the office. She had on a slipover and a pair of red shorts, just sitting there holding a broom, staring at nothing. I whistled at her.

She looked up and saw me and flung the broom and came running.

Then, watching her, I knew I'd done the right thing, after all. It had worked out right. I wasn't coming home empty-handed and I knew now I never wanted that to happen. Now she'd have what she deserved, or as near to it as I could deliver. It had been in my mind all along, I guess. If I'd come home the way I'd started, without Vivian—it wouldn't have been good.

"Roy!"

It seemed odd and sort of wonderful, hearing her call me that—after all that "Nichols" business.

How Bess could run! She wasn't too tall, just right, and built just right, too. With light blond hair that the sun was dancing in, and bright blue eyes, her slim legs churning. And those red shorts. She came running across the lawn past the sign, and down the sidewalk.

She hit me hard, the way she always did, jumping into my arms. "Roy—

you're back!"

I kissed her and held her and we started walking across the lawn toward the office. We had the apartment behind the office.

Like I say, the sun was in her hair and it was in her eyes, too. She had on a white terry-cloth slipover, and walking across the lawn she kept swatting me with her hip.

"Did you get it, Roy?"

"Sure."

She stopped again and jumped up and hung on my neck, kissing me. Bess was the way I wanted it and I never wanted it any other way. Just Bess.

I dropped my hat and she let go. "You mean, Albert gave you the money?"

I nodded.

She picked up my hat and looked at me and there was a flash of suspicion, only she chased it away. "That's a different suit, Roy. Where'd you get the suit?"

"It's—"

"Doesn't fit you quite right."

She reached out and flicked the jacket open and grabbed the waist of the pants and yanked. She was that way; quick as anything and I stood there, looking down at the gap. He'd been a lot bigger around the middle than I was.

"Al gave it to me."

"Oh?"

"Like it?"

"Where's your other suit?"

"I gave it the old heave-ho."

"But, Roy! That was your best suit." She began to look at me that way again.

"My only. And three years old. It fell apart."

"Oh, Roy!"

I grabbed her again and kissed her and we went on over to the office and on inside. I had a desk in here, and a couple chairs. It was a small front room.

Bess looked at me kind of funny, and took my coat. She flipped the coat on a chair and plopped the hat on it, and looked at me again.

"It's good to be home."

"You know it."

I took her in my arms as she walked up to me. She pressed against me, and when she kissed me, she really let me know. I got my hand snarled up in her hair and yanked her head back, looking down into her eyes.

"Gee, Roy!"

"Yeah."

"He came through!"

"That's right. He's going to send the money down. Don't know what got into him."

"You were right, then—in going up there. Instead of writing or just phoning, like I said at first."

I kissed her again, kissing her lips, her chin, with my hand snarled in that golden hair.

"Roy, you better stop."

I was trying to hold the rest of the bad stuff away from my mind. It was rough, because I hated lying to Bess. I remembered Vivian, and kissed her again and said, "You son-of-a-gun!" Then I let go of her and turned around, looking at the office, rubbing my hands together. "Boy, it's sure good to be back! Any customers?"

"A couple. Listen, you're not getting away that easy. How come you're late? I figured the day before yesterday. Where've you been?"

"Got a ride down. It saved some money. Folks coming south to Tampa, and I bummed over from Tampa." I cleared my throat. "For free. I drove them down, see?"

She kept looking at me. "What did your brother say?"

I shrugged. "Well, I laid the cards on the table. I told him what kind of a fix we were in. He saw it, all right." I laughed. "Wouldn't trust me with the money, bringing it down myself. Thinks I'm still wild, or something. Said he'd send it."

She came over and put her arms around me again. "You're sure he will, Roy?"

I nodded. "Anything new about the road?"

She shook her read, laying her cheek against my chest.

"I missed you, Roy. And you look sick. You need a shave and you're pale. Is something the matter?"

"I'm fine. No sunshine up there. Freezing. Snowing in Georgia, even."

I kept trying to look out the window. I knew damned well that Ford would be along any minute. She was plenty anxious. Then I got to thinking, "What if she doesn't come? What then?" It hit me just exactly how much I was depending on that money. It was like caving in—I had to have it.

"You went and started trimming the hedge. I told you not to do that."

"It's just started growing again. I had to do something."

"Yeah, I guess." I caught myself pacing.

"Roy, you sure you feel all right?"

I turned and looked at her. "Just happy, getting home and all."

She started to come over to me and I heard the car drive up out in the street. Bess looked at me. I didn't look out the window, I didn't dare.

"Somebody's stopped out front." Bess said. "Maybe business is picking up." She yanked her sweater down and headed for the door. "I'll go see, Roy."

"No. You take it easy. I'll check this one."

We stood there, looking at each other, by the door.

"You listen to me." she said. "One look at you, and you'd scare anyone clear down to Key West. You look like you've been shot out of a cannon. So I'll see who it is. You sit right here and relax."

The screen door slammed. I watched her cross the lawn, her legs scissoring, the red shorts in and out of shadow.

Sweat popped out all over me. I stood watching them through the window. Vivian got out of the car and stood there, looking at the motel. When she saw Bess coming across the lawn, she kind of shrunk back against the car, then straightened and reached for her purse on the seat. She turned as Bess stepped up.

They were talking, and I sweated and sweated, sitting at the desk, my head propped on my fist, watching Bess and Vivian. Vivian was nodding about something. Her hair was real black. Bess was shorter than Vivian, standing there with her hands on her hips.

They both started up toward the office.

It was all wrong. I got up and walked out of the office, into our living room. I couldn't stay there, so I came back. They were talking out on the front lawn. It was enough to drive you nuts.

I had to have a cigarette. I found a pack in the desk drawer and lit up and stood there sweating and fuming. I went out into the kitchen and got a drink of water.

I didn't want to see the two of them together. Not now, I couldn't face that. Bess was too wise.

I heard the front screen door slam. I walked as slow as I could back to the office. Bess was beside the desk, counting some money.

"Two weeks!" She turned and waved the bills and smiled. "Just like that. Isn't it swell? I gave her number six. A woman, all alone. She's a real looker, too. You stay away from her door, Roy. Hear?"

I looked at her, but she had her eyes on the money. She took it over and put it in the cigar box in the desk drawer. I felt real bad about this. Now it was beginning.

"She's coming over to register."

The blood began to pound behind my ears. "Did you tell her where to park the car?"

"No. You can show her later."

"I think I'll take a shower, Bess."

"Right. I'll take care of her. I'll fix a good dinner." Then she left the desk and came over by me. "It's swell about Albert. Maybe we can make it now."

"Sure, we'll make it." I kissed her and gave her a good smack with both hands and went back into the apartment and closed the door. In the bathroom I started to take that suit off; I'd never put it on again.

I was taking off my shoes, when I remembered the broken finger and the ankle. Bess hadn't said a word about the finger. It looked like a miniature baseball bat and it was as black as midnight. She couldn't have missed seeing it.

The ankle was a mess. I took the sock off, then untied the handkerchief. When I yanked the handkerchief, it started bleeding again. I got a Band-Aid and fixed it up with some iodine and then remembered the shower.

I'd fouled things up just dandy....

"You can show her the garage, Roy."

"All right. Did she register?"

"You bet."

"You didn't say anything about my finger."

"Uh-uh. I saw it, though. Did Albert bite it?"

"It's busted. Caught it in the car door, coming down. Not my fault, either. This old biddy slammed the door on it."

She looked at it. "You'll have to see a doctor." Then she looked up and smiled at me. "You look lots better, shaved and in your own clothes. They fit, at least."

I had on sneakers, a pair of gray slacks and a T-shirt. "Fix some dinner, huh?"

"She's out by her car. Go show her the garage."

I went on out there, walking across the lawn like it was a big basket of eggs. The sun was way down now, right smack in your eyes from across the street in the park, glinting between the branches of the oak trees—long slices of fiery orange peel.

"Hello, there."

I nodded at her.

"Wonder if you could show me where to park the car?"

"I'll drive it around. Get in."

She slid under the wheel and over to the other side of the seat and I climbed in after her. I slammed the door, not looking at her, started the engine and took it down around the block and in the drive behind the apartments.

"Nice wife you have, Nichols."

I showed her the garage for number six. I drove the car inside and got out and stood there in the semi-dark. She got out on her side and came around and stood in the doorway, looking at me. She wasn't self-conscious.

"You've got a swell place. You're very lucky."

"Thanks. And listen: Be careful around my wife."

"Relax, Nichols. I'm a woman, too."

She was telling me! "You go that way, I'm going around the other way."

"But, Nichols—!"

"You heard me."

"You've got to stay by me. Suppose somebody—?"

I left her standing there and cut around the other side of the garage. She worried me plenty. I heard her walking the other way on the gravel. It wasn't good having her here. I had to keep elbowing out of my mind who she really was, the things she'd been mixed up in, the people she knew. But that money kept chewing away at me.

I headed for the back door. Bess was waiting, holding the door for me.

"I've got my eye on you, Roy."

I knew she was kidding. Bess was real smart, but she was usually trusting. I wondered just how far that could go. It made me sweat, the way she was standing there and the way she said that.

SIX

With Vivian in number six, my nervous system started to kick up. I couldn't stay still. Thing was, I didn't know what she might do. She was scared and wound up tight and anxious to get on the move. There was always the chance she might crack and come running over to our place, yelling, "Nichols—Nichols!"

That would be all I'd need.

I couldn't see any way to get to her tonight. If I took a chance and went over there, Bess might wise up. She was watching me like a cat, anyway. I figured she was thinking about what I'd done up in Chicago. She probably thought I'd got drunk.

"Last day I was up there, I stayed in a cheap hotel. Waiting for these folks to get ready for the trip down. I bought a bottle, Bess. I shouldn't have, but I felt like celebrating."

She seemed to take it all right. Celebrating! That was hot one, all right.

"It was bad stuff. I got sick."

"You looked pretty bad when you came home. Lots better now, though."

"When I saw you, I felt better right away."

"Now, Roy, you know what whiskey does to you. You shouldn't take the chance in a strange town. You don't have any sense when you're drunk. Somebody tell you, 'Let's rob a bank,' you'd be all for it. Whoopee!" She shook her head, standing there by the oven in the kitchen with the roast going. "No sense at all, Roy."

"Let's not talk about it. All right?"

We looked at each other. Then she started smiling and she laughed and it was all right. For a minute there, she had me worried. The way she looked at me.

It was a good dinner. Roast beef, mashed potatoes, fresh peas in a cream sauce, apple pie and coffee.

"Wonder what she's doing down here?"

"Who?"

"That woman I put in number six. One that came in before dinner."

"Oh. Why?"

"All alone, like that. You don't see them like her alone. Miss Jane Latimer, from Yonkers, New York."

"That's her name?"

"Didn't you introduce yourself?"

I shook my head.

Bess drank some coffee. "She didn't go out for dinner. She hasn't left the place."

"It's early yet. Who else we got aboard?"

"There's an old guy in number fifteen. He's a shuffleboard bug. I think you ought to clean off the courts. He'd play all by himself. His wife's going to join him in a month or so. They're looking for a house down here. So we've got him for a month. Mr. Hughes, he is... Say—maybe I should introduce him to Miss Latimer?"

I began to wish she'd lay off.

"Then there's a couple—middle-aged. The Donnes. She drinks an awful lot, always got one in her hand. I don't blame her, though. The way her husband sits and broods. They came down from New York, so he could get some rest. They never do anything, just sit. Every day a taxi comes up with a load of papers for him. He's an editor. Some New York publishing house. Got great big circles under his eyes. He walks up and down, talking to himself. She told me she's scared he's going to crack up."

"Anybody else?"

"Honeymooners in eleven, only here for a couple of days. Real cute. And a woman whose husband just died, in nineteen. That's all."

"I think that's damned good, the way things been."

After supper I got out on the lawn and monkeyed with the sprinkler system, trying to work myself over by number six, so I could see what was going on. It was real quiet over there, but she had a light burning.

I turned the sprinklers on. I knew if I was going to speak with her, it would have to be fast, while Bess was doing the dishes.

We had the floodlights cut off to save juice, what with the electric bill we had. They turn them off on us, and it'd really be rough, but I had the lights turned on the lawn at the two corners of the block. And the sign was a big one.

What I did was turn all the sprinklers off, then start turning them on, one at a time, by hand. I followed around, working toward number six. The sprinklers ticked and swished. They looked real good. If only there was lots of traffic, and I could have put the floodlights on. It looked good from the road, but the road was like a mortuary.

"*Psst!* Nichols!"

I almost went right out of my skin. She was standing there behind one of the double hibiscus bushes at the corner of number seven.

"Get back."

"I've got to see you"

I just walked straight off across the lawn. I leaned against the royal palm by the sign. I heard her go back toward number six. So then I went over to the sprinklers again. I got the one by seven going, then moved on down beside six. It was in shadow.

It wasn't good to whisper and sneak. But it wasn't good to play it straight, either. Let Bess catch me running over here every chance, she'd put the clamps on—trusting or not.

I heard Vivian breathing through the screen windows from inside number six. She had the lights shut off except for one burning in the kitchen.

"You've got to get a move on." she said. "I mean it. I can't stay here forever."

"I'm not doing nothing till tomorrow. That's the way it is."

I could still hear her breathing; kind of rough, like she was breathing across a washboard. "I haven't anything to eat."

"Well, go out and buy yourself something. You got enough money."

"I can't go out, Nichols. You'll have to get me some groceries. Something. Buy me a hamburg."

"Get it yourself."

Her voice cracked, high and shrill, whispering through the window. "I can't go out, damn you! They'll be watching! My God, they'll—!"

"They won't be in St. Pete."

"But I can't take that chance!"

"All right. I'll be in front of our place. You come on over there—by the office, and ask me real loud. Hear? And bring some money. And no hundred-dollar bills."

She started to say something, but I was already walking away toward the office.

Well, I waited and nothing happened. She didn't come and she didn't come.

"Roy?"

The front screen door slammed. It was Bess, coming around front where I stood. Now, *she* would come. That's the way it always goes.

"Roy, that Latimer girl asked if you wouldn't go someplace and buy her some groceries."

"What?" It was a good thing she didn't get a close look at my face.

"She came to the back door. Not feeling well, but she's hungry. Tired from the trip down. She made a list, here. And here's some money. The corner store's still open. I told her you'd be glad to do it."

So I got the Chevie out of the garage and bought her groceries and came back. She and Bess were talking out in front of the office, on the lawn. I wanted to talk with Vivian.

I came across the lawn. "Here you go."

"Oh, fine. Thanks so much." She was wearing white slacks and a black cardigan sweater.

"Well, don't stand there." Bess said. "Take them inside for her."

I went on across and into number six. There were the two suitcases, sitting in the middle of the floor, one of them open. I didn't see anything of the brief case. I left the groceries on the table in the kitchen, with the change, and started out.

She came in the front door. She didn't say anything. She just stood there, wringing her hands. "I feel trapped."

"Tomorrow. I'll do something tomorrow."

"You've got to get me out of here fast."

"Leave, then."

"I can't just leave. Nichols, I've got to get a plane, or a boat, or something. And I can't do it myself. They'll have every place covered!"

"You're nuts. They can't do that. You think they got the U. S. Army?"

"It's worse than that." She stood there, not looking at me. "I wish you were staying with me tonight. I'm scared, Nichols."

"Where's the money?"

"Under the seat of that chair."

I could see the tip of the brief case and some of the red scarf. "Why don't you fix the clasp on that brief case? Give you something to do."

"Better the way it is. I've had that scarf for years. It's a kind of talisman."

"What in hell's a talisman?"

"Good luck charm, like."

Bess was coming back from the curb, brushing off her hands. She was looking toward number six, squinting a little.

"We'll work something out tomorrow."

She turned and kind of leaped at me, both hands out. I got over by the door. "Nichols. I'm scared."

I watched her for a second, then went on outside. That Vivian, scared of her own shadow! How could they cover all the airports? They didn't even know she was down here. Maybe they didn't even know she existed. It was Teece they would be wondering about. And they wouldn't wonder about him for long. They would wonder about the money.

But who were "they?" She was really frightened, there was no getting around that.

Well, I'd have to get her out of here. And I was going to hit her hard for doing this. It was costing me a few years.

I went on out and put the Chevie in the garage....

"I phoned the doctor."

"What?"

"About your finger. You've got an appointment for tomorrow afternoon. Two o'clock. I tried to get it earlier, but he was filled up."

Bess closed the Venetian blinds on the bedroom windows.

The next morning I couldn't get near number six no matter how hard I tried. She came out and walked around and you could see the nerves. She had on the white slacks and the black sweater.

The best we could do was wave at each other. There was so much to do, I didn't really accomplish anything, what with the worrying.

The front of number twenty was beginning to peel. I mixed some paint, trying to get the same pastel shade of blue it was in the first place. When it began to dry, it was a lot darker. It looked bad.

"You'll have to paint them all, Roy. They need it, anyway."

And all the time Vivian was back there in number six, going crazy. Every time I walked past on the lawn, she'd come out on the little porch, kind of frantic, making eyes. I didn't even dare look at her much.

Roy this; Roy that. The grass needed cutting. The garage roof leaked in two places. The hedges needed trimming and the fronds were withered and brown on all the palms. The lights had gone bad in ten. The sink was plugged up in number five. Mister Hughes said his toilet wouldn't flush.

I ran around the place, getting nowhere, and then it was one-thirty.

"How'd you do this to your finger, Mister Nichols?"

"Well, Doc, you see, I caught it in a car door."

He looked at me, blinking his eyes behind enormous black-framed glasses. He was a young guy, heavy-set, with shoulders like a fullback, with those eyes that say you're lying no matter what you say. He kept looking at the finger and shaking his head.

"Have to set it. Have to get the swelling down first."

"Anything. Listen, just set it."

"With the swelling, the pain would be bad."

"Go ahead—go on."

Well, he liked to kill me. So there I was, finally, with it in a neat little cast. My finger sticking out so it would be in the way of everything.

"Bill me, Doc."

"Well, all right, Mister Nichols. And, say—be careful of car doors after this."

His grin was real sly....

His office was alongside the Chamber of Commerce building. I went on out to the car, figuring I'd have to see Vivian if I was ever going to get my hands on any of that money. I climbed into the car and started her up.

The sun was bright and hot.

I looked back to check traffic and happened to glance over toward the front door of the Chamber of Commerce building.

It was like being shot in the face. But it was no mistake. I would never forget that face,

Noel Teece was limping across the sidewalk.

SEVEN

I sat there, staring, with my foot jammed against the gas pedal, my hand just resting on the gearshift. The engine roared and roared without moving.

Teece was limping badly, dressed in a white Palm Beach suit. His left arm was in a big cast and sling. One side of his face was bandaged, so he only could use one eye.

I didn't know what to do. All the things Vivian was afraid of were beginning to come true.

He walked right by the front of the car, starting across the street. Then he looked directly at the windshield, and you could see him frown with the way the engine was tearing it up. I let go on the gas. He turned away. The sun was on the windshield, so he hadn't seen me. Then he went on across the street, limping, moving in a slow slouch.

He was real beat up and in pain. You could tell.

I watched him go on across the street and stand on the corner. He stood there arranging the sling, kind of staring at his arm as if it was something foreign. Then he patted the bandages by his left eye. He was wearing a Panama hat and it rode on top of the bandages on his head. He kept trying to pull the brim down.

I had to tell Vivian. When I did, there was no telling what she'd do. I sure didn't like seeing Noel Teece—alive. Because I knew why he was in this town.

"You get your finger fixed?"

"Yeah."

I had tried bringing the car around to the garage, figuring I'd be able to sneak over to number six. Bess must have seen me coming, or else she was just waiting back there. Anyway, she watched me park the car in the garage,

"That's good."

"The doc set it. It sure hurt."

"Tough." Bess said.

I looked at her. She had on a two-piece white swim suit. She'd been working in the back lawn while I was gone, and she was wet from the sprinklers. Only there was something else in her eyes. She had some mud on one hand, and she wiped her face and some of the mud smeared off.

We stood there watching each other. Finally I started for the house. Somehow I had to get to Vivian, because Noel Teece knew my name. I remembered telling him in the Lincoln. All he had to do was check a little, and he'd be along.

"Where you going?"

"Inside. This damn finger. You wouldn't think a little finger could hurt so much."

She came along behind me, her feet swishing on the grass. "Roy?"

I stood there holding the screen door open, half inside the kitchen. You could tell it from the tone of her voice. She had something on her mind. "A letter came for you."

"Oh?"

"It's in on the desk."

"Well, fine."

She just stood there. She didn't say anything.

I went on into the kitchen and let the screen door slam. It was like everything had gone out of the place, all life. There just wasn't any sound at all.

I kept thinking of Vivian. I went in and the letter was on the desk. There wasn't another thing on the desk. Just that letter. Now, I knew Bess was pulling something.

It was from Albert, and it was open.

I started reading and I heard her coming. It was short and sweet, just like that creep. Explaining everything, just fine.

"Why did you lie, Roy?"

"What in hell else could I do?"

"You could have told me he wouldn't give you the money. I didn't mean to open it. I thought it was all right. I thought it was the check."

Albert had said how sorry he was about not giving me the money. The same old line all over again. Hoe your own row. Maybe some time ten years from now....

"Roy?"

"Huh?"

"You didn't answer me. Why'd you tell me he was sending the money?"

I stood there with my mouth open. Vivian was walking across the front yard. She went over by a palm tree and stood there. I could see her gnawing her lip.

"You want a telescope, Roy?"

"Cut it out!"

"Answer me, then."

I had to get Vivian back into the apartment. My God, what if Teece came along now? She didn't even know. All day long she'd been waiting for me to do something and I hadn't even been able to talk with her.

I turned to Bess. "I had to lie to you. How could I tell you the way he acted? It was lousy—crumby. You never saw anything like it. My own brother!"

"You don't have to talk like that, Roy."

"Well, damn it, it's true. I didn't know what to do."

"So you let me get my hopes up. And the suit, Roy. Did he give you the suit of clothes, too?"

"Sure, he did. Certainly. My gosh, Bess!"

"Don't blame me. I don't know what to believe any more."

She came over and perched herself on the corner of the desk. Her hair was all messed up and there was that mud on her face. "Take it easy, Bess."

"I'm taking it easy. I'm just so damned mad I could choke you."

Vivian was staring over here at the office. Then she started back across the lawn toward number six. She paused and glanced toward the office again.

"You notice? She cut off her slacks and made a pair of shorts. She's got nice legs. Hasn't she?"

"Bess, for gosh sakes!"

She came off the desk and started toward the kitchen, and whirled and stood there. "You saw him four days ago. Where were you all that time, Roy?"

"I told you—waiting for a ride down here. Listen, I didn't have much money, you know that. The hotel bill took everything. I had just enough for that damned bottle. So I bought it. Not enough dough to get home, even. I didn't even eat, Bess. Last night was the first meal in two days."

"All right." she said. "I'm sorry." She walked up to me and put her arms around me. She was soaking wet, but I held her tight and kissed her.

"Forgive me, Roy?"

"Sure. What's there to forgive?"

"I shouldn't be that way. Only you were gone so long, up there in Chicago. And I know Chicago, remember? I thought all sorts of things. Then to find this out—that you didn't get the money."

I kissed her again.

"What are we going to do, Roy?"

"I'm figuring something. But I can't tell you now. Something'll work out."

"All right. I'll lay off. I'm going to take a shower. I'm sorry what I said about her, too. But she's been walking around in those home-built shorts of hers. She cut them so close up it's a wonder they don't gag her."

"Go take your shower."

The minute I heard the water running behind the closed door, I started over toward number six.

Hughes was a fine-looking old gent. He stopped me right outside the office. I tried to let him know I was in a hurry, but he wasn't having any nonsense.

"Mister Nichols?"

I nodded and tried to brush by.

"Wait. I want a word with you."

"What is it?"

He was tall and thin and stooped a little; the scholarly stoop. He had on a gray business suit and a red bow tie and his eyes were like a busy chipmunk's. "It come to me that you should do something about that shuffleboard court of yours, there. Now, if you like, I could get to work and clean it up just fine. We could—"

"All right, you just go right ahead and do that." I could still hear the shower going, but it wouldn't be for long.

"Now, there's one thing—"

"I'm sorry. I've got to run."

"Well, it's just—"

I whacked him a light one on the shoulder. He darned near collapsed, but I was already cutting across the front of the apartments.

"Teece is alive."

She was sitting there in a chair, with a newspaper in her hand. It was shaking like crazy.

"I knew it." she said. "I knew it."

"I saw him. Downtown."

"Oh, God—Noel."

"You'd better stay inside and not go out."

She dropped the paper on the floor and Bess had sure been right about those shorts. Then she grabbed the newspaper up and shook it at me.

"It's in the paper about the wreck. They found the Lincoln, Nichols. Only they didn't find anybody in it... Nichols! What in God's name am I going to do?"

She stood up and threw the paper down. I picked it up and she pointed to the little news item.

According to the report, there'd been blood all over everything. The pine trees were sprinkled with it. They'd found a smashed whiskey bottle, and that was supposed to account for the wreck. There had been no sign of any of the car's occupants. They located a trail of blood leading up along the bank of the stream to the road and down the road, only it stopped. They had no idea what happened, but decided the person or persons involved had picked up a ride on the highway.

Vivian was breathing down my neck, trying to read it again over my shoulder, trying to thoroughly digest the bad news. Then she stepped away, flopping that thick black hair around. "You've got to get me out of here, Nichols."

"Relax a minute, will you? Let me think."

"There isn't time to think. Noel's after that money, now. He's out to find me. He'll be here. You know he'll be here!"

"Quiet." I remembered Bess. I had to get out of the apartment. "We can't talk here. You just stay inside. There's nothing to worry about. If he comes, I'll talk with him. He may not even come."

"Stop it!" she said. "Will you please stop it!"

"Well, we can't talk now. If my wife spots us together and thinks anything at all, she'll have me boot you out of here—and quick."

She had her hands folded the way she did, praying again.

"If I didn't move you out, she'd call the cops."

She shook her head. "Oh, no, Nichols. I'd tell her you slept with me night before last. In that hotel. How would she like that?"

"You think she'd believe you?"

"Nichols, we've got to hide the money. At least you can do that much?"

She had me going. It was like my mind had shut down like a door. What she'd said about telling Bess had jarred me. Because Bess would believe it, the way things had been going. I tried to calm down inside, so I could think straight. I couldn't do it. I was all tied up and everything was going wrong.

She'd never let me try to ditch her and back out on this now. And Teece was alive and he knew me.

I had to take the chance of Bess finding me here, so I told Vivian I'd help her hide the money. I didn't know what good it would do. But if Teece did raise any hell, at least he wouldn't get that money.

"You know." she said. "It's not just that brief case any more, Nichols. It's me, now. And it's you. Noel's not dumb. He's probably worked it out, what's happened."

We hid the money in the bureau. I took the top drawers out and wedged it in against the back of the bureau. The drawers wouldn't close all the way, so I took some of her clothes and dribbled them over the drawer. It looked like the drawer was jammed with black lace.

"Now, I've got to scram."

"Nichols, Nichols." She got her arms around my neck and slung herself against me. "I'm scared."

I pulled her off and checked the back way from the kitchen door. No sign of Bess. I went on outside and started toward our place. Bess stepped onto our back porch from the kitchen, and looked at me. She had on a bright-colored skirt and a peasant blouse. Her hair was brushed to a soft gold.

"Where've you been, Roy?"

"Just checking the paint on the rest of the place. Sure needs a paint job."

"Wait, I think I heard a car stop out front."

It felt as if the porch steps began to rock and heave.

"Roy, you're pale as a ghost. What's the matter?"

"Nothing, honey. Nothing at all."

I pushed past her on the porch. She followed me through the house and I was sweating all over. Sure enough, a car had stopped out front. It was a big black baby, a Cadillac, and the sun shot off it like a mirror. It was huge.

I stared till my eyes watered. Then a man got out and stood there a minute, staring at the motel sign. It wasn't Teece.

"Look at that car. It's like a hearse."

I didn't answer. My heart gradually began to slow down and we stood there together, watching him.

"Think he's coming here?"

He was. He threw a cigar away, turned and started up across the grass. He was a big guy, wearing a single-breasted powder-blue suit and a light gray felt hat. I didn't like it, the way he came at the office. His head kept going back and forth, his gaze checking.

"Could it be somebody from the bank?"

"I don't know."

"Well, go out and meet him, Roy. He probably wants an apartment."

"His kind don't stay at motels."

I went on outside and waited. He saw me and his face didn't change expression. Then he grinned and paused by the porch steps. I came down a step.

"Roy Nichols?"

"That's right."

"My name's Radan, Mister Nichols. I've just come over here from Tampa. That mean anything to you?"

"No. Why?"

He pursed his lips and lifted one foot to the first step of the porch. Then he took off his hat and held it in both hands on his knee and watched me. His hair was immaculate. It was black hair and it was perfectly combed. His eyes were level and steady. There were tiny nips at the corners of his mouth and, standing there, he gave an impression of great leisure.

I heard Bess moving around inside. "Looking for a place to stay?"

He shook his head gently. "Nothing like that. Not yet, anyhow."

"Well, what is it?"

"That's not the question, Mister Nichols."

"Maybe we'd better talk inside?"

"That's up to you. I believe perhaps it might be best that we talk alone, privately. At least, for now."

"Oh?"

He took his foot down and lightly banged his hat against his leg. He seemed to be waiting for something.

I stepped down beside him. He edged a little toward the front lawn, looking at me with his head a shade to one side. Then we both walked out on the lawn.

"Is that your wife inside, Mister Nichols?"

"Yes."

"I didn't want to embarrass you."

I didn't say anything.

"I understand how these things are, Mister Nichols. Now, where is Vivian?"

"Vivian?"

"Yes. Vivian Rise. You know what I mean, Mister Nichols." He cleared his throat carefully. "Unless you *would* rather go back inside and discuss it with your wife."

"I don't get you."

"I'm sorry about this." he said. He kept his voice low and his manner was apologetic. "But I can't do anything about it. You see, I've been sent over here to clear this up. You recall Noel Teece, don't you, Mister

Nichols?"

The screen door slammed and I heard Bess coming toward us. "Roy? Could I be of any help?"

The guy turned and jerked his head in a neat little bow. "We'll see, Mrs. Nichols. We'll see."

EIGHT

Bess smiled at this Radan. She had slash pockets in her skirt. She jammed her hands into the pockets and stood there, smiling and rocking back and forth on her heels.

Vivian might not know who Radan was. More than likely she'd never heard of him. So all she had to do was wander out here now, in those shorts of hers and make things just right. I got a tight feeling at the base of my skull, as if somebody'd put a clamp on there and was screwing it tighter and tighter.

Radan cleared his throat. "You have a very nice place here."

"Thank you. We love it, don't we, Roy?"

"Oh, yes."

Radan looked at me and smiled pleasantly. He banged his hat against his leg. He looked at his fingernails. He banged his hat against his leg. He looked at his fingernails, and then at the apartments. He checked the roofs, glancing at Bess from the corner of his eye.

"Thinking of staying in St. Pete?" Bess said.

He frowned at her.

I glanced over at number six. There was no sign of life. But I knew she was there, behind the Venetian blinds, watching, waiting.

"Let's see around back." Radan said. "I'd like to have a look at your garage, Mister Nichols."

I started to say something and changed it fast. I didn't want him to see the Ford with Georgia plates. If he got a look at that, there was no telling. I didn't know exactly who he was, but I had a good enough idea. I wished to God I was out of this. But there was no way out right now.

"All right."

"Sure." Bess said. "We'll show you."

"Well—Mrs. Nichols."

"Bess, you know—" She stared at me.

I tried to give her the eye, making it look as if this guy was nuts. As if I didn't know anything about what he wanted, one way or the other. I winked at her.

"Guess I'll see about dinner, Roy."

Radan nodded and Bess went back inside.

We walked on across the grass toward the far side of the block, over to the edge of the apartments. "I'm afraid you're in over your head, Mister Nichols. I don't think you have any idea what you're really mixed up with. Or have you?"

I didn't say anything.

"You understand?"

"I don't believe so."

He paused and got in front of me and lightly tapped the brim of his hat against my chest. Then he pursed his lips and turned and walked toward the corner of the apartments. The shuffleboard courts were just beyond, under some pines.

"Come along, Mister Nichols."

We went on past there. I had this one court. Hughes was on his hands and knees on a pad, scrubbing the cement with a G. I. brush. He was working with a pail of soapy water, wearing khaki shorts. He kept coughing as he worked. There was soap and water all over everything. He was really scrubbing.

"Now, Mister Nichols." Radan said. "You've got to understand that we want to know where this girl is."

Hughes saw me. He got up, straightening like a rusty hinge, and came toward us, stooping. He waved the brush and a string of soap and water dribbled wildly. "Mister Nichols?"

"We'd better go the other way."

Hughes reached us. Radan sighed.

"How you like that, Mister Nichols? Getting her really cleaned up around here." Hughes' eyes sparkled. He waved the brush and a long stream of soapy water sprinkled on Radan's suit. Radan kept on smiling, brushing at it with his hat.

"I'm sorry." Hughes said. "Excited, I guess. You can't blame me, getting the courts all fixed up and all."

Hughes moved in closer and stood there, holding the brush so it dribbled gobs of soap on Radan's shiny right shoe.

"I'll have her cleaned up in a jiffy. Then I can play. We'll get up a game, right, Mister Nichols? You and your wife can come out and we'll have a fine time. I think the Donnes are becoming interested in the sport." Then Hughes nudged my arm, looking at Radan. "Is this somebody new—going to stay here, Mister Nichols?"

I shook my head.

"I'm afraid not, sir." Radan said. He walked toward the rear of the apartments, past some benches I'd put beside the shuffleboard court.

"Mister Nichols?" Hughes called.

We kept going. At the corner of the apartments, Radan paused. He got out a handkerchief and bent down, rubbing at the soap and water on his shoe. It took all the shine off. "I don't exactly go for this." he said.

"Sorry."

He straightened. "You smash your finger in the wreck, Mister Nichols?"

"What wreck?"

"That won't do any good. There's no use pretending. We know all about it. Either you take action, or we take action. That's the way it is." He was still very apologetic.

"You haven't made yourself clear."

"Whether you like it or not, you're mixed up in it now, Mister Nichols. I don't believe you realize that."

"I still don't understand."

"Yes. You do. Don't be foolish. We don't like to get rough. It's silly, this day and age. You should understand that."

"Are you threatening me about something?"

"Mister Nichols, for Lord's sake! Now, look—you certainly wouldn't want to see your place burned down, would you? Your motel, I mean? Now, would you?"

He talked very pleasantly. He was almost pleading, and very matter-of-fact about everything. Looking at him, talking with him, you would think he was some kind of a businessman. He was obviously prosperous. But there was something deadly about him all the same.

"We just can't let it go on, Mister Nichols."

I could hear Hughes working on the cement with the scrub brush, and his dry, papery cough.

"All right." Radan said. "I take it that I have your answer. Right?"

I still said nothing.

"All right." he said. "You've had your chance. I was told to give you ten minutes, and I have. You've used them up, playing this all wrong. Now, where's Vivian Rise?"

"Never heard of her." He was beginning to make me mad, now. Damned if I'd tell him anything.

"Have you seen Noel Teece, Mister Nichols?"

I didn't say anything.

Radan put his hat on. He watched me levelly. "You've had it, Nichols."

He turned and walked rapidly away. I started after him. He walked on past Hughes, then paused and stepped over beside the court. Hughes was on his knees, scrubbing the cement.

Hughes looked up and saw Radan and smiled and bobbed his head. Radan looked at him for a long moment, then he lifted his foot, placed it against the old man's head and shoved. Hughes slipped down onto the soapy cement.

"Listen here!" I said, going after him. Radan paused and looked back at me, turned sharply and cut across the lawn. He reached his car. I stood in the middle of the lawn by the sign and watched him get in the car.

Radan took a last look at the motel, started the engine and made a fast rocking U-turn on the broken road. He vanished around the corner, the engine hissing.

I went over to Hughes. "I'm sorry about that."

"It's all right, Mister Nichols. I could tell he was a sorehead when I spilled that soap on him. He didn't hurt me. There's all kinds in this world. Now, listen—I think the court should be renumbered. Have you any white paint? I'm really good at lettering."

"You'll find some in the garage for number one."

He nodded happily and I started back toward the office. I had to see Vivian again, but I didn't know how I was going to get to her.

This Radan was a beaut....

"Roy?"

"Yes?"

"What did he want?"

"Oh, that guy? Kind of a funny character. Says he, well—wanted to build a motel. Comes from over in Tampa. He's been riding around looking at motels. He likes this one. Asked me a few questions, that's all."

"Sure peculiar."

"I know it. Hard to figure. Wants to build a motel. He sympathized with us, being stuck the way we are, with the road not through yet. He mentioned taxes."

"Please. Don't even speak of them. What'll we do, Roy? What are we going to do about money?"

"I'll think of something."

We were in the office and she was standing in the doorway leading to our living room. She turned and went back into the kitchen.

I wished I could think of something to send Bess out for, so I could go talk with Vivian. But there wasn't a thing I could do. And there she was in the doorway again. When Bess looked at me, it was in that funny way that I didn't like.

"Roy, you look sick. Honestly, I never saw you look so bad. Try not to worry about things. Everything'll be all right. You wait and see. Hasn't everything always worked out all right?"

"Sure."

"Or is it just that you had a hot time up there in Chicago?"

"Nothing like it. I just got drunk, that's all. But it was bad stuff. Maybe

I can't take it any more." I had to get away from her and think. Try to.

"You don't suppose that man had anything to do with the bank?"

"No." She was so worried, and there was nothing I could do to straighten her out about things. Not now. I wanted to and I couldn't.

"Maybe they've put the place up for sale, or something. Without telling us about it."

"Stop it, Bess!" My voice was hoarse. "They can't do a thing like that. You know that."

"What's the *matter* with you, Roy?"

I went outside and stood on the porch and looked down across the lawn. There was no sign of Vivian. I knew that was no way to act if I wanted to keep Bess quiet. I went back inside. She was standing by the kitchen table with both hands flat on top. She didn't look up as I came in.

"I'm sorry about that."

"It's all right."

"Everything's got me down. Trying to figure a way out f this mess."

"I know."

Oh God, I thought, if she only did know....

A few minutes later she was in by the desk, checking the bills. "Roy—that man just drove past again."

I went over by the desk. "What?"

She turned and looked at me, frowning. "The man in the hearse, Roy. I've seen him go by the place twice now."

I stared out the window. It was quiet on the street, but I knew she had seen him. And I began to know she would keep on seeing him.

NINE

"Mrs. Nichols. I've got to see your husband."

"Oh, hello, Miss Latimer."

"Is Mister Nichols around?"

"Yes. He's in the other room. What is it?"

"Well—I think he'd better have a look at my stove. There's something wrong with the stove."

"What seems to be the matter?"

I went on out there. She was on the back porch, talking with Bess. She was still wearing the shorts and she looked wild. Her hair was like she'd been combing it with her fingers. She had on lots of lipstick, but the rest of her face was the color of flour.

She saw me over Bess's shoulder and her eyes got kind of crazy. Bess heard me and turned, holding the door open.

"Miss Latimer's having trouble with her stove." She gave me the eye.

"Well, all right. You want me to have a look?"

"Would you?" Vivian said. "I hate terribly bothering you like this."

"Sure." I brushed past Bess, Vivian went off the porch onto the grass and Bess stepped after me. I didn't dare say anything. If Bess came along, there was nothing you could do.

"Think I'll see how Hughes is making out with the shuffle board courts." Bess said.

"Every time I light the gas, it pops." Vivian said.

"Air in the line."

Bess went off along the rear of the apartment.

"God, Nichols!"

"Wait'll we get over there."

As soon as we were in her kitchen, she whirled, and it was like somebody was running a knife in and out of her "I saw him. Radan! That's Wirt *Radan!* I know about him. I know why he's here. You don't even have to tell me. He's famous, Nichols—famous! I met him once in New York. He moves around the country. You know what he is?" She was breathing quickly, her eyes very bright, and she had her fists bunched tight against her thighs. "He's a killer."

"Cut it out...."

"Sure. You wouldn't believe that. I knew you wouldn't, you're such a damned square. But it's true. That's his job. He's one of them that works to a contract. You think they don't do that any more? Do you? You're crazy, if you think that!"

"Take it easy."

"Noel told me about him just a few days ago." She paused and turned and held her back to me that way, and her shoulders began to shake. She whirled on me again and I thought for a second she was going to yell. She didn't. She just kept talking, with her voice held down in her throat, and she was really scared now. "Noel said Wirt Radan was getting so tough the men are afraid to work with him, even."

"And you told me you weren't mixed up in any of this."

"I'm not. I was Noel's girl. That's all."

"Only that wasn't enough."

"Nichols! You've got to get me out of here!"

I wanted that as much as she did. Only, how? "Did you ever stop to think of the mess you've got me in?" I said. "Did you?"

"I'm paying you. Remember?"

"Vivian, all you think about is that money. Money can't take care of everything."

"You're thinking about it, too! Plenty. True, Nichols?"

"All right. How do you want to work it?"

"I want plane tickets to South America—Chile, probably. You'll have to get me to the airport, see me on the plane. Somehow. Then you'll get yours."

"Why not just get the tickets? Can't you get them yourself, for that matter? You can drive to the airport yourself. It's not far."

"Can we still get them now? You think it's open, downtown? The ticket office?"

"I guess so."

"Then let's get going. I can't go alone. I know they'll be at the airport."

I just stood there. She turned and rushed out of the room and I heard her in the bedroom, yanking the bureau drawers. I went in there.

She had the brief case. She got her suitcase off a chair, snapped it shut without putting anything extra back inside, and looked at me. "Let's go, Nichols."

She was off her rocker. She wasn't thinking; traveling in some kind of a vacuum, she was like a hound dog on the scent, flying like the crow.

But I thought about that money, and not only that—if I could get her out of here now, I could tell Bess I'd taken her downtown. Tell her anything. Because she'd be gone and there wouldn't be any chance for argument.

She glanced down at her shorts, turned abruptly, dropped the brief case and opened the suitcase and whipped out a blue skirt. Her anxiety was almost comical, except you knew how real it was.

I heard Bess call to me from outside.

"No." Vivian said. "Please—don't go." She grabbed me. "Tell her something—anything. You know I've got to leave here now."

I shoved her and she went windmilling across the bedroom and landed against the wall. I beat it out into the kitchen and Bess was just coming up on the porch. I opened the door. Bess tried to look past me. I let her look.

"Did you fix her stove all right?" There was a slight touch of sarcasm in her voice. But as she looked at me, she began to smile.

I grinned at her. "You go fix dinner. I'll be along."

She turned and went back toward our place. Vivian came out of the bedroom wearing the blue skirt. That wild look was still in her eyes. There was something about the way she held her mouth, too; a tenseness that told you a little about what went on inside her. Just a young kid, really—only not a kid—and her life all twisted out of shape. And she was trying to save her life in the only way she knew. Watching her, I felt a sense of hopelessness.

"All right. Let's get going."

She picked up the brief case and the suitcase and I saw the filmy red scarf fall softly, lazily, from the brief case to the floor. She jammed the case under her arm and we went out into the kitchen.

"Wait'll I check." I looked outside. Nobody. "All right. You get in your car. I'll be along in a minute, so it won't look so bad. Make it fast, now, to the garage."

"Yes." She gave me a quick harried look, turned and went outside. I watched her cross the grass swiftly and slip between the garages toward the drive, her shoulders held rigid, as if she were trying to hide behind them. Twinkle-toes.

I waited another moment. I knew it was better this way. She'd be gone, and the worry would be gone with her. She'd carry that part wherever she went, but it would be off my back. Somehow, I knew it was going to work out all right.

I stood there, trying to get my breath evened out, and then I went on outside and closed the door and started across the grass. She came running at me.

She tripped, stumbling, and the suitcase fell out of her hand. She made a wild grab for it, missed, and came on, her mouth open and her eyes stricken and sick.

"Get back!" She kept running. "He's out there. Radan just drove through the alley!" She came past me and rushed inside.

I went on out and got the suitcase and made it back to the porch. I entered the kitchen and looked at her. "Did he see you?"

"No. No, he didn't see me." She kind of turned and bent over like an old woman, and let her head hang, and went into the living room, moaning to herself. She still had the brief case plugged under her arm.

"Did he stop?"

"No. I saw him coming. I was right out in the drive, there. He'd just turned in off the street with that big black car. I could see his face—looking. Not at me, though. Oh, *damn it!*"

"That's bad."

"I'll never be able to get out of here now. He'll watch, and he'll watch." She flopped down into a chair, hugging the brief case and she began to cry. It was wild, angry, hurt crying.

"The money. We'd better hide the money again." I said. "But not in the bureau. I got a better place. Come on."

She just sat there. I went over and grabbed her arm, pulled her up, and she leaned against me, shuddering. She was an awful sight and I felt sorry for her.

"The apartment next door's empty. That'll be a better place—just in case. We'll have to run for it again. The front way this time. So come on."

We went outside, and there was no sign of Radan. The sun was beginning to dip. Another day gone, and things just that much worse. We went in next door. It was hot and stuffy. It hadn't been aired in weeks, and our footsteps were loud on the floors. "Suppose somebody moves in here?"

"They won't. I'll see to that. Listen, I'm going to drain the tank behind the toilet, shut it off, and we'll put the brief case in there."

She was lost again, praying. I got the brief case and there was an immediate thrill, knowing what was inside it. It was heavy and full and it made you want to run some place, hanging onto it. I took it into the bathroom, turned the water off, flushed the john, and put the money in the tank.

"What are you doing over here, Miss Latimer?"

"I—we—he's checking the stove for something."

I came out of the bathroom, dodged into the kitchen and stood there sweating. Bess was talking in the living room now, about it being so hot. I went out the back door and let it slam real hard. I went over to number six, and stood there fiddling with the stove, turning it on and off, hating every minute of this and wishing I didn't have to treat Bess like a stranger. I could hardly see the stove.

Pretty soon they came along. Bess entered the kitchen first and I didn't look at her. I got out a match and lit the stove, and the gas caught just fine.

"Hi. She's okay now."

"That's fine." Bess said.

"Thanks so much, Mister Nichols. Honestly, I hate all this trouble I'm causing."

I looked at Bess. Boy, was she sparking! Vivian moved past us, on into the living room and stood by the front window.

"You just call me if there's any more trouble."

Bess and I went outside.

"You're sweating, Roy."

"Roy. She's got a man's suitcase in there."

"What?"

"Miss Latimer. She's got a man's suitcase, and it's full of a man's clothing."

"What've you been doing in her apartment?"

"I just looked in, that's all, while you were next door. I saw it. What would she be doing with another suitcase, like that?"

"Darned if I know. Maybe it's her husband's. Maybe she's married, just doesn't want to say anything. Some women are like that."

"She acts pretty queer, you ask me. Has she said anything to you about being married?"

"No"

I had to shut her up, or get away from her. I couldn't take it, because I knew now that I was in on everything with Vivian, and I was scared. Just plain scared. I didn't know what to do. With Radan skulking around like that. Only you couldn't call the cops. Not on a thing like this, not even if you did want to back out of the bad part.

Besides, that money. It was there, and I *had* to have some of it. Somehow. It was the only way I could see—even if it was a wrong way. When the taxes for this property came due, we'd really be in the soup. I didn't want to lose this motel. I wasn't going to lose it. I couldn't let Bess take it on the chin any more. She'd never had any peace, never—all our married life, it had been like this. From one thing to another, never any peace, and by God, she was going to have peace and some of the things she wanted.

One way or another.

Even if I had to get hold of the brief case myself, and run.... God, I was in a sweet mess and I knew it. But something had to be done.

"Roy." Bess said, "I hate to keep at you like this. But I know darned well something's the matter with that woman. You must have seen that. She's afraid of something. We've got enough around here without somebody tossing their troubles in our laps."

"How do you mean?"

"I don't know. I can't figure her out, but I do know something's wrong. You think I should ask her?" I knew Bess had been doing a lot of thinking. There was no way of her catching onto the truth, but I didn't like her this way. It was my problem, not hers. She said, "I'll bet she's in some kind of trouble, Roy."

"Well, maybe so. But let's not stick our noses in, huh?"

"Yes. I know you're right."

I went into the bedroom and lay down. I finally dozed a little. Once I heard Bess come in, very softly, and stand there looking at me. I didn't open my eyes. She went away.

I woke up and it was dark. I could hear Bess breathing quietly. I rolled off the bed carefully, so as not to disturb her and stood there in the dark. It was after midnight by the clock ticking away on the dresser. I had conked off for sure. I hadn't even eaten and Bess had let me sleep. The poor kid was plenty worried about everything.

I started to undress, then looked at her again. She was really knocking it, breathing deep and heavy.

I left the room. In the office, I looked out through the window. The sign was still lit up and I sat down at the desk for a while, trying to think of something. I got nowhere.

It was real quiet, inside and outside. And it got real lonely.

I finally got up and went and looked into the bedroom again. She was sleeping quietly. There was a dim shaft of light down across her face, from where one of the slats in the Venetian blinds was tilted open. She looked worried, even in sleep. I knew she was catching on to things, to something anyway, and it troubled her plenty, even if she didn't know what it was. She knew me too well, and she trusted in me too much, and God, I loved her and I wanted her to be happy.

I left the room and slipped out of the back door and around between the apartments. It was quiet over at number six, but there was a light inside. I went up onto the porch and kept checking out there on the lawn. I opened the door and stepped inside, and closed the door.

"Yeah." Noel Teece said. "*Yeah*. Here he is now."

They were sitting there. She was on a chair, with her hands clenched in her lap, holding her thumbs, staring up at me, round-eyed and hopeless-looking.

Teece was humped on the studio couch. He was all bandaged up, the way I'd seen him. His hat was on, jutting above the bandages on his face.

TEN

Teece had an evil-looking eye.

That eye watched me, blinking under the hat brim, and you kind of wished you could see the other eye, too. But the bandage covered that. The eye that watched me was bloodshot and tired, yet kind of frantic and steady, even behind the blinking. His cheek was mottled and his lips were pale and thin and he needed a shave. He just sat there, blinking that damned eye at me.

"Noel just came in. He sneaked in the back way." Vivian said. "Noel, honey—we thought you were dead. You know we thought that."

He kind of laughed. It sounded a little like he was crying inside.

"You two been happy?"

Neither of us said anything. I didn't like the looks of him at all. Like I say, there was something frantic about the way he looked. As if he was out of hand and knew it and didn't care. He was breathing pretty fast.

"All afternoon I've been trying to get in here, you two. Now, I'm here."

His eye was watering. Vivian just sat there, holding onto her thumbs.

"Thought I was dead, did you? Well, I'm not dead."

Still we didn't speak.

"You know why I'm here?"

Vivian began nodding slowly.

Teece stood up. Now I could see what it was. The man was scared. He was so scared he didn't know what to do next. It was knocking the hell out of him, the way he was.

"I talked with them on the phone." he told us. "I can't go see them. They'll kill me. Oh, yes. But if I get that money back to them, maybe I can swing it. Maybe they'll understand."

He said it like that, but you could tell he didn't really believe himself. He knew they wouldn't understand. That's what you could read in the half of his face that showed, and in the way he began prowling up and down the room.

"All right. Where's the money, Viv?"

She looked across at me.

"We haven't got it." I told him. I heard myself say it and went along with it. "They beat you here, Teece. You worked too slow."

He was like an animal. His mouth came open and the way I'd said that had hurt him. He stood there, blinking, with the light gleaming in that bloodshot eye.

"We gave the money to some guy called Radan."

"Wirt Radan?" He turned on her and she bobbed her head fast.

"That's right, Noel. He came and we gave the money to him. We had to."

"But, he's—"

"Radan said they were going to get you, Teece."

"You lie! Both of you lie! You and Viv, you think I can't see through this? You're planning it together. But you're not getting away with this. Now, where's that money?" He reached into his coat and came up with a gun. It wasn't very large, but it wouldn't have to be. Only he wasn't sure of himself. He wasn't certain that we were lying.

"That's not going to do a damned bit of good. I told you, this fellow Radan came here today. This afternoon. He drives a big black Caddy. He knew all about everything—you, the accident, the works. We gave him the money, and that's it."

He moved his head slightly from side to side.

"It's the truth, Noel." She came up out of the chair, with an imploring look on her face. It was a real art, the way she did it. "It's true, Noel." She stood there, looking straight into his eye. "He told us what they were going to do. There wasn't any other way. *You know Radan.* Sure, I was going to try and get away with the money. Wouldn't you have done the same thing? What else was there to do?"

He kept on moving his head from side to side.

"Noel, honey. We thought you were dead. I did the only thing I could do. I've been trying to get Nichols to help me, see? So I was going to pay him to help me get out of the country. He needs the money for his motel, here. Can't you understand that?"

The gun began to droop a little and the headshaking slowed down almost to a stop.

"So, then Radan came here this afternoon. He burst right in here, Noel. He saw the brief case we had the money in—remember? I gave it to him. There was nothing else to do."

A crafty look came into the eye. "Radan just took the money? Didn't he do anything else?"

I said, "He threatened a lot of things. Maybe it's all still up in the air. He hasn't been back. That's why I came over here now, to ask her what we should do."

He wheeled on me with the gun, and it scared me. I made a pass at the gun with one hand. It connected. The gun clattered on the floor.

"Don't!"

He came at me with that one arm, his head back, cursing. It was comical. Him with his arm in a sling and his head all bandaged up and that scared look in his one bloodshot eye. But he swung, just the same.

I tried to hold him off. Then I took a poke at him, shying away from his face. I hit him in the chest. He staggered back toward the door and the door opened and Bess stood there, blinking sleepily and hitching at her housecoat over her pajamas.

"I heard a noise." she said.

He fell against her. She shoved him off and looked at us. He turned and saw her and his face reddened.

"What's going on?"

"It's nothing, Bess. It's all a mistake."

Teece eyed me and swallowed and looked at Bess.

There was the gun on the floor, but Bess hadn't seen it. Vivian saw the gun and she stepped over and stood just beyond it, so Bess wouldn't be able to see it even if she looked down there.

"But, Roy—" Bess said.

"Yes." Vivian said. "Sure. Look, this man—" she motioned toward Teece—"is a friend of mine. Mister Nichols must have heard something and made a mistake."

"That's right, Bess. I couldn't sleep after I woke up. I went out to get some air and I saw this guy snooping. I thought he was a prowler. Actually, I guess all he was doing was looking for Miss Latimer's apartment I'm sorry I was so bull-headed."

Teece's eyebrow shot up.

"He'd planned on coming down." Vivian said. "He was supposed to meet me here. He met with an accident on the way. Maybe you've noticed how worried I've been? Well, this is why. Mister Nichols thought he was doing the right thing. He came to help me."

Bess stood there and took it all in. Then she turned and stepped out onto the porch. "I'm sorry." she said through the screen door. "You coming, Roy?"

"Sure. Just a minute."

She went away and we looked at each other.

"The money." Teece said.

"We told you. Radan's got it."

Teece went over and picked up the gun and looked at it. He put it away.

"Radan, huh?" he said, and there was this funny new look in that eye of his. He stared at Vivian for a second and she looked right back at him, nodding slightly. Then he turned away and went outside. He disappeared along the side of the apartment, back toward the garages. I started for the door.

"Don't leave me alone!"

"I've got to get out of here."

I opened the door and stepped out on the porch. She came up to the door and stood there, scratching her fingernails on the screen.

"Don't you see?" she said. "I can't leave now. I can't leave!"

I went down off the porch and around toward the garage. I heard a car start up out in the alley. It drove away fast, showering gravel. I listened to it until I couldn't hear it any more, then I went back to our place....

"Roy, I'd like you to ask Miss Latimer to leave. I'd appreciate it if you'd go over there now and ask her to pack her things."

"Bess, don't be silly. I know how it looked. It bothered me, too. But everything's all right now."

"I'm sorry. But I'm asking you to do this for me. I don't like it, the way things are over there. Are you going to do it for me?"

"Look. Let her stay till morning." I reached out and drew her close, and kissed her, but she was kind of cold about it.

"Morning?"

"All right. In the morning, you go over there the first thing, Roy."

ELEVEN

In the morning I figured she forgot about what she'd said. Either that, or maybe thought better of it. I didn't get much sleep. I lay there thinking it through, but trying to stay away from the real part—how it was working out. I kept trying to figure how I could have got my hands on some of that money, or all of it, without this mess. There was no use telling myself I didn't want that money. There were too many reasons why I needed it.

The big thing I kept figuring was that it was crooked money to begin with. Somehow that made me feel better. I kept coming back to that, trying to figure some way. And then I remembered that was how Vivian had talked in the hotel room. It wasn't money that really belonged to anybody, she'd said. Or to that effect. And she was right.

But, there was no way. Not unless I went over there and took it and got out of here. I thought about that. How I could grab the money and run. Then I could mail Bess enough to pay off the motel, and … only it wasn't any good. It didn't have that part I wanted—the peace of mind part.

Because without the peace, you had nothing. And you couldn't buy that, cither.

Anyway, all I wanted out of this world was Bess and the motel. The motel. That was a laugh, and I lay there with Bess asleep beside me, thinking of her, and how I could make some decent kind of life for us together…

I figured I'd done enough to belong to a part of that brief case, anyway. Not a big part. Just enough to take care of immediacies. Where did that come from?

And then I saw that Radan's face, like it was hanging up there on the ceiling of my mind. And I knew what kind of a guy he was. I didn't want to mix with him.

It was all real crazy. Albert, and the Lincoln and Vivian and Noel Teece, and now Radan, like a parade through the bloody twilight. And the brief case with that red scarf tied around it. Only she'd dropped the scarf. Talisman.

"Go to sleep, Roy."

"Yeah."

What in hell was I going to do? The emptiness got filled with a kind of frantic rushing and my heart got to going it, lying there. I wanted to yell and crack my knuckles, or sock somebody.

Because it was all closing in. I could tell.

You recognize the landmarks, because you've seen them before, if you've been around enough. You go along trying to hold it all gutted up and hard and ignoring it all, then one fine day it busts wide open. And there you are. You got to do something, and there's nothing to do. You can't think, even.

Southern Comfort Motel—crawling with fright.

That Vivian was a dilly, sure enough. Getting herself messed up like she had. Shooting the works to Teece, and so scared now with what she'd done, she could hardly stand up.

It was like I didn't quite know them and I didn't want to. Just that brief case. A piece of that….

So I finished breakfast and she didn't say a word about anything. My second coffee, I said, "Maybe mow the lawn today."

She clinked the plates and coffee cups to the sink. She ran the water. She shut it off. She had on a kind of blue-flowered housecoat and she looked nice, only worried.

"Roy?"

"Yeah?" Here it was.

"Have you forgotten what I said last night?"

I kind of ran my hand across my face, trying to remember what she meant, letting her think that was it. "You know what I mean. About Miss Latimer. I want you to go over there and ask her to leave."

"I figured that was just a pipe dream."

"It's no dream. You want me to do it? If you won't, I will."

She sure had me there. Now what was I going to do? Tell Vivian that, and she'd freeze over there in number six, and you couldn't get her out with a derrick.

"Well?"

"You'd have to give her back her rent money."

"A pleasure."

She left the kitchen. "We can't have people like her running around, Roy. She'll hurt the name of the place. Imagine, that wreck of a man coming in the middle of the night. Maybe she picked him up off the street, how do you know?"

I tagged along and she went into the office, to the desk, and counted the money out of the cigar box and looked over at me.

"I'd appreciate it if you'd do it, Roy."

I took the money. "Can't we give her a little more time?"

"You want her staying here? That it? With her nice tight shorts and everything?"

I looked at her.

"I'm sorry I said that, Roy. Honest. I didn't mean it." She stared down at the desk, then up at me again. "It's just she worries me, being here. She isn't right, and you know it."

"Okay."

I left the office and let the screen door slam.

I came along by number six and looked it over. It was quiet. What was I going to do? I had to tell her what Bess said, but there was no saying how she'd take it. I knew how she'd take it. It had to be Bess's way.

Well, she sure had that red scarf tied around her neck.

Vivian was right there on the floor in the doorway between the living room and the bedroom hall. She was all crumpled up in a twisted knot, the blue skirt up to her belly, and her face was a hell of a color. Her eyes bugged and her mouth was open, her tongue all swelled up like a fat pork chop.

I turned around, wanting to run, then stopped. The scarf was tied around her neck so tight the flesh bulged around it. I got over there, still holding her refund money in my hand, and I touched her.

She was cold.

TWELVE

Well, Vivian was gone, all right. Only it wasn't exactly the way Bess had wanted her to go.

I knelt there for a long time, dizzy and half sick. Her shirt was torn at one shoulder and there was bruises on her arms. She was crumpled on the floor like paper gets crumpled.

That red scarf. Vivian's good luck. Her talisman.

Then I remembered the brief case. I got out of there, still carrying the rent refund wadded in my hand. I shoved it into my pocket and cut over next door. I kept thinking, What now—What now—? I went next door, let myself in and headed for the bathroom.

I got the lid off the tank and there was the brief case. All I could think was, Maybe she told whoever did this where the money was. I got it out of there, and the money was inside. I put the lid back on the tank, turned the water on and headed for the rear of the apartment.

I had to hide it again. But where?

I got out in the garage and stood there, wondering what to do with the brief case. So finally I climbed up on the hood of the Chevie and grabbed a beam and snaked myself up there where I had some lumber piled. I crawled back into the corner under the eave and shoved the brief case under some of the boards. You wouldn't find it unless you knew it was there. They'd tear the whole motel apart first.

They? They—who? And it kept hitting me that the law would be in on this now. There wasn't anything I could do about that. I climbed down onto the car again, and hit the dirt. There was no sign of anybody. I made a run for it, down between the garages and to the back door of number six. It was open. I walked through the kitchen, and she was still lying there on the floor.

"Roy?"

It was Bess. She called again from out front. I stepped past the body and walked through the living room fast, and out the door. I stood on the porch.

Bess came across the lawn. She'd been talking with Mrs. Donne who was settled in her beach chair, a half-filled drink in her hand.

"Well, did you tell her?"

I didn't say anything.

"All right. *I'll* tell her!" She tried to push past me. I got hold of her and held her still. She had on a white dress and she looked fresh and lovely, but I couldn't remember ever seeing her look so worried. Her eyes had that kind of not-quite-looking-at-you way they get.

"Don't go in there, Bess. Bess—" I couldn't bring myself to say it.

"I certainly *am* going in there! I'm going to tell her. Didn't you say anything to her at all? What'd you do, just stand there?" She pulled away from me and started for the door of number six. I turned and went after her. "Is *he* still inside?"

"No."

"Then, what?" She knocked lightly on the door, brushing some hair away from her forehead.

"Nobody's going to answer." I said softly.

Bess opened the door and went on inside. I followed her, thinking, What am I going to do? Bess just stood there, staring and I could see her start to yell. If she yelled, that was her business. She didn't. She cut it off and turned and looked at me and blinked. "She's dead."

"Yes."

Well, she just stood there, staring. She didn't cry or scream or carry on at all, like a woman might. And I was proud of her—that she was my Bess. Then she looked at me again and swallowed.

"Well." I said. "That's the way I found her."

She shook her head and went over and slumped into a chair. I got over there and pulled her up and held her. She was trembling a little. I held her tight.

"What d'you suppose happened, Roy?"

"That's better."

I wondered for a moment if she'd thought I'd done this. Sometimes they can cook up some weird things in their heads.

She looked over there again and whipped her head away. "It's awful!"

She didn't even begin to know how awful. It was just hitting her, what had really happened. You could see it come across her face. A shadow of fear, and something like hate.

"Mrs. Nichols?"

I whirled and it was the young girl who was on her honeymoon, in number eleven. We hadn't seen anything of them, but now here she was. Her yellow dress was one of these fluffy things, and she had brown hair and brown eyes and she smiled and said, "Mrs. Nichols."

"No." I said. "Wait."

But she was already coming through the door. Bess started toward her with one hand out.

The girl said, "I was just looking for you. I saw you come in here, so I—"

and she stopped. She saw that over there on the floor and she screamed. She put both hands against her face and filled her lungs and let it rip. It rocked the house. She really had lungs. Her face got red and she kept on screaming. She turned and ran smack into the screen door, and got it open and went outside, screaming and running for number eleven.

I looked out the window. Mrs. Donne was standing out there by the beach chair. She held the glass in her hand, but it had all spilled down her front. She watched the girl run across the lawn, trying to brush the spilled drink off her dress. Then she looked over here at number six.

"We've got to phone the police."

"Wait."

"What d'you mean, wait, Roy? We can't wait."

"Wait, anyway." I went and sat in the chair and held my head. I felt blocked. I knew there was something I could do. There had to be—

"We've got to phone the police right now. Is there any reason why we shouldn't?"

"Wait." I didn't want her to call the cops. I couldn't help it, I just didn't want it, and there was nothing I could do about it.

"Roy, let's get out of here. I don't want to stay in this place."

"Yeah."

She came over and grabbed my arm. I stood up and we walked over to the door. "What's the matter with you, Roy?"

"All right."

The girl from number eleven was standing down there by her porch. She was talking with her husband through the window, waving her arms around. I quit looking at her, but I could hear her damned piping voice talking and talking.

We got over to the office and Bess sat down at the desk. "What'll I say?"

I stood there watching her.

"Roy!"

"Just go ahead. Call them."

So she did....

"How long d'you think it'll take them to get here, Roy?"

I sat there on the couch, staring at the floor. I could see Bess's feet going back and forth on the rug, back and forth. She walked up and down.

"Roy. You just sit there."

I stared.

"Did—did you touch her?"

"Yeah. She's cold."

"What could have happened? It must have been that man, the one with his arm in the sling. This is awful, Roy! It can ruin business here, too."

Business. Business.

"Here come the honeymooners."

I looked up and they came along and knocked on the office door. Bess went over and started to open the door, then decided against it.

"We're leaving." the guy said. He was a tall, thin guy, dressed in a gray suit. He had red hair and freckles, and the girl stuck close to him. "We were going to stay another week, but now we want this week's rent back. We've decided to move along. That's how—"

"All right." Bess said. There was a kind of a sting to the way she said it. "Come on in."

"No." the girl said.

They stood there, shuffling on the doorstep. Bess looked at them for a moment, then went and counted some money out of the cigar box and looked at me and went over and opened the door. She handed the guy the money.

They turned quickly and walked away without a word. The girl was talking like crazy the minute they were on the front lawn. I sure didn't envy him his married life with that one. A few more years and she'd really be a dilly.

"I wish they'd come."

"They will, don't worry."

"Roy. Who d'you think she was? Murdered—murdered right here in our place. I didn't hear a thing. Did you hear anything after we came back from over there?"

"Nope."

I got up and went out into the kitchen and washed my hands in the sink. I dried them on the dish towel. Then I took a glass down from the cupboard and filled it with water and stood there drinking. You could taste the chlorine, and the water wasn't very cold.

"What are you going to tell them, Roy?"

"What *can* I tell them?"

She was in the doorway. She came over and stood by the kitchen table. I didn't want to look at her. At the same time, I wanted to tell Bess everything I knew, all I'd been through with Vivian.

"You're spilling water all over the floor, Roy."

Well, I took that damned glass and I let her go. It whizzed across the room and smashed against the cupboards and busted, and water and glass showered. She didn't move. Just stood there, watching me. "Honey." she said, "what's the matter?"

"It's all right." I said. "It's nothing. I'm sorry I did that. It's just things, that's all. *Just things!*"

78   **GIL BREWER**

THIRTEEN

We stood there for a time without saying anything. It began to scare me a little, understanding how easy it is to start a canyon of doubt between two people. We'd been as close as any two people can get in every way, and now I could sense the separation because of doubt, and because I couldn't, or wouldn't tell her about things. I couldn't. And then I knew I wouldn't ever let it be like that.

"It's nothing, Bess. I'm just wrought up, I guess. Not getting the money from Albert, and then I went and lied to you about it all, and he writes. All the money we owe, and I can't see my way clear."

I went over to her and put my arms around her. She was kind of stiff, then she let loose and laid her head on my chest and it was like old times.

"And now this." I said. "Can you understand how I feel?"

"It scares me, Roy."

"It's damned well enough to scare anybody."

"I mean the way she looked. She was beautiful, Roy."

"I guess maybe she was."

"How could anybody *do* a thing like that? And us finding her. Why? Why?"

I patted her head and squeezed my hand on her arm. I wanted it to be right with us. But how could it ever be right from now on in?

So finally I let her go, and went in and flopped down on the bed. And I kept seeing that face, red and black. With the tongue.

Well, you either win—or you lose.

"Roy, that man in the car like a hearse drove by again."

"Oh? Yeah? Him?"

"He just keeps driving by. It's the third time I've seen him today, Roy. Maybe he's gone past other times. Just driving by, like he's going around and around the block. I wonder what he's up to?"

"I don't know."

"Well, he's sure up to something."

"Maybe."

"Please don't act that way, Roy!"

I lay face down on the bed, with my head buried in the pillow.

"I wish the police would come. Why don't they hurry up?"

They came quick enough for me. They came to the office and Bess went out there. I stuck with the bed. She told them about number six and they went over there. You could hear them, like elephants.

You could hear them talking.

There's something about the voice of the law. It's a jumble of solemn and righteous sound. It reached me all the way in the bedroom and I lay there, listening, wondering what I was going to do. What would I tell them? My mind was all cluttered up with that brief case, and how it had been for the past few days. I kept being with Noel Teece and Vivian in the Lincoln, off and on, cracking up on the Georgia road. And then the hotel room, and the brief case again, around and around.

"Roy?"

I didn't move. She came into the bedroom and over to the bed. After a little while, she sat on the bed and put her hand on my shoulder. What did she figure was the matter with me? I'd make a fine crook, all right—running off and trying to hide my head like an ostrich.

"They're still over there." she said. "One of them says he wants to talk with you. He said he'd be over here."

"Okay."

"They're going to take the body away. They've been over there an awful long time." She paused, then said, "I think you'd better come into the office—kind of show yourself. That one, he said—"

"I heard you."

"Don't snap so." Her hand rubbed on my shoulder, the fingers squeezing. I rolled over and looked at her and she grinned at me. So I grinned at her, and it was like she'd come back to me, after she'd been away a long time. And then I knew she wasn't really back at all. Because she still didn't know. But she was with me. That much of it paid for a lot.

I sat up on the edge of the bed. "Okay, honey." I said. "Thanks."

We watched each other, and she put her hand on mine and I took her hand and squeezed it and it was almost as if she knew everything and was with me. So I knew everything was all right, even if she didn't know.

"What are you going to tell them?"

I kept looking at her, kind of drinking her in. Then I grunted and got up and went into the bathroom. When I came back, she was still sitting there on the bed.

"They took the body away. I told them we found it together."

"But, Bess—we didn't."

"I told them that, though."

"Well, all right."

"I haven't seen him drive by any more, Roy—not since the police have been here."

I looked at her and she looked at me, then down at the floor, then up at me again. I grinned at her and turned and went into the office and sat down at the desk. I felt plenty shaky inside. Maybe she really thought I did it. She was acting funny. Acting good, but—would they think that?

I heard her come through the hall. She leaned against the jamb in the doorway, with her hands together just the same way Vivian used to do. "Here he comes, Roy."

"Okay. Everything's going to be all right, now."

"*Shhh!* Here he comes!"

I stared at her. Her eyebrows were all hiked up and my God, I didn't know what to do. Really, I hadn't done anything, and yet she suddenly had me feeling so guilty I was rotten with it. And then I knew it wasn't her fault. She was trying to do right by me, and I was kicking her for it....

Knock—knock....

Bess went across the room, stumbling once on the rug, and opened the door. "Yes, Officer?"

"Mrs. Nichols, hate to bother you again. Is your husband awake yet?"

So, I'd been asleep. Great.

"Yes, Officer." She held the door open, stepping out of the way, and he came into the office and took his hat off. He stood in the doorway, so she couldn't close the door. He looked over at me. "Mister Nichols?"

"Yes?"

He stepped into the room and she closed the door and leaned back against it. I could hear old Hughes talking from outside.

The plain-clothes cop was a little guy, not big at all. His voice was very soft, kind of like purring. He wore dark-brown pants and a light sand-colored jacket, white shirt, and a clean maroon tie. The tie was clipped halfway down with a silver sword and his coat was open so you could just see the hump and the edge of the butt of his holstered revolver. On the left side, for a cross draw.

"Could we talk for a little?"

"Sure thing."

He had a moon face and it was buttered like a bun with sweat. There were little pouches under his eyebrows, and his eyes looked at you through slits in the pouches. Brown, bright eyes. This was the man whom I'd deal with.

I couldn't help staring at him. I'd been waiting to meet him for a long time. Almost ever since that Lincoln picked me up on the Georgia road.... His hat was brown, like a chocolate drop.

"I'm Ernest Gant."

I got up and went around the desk and stuck out my hand. He transferred his hat and we shook once and dropped clean. He had a waistline shake, palm down.

"Well, I guess I'll be in the kitchen." Bess said.

"That's all right, Mrs. Nichols. You needn't leave."

"I just thought—"

He smiled at her, then looked at me. "I wonder if you'd just step over to the other apartment with me a moment, Mister Nichols?"

"Sure thing."

He grabbed the door and held it open and grinned at Bess again. The grin went away and we were outside and the door was closed.

"What do you think?" I asked him.

He didn't say anything. We walked across the grass. A uniformed cop hurried across the lawn toward an official car parked by the curb. The Southern Comfort Motel had become a busy place.

Gant was nearly as tall as I was, after all—it was just that he seemed smaller, somehow. He wasn't, though. Not really.

We went inside number six. There was nobody there. The body was gone.

"Your wife tells me you found the body together?"

I started to go along with that. Then there was something in the tone of his voice, in the way he looked at me. It gave me a queer feeling and a certain respect for him, too. "I want to clear that up. She said that, but it wasn't quite that way. I came in first."

"I understand."

He went over and stood by a chair. Then he sat down. His actions seemed to be thought out beforehand. He put his hat over his knee and patted his pockets. He came up with a crumpled package of cigarettes.

"Smoke, Mister Nichols?"

"No, thanks."

"Sure?"

"Well, all right—I guess I could." I took one and fumbled for a match. By the time I found one, he had a Zippo going under my nose. It was nice and steady with a big flame. He went over and sat down again.

"Why don't you sit down?"

I got over on the couch. I kept looking toward the hall doorway, the area drew my gaze. They had cleared the body away and there wasn't a trace.

Somebody came clomping heavily through from the back way. I looked up and it was another harness cop. He walked into the room, his leather creaking, and stepped around the place on the floor where the body had been.

"You want anybody posted outside, Lieutenant?"

"You stick around, all right?"

"Burke's with me."

"Tell him to stick around, too. I'll let you know. They're finished with the floor?"

"I guess so."

The cop looked at me. He was a man of perhaps thirty-five and there was nothing at all in his look, the way they look at you. He had very pale blue eyes, and his cap was on very straight. "We'll be out in the car, then."

Gant nodded and went on smoking. He had very dark hair, parted neatly on one side and brushed straight back. "You came in first?"

"That's right."

"When was that? What time, about?"

"This morning."

"This is this morning. Could you narrow it down some?"

"Well." I didn't have any idea about time. Time was suddenly all run together like syrup. "Maybe nine?"

He smoked. He would come back to the time later, after I'd thought about it a while. He really had me thinking about time now. When *had* I come in here?

"And your wife? When did she come in?"

"A little after I came in."

"Oh. I see. Let me get this straight. I thought you both came over here together, and you came in first. But she—?"

"No. That's not right. I came over alone."

He nodded. "That's straight enough. Then your wife came along. That it?"

"Well, she—yes. That's right."

"You just kind of—well, waited around until she decided to come and find the body, too—huh?"

I looked at him.

He held his hand up. He grinned. The grin went away and he began to smoke again, really working on the cigarette. He would take a drag and inhale, and hold it and then let it out, and stare at the cigarette, and do it all over again. The cigarette was finished, with that treatment. He held the lungful of smoke and ground the cigarette out in a standing ash tray. Then he let the smoke out in a long sigh, down into his shirt.

I was getting mixed up, and it made me mad.

"What did you do when you found the body of this woman—girl—in here?"

I started to blurt something, then paused, and that was all he needed. I could see it in his eyes, no real expression, just a shadow. I wanted to cover it, he was thinking. You couldn't cover it. You make your slip just once and it stands there, laughing, sneering at you for the rest of your life.

"Did you touch it?"

"No. Of—yes. Yes, I did."

"Why?"

"I don't know why. I just touched it, that's all. Wouldn't you touch it?"

"I would. But then, that's my job. It doesn't matter, Mister Nichols. Don't misunderstand, please. I've got to get everything as straight as I can. You see, your wife was rather, well—nervous? She tried not to be, but she was. A normal reaction."

I nodded.

His voice was soft, like velvet. Honest, it purred like a little well-oiled motor. There was nothing sleepy about his eyes. He just seemed to be holding cards, that's all. He hadn't said anything to make me know that for sure, but I couldn't help believing it. I was guilty of a lot of stuff that had to do with this crime, and it was stuff I didn't want known. I had to catch hold of myself, and keep the grip.

There was something about Gant … I didn't like him. So what could I do about that?

"Was the body cold?"

"Yes."

"Then what?"

"How do you mean?"

"What did you do then?"

I started to say something and he leaned back in the chair and held up his hand and cleared his throat. "Wait. I mean, let's get back a little bit. Why did you come over here?"

"Didn't my wife tell you anything about—?"

"Just answer the question."

"I don't have to answer anything."

He sighed and stared down into his lap. He lifted his hat and rapped it on his knee and looked out the window. Then he tipped his head a little to one side and said, "Would you really mind answering a few questions, Mister Nichols? You'll have to sooner or later. Why not now?"

"I didn't say I wouldn't. I just—"

"Fine! That's the way to talk."

I could feel the shaking start in my stomach and spread. "No reason in the world why I wouldn't answer some questions."

"Look." he said. "I have to go about this in my own way. This is a serious thing."

"I know it."

"This woman was murdered. Somebody choked her to death with a silk scarf. She took quite a beating, too."

"I know."

"Oh. You know."

"I saw the bruises."

"Mister Nichols, don't you think you'd better put that cigarette out? It's going to burn your fingers. It makes me nervous."

FOURTEEN

"Let's relax. All right?"

I jammed the cigarette into the dirt around the cactus plant on the table by the couch. I wanted to relax. I had to get hold of myself, but it wasn't working right. Like if I tried to lean one way, I'd really be leaning in the opposite direction. I looked at my hands and they seemed steady, yet I could feel them tremble. The shaking was all through me. I couldn't control it.

If I refused to answer his questions, it would only make things worse.

"You have a nice place here."

"Thanks."

"Been here long?"

"Oh, not too long."

"Must be expensive, the upkeep." He shook his head. "Especially now. Must be a headache, with the highway all torn up. Hasn't that done something to your business?"

"It's knocked it off a little."

He wasn't looking at me. Then he did. "Mrs. Nichols said something about a man's suitcase being in here."

I didn't say anything.

"Did you see it?"

"I didn't really notice."

"Did Miss Latimer mention anything about a man?"

"No."

"Nothing like her being married, anything like that?"

"I didn't talk with her much."

It troubled me that he thought her name was Latimer. I didn't know why. Then I began to realize just how snarled up things were. With me smack in the middle. And I was already off on the wrong track with Gant. There was nothing to do about that, either.

"What about this man who was here last night?" He had left it open. I didn't know what to say. "You met him, didn't you?"

"Yeah—I met him."

"How did you happen to meet him?"

I told him how I'd thought he was a prowler and had gone to see if Miss Latimer was all right. Telling it to him that way, it came out easy. Then after it was out I sat there and felt the sweat. Every word I said, it got deeper. Why couldn't I just tell him? Tell him everything?

I knew why, and it was hell. That money hidden in the garage. There was no reason why the law should ever find it, because they knew nothing about it. It didn't concern them. The only thing they were after was the killer of Vivian. I couldn't tell them that, either. Sooner or later they'd find out. And I hadn't killed her, so I was all right.

"Were they arguing, Mister Nichols?"

"Who?"

"This man and Miss Latimer. Did you notice whether or not they got along—seemed to?"

"Oh, sure. There might have been some argument."

"Your wife said something about it. When she came in she said you—"

"Oh, that. Well, the guy sort of resented my busting in like that. You understand."

"I see."

All I had to do was keep that brief case hidden the way it was and everything would be all right. Even if Gant was a snoop, and I was pretty sure he was. Then I remembered something.

I looked at him and it came to me and I almost fell off the couch. I had never had any thought hit me this hard.

"What's the matter, Mister Nichols?"

"Nothing. Pain in my stomach."

"Oh?"

"Cramp, like."

I put my hand on my stomach and made a face. "Listen, would you excuse me a minute?"

He looked at me and frowned slightly.

All I could think was, The car. The Ford. With Georgia plates taken out in my name. It was beautiful.

"I won't be long. Just wait right here, Lieutenant. I get these pains every once in a while. There's some stuff over at the house."

"All right."

We got up and stood there.

"I'm not through talking with you, though." he said. "I'll be out front in the car."

"Fine."

I went on out quick and cut toward our place. He walked across the grass to the police car at the curb. When his back was turned, I started down between the apartments, toward the garage. I ran.

Sure as the devil, they'd trace those plates. If they found them in my name, how could I explain that? If I could just hang on long enough, I felt sure something would turn up. They'd find Teece; they'd find who she was and they'd get him for it. If I could just hang on and keep them off my neck, so I wouldn't have to spill about that money.

They'd never say anything about that money to the law. They wouldn't dare, not a one of them.

I reached the garage for number six. Her car was there, all right, with the door closed and nobody'd been around yet. Her car hadn't been mentioned. Maybe they thought she'd come down by train, or plane. Maybe they wouldn't ever ask about her car.

Don't be a complete idiot, I told myself. You know better than that. But they might play it out that way. Worse things have happened than the cops slipping up.

I worked as fast as I could. I was so excited I really did begin to get cramps.

I went along the front of the garages to our garage and got back in there by my work bench. Under the bench I knew I had a last-year New York plate. Some folks had left it here. There was a week before the time expired in Florida, so it would still be okay down here.

I couldn't find the plate. I got down under the bench and rummaged around in the junk box. It wasn't there. Then I got up and saw it sitting on a side beam, like a decoration. I grabbed it and headed for number six garage.

I had to come back for a pair of pliers and a screw driver. I was kind of sobbing to myself by then, soaked with sweat, running against time. He'd begin wondering where I was and I didn't want him to wonder.

The Georgia plate came off easy. They had it snapped on with a kind of coil spring deal, so I didn't need the screw driver and pliers, after all. I flung them across the alley into a field beside a house. I got the plates changed and stood there with the Georgia plate.

I started back for number six and Bess came around the corner of the garage, emptying the garbage. She had the little tin bucket from the house and she was just taking the lid off the big garbage can by the garage, when she heard me.

"Roy."

I had the plate jammed into my belt, in back, up under my shirt.

"You through talking with the detective?"

"No."

"What are you doing back here?"

"I was just—oh, hell—I had a cramp."

"What?"

"Stomach-ache. I don't know."

I started past her.

"You want me to fix you something?"

"I was just coming over to the house. I'll have to get back there. I told him I'd be right back."

She looked back down the line of garages, then at me. She didn't say anything. I kind of grinned at her and patted her shoulder. I left her standing there and went for the house. As soon as I was around the corner of the garage, I ran again.

In the house, I had that damned plate. I didn't know what to do with it. I had to hide it. There didn't seem to be any place and Bess would be back in a minute. I heard her coming across the yard, then, the handle on the kitchen garbage bucket squeaking and her feet hushing on the grass.

I went into the office, still with that plate cutting into my back. I looked outside. He was leaning against the car, talking with them, watching the office.

The kitchen door opened.

I went over to the studio couch, lifted a cushion and jammed the plate down in back. I pushed it as far as it'd go and something ripped. I jammed it down in there and put the cushion back and sat on the couch to see if it was all right. It was, and I was plenty tired all at once.

"Your stomach any better, Roy?"

"It'll be all right. I was just going."

"Be glad to fix you something. Bicarb, maybe?"

"No. Never mind."

She stood there watching me and I could see she wanted to help, only I couldn't let her do anything. I didn't half know what I was doing. I got up and went out and across to number six. Gant saw me and started back over the lawn, walking with a kind of head-down shuffle, holding his hat.

I waited for him, trying to ease my breathing.

"Feel better, Mister Nichols?"

"Lots better. Thanks."

Then I saw the front of my T-shirt, and my hands. There was dust on my shirt and my hands were black with dirt and grease. He hadn't noticed yet, but he would.

"Wait a second. I'm going to turn on the sprinklers."

He looked at me and frowned with that nice way he had. I paid no attention, went down by the main faucet and turned the sprinklers on. Then I turned on the spare faucet that I used for the hose, and washed my hands the best I could and splashed some up on my shirt. I saw old Hughes walking around the corner of the apartments, toward the shuffleboard court....

"Can you talk now?" Gant said.

"Sure. Fire away."

"Let's start from where we were."

"Shall we go back inside?"

"Let's just stand out here."

I didn't like the tone of his voice now. It had changed; there was something new in it. It was no longer so soft. "This man who was in the apartment with Miss Latimer. You didn't happen to hear his name?"

"Not that I know of." It came out like that and I wished I hadn't lied about that. But I couldn't correct myself, not without making it worse, so I'd have to let it ride.

"What did he do? I mean, when you came in. Did he want to fight you?"

I laughed. "He couldn't fight so well. He had one arm in a sling. His face was all bandaged up."

It made me feel good to tell the truth for a change.

Gant went over and leaned against the wrought iron railing on the small porch of number six. He looked like a man who had maybe worked hard at his studies, always treating everything very seriously, and now he was exactly where he wanted to be. He seemed certain of where he was going now, and what he was going to do. He was a thinker, keeping everything peacefully and quite seriously to himself.

"Did he want to fight?" Gant said.

"Well, yeah. I guess he did. I took a little jab at him, just to warn him."

"Your wife said you almost warned him right through the door."

"Well, it might have been harder than a jab. I mean, he was off balance."

"Mister Nichols." He looked at me and took his hat off again, then put it on again, fooling with the crown until he was satisfied. "This is no way to go about things. Honest." He shook his head. "I know you don't feel well, but you've got to get your thinking arranged better than this. You keep making me think things."

I didn't say anything.

"The way you act, anybody would think you killed that Latimer girl."

"I didn't."

"All right, then. Why don't you make an attempt to help me? This is my job, and I like it. But you're making things tough for me."

"I'm just answering your questions."

"No. You're not. You're thinking just as fast as you can, and you're saying the first thing that comes into your head. Are you trying to cover up something? Because, if you are, it won't do any good. We *always* find out, Mister Nichols. It'll just save lots of time if you'll play it straight with us."

"I'm not covering up anything. What right have you to say that?"

"There you go again." He sighed and stared down at his shoes. "We deal with things like this all the time. I'm with Homicide, and sometimes we have to talk and talk. But I can't recall ever having talked with a guy just like you, Mister Nichols. You say one thing and you must know your wife has told me different. Why do you do that?"

"Well, I don't know. I didn't realize it."

"Are you trying to shield your wife from something?"

"No. Listen, I've got a motel to run. There's a million things—"

He held up his hand and stepped closer. "I don't want to have to run you down to headquarters, Mister Nichols. But if this keeps up, we'll have to. We question a little bit different down there. And you wouldn't be able to take care of the motel by remote control." He looked around. "Anyway, there's not really much to take care of. Your wife says business isn't good at all. I don't see many people around."

He began to scare me now.

"Now, try not to get excited." he said. "I never saw anybody get so excited and pretend they aren't."

I didn't dare say anything. I wanted to either poke him or walk away. I didn't do either, because I was beginning to see how I looked to him. From his side, I'd either done this thing, or I'd done nothing. I was just a motel owner, a guy who was a near-witness to a murder, and he was trying to learn what he could from me. But with the amount of lying stuff I had inside me, it was difficult to act right. I *was* trying to think every minute— I *was* saying the first thing that popped into my head. And now I knew it couldn't be any other way.

"Your wife says Miss Latimer drove down here in what looked like a Ford sedan. That right?"

I nodded, and the world seemed to tilt a little. "That's better. What say we have a look at the car?"

I motioned with my hand and we started walking toward the garage. Boy, it was that close. If only I wouldn't make any slips now. He wasn't fooling me now. He scared me some, but I was still ahead of him. And I had to keep it that way. That brief case was Bess's and mine, from now on straight down the line. It had to be.

Now, just take it easy... easy is the way.

Because the thought I kept on hanging to was that *I hadn't done anything*. Not anything real bad. Of course not....

"You're sure lucky, Mister Nichols. Having a place like this. I'd give my eyeteeth for something like this."

"Thought you liked your job."

"Well, sometimes it catches up with me." He didn't look at me when he said that. We came around by the garages and walked up to number six.

"You always leave the garage doors open?"

"I guess she must of left it open. I didn't check."

He nodded and we stood there and looked at the Ford. The New York plate on the back bumper would knock your eye right out, it was that bright. He looked at that and went up and flicked it with his fingers. It clanged. Then he stretched his neck to look into the back seat through the rear window.

"Don't touch the car. We'll have to dust it for prints. No use messing it up any more than it probably is."

"Oh."

"Probably won't find anything. Hardly ever do. We'll have to check it, though, just the same."

"I understand." Sure, with my prints all over it. "I drove it around here and parked it in the garage for her."

"Oh, well, that won't matter. Person would have to be in the car for a time, to really lay any prints worth while. Anyway…"

He didn't finish that.

He looked the car over, looking in every window, hanging his head in the open windows. He kept looking at me, now and then. I just stood there and waited, thinking about things.

His attitude was lousy. He had no right acting the way he did, saying those things he'd said. He was getting me on the defensive and keeping me there. He didn't have anything on me. There was something speculative in the way he'd look at me, kind of like he was trying me out on things.

I turned away and walked along the garages. He could come and get me when he wanted me. The hell with him, and the hell with everybody.

"Nichols?"

He called from back there. I waited for him and he came up.

"Didn't you hear a thing last night?"

"No."

"Well, this is a hell of a one, all right. It must have been that guy who was here last night. But why?"

"She said she'd been waiting for him to show up. She didn't say he was her husband, anything like that. Just waiting."

"And your wife claims she saw a man's suitcase in the apartment before he came?"

I waited while he thought that over. He shoved his hat back and scratched his head, looking at me through those slits of eyes.

"Look." he said. "There's something I've got to check on. Then I'll want to see you again. So don't go away."

"What did he want?"

"Just questions, honey. He thinks he's a hot-shot."

"I didn't get that impression."

I went into the bedroom and sat down on the bed. Then I flopped back and lay there looking up at the ceiling. She came in and sat down on the bed. I wished she would go away. Then I cursed myself for even thinking such a thing.

"Roy." she said. "You've got to tell me if there's something troubling you."

I didn't say anything. I reached out and patted her arm and let it go at that.

Gant had left things hanging, because he was planning something. I knew damned well that's what it was. There'd been a crafty look in his eye and he'd practically run back out to the curb to get in the car. What could it be? I had to stay a jump ahead of them.

"If there's anything you think you should tell this man, Gant, Roy—I wish you would."

I cocked my head up and looked at her. She had on her red shorts now, and a yellow blouse. She looked real good and she was smiling at me. Her eyes were very bright

"What d'you mean?"

"Nothing. Just that you should try to help all you can."

"What do you mean?"

She shrugged. I sat up and grabbed her arm. "You mean something. You're trying to say something."

"No, I'm not, honey. You're reading something into what I say."

We watched each other. She kept on smiling and I began to feel better. I'd thought for a minute there—but I'd been wrong.

"Roy?"

"Yeah?"

"Why do you think somebody killed her?"

"I don't know."

"You don't even like to talk about it. Do you?"

I didn't say anything.

"Roy, I hear somebody."

She started up. I heard somebody step on the office porch and then the rattle of knuckles against the door. "You answer it, Roy. It's probably Gant again."

Somehow I didn't want to answer that door. I did, though. It was Wirt Radan.

FIFTEEN

Radan stood there in the doorway and looked at me. He didn't smile; he didn't do anything. His face was without expression and he was wearing a gray suit and a blue hat, this time.He had switched colors, but he looked as natty as ever—and the threat in him was as quiet and contained as before.

"Hello, Mister Nichols."

I waited.

"Would you mind opening the door?"

I opened the door and went on outside. I heard Bess come into the office and glanced back.

"Hello, there, Mrs. Nichols." Radan said. He touched one finger to his hatbrim and the corners of his mouth pinched up a little.

"Oh." Bess said. "It's you." She smiled at him. "Won't you come in?"

"He wants to see something outside." I said. We went out onto the lawn. Bess stood by the screen door, then I heard her walking toward the rear of the apartment.

"Well, well." Radan said. "Here we are again."

"What is it this time?"

"It's like this." he said. "I saw them take her out. Feet first. She was here and Teece was here. What do you figure you'll do about this?"

"Take who out?"

"Let's get away from here." he said. "Come on." He started down toward the rear of the apartments. "Come along, Mister Nichols."

I followed him and he had that same jaunty walk as before. His shoulders leaned forward just a shade with each step, and he didn't look around to see if I was coming.

He paused by some bushes. "Where's the money?" he said.

"You killed her, didn't you?"

"Be careful how you talk to me, Nichols." he said, and something peculiar came into his eyes. It was only there for an instant, then it was gone. Something had come over his face, as if the skin had shrunk in that brief moment. Then it relaxed. But I'd seen all I needed to see. I knew that if you touched him, he'd be like a piece of steel ready to spring. There was that warning emanating from him, from the way he looked at you and the way he stood. It hadn't shown so much before, but now it did show. Just enough to let you know. He didn't seem to have any satisfaction about it, either. It was, as was everything else about him, quite matter-of-fact, edgily contained.

"You're learning." he said. "Aren't you?"

I wanted to get away from him. I'd read about them, the way he was, but I'd never really met up with one. He was a killer, and in no joking sense. It was written in every line of the man. He was woodenly conscienceless.

"Where's the money?" he said.

I still didn't say anything, but I moved slightly away to not say it.

"We can save time, Mister Nichols—and energy. Your energy, if you'll just tell me quickly." He sighed and shoved his hands into the pockets of his jacket and stood there looking at me with his shoulders hunched. "You know." he said. "I've never met a guy just like you." He shook his head. "You know who I am, and why I'm here—yet you act this way. It's a dumb way to act. I wish you wouldn't do it."

I grinned at him. He didn't move.

"Was she here when I was here last time?"

"Did it ever occur to you I won't be pushed?" I said.

"No."

I didn't say anything.

He took a single step, bringing him up close to me. His eyes were very clear, the whites as clear and innocent looking as a baby's. "Mister Nichols." he said. "You know the kind of a man I am, and you know the job I'm on. I'm paid very well for this job, believe me."

"So?"

"I'm going to kill you right here in your own yard, if you don't tell me what I want to know."

He waited. That's all there was to it. You knew absolutely that he would do exactly as he said. It would be, to him, like turning around and walking away. A single movement.

"We gave the money to Teece. You're too late."

"You're not lying?"

"It's the truth. I swear it. We gave it to this Teece. All right, yes—she had it. I didn't. I didn't have anything to do with this. She told me about it—wanted me to do some damned thing for her. She gave it to Noel Teece. It was in a brief case."

He kept standing there like that, watching me. I saw the skin on his face shrink up again and stay that way, and his color under the tan was pale. There were tiny pinpoints of perspiration on his nostrils. Otherwise, he didn't change at all. He didn't move.

"What did she tell you about it, Mister Nichols?"

"Nothing. She just wanted me to help her."

He thought about that for a time, watching me steadily.

"This is something that has to be cleaned up right away." he said. "You can believe that, can't you? And it's not getting cleaned up—not at all. It's getting gummier all the time."

"The hell with you, Radar."

"You can say that, yes."

I turned and walked away from him.

"All right." he said, from back there. "I'm going to move in."

"What?"

"I want her apartment. Number six."

I paused, then went back to where he was standing. "The hell you say!"

"I'll take the one next door, for now. As soon as the law's through, then I'm moving into her apartment. You can understand what that means, of course?"

"You can't do that!"

He laughed quietly, reached out and tapped me on the arm. "Come on." he said. "Will you show me the apartment? Or shall I take care of that myself?"

I just had to stand here and take this, along with all the rest. And it was getting to be too much. Wouldn't the law know him? Apparently not. He wouldn't be here if they did, and he was damned certain I wasn't going to say anything. He had me over a barrel.

"Let's do it right." he said. "Like any decent landlord, Mister Nichols." He started walking out toward the front of the motel. Then he turned. "You going to change your story, Nichols?"

"She gave Teece the money. Honest to God she did. He did something, threatened her—listen, she wanted me to help her get out of the country. That's how I got mixed up in this. It's all over now. It's done, can't you see? Teece is probably in South America, by this time. Can't you go away and leave us alone?"

"Nobody got that money, Nichols. You're lying."

"I'm telling you—"

"All right. I'm moving in. We'll see. I'll have to work it out."

Well, he moved into number seven. And the first thing he did, with me right there, was walk into the bathroom and lift the lid off the toilet tank and take a look. He clanked it back on and didn't say a word.

"I have some things out in the car." he said. "Come on, help me carry it in."

"You can go to hell."

"All right." He shrugged and went out, whistling. He got into the car and started it and drove off. My cripes, was he leaving? I rushed out there and watched him drive along and turn the corner. I waited. He turned into the alley and I heard the plump tires of his Caddy on the gravel back there and I heard him stop at the garage for number seven. The door squeaked as he slid it open. He drove inside.

Pretty soon he came along, carrying two great big suitcases, so he'd figured on something like this. He walked past me without looking at me and went on into number seven.

I went after him. I stood in the doorway. He had taken the suitcases into the bedroom, and he came back into the living room and glanced at me, then went over and opened the blinds.

"You can't stay here." I said.

"Why don't you prevent me?"

"I told you all I know."

He began to whistle. It was shrill and harsh on the ears, tuneless. Just ceaseless, endless, hard. He walked around and put all the blinds open, took off his hat and set it on an end table, with care. Then he took his jacket off and went into the bedroom. When he returned, he wasn't wearing the gun, either. It had been a big gun.

"I like these assignments, Nichols. Everybody knows what's going on, and only one is lying or not lying, and eventually you find out."

He wasn't sure about believing me. I could tell the way he looked at me. His instinct told him I was lying, and his instinct was right. Only he had to believe me.

"Too bad I can't have a dame around here." he said. "But I'm traveling under orders, like I said. Too bad. It'll be lonely—unless something happens. And it probably will."

We stood there and watched each other. He reached up and loosened his tie, stretching his jaw, his eyes never leaving mine. Where his shoulder harness for the gun had been, his shirt was wrinkled. It was no light harness, either; it was thick-strapped and Radan was a tried gunman. You knew it, you didn't have to be told. And there didn't seem to be any fear in the man, and he wasn't ignorant.

"There a phone in the office, Nichols?"

He shoved by me and went on outside. I had thought about shoulder pads in his suit jacket. It wasn't so. Radan's shoulders were broad, pushing at the seams of his shirt. He was loaded with energy, and very fit, and I felt that in his own secret way, he was very proud of this. So far, I hadn't seen him smoke. I wondered if he drank.

He started across the lawn toward the office. I went after him and caught up with him.

"Listen: Be careful what you say over the phone. My wife's around."

He didn't bother answering. He stepped jauntily up on the porch and opened the door and called, "Mrs. Nichols—I'd like to use your phone. Will it be all right?"

Bess came into the office. "Why, hello, there."

"I've moved into your motel, Mrs. Nichols."

She looked at me and I nodded. "Number seven."

She swallowed and said, "You've probably heard what happened here this morning."

"Wipe it straight off your mind. The phone?"

She pointed to the desk and he went over and picked it up and dialed once and asked the long-distance operator for a Tampa number. Then, waiting, he looked first me, then at Bess.

Bess tugged at my arm. We were bothering him, and after all, when a

person's phoning, you should have the common decency not to listen in,
"Hello." he said into the phone. He waited as somebody spoke on the other
end. "Yes." he said. "All present and accounted for. I moved in. Yes." He
hung up, turned and grinned at Bess.

"Thanks." he said. He stood there by the desk and said, "How much for
a week? I figure a week should take care of it." He looked at me when he
said that.

She told him and he paid her, and he went outside, whistling. "He's rather
nice, in a funny way, isn't he?" Bess said.

"Yeah, sure."

"What did he say when you told him about what happened?"

"Nothing, Bess. It didn't seem to trouble him."

"You think they've caught the man, yet?"

"How's about fixing something to eat?"

She hesitated, watching me. Her eyes were soft and blue. I looked at her
and there was this expression of patience on her face, in her eyes, and she
smiled at me. Then she came up to me and put her arms around me. I held
her tight, wanting to crush her, loving her maybe more than I ever thought
I could love her. I was lost and all these things were crowding me. I didn't
know what to do now. And she didn't know what it was all about and I
couldn't tell her. That's what hurt most, I guess. I wanted to tell her—but
I never could. She believed in me and trusted me, and I'd slipped up.

Only the money was out there, and it was our money. I wasn't going to
lose that now.

Her lips were warm and I kissed her temples, feeling the soft golden hair
against my lips, and her forehead and her chin. I pulled her tight against
me.

"I love you, Roy."

We stood there like that.

And him over there in number seven, with his gun and his suitcases,
waiting for God knew what. And Gant. And Noel Teece.

Remembering Teece brightly was like a kind of added pain.

Maybe if I could talk Bess into taking a vacation. Just close the place
down, kick them all out, and go away. Let it all blow over. We could take
what money we had and just leave that brief case. When we came back,
Lieutenant Gant would have the murder solved, and we could …

After we ate, I went around trying to catch up with things. Trying to keep
my mind off what was happening—what could happen. It didn't work. I'd
be in the yard and find myself sneaking around the apartments to have a
look at the outside of the garage. Six or seven times I went into the
garage, for nothing. Just to find myself standing there by the Chev, staring
up there at the beams where that brief case was. Or I'd look over at number

seven, and sometimes he'd be standing on the porch with a tall glass in his hands. He'd look across at me and I'd turn away.

Once he waved and called, "Hot, isn't it?"

I began to quit trying to duck everything, and face it up instead. I'd have to, sooner or later. And maybe right then, for the first time, I really began to understand what I was up against. I'd thought I had before. Now it all came up into me like a big choke. These people who had sent Radan over here weren't fooling, and I'd been kidding with it. And Radan had said he had a plan.

What kind of a plan? I didn't want to think about that. I began to get scared, more than ever before in my life, and I knew I had good reason. Bess was in there and what was she thinking? And Gant, what was he going to do—would he be back today? I went back inside our place and just sat. Bess would come and look at me, then go away. I didn't care what she thought. It didn't matter.

I felt empty inside, as though there wasn't anything left—no place to go. Yet, I had to hang on. If I weakened now, then it was all shot and we wouldn't have anything. It was the chance I had to take. All down through the years there'd never been anything but fight, fight, fight—for nothing. Whenever we got anything, we'd lose it.

Now, just this once…!

I'd just sit there and Bess would come in and look at me. Sitting on the couch in the office, waiting. I didn't know what for. For that guy over there in number seven to do whatever it was he was going to do—or for Gant to come back and shackle me and I'd still fight, and if I fought, I'd have to lie. And that would put me in deeper and deeper, only I couldn't stop.

It happens that way sometimes. If you ever have it that way, then you'll know what I mean.

And there was a deep concern in Bess's eyes; something I couldn't quite read. It bothered me, but what was I going to do?

"Come and eat, Roy. Supper's ready."

"All right."

I went into the kitchen and sat down and stared at my plate. I didn't want to eat. There was this rotten black feeling all through me and I couldn't shake it.

"Eat something, Roy. What's the matter?"

"Nothing. I just don't feel so hot."

I wanted to go over and take this guy Radan and knock the hell out of him. Only I knew I wouldn't. You know when it's not ready; you know when something's going to happen.

Something had to happen. It was like before a big storm, with the black clouds out there on the horizon. Everything goes calm and dead, and then…

It happened about four o'clock in the morning. It was still dark when somebody began pounding on the office door.

I got up and wandered around, kind of hazy, there in the bedroom. They pounded on the door. I didn't want to go out there. Finally I put on a robe and went.

I opened the door and a cop stood there, his face shining in the darkness. I saw a car out by the curb, with the headlights gleaming cold and brilliant on the road.

"Get some clothes on, Mister Nichols." he said. "Lieutenant Gant wants you to come along with me."

SIXTEEN

We went out to the car. There was nobody inside. The motor was quietly idling and the door on the driver's side was open. He sure didn't give a hang about the city paying for his gas. I went around and climbed in and he got in and we slammed our doors at the same time.

He started up and we went down the street and took the turn at the corner and headed toward Tampa Bay. He drove along through the quiet Southside residential section, his face turned rigidly front.

"Well." I said. "What's up?"

He didn't answer.

It makes you feel like hell when they act that way. They get that superior air and I suppose they teach them that. Only I was a taxpayer, at least on the books, and I paid his salary.

"Lieutenant Gant, eh?"

"Look, Mister Nichols. It won't do you any good to keep asking. I'm not going to tell you anything. Those are my orders, and I reckon I'll keep them."

We turned left on the street along the park by the bay and he stepped it up a bit. You could see the reddish halo of light across the bay, over Tampa. Like a hooded, glass-enclosed Martian city, maybe—or just a pale hell on the not-too-distant horizon.

The park looked shadowed and quiet.

Then it changed.

There were some cars parked along the curb up there. Men were grouped in three or four places and they wore dull uniforms upon which sparks of light winked. Two spotlights were shining a silvery wash down there in the park, focused on the ground just beyond a tremendous live oak. The light was somehow off-white, bringing that odd cast of known green but seen gray to the brain and eye. The two cars were parked down there in the park on the grass.

We rolled along and he put on the brakes. He scraped the curb with the tires and we stopped.

"Get out, Nichols."

I got out and waited, looking across the park where the spotlights were. A man detached himself from a group down there and the group dispersed. The man came along with a kind of head-down shuffle.

He came along and flipped his hand at me. "Something I want you to see, Nichols."

It was ominous and I didn't like it. This Gant was too somber. He motioned to the cop and the cop went around and got behind the wheel of the car and drove off. For a moment Gant and I stood there. The palms along the road sent crazy shadows leaping from the streetlights. "Come on." Gant said.

I started along with him, down through the park. There was nobody down there where the spotlights from the police cars shone. I couldn't see where we were going, because there was a huge bush in the way.

We came into the beams of the spots. We rounded the bush and Gant looked at me, waiting.

Well, it was Noel Teece.

He had been what you might say torn limb from limb. A long streamer of bandage from the cast on his left arm lay tugging and fluttering in the wind, up along the grass. The cast on his arm had been smashed. His eyes were half-open. The bandage had been torn off his face and it was all scabs. He was lying flat on his back, looking up into the dark sky.

Then I saw how he'd been slit up the middle with a knife, or maybe an axe. I turned and walked around behind the bush and was sick.

When I came back, Gant hadn't moved. He was standing there, looking at Teece.

"Like a fish." he said. "Just like a fish."

"What'd you bring me down here for?"

"Don't you know?"

I couldn't look at him again.

"Go ahead." Gant said. "Look at him. That's Noel Teece, Nichols. He's the man who was down to your place, visiting that Latimer dame. Recognize him?"

I still couldn't say anything.

"He's a little hard to recognize, I admit." he went on. "But that's him, all right." He turned and looked at me and frowned. "Do you say it's him, Nichols?"

"I don't know."

"Well, make up your mind. We brought you down here just to make sure. Not like there's two of them running around, dressed the same—and with a broken arm and a patched-up head. What do you say?"

"It might be."

"'It might be!' You—" He paused and rubbed his hand across his face. "All right We'll bring your wife down here. She saw him, remember?"

"I guess it's him, all right." I still didn't look down there again. "I'm sorry. I don't know why I said that."

"Thanks. For nothing." He turned and started away, then whirled and came up to me again. "Why do you do this? Why do you act this way? Isn't it enough—?" He shook his head, breathing hard, real mad.

I felt like hell. I wanted to help him. But if I helped him, I'd be helping myself right out of that money.

Then I thought of Radan and it was as if the back of my neck turned to wood. He'd done this, as sure as hell—Radan. So why hadn't he come to me? If he did do this, he sure would head for me right after, because by now he'd know Teece didn't have the money. And that was all Radan wanted.

I could hardly move, the way I felt.

"What's the matter, Nichols? What's cooking in that peaceful little mind of yours?"

"If you knew who this guy was, why'd you bring me down here? What's the point of that?"

"Nichols, I wish to God you weren't what they call a citizen! I'd run you in and I'd work you over."

"Why don't you? I'd like to know what you're getting at. You act like I've done something."

He went absolutely still. His mouth hung open and his eyes got wide and he shoved his hat back on his head. Then his eyes went normal again. "Done something." he said. "You're lying, Nichols. You know something. You're scared. There's something inside you that's eating at your guts till you can hardly stand it. It's going to bust out, too. Wait and see."

"You think I did this to that guy?"

"I don't know." He turned and walked away again. I went up by him and he turned and stopped me with his hand out. "Why don't you come clean, Nichols? This is getting you no place. *What is it you're trying to hide?*"

"You've got it wrong. A woman was murdered at my motel. Now you think I'm mixed up in it."

"We're running lab tests, Nichols. What are you going to do then? Because I know we're going to find something. All right, suppose this one killed the Latimer girl. Then who killed him? And why? Why at your place?"

Why do you act so scared? Why do you lie about things that don't matter, that couldn't matter to you? I'll tell you—it's because they somehow *do matter*. Do you know who that dead man is? Noel Teece. Do you know who *he* was? We know, Nichols. We know all about him, and why he was going to end up this way, for sure. You think it's going to take long to find out all the rest of it?"

"Who was he?"

He just made another face and I was plenty sick about the whole thing. "You're damned good at this." I said. "You've got it all straight in your mind, haven't you? You've got the guilt all leveled at me. You can do that fine. What do you do about protecting the public from things like this?"

He cursed in a soft whisper, watching me. "Yes." he said. "You'd say something like that, too. But I'll tell you—even you, and you know what I'd like nothing better than to do to you, Nichols—even you … I have two men stationed by your place all night—just waiting. Know what they're there for? For your health, Nichols—so you won't get hurt, because we might be wrong, and you might be right, and that's the job the way I see it. I have to do that. And it was done because you were a suspect in the killing of that girl, too."

Now I saw why Radan hadn't been around. Radan would be half nuts with wanting to get at me. I hadn't seen any guards by the house, but Radan would know. It explained a lot of things. And now what was going to happen when I got home?

Radan wouldn't move too quickly; haste could mean a big bill of waste in this instance. He had orders to get the money. He knew I wasn't going any place with the law barking down my collar. So he would wait until everything was clear. Then he would move in on me, because he knew now that I'd lied to him about the brief case.

"Nichols?" Gant said. "You aren't listening."

"What?"

"I said, 'What happened to your finger?'"

"It's broken."

"That's damned enlightening. I mean, how broken?"

"I caught it in a car door."

"When?"

"What's that to you?"

"See, Nichols? See what I mean?"

We stared at each other.

"Nichols, there's hardly a thing I can ask you about that you don't get scared and want to run. *What is it!* By God, I'll bet you can't bring yourself to tell me about that finger, even. Not the truth. You can't force yourself to tell me how it got caught in what door, or when, or where? Right?"

I didn't say anything. He had me really going. I wanted to pile into him, and I couldn't. And that was bad, because I knew I was the one who was wrong.

He was doing his job. He had every right to be this way, and I could see that much of it clear now. And I was withholding the very grains of knowledge he had to have.

"Nichols, all I have to do is ask your wife."

My neck got hot. If he asked her, she'd tell him about my going to Chicago. I felt trapped.

"Well?" he said. "Where *did* you bust your finger?"

There was a kind of gleeful tone to his voice, as though he was really enjoying this, or maybe a little crazy or something. And I knew he wasn't enjoying it.

"A car door."

"'A car door.'"

He turned sharply and started up toward the road, muttering to himself. I watched him go with this tight new feeling of being trapped inside me. If he went to Bess, what then? I hadn't done anything! I wanted to yell it at him. If he really had anything on me, he'd have run me in fast. I knew that. So I was all right. I was still ahead of them—'way ahead.

Only how long would they keep it up?

All I had to do was tell them. Only I couldn't tell them a thing, and they didn't know that. And by keeping my mouth shut and lying, it looked as if I was really mixed up in this. Maybe even committed murder.

I started on up across the park toward Gant.

So Vivian was dead. And now Teece, too. And it struck me what Radan might be doing, and I was damned well scared. I wanted to get home....

"I'm going to haunt you, Nichols."

"Listen, if I could help you, I would. There's nothing I can do to help you. You think I know a lot of things that I don't. You're reading a lot into this that isn't there. I mean it. Why should I want to stand in your way?"

He turned to a cop standing about ten feet off on the curb. "Pete, will you run Mister Nichols home?"

"Listen." I said, rapping his arm. "You didn't answer me."

He looked at me and grinned. "I'm going to haunt you." he said. Then he turned and walked off across the park toward where the spotlights were focused.

"Coming, Mister Nichols?" the cop said.

"Yeah."

Way off there toward the Gulf, you could see the pale, gray-pink line of dawn, blurring the horizon.

I headed for our place in a hurry. I hoped that Gant still had his guards posted. But it could be that Radan would wait to make certain about everything.

Bess lay there in bed with her eyes closed. But she was awake. Already the gray morning was probing through the Venetian blinds. Still fuzzy with sleep, she sat there on the bed, staring at me, her pale golden hair mussed, and looking as warm and cozy as crackers.

"Wh-what did Gant want in the middle of the night?"

While I undressed, I told her about Teece, and she put her hand up to her mouth, her eyes round. "Roy." she said, and her voice broke a little, "I've had all this on my mind and I can't stand it...."

I could feel the sudden tensing behind my solar plexus. "Will you tell me? Will you?"

"What, Bess?"

"You're mixed up in something, I know you are. How long do you think I can go along with you like this? You knew that girl, Roy—I know you did."

"I don't get you at all."

"Listen, Roy. I've been playing dumb, for your sake. But it can't go on. I live with you. I love you. I can't help feeling things—knowing something's wrong. All I know is this—you're in trouble and you won't tell me what kind of trouble."

"Listen, Bess." I said finally, "if there was anything I had to tell you, I would. I didn't know that girl, and I'm not mixed up in anything. Now, just relax, and let's try to get a little sleep before we have to get up. Huh?"

She turned over and didn't answer. I could tell she was mad, and she knew darned well she was right about a lot of things and all of it was eating at her. Just like things were troubling me....

Well, just for now, to hell with them. I was real beat, and I had to get some rest in, because God knew what was coming up in a few hours. Before anything else, I had to check the garage. Just an hour or two of sleep....

SEVENTEEN

Maybe when you get in more real trouble than you can handle and get dead beat-out the law of subconscious gravity or something slides the whole load off somewhere. Anyhow, I didn't know a thing until dark, and Bess brought me some stuff in on a tray, like I was an invalid. It made me feel worse than ever, and now all the things were catching up with me, and I got dressed, and carried the tray out to the kitchen. But I couldn't eat. I had some black coffee and all the worries were crowding me again.

I was telling Bess that she should have gotten me up, when someone knocked on the office door up front. I went over and swung it open.

Gant stood there. He nodded at Bess, who had come up behind me. He gnawed his lower lip and thrust his hands into his pockets. "Mind if I step inside your place for a few words? The two of you together?" He looked carefully at me when he said that.

"Sure." I stepped aside and he came in.

"Shall I go make some fresh coffee?"

We both looked at Bess and Gant smiled pleasantly. He took his hat off. "That would be nice. But would you mind waiting a moment?"

She nodded and her gaze sought mine.

There was something in the air that I didn't like. Something smug about Gant and the way he spoke. He walked across the room and stood by the studio couch.

"Sit down." he said. "There are a couple of things I'd like to clear up."

"But." Bess said. "I don't understand. About what?"

He smiled. "Please, sit down and take it easy." And he sat down on the couch and there was this *clang!*

He stood up immediately. The *clang* had come from behind the couch. I knew what it was right off; that Georgia license plate, and my world quietly exploded.

"What could that have been?" Bess said. She went over by the couch. It had been much too loud to be ignored. Gant frowned and stepped away from the couch. He was watching me. His interest wasn't behind the couch.

"Let it go." I told Bess. "Probably just a spring busted."

"No; it wasn't that. Here, help me move the couch."

Gant frowned and frowned.

I went over there like a sleepwalker and helped her move the couch. She skinned behind there, up against the wall, and bent over and came up with the plate. "Why, it's a license plate. It slipped through the back, where the lining's torn."

Gant was already halfway over the back of the couch. He snatched it from her and looked at it and started nodding his head. I went across the room and sat down. Bess put one hand against her face and stared at me. She came out from behind the couch and shoved it back with her knee, as easy as anything, and stood there.

Gant looked at me and sighed. "This shouldn't take long to check, should it, Nichols?"

I sat there and stared at him. I felt this grin form on my face and I couldn't erase it. He tapped the plate against his other hand and stepped over to the telephone.

He called police headquarters and asked them to run an immediate check on that plate and he read the numbers.

"How ever did that get there, Roy?"

I didn't bother answering that. Gant hung up and moved to the couch again and sat down. He laid the license plate across his knees. "Bright and new, too. Hardly used at all. Odd." He patted his pockets and came up with a package of cigarettes. He didn't offer me one. He took one and lit up.

Bess watched me closely and I hated seeing the look in her eyes. She didn't know what was up, but she knew that whatever it was, it was no good.

"Mrs. Nichols, why don't you go make that coffee you mentioned? I reckon I could go for some, I reckon we all could."

"Sure thing."

"We may have a little wait, here." He paused and glanced my way, not quite meeting my eyes. "All of us."

She left the room, her heels smacking the floor....

"Well, Nichols. You want to say something?" He had lowered his voice and I liked him for that.

"No."

"All right. We'll just wait. You see, Nichols, it's a funny thing. License plates was exactly what I came to see you about. We checked that New York plate through." He shook his head and smiled to himself. "Thought we had it all in a hat. Boy, how wrong can you get? Where'd you think it would get you? Never mind, you'd lie like hell, anyway—we'll find out." He shook his head again. "That New York plate was owned by people living right here in town, Nichols. They were staying here at your motel a while back and they bought their Florida plate and exchanged them in your garage. Maybe you even helped them, hey?"

"No."

"Boy, you've got a real stubborn streak, haven't you?" He stood up. "Second thought, I'm afraid I'll have to take you downtown. Might have a long wait and I don't think this is the best place."

He waited. I stood up. "Whatever you say, Lieutenant. You're the boss."

"How right." he said. Then he turned and called to Bess. She came into the hallway. She was very pale.

"Your husband and I are going to run downtown for a while. I'm sorry about the coffee. All right?"

"But—Roy?"

"It's all right. I'll be back."

"Sure." Gant said. "Sure." He looked at me.

"Roy."

I didn't look at her. I moved across the office and out the door and he came with me. Bess ran over to the door and called my name again.

"It's all right, honey. I'll be right back."

"Good-night, Mrs. Nichols."

We walked out across the lawn. He kept banging that license plate against his leg. We climbed into the car and he started the engine and drove off.

"You want to hold this, Nichols?" He handed me that Georgia plate.

"You're not going to try anything, are you, Nichols? You're not *that* crazy, I hope."

I just sat there, trying to think.

"Gee. It's sure something, isn't it, Nichols …?"

It was a small room, not much larger than a good-sized closet. There were no windows and only one doorway, with no door. At one end of this room, there was a platform perhaps ten inches high. On the platform was a straight-backed chair, nailed to the floor.

I was on the chair.

Over my head, swinging about a hand's breadth, was a 150-watt bulb, with a green tin shade. Nobody had touched the bulb, hanging from the high ceiling by a black length of wire, but it never stopped swinging and their shadows leaned and lengthened and shortened against the wall, breaking up against the ceiling. And my shadow was on the floor. It was crazy, any way you looked at it.

Gant had brought me in here, and for quite a while I sat alone, brooding. Then one by one they came and looked at me. They would stand in the door, with their uniforms all creased and their harness creaking, and just look at me.

They talked in the other room. Now and again one of them who had looked in once before, would come and stick his head in and then step away again.

Gant finally came into the room and stood against the far wall, watching me. It was a little hard to see him, because of the light. The light was hot, too. Then another man in plain clothes joined him. This was a big one, smoking a stub of cigar and he looked like the nasty kind. He was in his shirt sleeves.

"This is Armbruster." Gant said. "Armbruster, meet Nichols."

"Hello, Nichols."

I nodded.

Armbruster smoked his cigar, standing there. He had a red face, round and beefy, and when he breathed it made quite a noise. He had a barrel chest and it was like he had a pain in his stomach. He would kind of groan a little to himself every now and then.

"You want to say anything, Nichols?"

"What in hell is there to say?"

"Still chipper." Armbruster commented.

"Oh, he's chipper."

They stood there. Armbruster smoked and Gant just leaned against the wall, looking at me. It's pretty bad when people just stand and stare at you, like that. It begins to annoy you. You itch. You try to look away. You can't do anything. You begin to sink into the chair. You sweat. You think of a million things to do, all of them wrong.

"They've traced the plate." Gant said.

"Oh?"

"Yes. It didn't take long, did it? The Ford car was in your name, Roy Nichols."

"Isn't that something?" Armbruster said.

I swallowed. I wanted drink of water, but I knew better than to ask for one,

"That's all there is to it. Just that quick. We made it with two phone calls. Now, what do you say, Nichols?"

"Hell, man." Armbruster said. "Don't be a damned fool. Tell us about it."

A uniformed cop pushed past Armbruster and looked in at me. "Why'd you do it, Nichols?" he said. "Why'd you kill Vivian Rise?"

He went away. I stared at the space where he'd been. They knew her name.

"Yes." Gant said. "Vivian Rise. Did you know a girl by that name, Nichols? Or did you just know her as Jane Latimer? Or are you really Ed Latimer? Or what?"

"Or what?" Armbruster said.

"Come on, Nichols." the cop said, sticking his head in the doorway. "Why did you do it?" He looked at me for a minute, his face without expression. Then he stepped inside the room. He took a package of cigarettes out of his pocket. "Have a smoke, Nichols?"

"Thanks."

"That's all right." He lighted my cigarette, put the lighter away, stood there a moment, then left.

"Well, Nichols?" Armbruster said. "Are you Ed Latimer, late of the Ambassador Hotel?"

Gant looked down at the floor. "Come on. Let's not be here all night long."

Armbruster looked at Gant. They both left me sitting there.

The cop came in, the one who had given me the cigarette. He stood in the doorway, smoking and looking at me. "We know you didn't kill her." he said. "But how about the other one? Did he make you mad? That it?

Was he going to tell your wife about her? That it?"

I looked at him and opened my mouth. He turned quickly away and I heard him walk across the room.

They began talking out there. I couldn't make out what they were saying. I dropped the cigarette and stepped on it and sat there, staring at my hands. What to do?

That money. I had to keep it. Somehow.

It beat like a very small drum in the back of my head. A small and very distant drum....

EIGHTEEN

Armbruster came and stood in the doorway.

"Tell Lieutenant Gant I want to see him."

"Sure thing, Nichols."

He went away. A telephone rang. I could hear them talking out there. I was in a terrible sweat and I was going to tell it—my way. I had to tell something, and it would look all right. Anyway you looked at it, that money was still up there in the garage.

Gant came into the room and stood there.

"All right." I said. "Here's the story." I told it to him straight. All of it. Only I left out the money and I left out Radan. "I don't know why she wanted me to help her. She wouldn't say. She just said she'd pay me. That's all. I needed money. I need it bad. So I told her all right, it was a go."

"You thought this Teece was dead?"

"Yes."

"Did you check to make sure?"

"He looked dead. I thought he was dead, that's God's truth, Lieutenant. But he wasn't, that's all."

"It could happen. Then why in hell did you keep on lying after she was dead?"

"I don't know. I was scared."

"Oh, hell, Nichols. You don't scare that easy. I can tell."

"It's the truth. I was scared for Bess—my wife."

"And how about when you saw Teece dead?"

"I didn't know what to do. I figured you thought I'd killed him."

"Hey, Ernie!" one of them called.

Gant left the room. Pretty soon he came back. He looked at me for a long time. "You telling me the truth, Nichols?"

I could sense something. It smelled good. But I had to doubt it.

"Yes. It's the truth."

"Get out of the chair and come on."

I stood up. My back was stiff. I followed him through the other room, past Armbruster and three cops who were standing there. They didn't look at us. I followed Gant and he led me out and into a hall. We walked down the hall, our heels echoing on the marble floors.

We reached the front doors and the street was out there, with cars going up and down. A girl and a guy walked along the street out there, holding hands. He kissed her on the cheek and she laughed and they walked along out of sight. A truck went by, backfiring.

"All right." Gant said. "Go on home, Nichols."

I looked at him. "But, what in hell?"

He turned and walked back down the hall. And I smelled a rat. A great big dead rat. But I went on out through the doors, and onto the street. It was like just waking up in the morning.

Down the street I hailed a cab and went home. During the ride, I sat there and I was numb. I couldn't figure it. And I knew I had to do something.

It was crowding me hard. I knew it wasn't over.

Not yet ...

"You're back, Roy!"

"Yeah. I'm back."

Bess had been sitting on the studio couch, waiting. When I opened the door and saw her, she looked up, scared to death, with worry all over her face. Then she ran across the room and jumped into my arms, like the old days.

"What did they want you for, Roy?" Her voice was tight

I held her away, looking into her eyes. "About those two murders. They thought I was implicated."

"But you weren't—*you weren't!*"

"No. Listen, Bess—I've got something to tell you. Something I should have told you long ago."

"Yes?" She was smiling. I grabbed her and held her as close as I could. Then I thrust her away again and led her over to the couch. We sat down.

"I'm not asking you to forgive me." I told her. "But I've been lying to you, Bess. Up and down and crosswise. I'm in a terrible jam. But I want you to know the truth. All of it. The police already know."

"You've told them?"

"Yes. Only not all of it. Not the part I'm going to tell you."

And I told her. I gave it to her straight and hard, without any holding back. The whole business, from the very beginning on the Georgia road when the truck driver let me off, to the barbecue joint and the Lincoln. The hotel room. Vivian and me, in that room, and the money. I told her everything and she sat there, listening, with no change in expression and her eyes got wet just as I finished. "So, I'm not asking you to forgive, unless you can. If you can't, I understand. I had to tell you. I just found out I had to tell you, coming home tonight from the police station. I was sitting in the cab and I knew you had to know. That's why I've been like I've been. I couldn't stand it. That girl—it was only the one night, I want you to understand that."

"You were drunk, weren't you?"

"It makes no difference. I'm not making excuses." I wasn't. She had it in her lap now. All of it. "That guy Radan, he's right next door."

The only thing I didn't tell her was where the money was.

"All right, Roy."

She got up and turned her back to me and I saw her shoulders stiffen a little. She walked over to the hallway, turned and looked at me. She wasn't saying anything. Her eyes were a little cold now. I couldn't blame her. It was bad, but she had it straight, anyway.

"I've known something was wrong for a long time." she said. "I just didn't know what. You told the police about the money?"

"No."

"But, Roy—!"

"It's our money, Bess. You're not going to tell them, either. I've been through too much for that money. It's got to be somebody's money, and it's ours."

"No, Roy."

"I mean it."

"Where is it?"

"I'm not saying. If you tell the cops, Bess, say it's all the bunk. I'll lie up and down, all over again. They'll *never prove different.* I mean it, honest to God, I do,"

"Yes. You and that girl. Yes."

I watched her put her hands to her face. But she didn't cry. She brought her hands back down and came over to the couch and stood there in front of me.

"You've got to tell the police, Roy. You've got to!"

I shook my head. "I'm sorry, Bess. I can't do it. I've had that out with myself. It means too much for us, and they don't know anything about that."

She turned around and stood with her back to me. I looked at her hair, falling thickly to her shoulders, and the line of her back and her legs and her feet. I saw her hands along her sides, the fists half-clenched and she was perfectly still. I wasn't sure how she was taking it, or what she was thinking.

"All this time—" she said.

"That's right. I've lied, and I've lied."

"When that girl was here, Roy. Did you go over to number six and be with her? Did you?" She turned and looked at me, then. "Because, if you did—if you—"

"No."

"I believe you. God only knows why."

I couldn't look at her face. I didn't feel any better, having told her. I felt worse, because it was hurting her. I didn't want that. Yet, she had to know.

"Roy," she said. She came to the couch and sat down and looked at me. Her voice was pitched low. "You've got to tell them. We don't want that money. It'll stand in the way of everything for the rest of our lives. We'd never be happy with it."

"We'll never be happy without it. We've been without it all along, and it's not going to be that way any more."

"Roy, I'm telling you—you've got to listen."

"I'm not listening." I stood up.

"For me, Roy."

"Not for you—not for anybody. The money's ours. It stays that way." I leaned over and looked her in the eye. "I went through a lot to keep it. And now we've got it."

"Not 'we', Roy. You. You've got it."

I turned and walked out of the office, and down the porch steps. On the grass, I half expected her to come after me. She didn't. I looked back in the screen door and she was sitting there on the studio couch, staring vacantly at the wall. I walked away from there.

I heard the hiss of feet on the grass and somebody grabbed my arm, whirling me around. "Nichols."

It was Radan.

I was mad and I went straight into him. He stepped back and I saw the gun.

"Take it easy, will you?" he said softly.

I stopped, watching him.

"Come on, now." he said. He stepped up to me and rammed the gun into my back. "Move. Over to number seven."

In the apartment, he closed the door and looked at me. He needed a shave, and he looked harried and I realized he'd been drinking a lot more than he should. But that gun was very steady, and so were his eyes.

"What do you want?"

"You know what, Nichols. You're going to tell me where that brief case is. You're the one who hid it, and we know that. You're going to tell me— all alone—just me."

"That's what you think."

"So. At last you admit it."

We watched each other. He stepped in toward me and brought the gun down. It raked across my face. I grabbed his wrist and he grunted a little and his other fist flashed around and I saw the brass knucks.

I went down and sat against the wall. My face was ripped open and bleeding from the knucks,

"All right, Nichols. Tell me."

NINETEEN

He stood up there looking down at me with the gun in one hand and the brass knuckles in the other. I was seeing Wirt Radan for the first time. I brought my hands down, braced against the wall and pushed. He wouldn't use the gun, I was sure.

I hit him hard in the legs. He didn't fall, but his fist did. The gun bounced off my skull and the pain flashed through me. I raked at him with my arms and got a leg and pulled. He fell on top of me.

I felt the quick impact of the knucks against my head. *Once—twice— three* times and I got groggy and lay back on the floor, staring up at him. He brought his foot back and let me have it hard in the head. My teeth jarred and I bit my tongue. I tried to catch his foot, but it was like working in slow motion. My head was one great big knot of pain and the pain shot down in my chest.

Then it was quiet and I gradually began to hear him breathing. I looked up and he was over there, sitting on the edge of the couch, resting, holding the gun, and the knucks glistened in the dim light from the lamp on the end table. He still wore his suit jacket and his tie wasn't even out of place. His breathing began to slow down.

"Where is it, Nichols? You may as well tell me. I think you understand that by now?"

I didn't say anything. I just lay there, looking up at him, trying to get my breath and let the pain chip away. The pain came into my head in great sheeting waves, and my eyeballs hurt. Finally I began to get up. He rose quickly and stepped over and lashed out with the gun barrel, hitting and raking, back and forth. He did it mechanically, without emotion—as you might swing a hammer at a nail. I tried to catch his wrist.

I caught it and the knucks landed again. I was on the floor, flat out again. He was killing me. He was quick and I knew he wanted that money, and if he got it he would kill me, and that would be that.

It was quiet. I heard water dripping in the kitchen sink and the sound of our breathing whispered harshly in the room. There was no other sound. It was as if everything was dead and gone and there was only this pain, throbbing inside me.

"You'd better tell me." he said. "You're going to, you know." He cleared his throat gently. "Honestly, you really are, Nichols. Can you believe that?"

I watched him. "I gave it to Teece."

"No, you didn't. I killed Teece, Nichols. Just as I'm going to do to you. He told the truth, I know that. He was crying and pleading like a small child. He said he didn't have the money. Those were his last words, Nichols."

"He lied."

"We know he didn't. I've been sent on this job, and I'm going to finish it. I always do. It's my turn for the brief case now."

"The double cross from you?"

"Only halfway. They aren't sure how much is in that brief case."

I came up off the floor and at him fast. I got him. I sank one into his gut and chopped with my other fist and he started to go down. I saw it in his face, the hanging on. Those damned knucks flashed again.

I lay there. He leaned down and smashed at me with the gun. Then he stood up and cleared his throat. Then he waited.

"All right. I wasn't going this far, Nichols. But now I am. I'm going to tie you up and I'm getting your wife over here. Then you're going to watch something. And you'll talk, Nichols. They always do. It's the last thing we try. We don't have any other way. But it's a good way. It produces."

I looked at him and I knew he meant it. There was nothing to do.

"O. K., Nichols? You know I would?"

"Yes. All right. I'll show you."

"One wrong move. That will be all."

"It's all right. I've got the money."

"Get up."

"I can't, yet."

He waited. After a time the pain began to drift away and I got to my knees. Finally I got on my feet. The blood was in my eyes and I rubbed my hands across my face, knowing it was all done.

I'd let myself down. And Bess, too, I should have got Radan before, on my own. It had been the only way, and I'd missed it.

"Coming, Nichols?"

We went on out the door. I staggered off the porch and nearly fell. He stood back. He watched while I hung onto the porch railing, trying to see right. I couldn't see right.

"Around back, Radan."

We started down between the apartments. It was a cool night and the wind washed against my face. Everything was a big blank, and I had drawn it. There was no use.

We came around behind the apartments. I still couldn't walk right. Something inside my skull kept crackling, and my teeth hurt bad. I knew I was spitting blood and I didn't give a damn, not any more.

We came by the garage and I reached up and grabbed the door and flung it open. "You climb on the hood of the car. Then pull yourself up by a beam and the brief case is up there under the far eave, under some loose boards."

"Stand right there, Nichols. Remember, I've got a gun. I can see you against the light. Don't go away."

I didn't say anything. I stood there waiting. I knew I was waiting for a slug. It was almost as if I didn't care about that, either. He would kill me as sure as the night was dark. Then I thought, Maybe he won't.

He was up on the hood of the car. "Stay right there." he said. "I can see you."

I watched him pull himself up. Now was my chance to run. I didn't. I waited. I heard him up there, prowling around in the darkness. He was on the boards, over against the eave.

"God!" he said. "I've got it."

He came down fast, in a single leap from the beams to the car's hood to the ground. I turned and started walking toward the house.

"Nichols!"

"The hell with it."

I started up along the side of our apartment, heading toward the office door. I heard him coming fast on the grass.

"Nichols!"

Somebody else said, "Hold it right there, Radan!"

I whirled and saw him lift his gun and fire at the dark. He fired twice and I flattened myself against the side of the house and he came by me, running like hell.

He took a shot at me as he passed. It *thocked* into the wooden side of the house. A car moved along out in front by the curb and a spotlight blinked on, coming slowly bright and it picked him up.

I ran out after him. I saw him stand there on the front lawn all alone, with that brief case swinging and he fired at the spotlight and missed.

"Stop—*Radan!*" I recognized Gant's voice.

Radan didn't stop. Somebody fired rapidly twice from down by the corner and Radan turned and knelt down and fired. Somebody fired from the car out there in the street. Radan stood and whirled on the car and his gun clicked empty.

The front sign went on, bright and glowing. Then the floodlights came on and it was like daylight out there on the grass and he stood there holding his empty gun. He drew his arm back and flung the gun sailing at the car. He turned and started across the lawn, running toward the far corner and I saw the brief case come open. That broken clasp. Money streamed and tumbled out as he ran forward.

They shouted for him to stop. They gave him every chance.

But he didn't stop. They cut him down. He skidded into pile right by one of the floodlights, landing on his face. Then everything became still. It had been sudden. Now it was over. I walked out across the lawn.

"You all right, Nichols?"

"Sure."

It was Lieutenant Gant. He came across the lawn in a steady shuffle, putting his gun away. I walked over to Radan, lying on the ground. There was nothing left inside me.

We stood there and looked at him. About six slugs had nailed him. He was crumpled over on his face, with his grip still tight on the handle of the brief case, only most of the money had spilled out. He'd left a scattered green trail of it all the way across the lawn.

A cop started toward us, picking up the packets of money, softly whistling through his teeth.

"Well?" I said.

Gant looked at me. He shrugged. "It was your wife. She knew about that money, Nichols. She saw you put it in the garage. She checked and found the money, only she didn't tell us until just now, when she phoned. We'd freed you, thinking maybe you'd lead us somewhere. She wanted you to find it in yourself, to straighten it out without any help. That's why she never said anything to you about the money. I don't know. The hell with it. You know how women are. You should know how your wife is about things."

"Yeah. I know."

"She's over there. I'm not sure whether she wants to see you, though. Can't say as I blame her."

Bess was standing there by the royal palm at the near corner of the sign. She was watching me. I lifted one hand toward her and let it drop. She didn't move.

Three officers came across the lawn.

The one who'd been picking up the money went over by the dead man and got the brief case loose from his fingers. He began packing the money inside the case, still whistling through his teeth.

"I'm afraid you'll have to come along with us." Gant said. "We know Teece killed the girl and Radan killed Teece all that. We couldn't move in any quicker because we didn't really have anything on Radan, see? We've wanted him for a long while, Nichols. As I say, you'll have to come along, too. There'll be some sort of a trial. Maybe you'll get a suspended sentence. Maybe not."

I turned and walked over by Bess. There was just nothing left inside me, but her. And she didn't want any part of me.

We looked at each other.

"Lieutenant Gant says the highway's coming through." she said. "He told me that tonight, when we were talking about you. Why you did all this."

"I'm sorry, Bess."

She looked up at me. We stood there that way for a second or two. Then I saw Gant coming toward us.

"It's all right, Roy."

I didn't know what to say. It was all over.

"It's all right. I'll be here, Roy."

Gant touched my arm. "Coming, Nichols?"

We started off across the lawn toward the curb. "There's a few things you'll have to clear up." Gant said. "I don't exactly get it all yet."

"Me either, Lieutenant."

As we got into the car, I looked over across toward the sign. Bess was still standing there. She waved her hand at me.

Gant slammed the car door. His voice reached me through a haze, "You care for a cigarette, Nichols?"

THE END

A Killer is Loose
GIL BREWER

Chapter One

If I can tell all of this straight and true, and get Ralph Angers down here the way he really was, then I'll be happy. It's not going to be easy. There was nothing simple about Angers, except maybe the Godlike way he had of doing things. He was some guy, all right. In the news lately, you've read of men doing some of these things, like Angers. They were all red-hot under the same cold star when the wires snapped and Death became a pygmy. So I figure I'd better get this told. There are plenty of Ralph Angerses now on the streets, on the trains, in the bars, in the hotels, in the houses, at the ball game, and there's no way on earth you can tell *who*, until it happens. Hell, no. So this is my story and how it happened with me, and how it ended. It ended simply, come to think of it. I guess it had to. It would take some devil of a mind to conceive horror enough for … But listen.

You know how luck works a cycle, good or bad, with both kinds equalizing when you score it out; so after enough bad you don't worry at all because it's got to change. Well, I'd gone six months beyond that, even. For three weeks I hadn't bothered lying to Ruby about leaving the house mornings to look for work that wasn't to be had. The game was played out. So I stayed home. I sat on the couch in the living room and watched her grow bigger and slower with our first kid, knowing he would be born any day now. Only this morning I couldn't take it any longer. I knew what I had to do. I left the living room, went down the hall into our bedroom.

She was there on the bed, resting between mopping the porch and cooking lunch with nothing to cook. What a Ruby!

"Steve," she said, "I had a pain when I was working. Maybe it's a false alarm. But it won't be long now."

I didn't look at her. I went over to the bureau and stood there with my hand on the second drawer. I knew she was watching me and I stared at the things scattered on the top of the bureau. A hairbrush and two combs and a nail file in a fake leather case with chromium trim and a dime-store hand mirror and a crumpled dollar bill and a ten-cent piece and a six pennies, one of them looking as if it had been socked two or three times with a drill press.

"It's probably a false alarm," she said behind me, and I heard the bed creak as she turned. "There hasn't been any pain since I've been lying here."

"Sure," I said. Only it probably wasn't any false alarm because the only false alarm in her life was when she married me. Quit thinking like that, I told myself. "Sure," I said. "You just take it easy." I pulled a little on the drawer. It was stuck.

"What are you doing?"

"Nothing."

"I hate to think of an ambulance, or anything like that," she said. "Be sure, Steve—just a cab, now."

"Absolutely."

"I wish I could have it home, like they used to."

"Don't talk like that. You know it's better in a hospital. They got everything to work with. They know just what to do. Besides, it's not sanitary at home."

"Things certainly do change, don't they? I was born in Daddy's car right in the middle of Times Square."

"I'll bet your ma had a fit," I said. "Knowing her."

"Steve, you shouldn't."

"Anyway, there's no Times Square down here."

"What are we going to do, Steve? The doctor's so nice, what he says about the bill and everything. But what will we do?"

"Like I say, don't worry."

I got the drawer open and stood there looking down at it all wrapped in the flannel cloth. I reached in and touched it and she began speaking again, only this time she was a little scared. She was thinking about it too much.

"Suppose it's born in a cab." The bed creaked. "Listen, hon, be sure and get me there in time. I don't know what I'd do!"

"Don't worry."

"What are you doing there?"

"Nothing, I told you." I took it out of the drawer and unwrapped the cloth and put the cloth back in the drawer. A Luger is a heavy good gun that squats in your fist the way a gun should, and just holding it you know what it's got and that it will do what you want it to right where you think it should. That's all you have to do with a Luger, just think where you want the slug, and it backs up hard and spits all at the same time, hard, solid, where you want it.

"I'm sorry about your guns, Steve. It's a dirty shame we had to sell them all." She meant it, she wasn't just talking.

"Yeah."

"You going to sell that one, too?"

"Don't know. Could maybe get thirty dollars for it. Twenty-five, anyway. Friend of mine."

"After all that work that gunsmith did on it for you?"

I shrugged.

"It's the last one from your collection."

"It's not an item. You can pick 'em up."

"You wanted to keep it. That's not enough money to help any, is it?"

"No." I still hadn't looked at her and I knew I might as well let her think I was going to sell the gun. Maybe if what I had planned for that bastard Aldercook worked, I wouldn't have to sell it. He was a fine bastard, all right. He owed me the money and now I had to take a gun. Maybe I would sell it anyway. The gun was a hunk of temptation lying in the drawer.

I closed the drawer and went over and sat beside her on the bed, holding the Luger, thinking how there was a full box of twenty-five nine-millimeter Parabellum Czechs in the candy dish on the buffet.

Damn that Harvey Aldercook.

"How much money have we got?" Ruby said.

"I don't know. Four dollars and sixteen cents."

"Steve?"

I looked at her, looking away from the fine soft hard feel of cold blue steel, machined like glass and more than neighborly.

"Don't sell the gun."

"We'll see. Listen, Ruby, I'm going downtown."

"You weren't thinking about selling it, anyway, Steve."

We watched each other for a time. She was propped up on her elbows with the pillows bunched behind her shoulders and head. Ruby was a beauty and a winner, all the way. She was long and full in the body, eager, and big-boned with the bones fine and delicately shaped, and there was grace in every movement she made, even with the kid, like this. She had a broad quiet mouth and hair like a thick mass of waving saffron and clear eager blue eyes with all that fine quality she had shining out at you, glowing quietly out at you.

I stood and patted the calf of her leg. "I better get on with it."

"Wait," she said. "Get on with what?" She patted the bed but I didn't sit down. She was wearing a bright blue dress with white collar and cuffs and white buttons all down the front shaped like hearts. She'd made the dress herself and she was a sweetheart. She looked fine.

"Something I want to attend to," I told her. I kept rubbing the gun with my thumb and it was hard, cold, but beginning to warm up. It had black ebony grips. It would sock them in there like a .32 revolver on a .38 frame, only the Luger was nastier.

She turned her head away. "I knew this would happen."

"It isn't what you think."

"Yes, it is. All those guns. I knew, I knew."

"What the hell you want me to do?"

"Not that."

I began to get that cramped feeling, like when somebody starts to crowd me. This was something I didn't want to talk about. Not to Ruby, not to anybody. Maybe the money was her business, but Aldercook and how I got what belonged to us was my business and I didn't want to talk about it. Just thinking about that pale slug of an Aldercook made my nose ache across the bridge.

"You think I'm going to stick up a bank?" I said.

"No. You're too smart to pick on a bank."

"Oh, Ruby, for God's sake!"

"Not now, Steve. Not now. If it wasn't for the baby, maybe I could understand. But now everything's different."

"You talk like I'm a crook. The only thing I ever stole in my life was two flashlight batteries out of a dime store when I was eleven, and a jug of cognac from a French *bistro* in Alençon during the war. And I got such a fool conscience I even sent the owner of that place five bucks when I got back in the States."

"Yes. But it's different now. I've been watching you, Steve." She looked at me and I could see in her eyes all the not-quite-fear, the praying-pleading that she was wrong.

"Then what?" I said. My voice was a little rusty, the way it gets, and I was keyed up. "You can bat your head against the wall just so long," I said. I said, "The South doesn't want us, Ruby. And we can't get back North, we can't even eat right, and every damned body you see is driving a Cadillac and eating steak and we haven't even got the Ford any more."

"Since when do you like Cadillacs?"

"All right." I walked over to the bureau and slammed my palm down on the top and the pennies and the dime jumped. Damned plywood.

"We own the house, don't we?"

"Some house."

"Can't you take out a mortgage?"

I turned and shot a little laughter at her. I wasn't thinking about how this was affecting her. I didn't think about that until later. "It's mortgaged to the throat and you know it. Another couple months we won't have the house."

"They like you here, Steve." She patted the bed beside her again, only I didn't take the hint. "Your father was born in this town and they remember him and they like you. Give it a chance. You have lots of friends in this town. Why, when we walk down the street everybody says, 'Hi, Steve, how's it going?' And—"

"Yeah," I snapped. "And they know just exactly how it is going, too. I tell you, they're still fighting that war down here. Why can't I get a job, then? This isn't the depression, Ruby—this is a high time on the calendar. I was on the force in Jacksonville and maybe it wasn't tops, but it was all right. Until that son-of-a-bitch jabbed his thumb in my eye and fixed it so

I can't see right. He ruined everything. I can't fly a plane any more. They won't renew my license. I'm an experienced mechanic until they see me trying to work with a screw driver or a wrench, or spot the way my hands get torn up jabbing them into the fan, or see the scars where I knock my head into every damned nut and bolt and sharp edge on an engine. 'Can't you see right, Logan?' they say. 'Is the light bad in yere?' 'I see fine,' I says. 'Just had a rough night, is all.' 'Well, we don't tolerate rough nights, Logan, not at this garage. Sho, now, I reckon you stay on this yere job another week, you-all will maim yourself with a spark plug or mebbe get constipated on a gearshift knob.' I hit him for saying that. He sat down in the grease pan. It's just I get excited, Ruby. I can see all right. Distance is a little cockeyed, I'll admit. But I can shoot a gun. Now tell me, how come I can shoot like that, but sometimes I have to feel my way up the porch steps? One-eye Logan. And that *one* keeps letting me down. I could cut that bird's throat, him with his dirty thumb!"

I stood there, watching her, still not knowing what it was doing to her, thinking only about my tough luck. "Ruby, I haven't held down a steady job in over a year."

"You're a carpenter, Steve."

"You should see me drive a nail."

She grinned, then chuckled. Then I got what she was thinking and had to laugh myself, even if my heart wasn't in it. It was a good thing you don't need eyes for that. I guess I'd have shot myself. What a Ruby!

"That was some speech," she said. "The most you ever talked in months. Steve."

"That's all right," I said. "It's all right about that." I sat on the bed, holding the Luger between my knees, looking at it and thinking about Harvey Aldercook. I was beat, that's all. I needed some raw meat or something. Then I stood up again. "I'm going downtown," I told her. "You hold the fort."

"Wish you wouldn't, hon."

I didn't say anything. I went over to the closet, took off my shorts, and dropped them on a chair. I laid the Luger on top of the shorts and it always looked good. I put on a pair of gray gabardine pants and a lightweight short-sleeved sport shirt.

"I wish you wouldn't," she said again. "I've got a funny feeling, Steve."

"You just hang onto it, then," I said. "I won't be long." I got the Luger and went over and kissed her and she tried to smile and it was no good because of what was in her eyes. I couldn't look at it, even. She was plenty worried, and not just about the baby, either.

I went into the dining room and over to the buffet. I stuck seven of the shiny Czech cartridges into the clip and slapped one into the breech and flipped on the safety. Then I worked the gun into my hip pocket, right side. It was heavy and anybody could tell I carried a gun, but what the hell? I went back and looked in on her. She hadn't moved from that position on the bed. She wouldn't look at me. She kept staring over there at the wall.

"Where you going, Steve?"

"Got some business," I said.

"Please," she said. "We'll make out all right."

"Better than you think," I said, and she still wouldn't look at me. "I'll be gone about an hour. You need anything, holler for Betty Graham, next door. She'll hear you."

She didn't say anything, just moved one leg a little.

I stood there a minute, watching her, and wishing I was somebody else with a steady job and a Cadillac. Only you're thinking all wrong, I told myself. So cut it out.

I went back down the hall, through the living room, and on out the front door. I hoped Harvey Aldercook was down at the basin, on his boat. But no matter where he was, I'd find him.

Betty Graham, a chunky red-haired girl in blue shorts and a green sweater, was watering her front yard with the hose. I stopped there on the sidewalk.

"Say, kind of keep an eye on the house for me, will you? I won't be gone long, but you know how it is with Ruby."

"Sure, Steve." She smiled and stood there watering her left foot, then she saw what she was doing and turned the hose onto the front porch. Cripes, I'd hate to be married to her, but she was a good scout. Her husband was a little nuts, too, so it didn't matter.

"Soon's I finish the lawn, I'll go in and see her," Betty said. "Don't you worry, now, Stevie."

"That's fine."

I went on down the street thinking about Harvey Aldercook, with the Luger pulling heavy at my hip pocket. It was a fine spring day and there wasn't a cloud in the sky. Some ragged-looking kids were playing tag in the alley across the street, and I got to thinking about Ruby, when the bus came along. So I invested a dime for a ride to the yacht basin and sat down next to an old man with a long yellow-gray beard who had eyes like blobs of thick gray dust and dirty bony hands that shook like crazy across the handle of his cane. I felt as sick as he looked.

The bus jounced along out of the residential section, turned east past some gas stations, and it began to get warm. Pretty soon we were between buildings and it was really hot.

I knew that if this didn't work with Harvey Aldercook, I was going to use the gun for something. That was for sure. Ruby wasn't going to go hungry and neither was the kid and that doctor was going to be paid.

Then I realized I was carrying the bright green box with the rest of the shells for the Luger. There it was in my hand. I jammed it into my pocket.

"Going a hunting, son?" the old man said.

"Yeah, Pop," I said. "That's right. Hunting."

"Used to do a mought of hunting myself, in the old days," he said, talking slow and dry behind his beard. "Never could abide fishing, now, but hunting—say, that's another thing." Then he held up one hand and we sat there watching it shake and jump and twiddle.

He didn't say anything else and I got to thinking how everybody has to get old like that, and die, and here he was, and here I was. Then I saw we were coming down along the yacht basin. I reached up and yanked the buzzer cord.

"So long, Pop," I said.

He didn't answer. He was way back there someplace in his dream, chewing his gums, his beard bobbing and curling where it lay down along his chest.

Chapter Two

I walked through the wooden gate and out onto the pier at the slip where Harvey Aldercook's yacht, the Rabbit-O, was moored. She still looked fine. The weather was touching her a bit here and there, but all that work I'd done on her was really holding up fine. I had scraped and sanded and painted and scraped and varnished and polished and refitted and painted and rebuilt and stripped both engines to nothing, overhauled them both, and put them back. She would need some work because Aldercook would let her go to hell. Only somebody else would get taken this time. Not me.

I stood there looking at her, thinking how he had paid me exactly ten dollars out of the two hundred and eighty that he owed me. That left two-seventy, and it would be like buying a pack of cigarettes to Harvey Aldercook, only he wouldn't pay.

Well, the bastard would pay.

A woman with whisky on her tongue laughed, then said, "Harvey-honey! There's a great big beautiful animal with yellow hair out there. I think he's watching me. Are you a Peeping Tom?" she called. "Harvey-honey, he's coming aboard just like a cat. Oh, boy, where's that bottle! Here, there! He's looking right at me. Hello, there."

"Hello," I said. "Is—"

"Fooled you, didn't I?" she said. "It's only Coca-Cola. I finished the bottle. Harvey's got to get some more."

She was an insult to the female gender, a short circuit in the voluptuous, tender woman flesh man dreams upon. She was one of these ash-blonde, bony, saucer-eyed, skull-grinning, jut-jawed, false-breasted, fake-fannied, angle-posing, empty-thighed in-betweens they stamp out like tin slats for Venetian blinds in some bloodless, airless underground factory to supply that increasingly bewildering demand for sexless models such as she for certain women's fashion magazines, where they loll backward gaping and pinch-nostriled in tight red and silver sashes, over an old freshly varnished beer barrel, holding long skinny umbrellas, point down in a sand dune. Sometimes you see them swooning pipe-lidded, paper-pale over a swirling Martini in a triple-sized cocktail glass with their long fleshless golden-tipped claws clamped buzzard-like around the stem. Give me curves, dimples, and swollen thighs, every time. I'm an easy man to please.

"I'd like to see the skipper," I said.

"Skipper? Skipper?" She went vacant, then erupted with vacant laughter and flipped her wrist. I wondered if maybe that's where Harvey Aldercook had picked up the gesture. "Oh, you mean Harvey, don't you?"

I nodded. All the time she'd been talking, she was stretched out on a padded beach chair behind the cabin screen door. She was dressed in one of these shorty nightgowns they wear and her legs were not like toothpicks, they were like matchsticks, with the heads of the matches her fine, full, excitingly curved hips.

"Logan?"

I turned and there was Harvey Aldercook. He must have gone forward, come up through the hatch, around the cabin deck, and into the stern.

"I'd like to talk with you," I said.

"Go ahead, Logan. Go ahead and talk."

"Honestly," she said from in there. "You're a scream, Harvey-honey!"

Harvey Aldercook was a big, droopingly handsome pale slug, dressed in white tennis shoes, blue linen slacks, white T shirt, and white yachting cap with a black bill. Somehow, even owning and living on a boat, he never saw the sun.

"Alone," I said.

"Look, Logan," Harvey Aldercook said. "I haven't got all day. Get on with it. If you have something to say, get it off your chest." He slapped both hands against his belly, glanced in over my shoulder at Spindleshanks, and winked at her, as if to say, "Be right with you, sweetheart. We've got a secret, haven't we?"

The Luger was like a melting chocolate cake in my hip pocket.

"Well?" Harvey Aldercook said.

"I need some money," I said, hating every minute of it, hating myself for forcing myself to ask him. "You owe me two hundred and seventy bucks."

I'm here to collect," I said.

"How do you figure?" Harvey Aldercook said. He was perfectly serious, a little amazed, maybe. His eyes even widened a little with astonishment and the whites of his eyes were perfectly white in a clean rim around the lids, but when the lids parted a bit it was all bloodshot and brown underneath. It was almost as though he had double sets of lids on each eye.

"You know how I figure," I said.

"Really, Logan, you're not joking, are you?"

"No."

"But, see here, Logan. I don't understand." Absolutely serious, earnestly puzzled.

We watched each other for a minute, like two dead men strapped to chairs across the newly dry-cleaned green cover on a poker table beneath a brilliant white light. Then somebody stripped a clean deck and tossed it on the table.

"Four and a half months ago," I said, "I worked on your boat, remember? For quite a time I worked. I have a list of the things I did, if you'd care to see it. For that job, you owe me two hundred and seventy dollars."

"Why don't you pay the poor jamoke?" Spindleshanks said from in there. "Or, better yet, send him for a bottle and tell him to keep the change."

"Let me handle this," Harvey Aldercook said.

"Well, for hell's sake, handle it, then!"

He looked at me again, still with that profoundly puzzled air, touched now with a veneer of hurt.

"Logan," he said, "you know as well as I that I paid you for that job."

"Ten dollars. You paid me ten dollars."

"Certainly," Harvey Aldercook said. He broke into smile now. "You remember, after all, Logan. Gosh, for a time there we were both befuddled, weren't we? How about a drink, now?"

"Wait," I said. "The job was two-eighty, you paid me ten of it. You still owe me two-seventy." I was onto his angle, all right, but I was going to play it to the end.

"See here," he said, serious again and allowing a little anger to show in his eyes. "You'd better get off this ship. I paid you what that job was worth."

"Yes!" Spindleshanks said from in there. "Tell him if he's blown that ten dollars, it's his worry. He shouldn't be so careless with his money." She broke into more vacant laughter. "What a jamoke!" she said.

"Besides," Harvey Aldercook said, "the job wasn't even done right. I had to do everything all over myself. It was a lousy job. You got ten dollars too much, Logan."

I had been going to use the gun on him, at least point it at him, scare him, because I figured he would scare. Now, somehow, I knew I couldn't even do that. He had me and he knew it, and he knew I knew it.

There was nothing to say. I could stand here and argue, but it would get me no place. I fumbled around for the gun, but it was jammed upside down in my hip pocket and I couldn't get it out without a struggle. I let it go.

"Get off the ship," Harvey Aldercook said.

"Listen," I said, swallowing whatever was left of whatever pride had survived these last few months. "My wife's going to have a baby—any day now. I need that money bad."

He shook his head. "Everybody's got troubles."

"I'll call it square for a hundred."

"I ask you for the last time, get off this ship."

"Why don't you throw him off, Harvey-honey? Throw the rummy into the drink."

"Maybe I will," Harvey Aldercook said, with what was supposed to be a sneer. He stepped toward me. I blew up. It was like Popeye with his spinach.

I reached out, caught the back of his neck, then swung with my right fist and sank it hard into his gut, just right. He doubled over, his eyes praying. I put my other hand on the back of his neck, laced my fingers, and yanked his head down. I brought my knee up fast and his nose made a noise and I felt it go, like pretzels in a damp bag. Then there was blood and he wanted to fall face down. I propped him up with my left hand and brought my right fist up again from down under. He arched backward over the rail like a big dead fish and struck the water and sank.

"All right," I said, turning to the cabin screen door. "You better do something, Gorgeous, or your boy friend will drown himself."

She was plastered up against the tiller, with her hands stretched out, screaming in a whisper. "Get away! Get away! Don't you *dare* touch me, you—*you horrid man!*"

Standing out there on the sea wall, I looked back at the Rabbit-O. Spindleshanks was helping a muddy, bleeding, soaking-wet Harvey Aldercook back over the side into the stern. As I watched, he flopped down onto the deck and lay there bleeding on the brightly varnished mahogany planks.

Then Spindleshanks saw his face and got sick.

I turned and started off toward town. As I moved along, two girls in bathing suits ran leaping across the lawn from the sidewalk and jumped from one of the piers onto the deck of a sloop. Both were really stacked firm and flashing and it was sure good to know they weren't all like that one back there aboard the Rabbit-O.

I didn't know what I was going to do. I was sick without being sick; numb and confounded and maybe a little crazy right then. Things could not get worse. I kept telling myself that, knowing all the time that I'd been telling myself that for months and it was getting worse all the time. I was confused. I walked, not knowing where I walked, and I was tired without reason.

The sun was hot. There was no wind. Along the park the trees hung green and dark and heavy, like dead hands, and the world was a winding tunnel, spaced with motionless shadow in black splotches, and the decaying lawns turned up and over into a pale yellowing sky, and far away through the dying bleat of traffic the City Hall clock tolled a slow and darkly maddening reminder of noon.

Noon and busy lunch counters, the restaurants, with business deals over cooling coffee, across polished tables and bread crumbs, among empty, gravy-stained plates, or the homes filled with searing sizzles of frying meat and laughter and sadness and the loneliness of empty waiting and the hushed whisper-touched trays of sickrooms or the cold stoves and silent unhungry patience of death.

I went on past the big hotels with the bright yellow or red or green marquees, their en trance ways touched with that nostalgic assurance of shadowed sanctuary beyond the depthless shade of muted lobbies where a switchboard buzzed and buzzed. Pretty soon I was in the business section of town, trying not to think at all any more, or remember. It was like being lost. There was no way to turn, nowhere to go, nothing to do. Ruby was waiting, and that's what I was really doing, waiting.

The streets were quite empty with noon. About a block away a city bus was tearing along toward me, with papers gusting in its wake. Then I saw him.

He was standing on the corner, looking down my way.

"Hey!" I called. "Watch it!"

He didn't hear me. Still looking absently down the street, he stepped briskly off the curb into the path of the speeding city bus.

Chapter Three

I moved fast. I left the curb and ran up the street toward the bus. Already I saw the driver in the window up there, over the big flat wheel, wrestling, and probably trying to find the brakes, only the brakes weren't doing anything and the bus kept coming.

"Jump!"

He didn't jump. He just ceased walking directly in the path of the bus and stood there staring at me as I came up to him. The bus was on us. I heard the brakes then. Somebody across the street screamed. I rammed my right arm under his left with all my weight, diving. We rolled over against the curb and the bus screeched to á halt in the middle of the street.

I stood up and my leg hurt. He pushed himself onto the curb and sat there with one shoulder against a big aluminum can lettered with the black warning:

DUMP TRASH HERE HELP KEEP OUR CITY CLEAN

He didn't answer. I had fallen on my knees and left shoulder, so the Luger was all right. I wanted to haul it out and look at it, but I couldn't because people were crowding around now.

"You all right?" I said.

The bus driver came around the rear of the bus. He had left it parked in the middle of the street now. Some bus driver. He'd been going like hell and he knew it and he was scared, it showed in his face.

"What you trying to do?" he said. "My God," he said. "Look where you're going. My God."

"What's the matter?" I said. "Did your foot go to sleep? Or was it your head?"

"Where's a cop?" the driver said, looking wildly around.

"He's probably having a sandwich and a beer someplace," I said. "Like everybody else. Maybe you've had the beer," I said. "Is that right?"

"I want a cop," the driver said. He had a pad and pencil in his hand now. "Hey, you," he said to an old lady in a straw hat, holding a shopping bag. "You see this thing? Eh? Eh?"

"Yes," she said. "I saw it, young man."

"What's your name?"

"What's *your* name, young man? You were going too fast."

He turned quickly away from her, brandishing the pad and pencil. The crowd was already dispersing. "Somebody must of seen it," he said. He took a step toward me. "He hurt? He ain't hurt. He's drunk, that's what."

The man seated on the curb stood up. His face was very pale. He leaned over and brushed his pants two or three flicks with his hand, hitched at his belt, stepped up to the bus driver.

"Case out," he said softly.

The bus driver blinked at him.

"Look," the man said kindly. "Go back to your bus, get in, and drive away." He turned, came over to me, rapped me lightly on the arm. "Come on, pal," he said softly.

I stood there a moment as he walked off.

He stopped, turned, grinned at me. He jerked his head. "Come on," he said. "Let's go have a drink."

I went on over. He looked at the few people still standing around and they got out of our way and we went on up the street. I glanced back once. The driver was climbing into his bus. I heard it start with a roar.

We walked along. It was a fine, sunny spring day, as I said, with not much traffic and very few people on the streets, and we walked along.

He was whistling through his teeth, no tune, not even a whistle, just hissing something or other through his teeth with the melody back there in his head someplace. He walked fast and purposefully, rolling his shoulders some. He wasn't quite as tall as I was, but broad in the shoulder and with a big chest and cross-swinging arms. He wore a dark gray single-breasted suit with the coat flapping open across a white shirt that was unbuttoned at the throat. He wore no tie. The suit was too heavy for down here at any time of year. The suit looked brand-new, yet it was a mass of wrinkles, as though it had been slept in on a clean bed for maybe three days running.

We walked along like that, with him whistling through his teeth, for a good three blocks. He walked too fast for down here. I was sweating plenty, but he wasn't. He looked pale and cool.

"You feel O.K. now?" I said.

He turned his head, still whistling through his teeth, swinging his arms. "Sure, pal." He started whistling again and we walked along.

The hell with this. "Well," I said, "I'll see you. I turn off here."

"Me too, pal."

We went around the corner and walked along for a while. The Luger was banging against my hip and beginning to chafe, what with all this fast walking and the sweat. Up ahead on the far corner by the railroad tracks was Jake's Place. Jake Halloran owned the place and he had seen the Luger and wanted to buy it. Well, maybe I should sell it to him. We'd have a little money, anyway, enough to stock up on some food. I didn't feel much like holding up a gas station any more, not much like anything. And now this guy.

A car stopped by the curb and somebody called my name: "Steve!"

It was Betty Graham.

I went over to the car. The guy in the suit stood there watching, then he looked down the street and just stood there.

"Stevie, Stevie!" she said. "You get your tail right over to the hospital."

"What?"

"It's happening," she said. "Ruby called me over and she was having pains and I took her to the hospital and the doc says any time. She told me you might be at Jake's—that's where you used to hang out, anyway. What a break, my finding you!"

"The baby," I said.

"Get over there, Steve. Ruby's worried about you."

"Yes."

"Shall I drive you over, Steve?"

"No, I'll walk. It isn't far, only a couple blocks."

She grinned behind the wheel of her old blue coupé. She was still in the shorts and sweater and her red hair was in damp ringlets across her forehead. She looked over my shoulder where I leaned on the door of her car and whispered, "Who's that guy there? He with you?"

"I don't know," I said. "Listen. All right. I'll get right over there. Is Ruby all right?"

"Sure. She's fine." Betty frowned. "Only she's worried about you, Steve. She wouldn't tell me what, but she's plenty worried. Everything all right, Steve?"

"Sure," I said. "Everything's fine. You go ahead now. I'll get right on over there." I backed away from the car. "And thanks, Betty. Thanks for taking care of Ruby."

"Forget it." She grinned, slapped the car in gear, shot another look at the guy who still stood waiting, and drove off.

"Baby, huh?" he said.

"Yeah."

"That's great, pal."

"I got to get right over there."

"Sure, pal. Sure. Here's a place, down here. Let's have that drink." He nudged me and we walked along toward Jake's Place. I could use a drink. Maybe that was his way of saying thanks, or something. The hell with it. Anyway, it would give me a chance to sell the gun, if Jake still wanted it. I was pretty sure he did. Then I'd get on over there to the hospital with our twenty-five or thirty bucks. It was like a thick black cloud inside me, empty and sick and black. Lost, that was it; lost and lost and lost. Like being way up there in the sky in a goldfish bowl with Ruby down here calling for me and no way to get to her with any good. Like when you need a drink of water, or you'll die, and all the taps run dry. You crazy bastard, I thought, go sell the gun and get a drink and eat a hamburg and get the hell over to the hospital and shut your face.

The world hasn't changed, or ended, I thought. It's just you're hungry and broke and you need a job and things are a little tough right now, so quit knocking yourself just because you're out of gas. So your wife's going to have a baby, so what? That's what women are made for, having babies. Almost every one of them has a baby sometime or other. You've got the house, haven't you? Well, all right, so the bank's got the house, but you're living in it, aren't you? You'll pay off the bank and everything will be fine. What's this about not letting them leave the hospital until the bill's paid? Now, that's a great one, isn't it? Well, we'll pay the bill, somehow. There's a way. There's always a way.

"Something bothering you, pal?"

I had forgotten about him. He was still with me. We were in front of Jake's now.

"No," I said. "I'm all right. I got to go in here."

"Good a place as any."

I started inside. He took hold of my arm and held me back. He looked at me levelly.

"Thanks, for that back there," he said.

"What?"

"Thanks," he said. "I'm just telling you thanks. You saved my life. We're buddies now, pal."

"Forget it," I said. "You didn't see the bus, is all."

"No."

"Anybody'd do the same thing."

"No," he said. "Not anybody."

"What do you mean?"

"You," he said. "We're buddies." He banged me on the shoulder. "See? Like that. You're my pal."

"All right."

"You saved my life. I'll never forget that. Never."

"All right," I said. "But-" Then I got a look at his eyes and changed it, and said, "O.K."

"Let's have a drink on it."

"Sure, but I got to get right over to the hospital."

He said nothing. We went on inside. I had got a look at his eyes and there hadn't been anything there. That's what was the matter. There was not a damned thing there, nothing. Just eyes, like a blind man. Nothing registered, you could tell. Just plain eyes. They were gray eyes and they were open and that's all you could say about them.

Otherwise he seemed a very energetic young guy who had maybe done considerable farm work, lots of energy, talking soft and fast and moving around a lot, even when he stood in one spot.

It was cool and shady in Jake's Place. I liked it because it was one of the last of the real bars you find anyplace. There was no red plastic and no chromium and the bar was wood, all the way. There was sawdust on the floor, good clean, fresh sawdust, and you drank wine, beer, or whisky just the way they were. If you asked for a Whisky Sour, you got a glass of whisky. You asked for a Martini, you got a glass of gin. And that's the way it was, because Jake didn't believe in cocktails or in mixing "the grape," as he called it, with anything but water. Everything was "the grape," and "water ain't good for the grape, either, but you want water, you get water. Now why not catch hold of yourself, man? Drink the grape the way it's naturally got to be drunk. You want ice, I got ice, sure. You want ice water, drink ice water. You want the grape, for your own sake, drink the grape. God wants it that way." And his name was Jake Halloran. Big and black-eyed and black-haired and loud-laughing, and there was always a plate of cheese and crackers on the bar, and it never went empty for long.

If you asked for gin, Jake would pour and say nothing, then lean on the bar with the bottle in his big hairy fist and stare at you until you'd drunk it. "You like that?" he'd ask. "Sure, I like it," you'd say. "Have another, then," Jake would say. And he'd pour you another. "You like that one, too?" he'd ask gently, leaning there with the bottle, watching you drink it, and by now you feel like ha-ha … well. "You still like it?" Jake would say. "Then get the hell across the street to the Tangerine Bar and Grille and drink up. They got better stuff." Then he would stand there with the bottle and watch you soberly and pretty soon you'd grin because you for cripes sake had to do something and you saw that's what it was. That he was waiting for you to do something, so he'd bust out laughing and you'd say, "Give me a whisky," and he'd slap the bottle of gin on the bar in front of you and have a whisky with you, on the house. "The grape," he would say. "Good, hey?" And all the time you were there, the bottle of gin would stand in front of you, and every time Jake passed by, he'd lift the bottle and rap it on the wood. Well, if you didn't like it, that was too damned bad, and you could get out. Because he owned the place and that's the way it was. He didn't like gin. And by this time you didn't either. You'd never take another drink of gin without looking over your shoulder first, either.

There was a man and a woman at one of the booths, a couple of men drinking beer at the far end of the bar, and one tall fellow brooding in his whisky in the center of the bar. He was pretty well shot, too.

"Well, Steve," Jake said, balling up the bar rag. "No time long see."

"Yeah," I said. "You know how it is. Ruby—"

"Gosh," Jake said, "that's right. Not five minutes ago. Steve, your wife's at the hospital, an' you gotta get right over there. Mrs. Graham was in here."

"I saw her."

"You did?"

I nodded, and all the time the man in the suit, my pal, kept staring at Jake. Then he nudged me and straddled a bar stool. I went over and stood beside him. "Give me a beer, Jake," I said, and then to my pal, "What're you going to have?"

And he said, "Gin."

Jake looked at him, then turned to me. "Figure you got time?"

I was thinking about Ruby and I didn't answer. Then my beer came up and Jake reached back and got a bottle of gin and poured my friend a shot and stood there.

"Is that all right?" Jake said to the guy.

The guy ignored Jake and turned to me. "Drink up, pal."

I took a swallow of beer, thinking about Ruby, and he tossed off his shot, shoved the glass toward Jake. Jake watched him a moment. "You want another?" Jake said.

The guy just looked at him.

Jake poured another.

"Listen, Jake," I said. "You know that Luger of mine?"

"Sure, Steve."

"Still want to buy it?"

"Well," Jake said, watching the guy, "I dunno, Steve."

I'd been wrestling with it, trying to get it out of my pocket. Finally I got it out and held it in my hand, looking at it. It looked fine, all right. Anybody with the barest interest in any guns at all would like the looks of this Luger.

"I got it right here with me," I said. "Listen, Jake," I said. "I'll level with you. I need the dough and you want a good gun. This is a good gun. It's been worked over by Benny Stock, the gunsmith over on Sixth Street. All you do is hold it in your hand and it does the rest."

"You want another now?" Jake said to the guy who had tossed off his second shot.

The guy just looked at him. Then he turned to me. "Say, pal," he said, "what's the matter with your friend?"

I looked at him and then at Jake and said, "Here, Jake, have a look. Wait, it's loaded."

"Out for bear?" Jake said.

"Just a second." I dropped the clip and ejected the shell in the chamber. I handed the gun to Jake. All the time, my pal was watching.

"That's a nice-looking gun," my pal said.

"It's a beaut."

"Why you selling it, pal?"

"Broke."

"Me too, pal."

I looked at him, but he was watching the gun as Jake took it from my hand. Jake held the gun and looked at the guy beside me there at the bar and said, "You want another of that?"

The guy reached out and poured himself one, all the time watching Jake and never spilling a drop. Then he drank it.

"It's a nice gun," Jake said to me. "How much?"

"Thirty bucks."

Jake hesitated.

"I'll throw in some extra shells, too. Here." I fished the box out of my pocket and plopped it on the bar beside the filled clip and the one extra.

"Wonder if she'll fit in the cash drawer," Jake said. He turned around and rang the register and began fumbling around with the drawer.

I looked at the guy beside me and he was watching the back of Jake's head. His face was dead white and there was a pale film of perspiration covering it. His face looked as if it had been molded from white marble. It was a wax face. It was dead. Even his lips had no color at all. His hair was India-ink black and he wore it in a crew cut and the planed features of his face down to the slightly jutting jaw, with the cleft in it, looked as if it had been sliced clean of any roughness with a keen knife blade. It was smooth and hard and waxy-looking, just like death.

"I'll give you twenty-five," Jake said.

"All right."

"Let's see it," the guy said.

Jake looked at him. Then he handed him the gun and turned back to the cash register. He turned and handed me two tens and a five.

"Take out for the drinks," I said.

Jake took the five and gave me the change.

"Now," Jake said, "do you want another?" He stood there, facing the guy. He tapped the bottle on the bar.

The guy just looked at him.

"What's the matter?" Jake said. "Can't you speak?"

"It's a nice gun, pal," the guy said, turning to me. He reached over in front of me and picked up the clip and jammed it into the gun.

"Give me the gun," Jake said.

The guy just sat there looking at him.

The drunk down the bar leaned over our way and said, "That sure is a nice pretty nice where pretty nice see find out how play the game now where." Then he turned back to his drink and laid his head down, then he lifted his head and said, "I'm alcoholic, will somebody buy me a beer?"

"Is Ruby all right?" Jake asked.

"I hope so."

"You better get over there."

"I am," I said. "Right now." I put the money in my pocket.

"Give me my gun," Jake said to the guy.

The guy sat there. Then he grabbed the slide and whipped a shell into the chamber—*smack*—and sat there.

"I'm alcoholic," the drunk down the bar said.

"That's loaded now," I said. "Be careful."

The guy sat there and looked at Jake. Then he just tilted the barrel of the Luger on the edge of the bar and shot Jake Halloran in the head. The slug took Jake in the forehead, between the eyes, and went right on through and smashed the bar mirror.

Jake stood there a moment with both hands on the bar, holding a bar rag in his left hand. The two guys at the end of the bar ran for the back door fast. The woman in the booth with the man began screaming and scrabbling, trying to get out of the booth. Jake dropped like a rock. His chin hit the edge of the sink a hell of a crack and he tipped backward against the rear shelf where he kept the cigars. A box of cigars spilled out over his head and tumbled into his lap.

The woman ran past me, screaming, but the man who'd been in the booth with her stayed there, scrunched down. I was out on the floor, standing there, looking at the guy with the gun. He turned and stepped away from the bar stool, holding the gun on me, and walked toward me. His face was white and he wasn't smiling. Then he grinned a little without really grinning and said, "Pal. My name's Ralph Angers. What's yours?"

Nothing came out, nothing. I wanted to run but I couldn't move. I knew he would kill me or anybody just as easily as he had killed Jake Halloran. I was really scared. Out there someplace the woman was still screaming and you could tell she was running and it seemed as if the roar of the gun was still going on. Then it was silent.

"I'm alcoholic," the drunk said.

"What's your name, pal? We're buddies now."

"Steve Logan," I heard myself say from way back there where nothing mattered, where this was not true, where all of this had never happened.

"You saved my life, pal. I must try hard never to forget that. I must try very hard never to forget that."

A loose piece dropped out of the smashed bar mirror and tinkled down among the rows of bottles and finally shattered on the floor back there where Jake was.

Poor Jake....

Chapter Four

Ralph Angers turned and walked back bar. He picked up the green box of Czech cartridges and the one extra cartridge and put them in his coat pocket.

"Come on, pal," he said. "Let's go."

We stood there looking at each other. His eyes were still the same. They showed nothing. There was no excitement, no fear, no regret, no friendship. Nothing. Sure, I thought of jumping him, trying to, anyway. But the thought vanished the instant it was born. I would die, that's all. There would be no waiting.

"Did you know Jake?" I said.

He just looked at me. He said, "No. Come on, let's go."

There was a desperate edge to my voice. I tried to sound calm, but that taint of fear wouldn't leave my voice.

I said, "My wife. I've got to get on over to the hospital."

"She'll keep, pal. We have important things to do." He reached out and banged me on the shoulder with the gun. Then he seemed to notice for the first time that he was holding it. He glanced at it for a moment, then started to put it into his hip pocket, up under his coat.

Now, Logan, I thought. Now....

But he said, "No," and brought it out again. He held it down along his leg.

"A gun is a wonderful thing," he said. "Let's go."

We went out onto the street. There was nothing else to do. Back there the drunk still sat at the bar over his empty glass and the other man was down under the booth on the floor.

True realization of what had happened was slow in coming. It was all there. I knew what had happened, all right. But the true feeling of it inched up on me a little at a time.

"Here," Angers said. "We'll go down here." He poked me with his elbow, toward an alley entrance. I glanced up the street. A cop was coming down the street with three or four pedestrians tagging along, but he didn't seem to notice us, and then we were walking down the alley.

"I've got to get over to the hospital," I said.

"Why?"

He had forgotten. It was an innocent question, spoken and as quickly erased from his mind.

"I've got to go," I said.

A small-winged horror came drifting down through the alley and brushed me lightly and vanished. My heart rocked. Just once, hard, my heart rocked, then it went on beating like always. Only after that I was never quite the same.

We walked on along the alley, through the cool garbage-smelling shadows, across the iron grates above the sewers. When we came out into the bright white glare of sunlight at the opposite end of the alley, we turned right.

"Where we going?" I said.

"Pal, I'm not sure."

It was still noon as far as the city was concerned and few people were on the streets. It was quiet and unhurried over here, a block beyond death.

You could run, I thought. Run fast and hard. Who is he? What does he want? I've got to get over to Ruby. Somebody will see him with the gun, they'll do something. There'll be a cop who'll see him with the gun. Where are they? When you want one, they're never around. Go ahead and run, I thought. Find the answer to everything.

We passed doorways to stores, restaurants, where people talked and laughed in there beside the cool rush of fans. An occasional somebody walked by and one woman looked straight at the gun hanging at the end of his arm. She smiled at us, walking along, and he never looked at her. He made no move to hide the gun.

"Down here," he said.

You've got to run, I thought. You've got to do something.

"Over across the street," he said. "Come on, pal." We crossed the street. He walked fast and it was very hot. We came across by a hardware store and started down another alley.

"Look," I said. "I've really got to get over to the hospital."

"Sure, pal."

"My wife's probably worrying herself sick because I haven't shown up."

"Uh-huh."

"I could meet you later. Anyplace you say. Say in an hour or so? You name the place. It doesn't matter."

"No, it doesn't."

"I mean, you could wait for me someplace."

"We'll see, pal."

About halfway down the alley, he stopped and knocked my arm with the gun. "I don't like to say this," he said.

I nodded with the bright pale yellow-blue sky up there in a strip interlaced with fire escapes.

"But I've got to say it," he went on.

"I've got to get to my wife," I said. "I've got to see her. She's worried. You see, she's having a baby. It's our first child and she's expecting me at the hospital. You see," I said, trying to reach him, talking with the words running out of my mouth just fine, "I wasn't home when Ruby had to go. So it's only natural she— I'm worried, too, Mr. Angers."

"Ralph."

"I can't help but be worried too, some, you see?"

"There are many things to be done, Steve," he said. "We'll have a good time, too. There's no cause for you to worry about Ruby."

"The doctor will want to see me," I said.

"That's good," Angers said. "That's fine."

"So I could meet you later. Let's say right here, in an hour. An hour from right now."

He didn't grin, he didn't do anything. The urgency of this moment had me now. Maybe he would say O.K., all right. He stood there with the gun hanging at the end of his arm, his face pale white and shiny with sweat as though somebody had painted it on this cold marble with a brush. Not beads of sweat, just a cold film.

"I'll see you, then," I said. I turned away and started walking.

"Wait," he said.

I didn't stop walking. I just lounged along with every pump of my heart throwing hot blood up into my head and it was like a dam getting ready to burst.

I was passing some piled crates at the rear entrance to a restaurant when the gun blasted behind me. A slug ripped through some garbage in one of the crates and ricocheted off the brick wall, whining straight up into the sky. A little limp piece of lettuce flipped into the alley at my feet. I stopped and turned as he laughed.

It was the damnedest laughter you ever heard, wild and high and crazy as hell. It stopped cold. He looked the same as ever.

He came up to where I was standing. "Come on, pal," he said. "Take it easy, now."

We walked along down the alley.

"This is a grand gun," he said.

We came out of the alley and turned right again and kept on walking along.

"How much money we got?" he said.

"I don't know."

"I'm broke."

"I've got twenty-five, twenty-six dollars."

"We'll have to get some."

"You just killed a man," I said. "Do you know that?"

"Yes, sure."

"They'll be looking for you. You know that?"

"I know."

"Everybody knows me in this town," I said.

"Pal, have you got a car?"

"No."

"We need a car."

We came along by a gas station and cut over between the pumps, cutting the corner. The police cruiser came along swiftly and I saw it. There was only the driver in it and he saw us and slammed on the brakes and came out running. He knew who we were.

"Hold it there!" he called at us.

Angers stopped in his tracks and looked at the cop. He was a young cop with a ruddy face, wearing a short-sleeved gray shirt with the bright silver and gold badge pinned to the pocket on the left-hand side, like they do down here. His cap came off as he ran toward us. Then he saw Angers' gun.

"Drop the gun!" he said, and he stopped running then and stepped onto the curb and you could see it in his face. He was very young and maybe right then he thought about his girl or his wife or his family, or maybe just of being a cop. Maybe he didn't think anything. But as he tried to draw his gun he knew what was going to happen. He stood right in the open between two cabbage palms and Angers lifted the Luger and shot him in the face.

I whirled, running. I ran around the gas station, giving it everything I had. The attendant had been standing in the doorway by the garage part of the station. He made a flying dive at me and slid on his face along the grease-stained cement. He was some attendant, all right. He didn't know.

There was a board fence behind the gas station. I hit it hard, running, and got hold of the top and dragged over. I was in a back yard, walled in by the high board fence and a maze of clothesline. At the rear of the yard by the garage was a gate. I went through the gate. The fence back here, except for the gate, was tight up against a brick-walled building, two of them. A narrow passageway ran between the two buildings. I ran on down there, slipping on tin cans and broken bottles. It opened into an alley.

I hit the alley running hard and turned right.

He was standing down there at the alley entrance, leaning against the corner of the building, watching me.

"Come on, pal," he said. "We're going over to my room."

He slapped the clip back into the gun, rode the slide, thumbed the safety. He had reloaded the clip. He had fired three times so far and that had left three shells in the clip. Only he had checked that, too.

He was staying at The Palmdale. It was one of the best hotels in town. We walked in the front door past the doorman and on through the lobby to the elevator.

"I got my key," he said. "I always carry my key, pal. I never leave it at the desk."

A smiling, crimson-lipped colored girl ran the elevator. When she moved, her starched white uniform hissed crisply. Her hair was well oiled and fixed in large tight rings, plastered to her skull.

No one spoke. We went up, with Angers still holding the gun down along his leg. Both of us were breathing heavily, only he looked exactly the same. We finally bumped to a cushioned stop on the eighth floor. The doors hummed open and we went out into the thick-carpeted hallway. We walked on down the hall.

"Here we are, pal," he said. He opened the door.

I heard him close and lock the door behind us. I was looking at the girl who was stretched out on one of the twin beds. Seeing us, she made a wild grab at a sheet and yanked it up. She had been entirely naked.

She said nothing, just worked herself up on the bed until she was leaning against the head of the bed with the sheet pressed into the firm roundness of her breasts. Then she saw the gun in Angers' hand and said, "Oh, God!"

"I forgot to tell you, Steve," Angers said from beside me. "This is Lillian. I'm afraid she doesn't like me. Or am I wrong, Lillian?"

"Stay away! Don't!" She pressed herself back against the head of the bed. She was very beautiful, with thick mahogany-colored hair, cropped short, but very full. She was frightened as much as it was possible to be frightened. You could see her tremble beneath the thin damp covering of the sheet. Her dark blue eyes were big and round and her red lips formed a frantic O, behind which she swallowed. One long full-thighed leg lay outside the sheet and it kept moving slightly, jerking, with a life all its own. A fan whirred and buzzed at her from the top of the bureau by the foot of her bed, yet her forehead and upper lip showed fine beads of perspiration.

Her voice burst in the room, then, strident, afraid: "You took my clothes!"

"Yes, Lillian."

"So I couldn't leave! You took my clothes!" Her eyes flashed to me, frantic with mute appeal. Then she shook her head and turned face down on the bed.

"I hung the 'Don't Disturb' sign on the door, too, Lillian," Angers said. "You know the hotels obey that sign."

The hotel room was a good one with twin beds, bureau, night stand, television, radio, and two comfortable chairs. It was quite large. The sheets on the bed opposite Lillian's were twisted into long ropes and the mattress was half off the bed, on the floor. There were two whisky bottles on the bureau, one empty, one half full. The closet door stood open and it was empty in there except for a few cockeyed wire hangers.

Her face came up and she looked at us again.

"This is a friend of mine," Angers said. "Steve Logan. Right, Steve?"

I nodded and her-eyes danced across toward me, touched with pleading and appeal, and danced back to Angers' face.

"Lillian," Angers said, "go on into the bathroom. Take a shower or something. I want to talk with Steve, here."

"But I—"

"Hurry up."

"I want my clothes!" She kept looking at him. Then she quit looking and got out of bed, trailing the sheet, and went into the bathroom. Her thighs flashed, her hips leaned in two fine half arcs as she vanished through the door.

She closed the door until just a part of her frightened face peered through, her eyes on the gun in Angers' hand. Then she shut the door. She was obedient, just like a well-behaved dog.

"Sit down, Steve," Angers said. "I've got to tell you something."

I was tired, sick, bewildered, and maybe more than a little crazy. I went over and sat on the foot of the bed, among the twisted sheets. He stopped by the bureau, laid the gun up there by the two whisky bottles, and turned to look at me. He hooked his elbows on top of the bureau and leaned back with his white marble face gleaming, his eyes still and vacant.

"What I have to say is this: Don't try to run, Steve. You see? Please don't try to run, or think of doing anything like that." He paused and his eyes gave the lie to all the words he spoke. He didn't know it, about his eyes. He probably thought he looked serious, talking to me, just like anybody else would. And maybe that was a good thing. Those eyes were dead bright mirrors. They were empty reflector cups. "I would kill you, pal. I would have to kill you, see? I honestly don't want to kill *you*, pal. Honestly. You saved my life and we're buddies and you've got to stick with me, pal."

I sat there, listening, thinking about that girl in the bathroom. Who was she? She knew what he was, all right. She was scared all the way to the ground. There'd been no way for her to leave the room. He thought of everything, all right. But why was he holding her?

"They're after us now," he said. "They'll kill us, only we'll kill them first, see? Now I've got—" He paused.

From the bathroom we could both hear her sobbing.

"Shut up, Lillian," Angers said. He said it smoothly and quietly, with no warning, with no particular inflection, and the sobbing ceased as if he'd turned off a faucet.

"I've got a lot of plans," he went on, turning back to me. "And we're going to go ahead with them. They don't want me to. They never did want me to do anything, pal. It's going to be hard, bucking them. Only I've got plans. You see?"

He stood there, thinking about his plans.

I watched him, thinking about Ruby now, over there in the hospital, wondering where I was, what had happened. He went right on talking.

"You saved my life," he said. "I don't want to have to kill you. So stick with me, will you? Don't make me do that. It's been rough," he said, with his empty, lying eyes. "Five days in this room. Ever since we came down here. Thinking it over, working it all out. So will you stick with me? Share and share alike, pal?"

"Sure," I said. "I'll stick with you."

"Fine." He turned and held up the whisky bottle. "We'll have a drink. Money's no object, you know. Plenty of money. I was just testing you back there, when I said I was broke."

And I knew what I was up against. Ralph Angers was a maniac. He was a psychopathic killer and his mind had snapped. There was no going back now. There was no nothing.

"I should really get over and see my wife," I said.

He grinned, gave a little snort of a laugh. "Sure," he said. "Sure. Here," he said, handing me the bottle. "Take a drink."

I took the bottle and sat there, holding it on my knee.

"You know?" he said, looking all around the room with those bright, empty eyes, and rubbing his together. "Things will work out fine now. Just fine!"

Chapter Five

"Ralph."

Lillian's voice reached us from the bathroom.

"Ralph, may I come out now?"

Her voice was faint, dubious, constrained. It was also touched with a quiet hysteria born of clean-edged fear.

He stopped talking and turned toward the bathroom door. It was very quiet for a moment and out the window over there spring was beginning a sunny, blue-skied afternoon. He glanced back at me and shrugged.

"It makes me feel good, I tell you," he said.

"Please, Ralph?"

I sat there on the bed with the bottle in my hand and watched him. It was a hell of a feeling, all right, because there was no telling what he would do next. Listening, I heard her breathing in there. You could tell she was listening, too.

"I have no clothes, Ralph," she said from in there. I could almost see her pressed against the door, hoping, maybe even praying. Maybe we were both praying. It doesn't have to be conscious and it doesn't have to be words. Just a feeling; a realization.

"Ralph, get my clothes for me, huh?"

He was looking at me, shaking his head. Wasn't she a card, though? The way she carried on?

"Did you take a shower, Lillian?"

"No, Ralph."

"Well, go ahead and take a shower. You need one. You've been lying around too much."

"All right." There was a long pause, during which I knew she was waiting to add something. "Then—then will you give me my clothes? Will you, Ralph?"

"Sure."

Almost immediately the sound of the shower hissed beyond the hum of the electric fan.

Angers was staring at the floor now, his face pale. How was I going to reach Ruby?

"We can't stay here, of course," Angers said.

"No?"

"Of course not. They'll come around here soon. I don't want to kill any more people than I have to. But they've got to learn, that's all. We're going through with this."

"With what?"

"My plans," he said. "You see, Steve, having a pal like you means plenty to me."

"I see." I took a drink from the bottle. It burned its way down my throat, into my empty stomach. I nearly gagged and my throat went dry at the smell of the raw whisky.

Angers watched me intently. "Nobody believed in me," he said. "Even back there, nobody believed. They don't care about saving people. They just want to make money. That's all they think about. It doesn't matter if people are in want, in need." He grinned. "But now you'll help me."

I set the bottle on the floor and rose. "Why don't you and Lillian get cleaned up, then?" I said. "I'll run over to the hospital and see how Ruby is. Then I'll meet you."

"But they'll understand when it's done," he said, still looking intently at me. He either hadn't heard what I said, or chose to ignore it, knowing I'd understand what he meant. I understood.

Just then the bathroom door opened a crack and Lillian stuck her head out, smiling. It was a brave smile and she was trying something new now.

At least new to me. She said something but the sound of the shower drowned it out.

"Turn the water off, Lillian," Angers said.

Her chin jiggled a little, bunching up, and I thought she was going to cry. But she went away from the door and the hissing shower ceased.

"Ralph, honey," she said, "would you toss me some clothes, huh? You wouldn't want me to come out there the way I am." She smiled at him through the crack in the door. I knew she must have worked on that smile in front of the mirror, building it up, praying it wouldn't wash out.

I went over and sat in a chair beside the bed. The fan hummed and buzzed, and far away, down on the street, a car's horn blatted *shave-and-a-haircut....*

"Sure, Lil," Angers said. He glanced at me, shook his head again. Wasn't she the damnedest, though? He started for the door.

My heart flickered dry and light, like a woodpecker on a thin, loose plank, then I felt it beating right up into my throat. He paused with his hand on the knob, then turned and went over to the bureau and picked up the gun.

"No telling who I might meet out there," he said.

Lillian's eyes were at the door crack. He didn't look at either of us. He went on over and unlocked the door, vanished into the hall, closed the door. I heard him walking down the hall.

I came out of the chair fast and grabbed the doorknob. He'd locked it, all right. I headed for the bathroom.

"Quick!" I said. I flung the door open. "Listen, we've got to get out of here!"

She stood there looking at me. I held to the bathroom door, holding it open. She was very pretty; large-breasted, long-legged, and afraid. She grabbed up a wet towel, shielding herself with it. "It's no use. Are you in this with him?"

"In what?"

"I know, I know." Her voice became strident and wild and the words came fast. "He's insane—insane!"

"Hang on. We've got to do something."

"Please, please, *do something!*"

"Fire escape."

"No, no." She laughed in her throat. "There isn't any. It's just a platform out there. The fire escape's down the hall."

"Who is he?" I said.

"He's crazy. What's he got the gun for? He didn't have a gun."

"He's killed two people in the last hour," I told her.

She stared at me. Her fingers gripped white on the wet towel. She moved slowly backward and sat down inside the shower on the wet tile. The red and white shower curtain rustled against her shoulders.

"The phone!" I said. I whirled and saw the phone on the floor between the two beds.

The door opened and Angers came back in. He carried a valise in one hand with a huge, cumbersome roll of paper beneath that arm. The gun was in his other hand. He glanced at me, grinned, closed the door, and locked it.

"Get to know Lil?" he said.

"No. Hardly."

I eyed the phone and cursed myself for not having used it right away when he left the room. It might have been the one chance. I could have got the desk and had them send for the police. It could be we might have made it.

Angers came over to the bed, looked into the bathroom. She hadn't moved. The door was still open and she was seated on the floor of the shower, watching us with round blue eyes. Her mahogany-colored hair was partially wet from the shower and long curls clung to her face.

He dropped the valise and papers and rushed into the bathroom. "You didn't fall, did you, Lillian?"

"No. No, I didn't fall."

He shrugged, came out, and went over to the bed. He took the large roll of paper and placed it on the chair and opened the suitcase.

He brought out a white nylon dress, underwear, stockings, a pair of white pumps, and a leather purse that closely matched the color of Lillian's hair. The suitcase was empty.

Carrying these things in a bundle, he went into the bathroom and dropped them on the floor.

"There you are, Lil. Get dressed."

She stared at the pile of clothes on the floor.

He came into the bedroom and closed the bathroom door. "Not much of a wardrobe," he said. "But after all, utility is what counts."

I sat on her bed, wondering what he meant. Time was flying by and Ruby was at the hospital and here I was with a maniac.

"Soon as she gets dressed, we'll get out of here," Angers said. He began pacing the room. Once he paused by the chair and flicked the big roll of paper with his fingers. "This is it, Steve."

"Where'll we go?"

"Why, to your house, of course, Steve. You have a house, haven't you?"

"Sure." I talked to the floor now.

"That's where we'll go, then. We need quiet."

"But they'll—" I stopped.

"But they'll what?" he asked. "Who'll what?"

"Nothing." I'd almost let it slip. If anybody had recognized me with him, they might go to the house. The law might be waiting there right now and I'd almost let it out of the bag. "There won't be anybody there," I said. "Ruby's at the hospital."

I stood, walked over by him, and looked him in the eye.

"Listen, Mr. Angers—"

"Ralph, Steve—*Ralph!*"

"*Ralph. I've got to see how my wife is!*"

"Turn your head a little to the left, pal," Angers said.

"What?"

"Look at me. Look straight at me, pal."

My stomach began to roll. I looked straight at him.

"Now," he said. "Just turn your head a little bit to the left. That's it. Say, pal, something's wrong with your right eye."

"Oh, Lord," I said.

"No, pal. Look up—up at the ceiling. That's right. Sure, pal...." He reached toward me, fast. I backed away quickly, feeling scared. For the first time a dim light showed in his own eyes; a light that was indescribable and sadly insane. It was like seeing a candle flickering at the end of a long black tunnel.

I kept on backing across the room, with him following me, staring at me, craning his neck. He kept nodding to himself and smiling kind of quietly with that crazy flickering light in his eyes, his face like slick marble. He reached out with his hand, feeling for my face.

"Stand still, pal."

"Why?"

"Just stand still. Let me look at that eye of yours. Listen, pal, does that eye hurt you at all? Ever have both eyes hurting you, pal?" He stopped walking, dropped his hand.

"Some, a little. My right one, mostly."

He stood there nodding to himself with the light in his eyes brightening and waning, glowing and fading, almost as if he breathed with his eyes.

"Sit down in the chair, there," he said. "Here." He grabbed the roll of paper and dropped it on the bed. "Sit down, pal. I want to look at that eye of yours."

"I'm all right." I didn't move. I had my back against the wall by the door now. I wasn't going to sit down for this guy.

"Traumatic, too," he said. "I'd have to— Well, let's see." He scratched his head. Abruptly the light went out of his eyes and he turned toward the bathroom. "Lillian, you ready yet? Hurry up."

"Yes, Ralph. I'm hurrying. I'll be right there, Ralph, honey."

"See that you are, Lillian." He turned to me. "A man has to have a woman," he said. "You're married, you ought to know that."

"Sure." I heard her scrabbling around in the bathroom, probably anxiously intent on dressing. The fan hummed and buzzed and Angers' face was a white marble blank again. "Are you married?" I asked.

"No. I like Lil, but now I'm not so sure she'd make a good wife. Lately she seems stupid, pal. Coming across the country she wasn't that way at first. It's only lately I noticed it."

"Oh. You came quite a way?"

"Quite a way, pal."

I wanted to find out where he was from, what all this was about. But Angers didn't look like the type you could pump much. He looked a little too wise for that. It might take time. I hoped it wouldn't be long. So far I could imagine no way out of this. If we went to my house, things could come to a head quickly. The law might be waiting there now.

I stood there watching him and it seemed almost as if he were trying to remember something. There was no expression on his face, but he stood very still, looking over at the wall.

"Pal," he said, "we'll fix that eye up, don't you worry."

I took the plunge. It might as well be now.

"How do you figure?" I said.

"Was your eye infected?"

I quickly told him about that rummy up in Jacksonville with his lousy thumb. Right away I wished I'd said nothing, but it was a sore subject with me and one I talked too freely about. Also, it seemed to me that talk, right now, was important. It took up time. Talk about anything.

He kept nodding, still staring at the wall. "I thought as much, Steve. But we'll fix it, first chance I can get."

"What do you mean?"

"I'm a surgeon. An eye surgeon."

"Oh."

I began to fade right into the wall at my back. The fear that was already in me blew a big cold breath. Angers turned and glanced at me. But the crazy light wasn't in his eyes; he wasn't interested just now.

"Maybe you could be the first patient at the hospital," he said. But then he shook his head. "That might take a little while, though. And that eye needs tending to, pal."

He kept looking at me.

"Hospital?" I said. It didn't sound like my voice at all.

He was nodding his head. "Sure. We're going to build a hospital, pal." He gestured toward the big roll of paper. "Those are the blueprints, right there."

"I see."

Just then the bathroom door opened and relief spread through me.

"We're going to save lives," he said. His voice was flat and with no inflection whatsoever.

Lillian came out into the room.

"How do I look?" she said.

"Fine," Angers said, staring at the roll of blueprints. Then he went over and picked up the cumbersome paper. "Now let's get going."

Lillian was wearing the white dress and she looked very brave and frightened, but quite pretty, too. I wondered how she'd ever got mixed up with him. I hoped to find out and inside I could feel all the helplessness welling up, because so far both our lives hung by a very flimsy thread.

She glanced at me, then said, "Where we going, Ralph?"

"Going over to Steve's."

"Ralph," she said, "I've got to buy some clothes. This dress is getting dirty and I haven't another thing to wear."

He just looked at her. She tried to smile and it was a washout. Her dark blue eyes were sheened with terror of the man. He turned toward the door and she glanced at me again, then at the gun on top of the bureau. She didn't move toward the gun, though. And neither did I.

Angers paused with his hand on the doorknob, released it, went back, and put the roll of blueprints into the valise. I could tell right then that his mind wasn't functioning in top form. There were moments of relapse and I had a cold feeling that he knew it. He capped the whisky bottle and put that in with the blueprints and closed the valise.

"We'll probably need the gun," he said. "Better take it along, anyway. I like that gun, Steve."

"Sure."

He jammed the gun into the waistband of his pants and his jacket covered it.

"We'll go down the fire escape," he told us, as we entered the hall.

"In daylight?" Lillian said.

"Certainly," he told her. "I haven't enough money to pay the bill. Certainly in daylight." He shook his head at me again. Wasn't she a dope, though?

Chapter Six

We went down the fire escape into an alley. All the time I kept feeling Lillian's pleading, wild eyes on me. She was pleading and praying for a help I could see no way of giving her. I wanted to get out of this as much as she did, but I knew better now than to make a break for it. We'd be dropped in our tracks.

"We'll walk, Steve," Angers said. "I want to see as much of the town as I can."

"Why can't we just take a cab?" Lillian asked.

He said nothing and we came out of the alley onto the street and Angers paused, touched my arm.

"Which way, pal? Where do you live?"

I tried to make my brain work. Angers had planted so much fear in me that he'd become an obsession and it was hard to concentrate on anything else. I didn't know what he'd do next, and I had to stay one jump ahead of him. That was a laugh, because it was impossible. Already his actions worked on immediate impulse and there is nothing in the world that can beat impulse.

"Right down here," I said. "We can go this way."

We started out. I was on the outside, with Lillian in the middle. It was good to have her there. She was sane and solid and she wore the faint traces of a perfume that told me sanity still was someplace in this suddenly crazy world.

Somehow I had to reach Ruby. I didn't even know how she was. Betty Graham had said I was needed at the hospital.

People passed us on the street and we were just three friends walking along, with that fine, manly-looking fellow carrying a suitcase. It would seem he might be rather warm in that suit, though, wouldn't you think?

"I'm glad we chose this town," Angers said. "Aren't you, Lillian?"

She'd been walking along, gnawing at her lower lip. Quickly she looked at him.

"Oh, *yes*, Ralph. It's a *nice* town!" Her eyes flicked toward me and I felt the sharp lash of fear again.

We walked along and he didn't know it but we were going to pass the hospital where Ruby was. Somehow I had to reach her. Something might have gone wrong. First childbirths can sometimes be bad.

"Yes," Angers said. "There's something about this town. It's homey. What I mean is, it's not industrial. That's important. Isn't it, Lil?"

"Yes, Ralph."

We rounded a corner and I saw we were walking straight toward the gas station up there, where Angers had killed the cop. I held myself together. Somebody would see us, recognize us. They had to.

Only Angers could be sharp, too. "All right if we cut over another block, Steve?"

"This is shorter."

He grinned across at me and jerked his head toward the gas station. He and I had a fine secret, didn't we? "We'll just cut over another block, pal. It won't take us out of the way, will it?"

"No. It won't take us out of the way."

We crossed the street, returned to the corner, started along toward the next intersection.

"No use tempting fate," Angers said. "No point to that. Somebody might get mad. I couldn't stand that."

I nodded, listening to the sharp rap of Lillian's heels on the pavement. Somehow she didn't look like an ordinary pickup. Where had she come from? How had she ever got mixed up with this guy?

"Florida's the place, all right," Angers said. "I'm glad we settled on that, Lil. Climate means an awful lot and industry can destroy climate." He looked over at me. "That's why I couldn't see building in Seattle. The climate's not right, not right at all, pal."

"Seattle?"

Lillian turned to me and nodded, with her eyes scrunched up and her teeth in her lower lip.

"Those damned fools back there wanted to build in Seattle. They were fools, that's all. They're blind. They don't really want to save anybody, they don't want to help. They only think of their own pockets, that's all."

We were coming along by the parking lot beside the hospital when Angers realized where we were. He paused, glanced up at the new building shining in the sun. Palm trees, freshly planted, helped the landscape. But the building itself looked somehow new and raw. It had been finished only recently.

Ruby was in there someplace....

We walked along toward the front entrance.

"Now, take that, for instance," Angers said. "Indian Park Hospital," he read the inscription above the glassed doors. He shook his head. "I can tell you about it without ever having heard of it, or ever having been inside."

We stood on the walk before the main entrance and I began to sweat. Perspiration dribbled down my sides and it seemed almost as if I could hear her calling to me in there.

"Mongers," Angers said. "That's what I call them. Hospitalmongers. Build new hospitals. How long has the town had this one, Steve?"

"There's old Indian Park, over there through the trees," I said. "This was just finished a few months ago. The town's rather proud of it."

"I'll bet," Angers said. "I'll bet." That light was beginning to show in his eyes again. I saw it and all hope left me.

"Ralph," I said, "this is where my wife is. I want to go in and see her."

He shook his head. "Not a chance, Steve. There's no time for things like that."

I stepped in front of Lillian and faced him. "I'm going in there," I told him. "She's in there. She's having a baby. Did you ever have a baby?"

"Stop kidding, pal."

Lillian's voice was urgent. "Is your wife in there, Steve?"

"Yes. It's our first kid."

"Oh, God," she said. She touched Ralph Angers' arm. "Honey," she said, "you've got to let the poor guy go in and see his wife. You must, Ralph!"

"There isn't time. Besides, I want to tell you about this place."

"Maybe it would help you to see the inside," I said. "You could come in and wait for me. All I want to do is find out how—"

"Mr. Logan?"

It was one of the Gray Ladies. She was a friend of a neighbor of ours and I knew her slightly. She must have just been getting through work. She came along the entrance walk toward us in her gray dress with the little cap, carrying a plastic raincoat and something that looked like an overnight bag. She was stout, gray-haired, and wore glasses. She seemed concerned.

"Mr. Logan. I'm so glad you've finally come. We've been waiting for you. The doctors simply don't know what to do."

"Come on, pal," Angers said. He caught hold of my arm and began pulling at me. I had gone sick inside. These Gray Ladies knew what went on inside a hospital, and she obviously knew something about Ruby.

"Wait, Ralph! Wait!" Lillian said.

The woman looked at us, frowning. She didn't know what it was all about.

I tried to pull free of his grip, but he held on and looked at me. "We haven't any time for this," he said. "Come on, pal."

"Mr. Logan," the woman said, "I'm at the desk, inside. I'm just going home now. But you should hurry in there. As I said, the doctors—"

"Please go away," Angers said to her. "Please, just go away, will you?" His voice was quite kind.

"Ralph!" Lillian said. She went up to the woman and said, "Is Mrs. Logan all right?"

"No. She's not all right," the Gray Lady said. "I hardly think this is any way to act. She's been calling for her husband and Dr. Amory needs to talk to him about something."

"Lillian," Ralph Angers said. "Come on with us. I won't ask you again." His voice was soft and dead.

The older woman was trying to look over Lillian's shoulder at me. Her glasses glinted in the sunlight. Then I felt Angers move and saw him reach beneath his coat.

"All right," I said quickly. "All right, Ralph. Let's go." I was sick inside. I grinned at him, banged his shoulder. "You're right, we haven't got time for this. Let's go, eh?"

He stared blankly at me, a sheen of perspiration covering his pale face. His grip slowly relaxed on my arm and we started walking along the sidewalk.

"Well!" the old woman said. "I never!"

"Come on, Lillian," I said. "Please come on."

But Lillian had seen Angers reach for the gun. She hurried along behind us. Back there the woman stood on the walk and slowly shook her head. Maybe eventually she would find out how very close she had come to never leaving that spot.

"I'm terribly sorry, Steve," Lillian said, beside me.

I didn't say anything.

We walked along. Angers' tread was solid and he stared straight ahead. "It's people like that," he said. "They stand in my way. Ignorance. It's always been that way. I should have killed her. I knew I should have. She'll go around, spreading her ignorance, standing in the way of progress. They say it's not the individual, but they're wrong. You know that, pal?"

I nodded.

"Yes. It takes individuals to make a mob, remember that. And then the mob becomes the individual. With but a single thought. Destruction. They destroy whatever is good."

Lillian took my arm. "She'll be all right, Steve. Don't think about it. There's nothing you can do. In a hospital like that, she must have the very best of care. I'm sure it's nothing serious."

"Thanks," I said. "Thanks, Lil."

Something kept telling me to make a break for it. But I knew it wouldn't be any good. He'd drop me before I'd gone ten feet and that wouldn't help Ruby a bit. It wouldn't help anybody. I'd been picked for a job, all right, whether I wanted it or not. If he killed me, he'd go right on his merry way killing anybody else that crossed his path.

Only what was the matter with Ruby? Why did they want me in there? Maybe she was dying. Maybe there was some kind of operation that was needed and they were unable to go ahead without my consent. It seemed to me I had heard of such things happening.

We walked along. Angers looked cool again. The sheen of perspiration covering his face had dried, and save for that pallor, he looked quite normal. I wanted very much to get Lillian alone and talk with her. Maybe she knew something, could tell me something. But that was a laugh. It wouldn't matter what she knew. Nothing mattered save the moment itself.

"Much farther, pal?"

"No, it's not too far."

I tried not to think about Ruby. It was the only way. But I couldn't stop thinking about her. It was such a simple thing. I told myself I would promise anything to see her. I wouldn't tell anybody about him. But I knew that was a promise I wouldn't be able to keep. It wasn't a question of just stopping this guy. He had to be stopped all the way.

"This is a nice town," he said. "A good town, a clean town. I like clean towns, pal."

Pretty soon we reached my street. We were still several blocks from the house. But far down there, out on the sidewalk, I saw a pair of blue shorts and a red sweater.

Betty Graham. Maybe there would be some way of telling her, tipping her off. She could get the cops. She would be right next door. If only I could reach her. She had seen me with Angers this morning, and something told me she hadn't liked the guy.

"Ralph," Lillian said, "don't you think we should go someplace and eat? I haven't eaten since yesterday. The phone didn't work at the hotel."

He grinned at her. "I disconnected it," he said. "It would have been rather silly, leaving the phone connected, don't you think?"

"There's nothing to eat at my place," I said. "Maybe we could go to a restaurant, Ralph. I've got some money."

He just turned and looked at me.

Up ahead, Betty Graham was still standing on the sidewalk. She was watering her lawn with the hose again. We were a block and a half away, but she saw us coming. She waved and I watched her cross the lawn to shut off the hose.

"Isn't she the woman who stopped you on the street?" Angers said. "In the car?"

"That's right."

"I see."

Chapter Seven

Betty Graham came toward us across her lawn. She was frowning. She glanced at Lillian, then looked hard at Angers, and I saw she remembered him. Then she looked at me.

"Steve, you haven't been to the hospital yet."

We paused on the sidewalk and Angers watched her.

"No, I've been busy, Betty."

"Oh."

"Have you heard anything?"

She shook her head. "Just that they want you at the hospital, Steve. I think you should get right over there. I thought you were on your way hours ago."

"Yes."

"Let's move along," Angers said.

"I live right there," I told Angers. "Right next door."

"Steve," Betty said, "who are these folks? Couldn't you introduce me?"

"Friends, Betty."

We all stood there, staring at each other. I knew Lillian would have liked to talk plenty and Betty was suspicious of something. She had every right to be. She knew it wasn't like me not to be at the hospital.

"So that's where you live," Angers said to me. He was watching Betty Graham. He started up the walk toward Betty Graham's front porch. "Come on, pal. You too, Lil. I've changed my mind. We're going to stay here. There might be trouble next door. But if there is—" He shrugged. "We'll watch it, eh?" He turned and waited for us. Lillian and I looked at each other and went on up to him.

"What is this?" Betty asked. "What is all this, Steve?"

"I can't explain," I said. "Not now. Just do as he says, that's all."

"But I don't understand, Steve."

"Listen," Lillian said. She spoke to Betty and her expression was very intent. "The idea is that we're going to come into your house."

"Come on," Angers said. "Let's go inside. I want to get out of this coat. It's hot."

Betty didn't know what to say. She wanted to understand, but it was a little beyond understanding. She sensed something, I could see it in her face. But she didn't know what really was up.

"Why, sure, Steve. Go ahead. Go on in. Sam'll be home pretty soon."

"Sam?" Angers said. He paused on the porch steps.

"My husband," Betty told him.

"Oh." He went on across the porch. I had a single instant where a whisper might not carry.

"Do as he says," I told Betty. "Don't ask questions."

"But Steve!"

Angers turned by the door. "Come on, pal."

Lillian and I went up the steps and over to the door. Betty stayed down on the front walk, watching us.

"You, too," Angers said. "Come on, get inside."

"I'm watering the lawn," Betty said. She knew something was up now, all right. "I'll be along soon."

"Sure," Angers said. "Only come now. Never mind the lawn."

"Please, honey," Lillian said. "Please, just come on, like Ralph says."

Betty came up the porch steps and we all went inside her house. She kept looking at me and I knew she was bursting with questions. I hoped she'd keep her mouth shut. I didn't want trouble and there was no telling what Angers might do.

"This looks like a good place," Angers said. "We'll live here."

We walked on through a short hallway into the living room. It was a typical one-storied Florida house. Betty and Sam had been adding to it whenever they had enough money saved up, and it was quite nice. They were proud of their place. Sam Graham was a clerk in the City Power Building.

"Some friends you got," Betty said. "How about introducing me, Steve? This guy's a card. Live here, he says."

"Yes, Betty. This is Lillian and that's Ralph Angers."

They nodded.

Ralph dropped the valise on the living-room floor and flinched out of his coat. He tossed it over a chair and Betty stood there looking at the gun stuck into the belt of his pants.

Lillian sighed and sat in a chair by the front windows. There were some throw rugs, a large rattan couch, a large coffee table, chairs, lamps, and a television set over by the fireplace.

"Anybody been over by my place, Betty?" I asked.

She shook her head.

Angers looked at Betty. "What's your name?"

"Betty. Betty Graham."

"Well, Mrs. Graham, I don't know how long we'll be here, but it may be quite a while. Suppose you fix us something to eat. All right?"

All the smiling was gone out of her now. She looked at Lillian and Lillian looked at me.

"I hate to put you to all this trouble, Mrs. Graham," Angers said. "But you'll see it's for a good cause. Let's have a look at the kitchen, all right?"

Betty dismissed the whole thing. It was too fantastic. She just grabbed hold of that thing that women have in their minds and closed the whole matter out. She crossed it off the books.

"Steve," she said, "are you going right over to the hospital? I could run you over in the car."

"Sit down, Betty," I said.

"But I don't want to sit down."

The room was very quiet. Angers walked around, pulled the Luger from his belt, laid it on the television set. Betty watched him.

"Please sit down, Betty," I said. I took her arm and led her over to the couch. We sat down. Angers paced the room. Finally he went over to the valise, picked it up, and flopped it on a chair. He opened it, took out the roll of paper and the bottle of whisky, and placed them on the floor. Then he shut the valise and took it out into the hall.

"Do as he says," I told Betty quickly. I couldn't tell her any more because he returned to the room.

The house was very still. Lillian sat over there with her legs crossed and stared at the purse she held in her lap. Angers picked up the roll of blueprints and placed them on the mantel over the fireplace, then he went back and sat down in the chair. He reached for the bottle of whisky, uncapped it, and drank. Then he capped it and set it on the floor again.

Betty and I sat there on the couch.

She said, "But Steve!"

"Yes."

"All right. I'll go get something to eat."

"Not yet," Angers said. "Sit still a minute. I want to tell you something, Mrs. Graham. I forgot."

His face was as expressionless as ever. His white shirt was soaked with sweat. The Luger was within reach of his arm on top of the television set.

"When will your husband be home, Mrs. Graham?"

"Oh, God, I don't know! In an hour or so."

"I see. Well, Mrs. Graham, I don't think you'd better fix us anything to eat."

"But I thought you said—"

"We'll wait for your husband."

"Steve!" She turned to me. "What is this?"

"I don't want to have to kill you, Mrs. Graham," Angers said. "But please, keep an even temper, will you?"

"Steve!" Betty said. She was getting a little harried now, wild. "If this is a joke, you've worn it thin. I can laugh at anything, but this is getting to be too much, Steve. What is this?"

"Try to listen," I told her. "And believe. Mr. Angers has already killed two people today, Betty. Please relax and do as he says." I didn't look at Angers. I didn't know how he'd take it. Lillian kept right on staring at her purse.

"Killed? Killed?" Betty said. Her eyes were big and round, and the fright that was in Lillian was beginning to show in Betty now. It was a peculiar thing, how you could tell when they began to see the truth. The fear wormed its way slowly into their eyes, and you knew they began to get it. Betty wasn't the type of person to sit down and take things as they came. She had to have her finger in the pie. And if the pie wasn't just right, she'd want to bake another one. So she'd want to change this. But the fear was there and she kept trying to push it back, not to believe in what she couldn't help believing. These things didn't happen to you! You read about them in the newspapers, or you maybe heard it over the radio. But they never happened to you. They weren't real. They never happened.

"You mean this man hasn't let you go see Ruby at the hospital?" Betty asked.

"He doesn't think it's necessary," I told her. "It's not the important thing, right now."

Betty ran a hand across her forehead. Her tone was beginning to change now. I had been quite serious in everything I said and she was slowly, very slowly, beginning to get it.

Her hand dropped and she stared across the room at nothing.

"Steve," Angers said, "we'll wait for Mrs. Graham's husband before I show you the blueprints. I don't like interruptions."

"Sure."

Betty rose slowly. She looked at me, then started walking across the room.

"Where are you going, Mrs. Graham?" Angers said.

"Just out here," she said. "It's my house. If I want to walk around in my own house, I guess I will."

"Go sit down," Angers said. "Steve," he said, "I hadn't counted on all this." I was beginning to recognize that something in his voice now; it was the small something that told me he was bothered. It was time to watch out.

Lillian caught it too. She was out of her chair and across the room to Betty's side before Betty reached the door. Anything could have happened if she'd gone through that door. Having somebody else to help, having a companion to fear, was helping Lillian.

"Come on, honey," Lillian said. "Come back and sit down. Please, honey." She tried very hard to warn Betty with her eyes. But how could you warn somebody about a thing like this?

"But I don't understand," Betty said. Her face was pale now, her eyes a bit haunted.

Angers laid his head back on the chair top. He was staring at the ceiling.

"I don't get it," Betty said. "I just don't get it." She avoided looking at Angers, her eyes simply wouldn't go in that direction. Her eyes flashed toward him, but always missed seeing him because she didn't want that. It was getting to her.

"Know something?" Angers said. "I haven't slept in days. Yet I'm not tired, not a bit. Wonderful, eh? It's having something that interests you that does it. Everybody should have some vital hobby. Don't you think that's right, pal?"

"Could be that's it," I said.

"Of course, it's not a hobby with me. It's much more than a hobby."

"Sure."

Betty Graham came back and sat down beside me on the rattan couch. Lillian looked at me and shook her head. Then Betty began to cry. She sat perfectly rigid, staring across the room at nothing, and the tears streamed down her face. I had never seen Betty like this, but now I knew what honest fear could do. She didn't know what it was all about, but she had suddenly begun to believe the worst and she feared it. Right now she was an automaton, like the rest of us, controlled by that maniac over there in the chair.

Chapter Eight

He had no personality, actually. I had watched him change, realized the contradictions and confusions in his mind. I wondered about him, even in the midst of all the terror he inspired. Who was he? I didn't like thinking about the possibility of his being an eye surgeon. Perhaps it was some mad figment of his mad mind. Either way, I didn't want him coming near me. What sight I had I wanted to keep.

The hospital he spoke of. What a laugh! To save people. And with his next movement he might draw that damned Luger and commit murder.

Sam Graham had no idea what he was coming home to.

I looked over at Angers. He was still staring at the ceiling, with his head resting on the back of the chair. I judged the distance he'd have to reach for that gun. And somehow, I knew if I jumped him, he'd get the gun first. He would kill me. That simple.

If he didn't get the gun ... what then?

He wasn't soft. Why was he so pale? Prison? He'd been someplace where there was little sun, and I couldn't believe it was prison.

"It's peaceful here, isn't it?" Angers said.

"Yes."

Betty wasn't making a sound, but the tears streamed down her face. We all sat there, Lillian back in her chair, waiting.

I knew that Lillian and I were thinking of ways and means. Betty would be thinking about Sam.

I tried to make it friendly, for his ears. You couldn't tell how he'd react.

"How long you and Ralph known each other, Lil?"

Her head jerked around at me, that wealth of mahogany hair rustling across her shoulders. She tipped her lips with her tongue, glanced at Angers.

"Oh, quite a while. I knew Ralph in Seattle."

"Old friends," I said.

"Not too old."

The room went silent again. Betty ceased crying. She got a handkerchief out of the pocket of her shorts and daubed at her cheeks and eyes, still looking across the room. Her plump thighs were spattered with tears. She wiped them dry and spread the handkerchief across her knee. She gave a great sigh and, turning, looked at me. Her head bobbed up and down just a little, then she got hold of herself again.

"What—are you going to do about Ruby?" she said.

"I don't know."

"You've got to see her. The hospital called twice, Steve. Some—something's up, and they need you."

"I know."

Angers stood up. "Just thought of something," he said. "Come on, all of you."

We looked at him.

"Come on. We'll begin in here. It's a shame to have to do this, but you can't trust anybody. I know I can trust you, pal." He looked at me with that pallid face. "But just the same. Come on, now."

We all stood up.

He started walking around the room. He closed every window that was open, and locked it. "Now the front door," he said. "Just come with me."

We all went out into the hall and he locked the front door. Then, guided by him, we made a complete tour of the house, locking all doors and windows.

The telephone was on a small shelf in the bar between the kitchen and the dining nook. Betty caught my eye as I looked at it. It would have to wait.

"Let's go back in the other room," Angers said. "We'll wait for your husband. Then we can take it easy and I'll go over the plans with Steve, here."

We went back into the living room and all this time the gun had been on the television set. But Angers was smart. He wasn't a blank about things that went on around him. He watched everybody—a little too closely.

He had been watching Betty a lot.

He dropped into his chair, and as Betty passed in front of him, he reached out and caught her hand. She froze.

Sitting there, he looked her over. She had a roundly built body, the skin of her legs below the shorts smooth and full. She was large-breasted and round-hipped.

"You're nice, Mrs. Graham," Angers said.

She stood rigid. He leaned forward, still holding her, and with his other hand reached out and palmed her thigh. He ran his hand all the way down the back of her leg. She didn't move. He ran his hand back up and patted her behind. He looked up at her.

"You've got a lot of what I like, Mrs. Graham. Lillian here is a regular snake. Aren't you, Lil?"

"Get off it, Ralph."

Angers was not smiling. There was nothing in his eyes.

"I'll bet you make your husband very happy. Is that right, Mrs. Graham?"

She didn't say anything, just stood there. She was looking at a point over my head on the wall. I didn't know what to do about this, either. There wasn't anything you could do.

"I'm not sure about Lillian, over there," Angers said.

Lillian rose from her chair and came across the room. Her teeth were sunk in her lower lip. Betty still didn't move and Angers held to her hand.

"I like your body," Angers said. "It's an exciting body, Mrs. Graham." His voice was as flat, as inflectionless as ever.

Lillian was moving toward the side of Angers' chair by the television set. I tightened all over.

"Ralph," Lillian said, "don't you like me any more?"

"Go back and sit down, Lil."

She stopped moving and eyed him. He looked up at her. She smiled and again came toward him.

He spoke quietly. "Go back to your chair."

She turned and went back to the chair.

Betty was standing there and he still held her hand, and then he reached out and put his arm up around her hips. She was like a board and then she looked at me and I saw something in her eyes. Abruptly she turned toward Angers and moved in close.

"If you like me," she said, "why don't you do something about it? You're a big boy now."

She was standing in close to him. He took his arm down and she swayed her hips, just a little. "Or maybe you're just kidding me. Maybe it's all talk. Maybe you're just passing the time." The look she gave him would have melted butter.

"You're just right," Angers said. "You interest me."

She moved her hips just a little again, then nodded toward the hall. "My bedroom's right over there, honey." She leaned away from him, pulling at his hand, staring at him with all the lecherous longing she could summon. "Come on, honey. Maybe I could show you something, at that."

My heart yammered right on up into my throat. If she could get him into that bedroom … What a chance! But you couldn't tell a thing from his eyes, his face. You didn't know what he was thinking.

"We could be nice and private," Betty said to him. "I—I like you, too. Come on, honey. Let's go into the bedroom. I can't do what I want to with all these people watching."

I glanced at Lillian. Her hands were gripped on the seat of her chair, the knuckles white with straining. Every muscle in my body was tense.

Betty put her right leg out and rubbed it against Angers' leg. "Don't make me wait," she said softly.

He laughed. He threw his head back and erupted with wild, crazy, high laughter. It was insane. It was the same laughter I'd heard in the alley earlier that day.

"Whore," he said flatly. He released her hand, gave her a brutal shove. She backed across the room, lost balance, and sat down, hard.

The door chimes began clanging insistently and a man called, "Betty! Hey, Betty! For gosh sakes, open up!" The chimes clanged and clanged up on the wall beside the couch.

Betty sat on the floor, staring between her legs. Her shoulders were shaking. She had tried hard, mighty hard, but it hadn't worked. Angers was almost like a child sometimes. Almost …

"Betty, where are you? Open the door!"

"Go open the door, Mrs. Graham," Angers said. "It's your husband, isn't it?"

She rose to her knees and looked at him.

"Isn't that your husband?"

She nodded, looking at him. Angers came out of the chair, took her arm, and helped her up. "Come on," he said. "We'll both go and let your husband in, Mrs. Graham." He went over to the television set and picked up the Luger, turned and grinned at me. "Come on, pal. Lillian. We'll all go let Mrs. Graham's husband in, all right?"

Sam Graham stood in the open door and looked at us. He frowned, then saw me, and smiled. "Hi, Steve. How's Ruby?" "All right."

He walked inside and Angers closed the door and locked it and Sam saw the gun hanging at the end of Angers' arm.

"What's this?" he said. Nobody spoke, nobody moved.

Sam was round-faced, stocky, with curly brown hair and tiny twinkling beadlike eyes. He kept right on smiling, because that was his way. His face was red and peeling from sunburn and he carried the coat to his light blue suit. His shirt collar was undone and he looked tired and hot.

"You can call me Ralph," Angers said. "My name's Ralph Angers. This is Lillian, Mr. Graham, and that's Steve Logan, my pal. This girl here in the shorts is your wife, Mr. Graham. Now, if you'll just come in and sit down?"

Sam's smile tipped up on one side and slipped off his chin. "Holy God!" he said. "You're the—"

"Oh, God, Sam—Sam!" Betty flung herself into her husband's arm, hiding her face against his shoulder. She was slightly taller than Sam. He put his arm around her, holding his coat in his hand, and looked over her shoulder at Angers. "You're the guy who killed Jake Halloran, right?"

"Please," Angers said. "Let's all go in and sit down."

Nobody moved.

"We'd better," I said. "It would be better that way." I found myself trying to warn Sam with my eyes, the way Lillian had done with Betty. Sam patted Betty's shoulder and started walking toward the living room.

"Did he hurt you, baby?" Sam asked.

"No, Sam, no, no, no."

Lillian was beside me, with Angers behind us. I would have liked to talk with her. I kept thinking that, but what good would talk do?

"There's too many people, Steve," Angers said. "I didn't count on all this."

"It's all right," I said.

"I just don't like it, pal. We've got to get to work on those blueprints. I've got to send a wire regarding the hospital fund. We should get hold of a contractor."

"Won't be able to do anything now, anyway," I said. "Not until tomorrow."

"That's true. That's true, Steve. We'll spend the night running over the plans. You'll go wild about those plans, pal. It's new, it's something that's never been done. They won't laugh when they see it, pal."

Lillian shivered against me and I caught the look in her eyes. I suddenly wanted to hold her close. Of all these people, I felt closest to Lillian. Somehow, I felt, if anything was going to be done, it would be up to us. I had no idea how Sam Graham was going to act. He'd obviously heard of Angers and what he'd done, even heard his name. So news was getting around town. If we stayed put long enough, it would only be a matter of time before the law turned up. I didn't like to think about that. It could be bad.

Everybody sat down again, except Sam Graham. He dropped his coat on the couch and motioned to Betty to sit down and stood there looking at Angers.

Angers went over and laid the Luger on the TV set again. Then he flopped into his chair. His eyes were glassy as he looked over at Sam.

"You've got a nice wife," Angers said. "We're all glad you're home now, Sam. Maybe we can have dinner now."

"Who do you think you are?" Sam said.

Lillian turned her gaze on him. Then she looked at me and I knew what was in her mind.

"Sam," I said. "Relax. Sit down. Take a load off your feet."

"Were you with this guy when he killed Halloran?" Sam asked. "And

Lyttle, the cop?"

I nodded. Sam frowned. "That's what I thought. They think so downtown, too. A guy in the bar heard him say his name. It's all over town. Somebody thought they recognized you with him. I never gave it a second thought, Steve. Cops will be over to your place."

I wished he hadn't said that. Angers just looked over at me, then away. "What's your game, mister?" he said to Angers.

"Drop it, Sam," I said.

"How come you're with him?" Sam asked me.

I just shook my head.

"He's not with him, Sam," Betty said. "Please, just do as he says, Sam."

"I don't know what all this is about," Sam said. "But you've killed two people and I don't want you in my house."

Angers just looked at him.

I didn't know how to shut Sam up. He was turning belligerent and that was bad. Angers wouldn't stand for it; it was the one thing he didn't like.

"You've got to do something!" Betty said. "Steve, do something!"

Lillian got up and walked across to the far side of the room and stood by the window.

"If you don't leave right now," Sam said, "I'm going to call the cops. You don't scare me, you know."

"Sit down, Mr. Graham," Angers said.

"You think you scare us? Is that what you think?"

"Please, Sam," Betty said. Her voice was almost as toneless as Angers', though for a different reason. She had begun to lose hope now.

"This is my home," Sam said. "Now, get out of here." He started across the room toward Angers. Angers reached out and picked the Luger off the TV set. Sam stopped and looked at him, standing there in the middle of the room. His face was very red and he was sweating and he wasn't exactly sure of himself. He was being a fool, but I didn't know what to do.

"Did you hear me?" he said to Angers. "This is my home."

All along, since Sam had come in, I had supposed he understood the fact that Ralph Angers was mad. Now I knew he didn't know that. He had no idea what he was facing. And although we had talked in front of Angers about many things, I wasn't sure how he'd take it if someone said he was crazy. That was the one word everybody had avoided.

Angers had settled down in the chair, holding the Luger in his lap. He was looking intently at Sam Graham's feet.

"Steve," Lillian said.

I glanced over at her. She was still standing by the window. She beckoned to me and Angers did not look up as I walked across the room.

"Look," she whispered.

A police car had drawn up before my house, across the yard. Two cops climbed from the car and stood on the curb. They talked a minute, then stared at the house. It was nearing dusk outside and the light was very dim.

"I'm asking you to get out of this house," Sam said, behind us. "I mean that. You may have killed two men, but I'm not afraid of you."

"Why doesn't the fool shut up!" Lillian whispered.

The two cops started up the walk toward my front porch. They stood on the porch and one of them pressed the bell.

Sam was still talking behind us about how he wanted Angers to leave the house. Angers hadn't said a word. I didn't want to look at him.

"They'll come here," Lillian whispered. "They've *got* to come here. Steve, Steve, what'll we do?"

"What're you two doing?" Angers said. "Lillian?"

One of the cops pressed the doorbell again. The other got out a package of cigarettes and offered one to his companion, who refused. The cop lit his cigarette and they stood there, staring out at the walk now. Then one of them walked to the edge of the porch, and, leaning on the railing, looked over at this house. He was looking straight at the window where I stood, but he didn't see anything.

"What is it, Steve?" Angers said.

Lillian hadn't said anything, so neither did I. She stood very close to me, holding my hand with her cold hard fingers. It was growing noticeably darker.

"I don't think you'll even use that popgun," Sam said to Angers.

Lillian and I watched the cops talk a minute on the porch over there. Then the one with the cigarette shrugged and they went down off the porch and along the walk toward the car.

Lillian swore a string of sad, whispered obscenities.

"What did you say, Lil?" Angers said.

"Never mind her," Sam said.

The two cops got in the car and it started and began drawing away. Lillian and I watched it go and another chunk of me went with it.

The gun behind us roared three times. The shots came slowly, evenly spaced, and Betty Graham began to scream. I whirled in time to see Sam fall to his knees, a foot from Angers' chair. Sam was holding to his left side and blood pulsed between his fingers. Blood was coming from his throat, too, and his left ear was gone.

Betty ceased screaming sharply and Angers said, "Steve, turn on a light, will you? It's getting dark in here."

Lillian hadn't moved from the window. The Venetian blinds began rattling and jiggling as she trembled. Her lips were drawn back across her teeth and it looked almost like a smile.

I went dazedly over to a lamp by the fireplace and turned it on. Amber light spread warmly around the room, changing the position of things, changing colors and attitudes. I looked down and Sam Graham's left ear was on the rug there by my foot.

Betty was making funny noises in her throat. It was a kind of moaning. She crawled across the floor from the couch on her hands and knees, over to her husband. Sam Graham was kneeling in front of Angers, with his head bowed over till it touched the floor. He looked as if he were praying.

"He's dead," Betty said. Her voice was stilled, remote. "He's dead, Sam's dead, I tell you."

"Pal," Angers said, "I didn't realize it was getting so dark. Did you?"

"Dear God," Betty said. She sat on the floor beside her dead husband and rested one hand on his shoulder. He tipped over and sprawled out full length on his back.

Angers looked at Betty, then stood. Both the body and Betty were in his way. He stepped over the body and turned to look at her again and she began to get wild with the realization of what had happened. Her heart was broken and she screamed wildly at Angers.

"Stop it," he told her. "Shut up!"

I went over to the window where Lillian was and looked outside. There was no sign of the police car.

Betty's voice was an unending babble of anguish.

"You're mad!" she said. "You didn't have to do it!"

"No, Ralph! No! Ralph!" Lillian's voice was shrill.

The gun exploded.

Lillian broke, began slipping down against the Venetian blinds, sobbing, until she slumped on the floor against the wall.

"He's killed her too," she said.

Outside the street was silent now. Then suddenly the street lights came on and it was night.

Chapter Nine

"Lillian," Ralph Angers said. "I don't like to see you this way. Stop it, will you?"

She was on the floor, seated up against the wall, dry-eyed and sobbing. She kept casting her eyes up toward me all full of that terrible gone despair.

"Stop it, Lil," Angers said.

"Ralph," I said, "why did you ever do that?"

"What?" He stood in the center of the room and looked over at me, with the gun dangling in his hand. "You mean that?" He motioned with the gun toward the two bodies on the floor. He shrugged. "Lil, get on your feet. We're leaving this place."

She shook her head. "I'm not going anyplace," she said.

I got one look at that rebellious despair in her eyes and went over and grabbed her arm and hoisted her to her feet. She swayed against me, the whites of her eyes showing.

"Lillian!" I said. I shook her hard and her head rolled around on her shoulders. I held her against the wall, slapped her face good and hard.

"All right." She looked straight at me.

"That's better," Angers said.

I held to her arm and walked her across the room and out into the shadowed hall. The house was dead quiet, and whenever one of us moved, the footsteps echoed.

"My ears are ringing," Angers said. "This is some gun, Steve. Heard you tell that fellow you'd had it worked over by some gunsmith."

I didn't answer. I rubbed Lillian's arms, standing there in the hall. She kept looking at me, staring in the darkness. "Snap out of it," I whispered. I glanced into the living room. Angers was over by the fireplace mantel, reaching for the big roll of blueprints with one hand and looking at the gun in his other hand.

"Listen," I whispered. "The first chance we get, you've got to make a run for it. Try to get help. Tell them all about him. You've got to—" I stopped.

Angers was coming. As he entered the hall, Lillian began nodding to me. She'd heard what I said and she kept on nodding.

"What's the matter with her?" Angers said, watching her.

"Nothing. She'll be all right."

"She'd better."

She looked over at him and the nodding slowly ceased. Her face was as expressionless as his. Her lips were pale and her eyes were wide and dull and her fine breasts rose and fell erratically beneath the white dress.

Angers went and glanced into the bedroom on the other side of the hall. "We'll leave the back way," he said. "Come on."

"Where will we go?" Lillian said. Her voice was numb with shock and she clung to my arm.

Angers said nothing. He just motioned us ahead of him through the house. In the kitchen he paused by the refrigerator, opened the door. In the darkness, the bright interior gleamed on his white marble face.

Lillian was between Angers and me. I pulled her gently back and eased her aside. He was bent over, looking over the food inside the refrigerator.

As I moved toward him, he straightened, turned, and looked at me. Then he put the roll of blueprints and the gun on top of the refrigerator and reached in, still looking at me.

"Here, pal," he said. He handed me a chicken leg. "Lil," he said. "Have some chicken." He gave her two wings. "Just a minute." He reached in again, came up with another leg, bit a hunk out of it, and began chewing. "All right, let's go."

He slammed the door shut. Light from a street lamp filtered into the dark kitchen and I watched him take the gun and the roll of paper.

"Open the door, Steve."

I dropped my chicken leg in a flower bed beside the back porch. Lillian had left hers inside on the kitchen table. Angers was chewing steadily.

"Better cut right on through," Angers said.

"Ralph," Lillian said, "you don't even know where we're going."

"Maybe not."

They stood there on the back lawn, facing each other.

"We—we can't just—just go, Ralph."

I noticed then that she wasn't carrying her purse. She'd left it back in the house. But whether or not there was anything in it that could help the police to trace us, I didn't know. Probably not. It seemed even the neighbors had heard nothing of Angers' shooting. The cement-block house had muffled the shots. Angers had left the valise in the house, too, but that was empty. And he had donned his coat again. It was a very warm night and I wondered at his wearing that coat. The suit itself was all wool, and in this muggy heat, he must have been swimming in perspiration. Yet, even so, he looked cold.

Four people were dead now. He had to be stopped. But how? Leaping wildly at him would get me no place. All right, what was I going to do? I didn't know whether Ruby was dead or alive and the town knew about Angers and suspected me of being with him. That meant that they were maybe after the both of us, and if they spotted us, they'd shoot to kill. They wouldn't wait. They never do when they get heated up about something like this.

"Pal," Angers said, "we've got to find someplace where we can sit and talk." He swallowed the last of his chicken drumstick and tossed the bone away. I watched it bounce in the shadowed grass, bright and pale. "There's too much going on all the time. We haven't had a moment's peace. It's dark already."

"Let's—let's go back to the hotel," Lillian said.

"Lil, I gave you credit for more brains," Angers said.

I thought, Here it is night already, and how about Ruby? There was no way of knowing. I wondered if maybe he would miss if I made a run for it in the darkness. He could miss.

I didn't run. You just don't, somehow. There was too much of it, and nagging at me all the time was the worry of his being free at all. There was more of a tenseness about him now, he wasn't so free and easy as he had been. It was funny, all right, the way he knew what was going on, knew the law was gunning for him, yet thought himself invincible. That's the way it was. He didn't seem to care at all.

"They'll be waiting at the hotel for us," he said. "They'll be looking everywhere for us. You heard what that fellow Graham said. We'll have to play it smooth, from now on."

"Ralph," I said, "how'll we ever get to work on the hospital with things like they are?"

"Well, we will, that's all."

Lillian looked at me, her face drawn and pale, almost as pale as her white dress. I shrugged. We stood there in the darkness of the back yard with the crickets beginning to chirp.

"They'll try to kill me, you know," he said. "The fools! But I'll get them first. They can't be blamed for not understanding. They don't know what I'm trying to do. I'm trying to help them."

"You mean by building this hospital?"

"Sure, Steve. The hospital. It'll be the greatest thing that ever happened to them. I'll be known then, known all over. But they can't see it."

It was the first time I caught the little twist of selfishness in his plans. He was figuring on his own greatness, too.

"I wish you'd quit talking about it," Lillian said.

"You don't like it?" Angers said.

"Of course, Ralph. Of course I like it."

He turned to me. "Wait till you see it, pal." He slapped the roll of paper beneath his arm. "I drew up these plans myself. I gave it everything I had. I got the donations for the fund, everything. There's enough money to build two hospitals like this one."

"All right," Lillian said. "Let's go, then."

We started across the back yard, past the garage, and Angers paused by a tall hedge of Australian pine.

"Pal," he said, "I'm not forgetting that eye of yours. I won't let you down, don't worry. You saved my life."

"Sure," I said. "Let's go." I wished to hell he would forget that eye of mine. It didn't help my nerve any, having him talk about that eye.

"I'll never forget that, pal. Never."

"Were you in the war, Ralph?" I said. As long as we were going to stand here and talk, I might as well try to prolong it. Maybe somebody would come along. Then I knew I didn't want anybody to come along. It was a bad thing, the way things were.

Angers' voice was soft. "Don't talk about the war to me, pal." He looked up at the sky, with the roll of paper under his arm and the gun hanging from his hand. "Yes, I was in it, pal. I was in it, all right."

"We just going to stand here?" Lillian said.

Angers looked at her quietly. "I was thinking," he said. "Didn't Mrs. Graham have a car?"

I just stood there watching him. It was like being strapped down to a table, having a ceiling of knives coming at you, chopping away, and you talking about the weather.

"Sure she did," he said. "It was a blue coupé, a club coupé."

He sure had a sweet memory. It was something we could have done better without. I wondered if he remembered the dead as well as other things.

"I'll bet it's right there in the garage," he said.

"We don't want a car," Lillian said.

I was over close to her now, and I reached behind her and grabbed her waist and she shut up. Let him get a car. He started toward the garage and I jammed my head close to her ear quick. "This is your chance. When the time's right, run! From the car!"

She stiffened and her perfume was faint but good and I moved away as Angers turned.

"Come on," he said.

We went up to the garage. The doors were open and Betty's car was there, all right. I kept thinking, Maybe she'll get a chance to run from the car. I wondered if she would take that chance.

"Well," Angers said, "this is perfect, isn't it?"

It was dark in the garage; the light from the street lamps didn't penetrate far. He herded us in by the driver's side, up by the hood. He opened the car door and felt around and said, "The keys aren't here."

So we had to go back into the house again. The keys were on the dressing table in the front bedroom. As we came through the hall past the living room, I glanced in and my breath hushed in my throat. I could have sworn I saw Betty Graham move. I had never looked to see how she was shot. I'd figured he'd done the usual perfect job and I was a little sick of seeing it. She was lying on her face in there beside Sam's body, and as we walked by, I was sure she kind of propped herself up a little, then fell down again. If she could prop herself up after all this time, she had a chance.

"You drive, pal," Angers said. "You and Lil sit up there. I'll get in the back seat." He got in and sat in the middle of the back seat, with the gun in one hand and the big roll of blueprints across his knees.

It was an old Dodge. Lillian glanced at me, then got in under the wheel and slid across to the door. I climbed in behind the wheel and sat there.

"Here," Angers said. He handed me the keys. I stuck them in the ignition and started the car. She started right off and now I wished we hadn't decided on the car. It could be a trap.

I backed her down the shadowed drive, brushing against some bushes, and out onto the street.

"Where to?" I said.

"Just drive around a while," Angers told me.

As I started off, a woman came across the lawn of the house next to the Grahams'. It was Mary Fadden. Nobody on the block liked her much because she was a really terrific busybody. They had a double lot and the lawn was a big one, but she was bent on stopping this car. She waved and called, "Betty!"

Angers apparently didn't see or hear her, because he said nothing. She sort of ran toward the car. Lillian reached over and grabbed my thigh, her fingers like steel clamps. I stepped on the gas and we went on down the street. I looked in the rear-view mirror and Mary Fadden was standing there, watching us. Then she started slowly up the front walk toward the Grahams' front door. It was the first and only time in my life I felt happy about snooping females.

Lillian's fingers relaxed and went away.

I heard a sharp metallic *snicker-snack*, and glanced around. Angers smiled at me and held up the gun. "I loaded the magazine," he said. "A nine millimeter is a wonderful shell, pal. These here are more powerful than our standard factory loads, aren't they?"

They were, but I said nothing. I went back to driving the car, feeling all hollow and rotten inside. It was my gun. It was my fault from the beginning that all this had happened. If only I'd let the son-of-a-bitch get himself hit by that bus!

You're thinking cockeyed again, I thought. Get it straight in your head. You didn't know. Nobody could have known. All right, but you had the gun, didn't you? Sure, I had the gun. Well, then. You weren't supposed to have the gun, remember that. There's a law, friend. Concealed weapons, remember? Pistol permits. Remember? You laughed at it, but this would never have happened if you hadn't been walking around with the gun.

"I wish you wouldn't talk about that gun," Lillian said.

I wheeled the car around a corner, heading downtown, where there were people. Angers didn't seem to mind where we went. Nothing really bothered the guy. He just kept going right on through his crazy dream with his damned roll of blueprints.

And twice now he had reloaded the Luger without my catching him at it. He was wily. I made up my mind it wasn't going to happen again.

"We could stop over at the hospital," I said. "I could just run in and see Ruby." I made it as ordinary as possible, trying to keep the strain out of my voice.

"No, Steve," Angers said. "We haven't time for that."

I gripped the wheel till my hands hurt. "Look," I said. "We're just driving around. I wouldn't be a minute."

"He should," Lillian said. "Steve should go see how his wife is, Ralph. You know that."

He didn't answer, which was a bad sign. I flicked my hand over against her leg and she kept quiet about it. She was beginning to prove herself. She was a fine girl, and if she'd been with him for weeks, as she said, she must have gone through plenty of hell. Today was the payoff. He hadn't killed before. Now he'd snapped all the way.

I kept my hand on the seat between us, then tapped her leg again. She tensed; I could feel her leg tense on the seat. It was the first time I'd ever felt a girl's leg under these conditions and it was no joke. I squeezed her thigh hard this time. I felt her look over at me and I pointed across her lap at her door. She moved a little in the seat, toward me, relaxing, then laid her hand down on mine and squeezed and it was as cold as ice, her fingers just like ice.

But she'd got it. I figured she would take the chance, whenever there was a chance. Then I didn't want her to. He'd get her, sure. He'd blast the life out of her with that Luger and it was no good. It wasn't worth it.

Or was it? I turned down Central off Ninth, into the business section of town. It was all bright with neon and people were sitting around on the green benches and walking up and down, window-shopping, or sitting in front of stores watching TV. This town was becoming a regular back alley of crime lately. The boys were getting the call, coming in from all over the country. Pinellas County was getting it in the neck, all right. It had started with purse-snatching and now you could name it and we had it. Every day somebody took a dive off a building and smashed his head and every night somebody got himself murdered or robbed or both.

You'd think folks would get used to it. They don't, though. One thing, you never get used to death. I got to thinking about how true that was as we drew up by a red light. We were by a big radio store and they had a TV set mounted up over the entrance. We could see it fine, and it was loud. The sidewalk was jammed with people.

"Listen," Angers said. "Listen to that, pal."

We couldn't help listening. It was us. It was Bill Watts up there, from WSUN, over Channel 38, laying the cards on the table. He had a news program, but it looked as if he was devoting all his time to Ralph Angers & Co. I knew Bill, and right now he was more serious than ever.

"Lock yourselves in your homes and don't answer the doorbell," Bill said. He hunched up at the desk and looked out at everybody. "The latest report, just received, is that Mrs. Betty Graham is alive. Police are on their way out there now, and some of you can no doubt hear the ambulance. So it's that close to you. It's not something to dismiss this time, ladies and gentlemen. We know there are three people: a woman known only as Lillian, a man from this city whom many of you doubtless know, Steve Logan, and Ralph Angers. Angers is the killer. So far he's killed three and a woman is hanging by a thread. If Mrs. Graham lives and can talk some more, we'll let you know. I repeat, they are driving a blue Dodge club coupé, license number"—Bill glanced at some notes on the desk—"four-W-one-one-eight-five-eight."

A car behind us began honking. The light was green. I put the Dodge in gear and we crawled ahead.

Bill's voice faded behind us. "Steve Logan's wife is in the hospital, and if he hears this, he should make every effort possible to ..." Then there wasn't any more and we were in traffic headed down Central again.

"Try not to worry about her," Lillian said. "You must try, Steve."

I was choked with it. He'd been saying something about Ruby and I'd never know what. I stepped hard on the gas, driving down the center of the street.

"Take it slower, pal," Angers said. "They'll pick us up for speeding."

"I've got to see my wife!"

He leaned over the seat and rested his hand on my shoulder. "It's not important," he said. "You're just excited, that's all. Anybody would be, hearing a thing like that. Now get out of the business section. We don't want to be picked up, because I've got to build the hospital, remember?"

"Hospital! It's crazy, can't you see that? You can't possibly think of doing such a damned thing. You'll never get to first base with your damned hospital!"

I wheeled the car left on First Street, heading north.

He said nothing.

"Take it easy, Steve," Lillian said. "You've got to."

"Yeah, yeah," I said.

"Everything depends on this," Angers said. "Now just keep driving on out here a way. It's nice and quiet out here."

"Sure," I said, and the bitterness was showing in my voice now. I looked over at Lillian and she was staring at me. She shook her head just a little and she was gnawing her lip again. She wasn't sure what Angers would do if I began acting wrong. Well, I wasn't sure, either. But I was getting fed up. Life is precious, sure. But after a while you get so you don't care. You can get yourself worked up like that and not care a damn what happens. I was beginning to feel that way. I had to see Ruby, had to find out what was the matter over there.

I was driving fast now, then I remembered about Lillian maybe making a try to get away. That was something important. I didn't think she could make it now, and I didn't want her to try. It was probably all she was thinking about. I turned down toward the bay. We drove along by the big park out there, the great expanse of lawn a dim, cool gray in the darkness. Way over there you could see the lights of Tampa, across the bay, glowing red and fading against the black night sky. The air smelled of salt now, and there was a steady freshening breeze coming in from the bay. There wasn't much traffic out this way.

"I needed this," Angers said. "Driving is good for the brain. You think better. At least I do. It's the motion of the car, I guess."

"Sure."

I reached out and gave Lillian's thigh a hard squeeze. Twice I did it, then pointed emphatically at her door. She pressed my hand again with her cold fingers.

In the rear-view mirror I could see Angers resting back against the seat, with his head thrown back.

I began slowing the car a bit at a time, easy. We were coming along the end of the park now to where the street turned left along the bayou. At the end of the park were many palm trees and a lot of heavy shrubbery to the right.

I touched Lillian's leg again, and made motions with my hand, pointing up ahead, making a turn, then opening the door handle on the car door. She sat very rigidly. I looked over at her and I knew she had got it. It could be I was sending her to her death. We had to take that chance, I knew. Either way, she would probably die, and this was the one chance she had to take. I didn't want her to do it. But I knew it was the only thing she could do. I had no idea what was going to happen, if it worked.

I drew in close to the right side of the road, still slowing, with one hand on Lillian's thigh, resting easy, holding her gently back, waiting.

"You know, pal," Angers said, "I have to find where I want to build, too. It should be centrally located."

"That's right," I said.

I held my hand on her leg, and we approached the turn. A car passed us, gunning away fast. I came in very close to the right-hand curb, with the shrubbery almost brushing the car, then started the turn. I slapped her thigh, pushed her toward the door.

She slammed down on the door handle. The door swung open, and before I'd made the turn, she was out of the car, running for an instant beside us, then off toward the bushes.

I slammed my foot on the gas, all the way to the floor.

"Lillian!" Angers shouted.

The door banged closed and the engine began to pick up speed. It was an old car, and the engine was tired. Too much gas choked it up and I sat there cursing.

"Stop, Steve! Stop the car."

I kept easing it to her.

Angers got his window open, leaned way out, and the Luger began barking above the crazy whine of the engine. I looked back once, searching the road back there. I saw her running, her white dress bright against the night. She was running along the bushes toward the palm trees.

I heard the gun bang away, then stop, and Angers sat back in the seat. "Empty!" he said. "Damn that woman!"

We were going plenty fast now, right along the sea wall beside the bayou. And Ralph Angers' gun was empty.

Chapter Ten

The road followed the bayou for perhaps a mile and a half, I knew. It was all residential out here, and on the left there were large homes, fronting the water. Piers jutted occasionally from the sea wall and boats were moored to some of them. I figured I'd get as far away from Lillian as I could before I did anything. I couldn't let him get that gun loaded. The tires slid and grabbed on the glassy brick pavement.

"Stop the car, Steve!" Angers said. He reached out and grabbed my shoulder. "Lillian's back there. Stop the car!"

All right. I decided to stop the car. I slammed the brakes with everything I had and the Dodge was out of my hands.

We whipped to the left, slammed over a curb, and careened wildly across somebody's big beautiful lawn. We narrowly missed two coconut palms and I wrenched the wheel.

"Steve!" I heard Angers say. Something hit the back of my head.

I let her go then. I turned in the seat and went at him. He slammed at me with the gun, yelling something. The car came down into the street again, not going very fast now, and headed for the sea wall. It barked up against the short edge of wall, climbed it, followed it, then screeched to a rusty stop, teetering. The right-hand door was open again, and the car was tipped that way.

Angers was up on the back of the front seat and we started falling toward the water. Not the car, just us. I tried to hang on, but we went right on through the door into the bayou.

We landed in about two feet of water. I knew that just a step or two farther away from the wall the water was deep, real deep.

"Steve, what's the matter with you?"

I dove at him. He was standing against the wall. I didn't reckon with the gun. I tried to dodge, but he brought it down against my forehead. Once, twice, he whipped that gun against my head. I reeled backward and fell. It hurt plenty. I could hear him talking to me but I couldn't make out the words.

I kept trying to get up but the bottom was mud and silt and slippery. I fell back toward deeper water. I dragged myself toward the sea wall and he was standing there, loading the clip on that damned gun, talking to me. Through all the pain in my head, I heard him say, "Steve, you shouldn't do that. Don't act that way. I know you get excited, but there's no reason for you to take it out on your pal, Steve."

Somebody called up on the street.

"Hey, there! Anybody down there?"

Neither of us said anything. I went toward him and he was finishing loading the clip. I couldn't move fast on the muck bottom, my feet kept sliding, and I heard myself sobbing with the effort and the failure. Sobbing with him standing there, now, putting the box of shells into his pocket and standing there and slapping the clip back into the gun.

"Come on, Steve," he said. "There's some stairs, right there."

We were by a pier and I kept hearing myself sobbing. The car was nose down over the sea wall, with the right side hanging over the water, the right front wheel propped up on the wooden pier. If we'd missed the pier we would have gone all the way in. Damn the pier.

"Come on, pal. Up the stairs."

Angers pushed me to the stairs and I started up. I was still plenty foggy from being hit with the gun. He waited till I was on the pier, then he said, "Go ahead, pal. Walk out onto the street, there."

He was a wise bird now, all right. His eyes were kind of shining down there, where he stood in the water. He was plenty wise now. I stepped away from the head of the wooden steps, and he came up fast, watching me.

"You shouldn't have done that, Steve," he said.

A man walked toward us on the street. We stepped over the sea wall into the street. The man came on toward us. He was in his shirt sleeves, holding a pipe in his hand. He was probably around sixty years old, with a very anxious face. He looked over his steel-rimmed glasses and said, "You men all right? That was a bad one."

"Listen," I said. "Go back home, quick." I was reeling.

"Been drinking, eh?" the man said.

"The blueprints," Angers said.

The man said, "I heard the racket there and you tore up considerable of my lawn, I reckon. This is a bad one. A wonder you weren't killed."

"Please, go home," I said.

"Have to report this," he said. "You can use my phone."

"Please," I said. Angers was standing there, looking at the man.

"Didn't hurt the car much, though, I don't reckon," the man said.

Angers started for the car. The man turned and touched Angers' arm. "You all right?" the man said.

Angers turned, without pausing, and shot him in the chest. Just once he shot him, and kept on walking over to the car. The old man collapsed on the brick pavement. His pipe jumped from his hand and rattled along to the sea wall and I heard it go *plunk* into the bayou water.

"They're all right," Angers said.

I looked over at him. He was standing there beside the car with his beloved blueprints in his hand. The big roll of paper was all right.

"Come on," he said. "We'll never get this car out of here."

"Maybe we can," I said, stalling.

"Come on." He came over by me, glanced once at the man lying in the street. A car came along, coming fast from the other direction. "Cross the street, pal."

We went across the street in front of the car.

"Keep walking," Angers said. "There'll be a crowd of people around here in a little while."

We slogged along across the road, up over the curb, and started across a lawn. Our clothes were soggy and they stank of fish and muck. Every step I took, my shoes squished. We kept on moving.

The car out there had stopped and a man said, "Somebody's there in the road. An accident."

I glanced back. A man and woman left their car and went over to where the old fellow was lying in the road. I wondered if he was dead. He probably was.

"Hey, you, there!" the man called. He'd seen us.

"Keep walking," Angers said softly. "Don't turn around again and don't stop, pal."

"Hey, you guys going to phone in about this? Better hurry up! Get an ambulance!"

"He's not dead," I said. I heard myself say it from someplace far away. "You hear that? He's not dead."

"Yes," Angers called out. "We'll phone for one, right away!"

We walked on across the big smooth lawn and around the side of an immense home. I was numb. He had cleaned me out. There wasn't anything left. I felt empty inside and all gone, hollowed out, finished.

I stopped walking there beside the house. We were in a side yard that opened onto a street. I could see the sidewalk stretching out beyond us, pale in the street lights' saffron glow. I heard another car stop out there by the bayou.

"I can't go on," I told him.

"Cut it out, pal. Sure you can. You've got to."

"I'm knocked out," I said.

"You'll be all right. We'll get some clean clothes someplace, and—"

"Clean clothes—where?"

"We'll find some. Come on now, pal. Let's walk."

We walked. We left the yard and went out onto the sidewalk. We started up the street, walking west now. We were a block and a half over from the bayou, heading on a slanting, intersecting street. It would take us farther and farther away from the accident. I wondered vaguely where Lillian was now. How was she? Was she still running, and had she gone to the police? What good would it do?

Angers didn't seem a bit tired. We both looked like hell, but he walked along now just as he had when I'd first met him. It seemed years ago. It had been only a few hours.

"You'll feel fine in a little while," he said.

"I'll never feel fine again."

"Sure you will. Listen, remember what I told you earlier today?"

"What was that?"

"About trying to run away, pal. Don't do it, will you? Why did you act like that?"

I said nothing and we crossed a street and went along a new block. The trees swished and fluttered in what was left of the breeze that kept coming in across the bay. The night was cooling down and it was a fine night, all fight. A fine spring night.

"I know," he said. "You got excited because of Lillian, that was it. Wasn't that it, pal?"

I looked sharply. Maybe he didn't know it, but his mind was going worse and worse all the time. If he hadn't slept in days, he needed sleep and rest, whether he knew it or not. You could stand up under that sort of punishment only so long.

"Lillian was frightened, I guess," he said. "I don't blame her, all this shooting and everything."

"You don't blame her?"

"She's a woman, pal, after all. You can't expect a woman to take it like men can. She couldn't realize how much this means," he said. He said, "Nobody seems to grasp the fact. But they will in time. Well, you saved us from going over that wall, anyway, pal."

I couldn't think of anything to say.

"If people were just all like you, Steve," he said. "Even-tempered. If they just wouldn't get angry with me, stand in my way. That's what they do, Steve, and I have to kill them. It's the only way to shut them up. There's really nothing to it. If they just would understand ... It's so utterly simple."

Oh, utterly, I thought. I sneaked a look at him and he was trying to think. His face was expressionless, but it was getting so now I knew when the gears were meshing in that mad mixed-up brain of his. He was trying to catch hold of something so he could explain it to me.

"That old man," I said. "He wasn't mad at you."

"Sure he was. He was mad about his lawn. He was getting all ready to tell us how much we owed him for cutting up his lawn, pal."

I couldn't figure him. On some things he was right with it, all the way.

"He wanted to hold me up, too," Angers said. "He was in the way. He wanted to tell me his troubles. I don't want to hear people's troubles, Steve. I've enough of my own."

We walked along, crossed another street, and started on another block. The wind was beginning to get a little stiffer now. On the wind, from far away and very faint, but growing steadily louder, came the wail of a siren. The ambulance.

"Maybe he didn't die," I said. "The old man, there. Maybe they'll save him."

"If he didn't," Angers said, "it'll be a lesson he'll always remember."

"I guess you're right."

"Sure I'm right. They told me I was working too hard. They were wrong. They're always wrong. They didn't realize how much punishment the human body can take. They'll never find out, either, because they don't have the guts to try. Told me I needed rest. All right. But who would do the job? Nobody but me. The fund was getting no place. All they wanted to do was talk, or sit and fill their pockets, out there. That's all. So I kept on going, and I'm still going. I'll build that hospital, Steve, and then they'll see."

We walked for quite a while between the trees, with the light from the street lights flickering between the branches. Sometimes we passed somebody out walking, too. They paid no attention to us. People sat on the porches playing cards, or talking, or maybe just sitting. You could hear an occasional radio playing from inside some of the homes. Once in a while a car hissed by and I had heard the siren stop for a few moments, then start up again and fade away into the city. They would take the man to the same hospital where Ruby was. He might even be on the same floor, might even see her. It was that close.

We were in a very quiet residential section now, one of the most expensive parts of town. The homes were huge, with tremendous lawns and old live oaks covered with Spanish moss. Tall royal palms lined the walks like slim gray giants, guarding the vaulted silence.

Angers still had the gun in his hand, hanging down along his leg, swinging loosely with his stride. Under his other arm was the roll of paper. His walk was still the same, shoulders swinging, busy, as though he were really headed someplace. Maybe he was.

Then he stopped walking. I paused, looked at him.

"Listen," he said. "Listen to that."

I listened but I couldn't hear anything. A pale glowing street light shone on his face.

"Hear it?"

"No. The wind, maybe."

"I don't mean the wind, pal. Listen real hard."

What else was there to do? It seemed to me I could hear a piano from someplace. That was all. Maybe it was a radio, I wasn't sure. It was very faint. No, it was a piano.

"I don't hear anything," I said. I was sick. The hell with it.

"Wait. Hear that piano?"

"Sure, I hear it."

"It's beautiful, pal."

"All right," I said. "It's beautiful. Maybe it's a radio."

He shook his head. "Piano."

He stood there looking at me in the street light, with his head cocked a little to one side, listening. I'll tell you right now, it was a picture. With what I knew about this guy, it was a fine picture, all right.

"I've got to find it."

Goddamn.

"I wonder where it is." He listened some more. "It's from up that way, someplace. Come on."

"Why?"

"Don't you hear what they're playing?"

Now he had me listening. We both stood and listened. I couldn't tell what was being played. All I could hear was very faint piano music and that was all.

"It's 'Dancing in the Dark,' " he said.

I looked at him hard this time. But you couldn't tell anything, ever. There was no way.

"Hurry up," he said. "I've got to find where it is."

We went off along the sidewalk. He shoved me onto the grass. "Walk quietly," he said. "Try to find out where it is. It's beautiful. It's my favorite piece, and anyway, it's beautiful. You hear it, pal?"

"Yeah," I said. "I hear it."

Chapter Eleven

Well, we came along the street like that, walking on the grass so we wouldn't make any noise. There was only the hissing of our feet in the grass. It was quiet as a residential street is quiet in the early evening and from someplace came this piano playing "Dancing in the Dark." That was the tune, all right. I recognized it now that he'd told me. But it was still so faint and far away, it just barely tickled your ears, like. I would sneak a look at him every once in a while as we went along, but it didn't tell me anything.

It was funny how he carried on about that hospital of his, yet anything that came up could send him off on a tangent. I'd been feeling a little lower than usual since he reminded me about not trying to make a run for it. He was wise, all right, and that episode down at the bayou sure hadn't helped matters any. Lord, I wished the car had taken the dip into the bayou. It would have maybe rolled over the shallow part on its nose and gone down in the deep water. He might have stayed down there, or at least lost the damned gun. Then I would have had a chance. As it stood now, nobody had a chance if he so much as wrinkled his nose at him. It seemed he would take quite a lot off me, but I wasn't going to bend that too far, either.

"It's not getting any louder, Steve," he said.

"You're right. Let's drop it."

"No, pal. I got to find out where it's coming from."

He brushed my arm, and we went on walking slowly down the lawns fronting these big homes. I wished the piano would stop. If it stopped now, he wouldn't know where to go and we could forget it.

"Listen," he said.

We stood still and listened some more. It was louder now, all right.

"Come on."

"All right." I was tired. We still stank from the mucky bottom of that bayou. The muck was in my hair, drying a little now, and our clothes were covered with it. My pants were still soggy, but beginning to stiffen some.

The tireder I got, the worse it got about Ruby and everything. It seemed as if we'd been going on like this for centuries, and when I remembered it was only this morning I'd been with Ruby, and decided to try to wash out Aldercook with the gun, it was impossible.

"It's from over that way," Angers said. "Come on, pal, we'll cut through here."

"What the hell," I said. "It's only a piano."

He turned and looked at me with his eyes kind of glazed over and that little crazy candle was burning in them.

You're getting rattled, I thought. Quit thinking. It's not good for you. So when he motioned to me again, I went along with him.

We crossed another yard under some slash pines and the ground was damp and springy underfoot. We got out there in the back of this big house and I could see a man and a woman sitting in the kitchen, all brightly lit, drinking coffee and eating pie. The woman was talking with a mouthful of pie and waving her fork at the man with her elbow resting on the table.

The piano was much clearer now. It was good playing, but maybe a little mechanical. One thing, it wasn't a radio. Angers was right about that.

"This way," he said.

We went along through back yards then. They were some yards, let me tell you; they were regular parks. I'd never really seen them before. Money could sure do things, all right. Yeah, money. Well, that's the way it was and I had about twenty-six dollars, didn't I? Money wasn't important any more. I could have lit cigarettes with those bills I had, if they were dry, and it wouldn't have meant a thing.

Funny about back there at the bayou, I kept thinking. He accepted my tackling him the way I had, just as though it were normal. He was on guard a little more, sure, but he just thought I'd got excited. I wondered if that's what he really thought.

"It's across the street," he said.

So we went through some more yards and across the street under the street lights, and the piano was coming from a house about half a block up. You could tell. It was clear now, all right.

"Lord, that's beautiful," he said. "Come on, pal."

"Why don't we just stand here and listen?"

"I've got to see who's playing that piano."

I began to get a funny feeling in my stomach. I should have been used to it by now.

We went on along the sidewalk and then we were in front of this house. If anything, the homes over on this street were larger and richer and had more lawn and trees than those back where we'd come from.

This house was set way back at the end of a U-shaped drive and the only lights that we could see through the trees were in an immense window-walled room, like a sun room, over on the right.

"Come on, pal," Angers said. His voice was like glass, hard and smooth. He waited till I was beside him, then we started across the lawn. We were underneath pines and cedars. The lawn was covered with a slippery carpet of needles and now and again you'd kick a pine cone and it would rattle and bounce along the ground.

Then the piano stopped.

He stopped as if he'd been hit and turned and looked at me.

"Wait," he said.

We waited a minute. Then whoever was playing the piano began to hit one key slowly, over and over and over. He motioned to me and we started toward the lighted room again. The lights were soft, shining out of the windows, a soft orange. The house was made of stone, I could see now, something you don't find much down here, and that alone spoke of money. Well, we crossed the drive and whoever it was kept slowly hitting that key. It began to get on my nerves, what with everything else.

There were big bushes beside the room, but they were trimmed in an oval shape, with space between. The ground between the bushes was clean and dark-looking, cut back from the freshly shaved lawn.

I took hold of his arm.

"Listen, we don't want to do that."

"I've got to see who's playing that piano."

"Whoever it is is just fussing now," I said. "Can't you hear? What does it matter?"

Then whoever it was began playing "Dancing in the Dark" again and I felt his arm tense under my hand, as hard as rock, and the roll of paper under his arm crinkled and snapped.

I could hear him breathe. He was breathing real fast, and when I got a look at his eyes, it was awful. I didn't want to look at his eyes any more after that.

"Come on, pal."

We went in there between the bushes and stood by the windows. There were Venetian blinds and heavy drapes, but they were all pulled back and it was wide open.

It was a little girl.

Her feet didn't even touch the pedals on that big gleaming grand piano in the middle of the room. She was perched on the broad piano bench with her back to us. Long golden curls dangled down her back and she was playing away, rocking her shoulders a little, having fun with it. She was good, too. Real good. Not the best, naturally, but good.

"Listen to that, will you? Listen to her play," Angers said. "So."

"Let's go," I said. "We've seen it. Let's don't stand here."

He didn't answer. He just stood there, listening and watching, then he turned and pushed me out of the bushes. He kept tapping me on the arm with the gun, kind of pushing me along toward the front of the house. Our feet crunched on the gravel drive as we came around to the front of the house.

The front was like a hotel entrance. There were two big glass doors, and you could see into a very dim hallway. I could see tiny dim lights ranged along the wall of the hall inside.

"What are you going to do?" I asked him.

"We're going inside," he said.

"Look, we can't do that. We can't just walk into somebody's house. They'll kick us out," I said. I laughed, forcing it, trying to reach him, and I was scared worse than ever.

"Bet nobody's home but her," he said. "Come on." He pushed me up a couple of steps onto the flat porch. We were in front of the door. He reached out and tried the knob and the door swung open, heavy and without a sound. You could smell the house now. It smelled rich.

"Listen," I said. "Ralph, listen. Don't go in there."

He tapped my arm with the gun, looking at me, but still not looking at me. His face was just the same, it hadn't changed, but there was an eagerness in his actions.

I went in. We stood in a kind of vestibule and he reached for the other door that opened into the hall and it opened just like the other, without a sound. It swung heavy and sweet.

We went on into the hall and you could smell the house even better now. It must be something to live in a house like that. I didn't know whether it was a good something, though. It would be like living in a library, or a museum.

The piano kept right on playing.

There was a big mirror there in the hall and in the dim orange-colored wall lights I saw Angers and myself. It scared me right to the floor. The different perspective showed me how crazy he looked, and I didn't look much better. Him with his pale, strained face, his roll of paper, and the gun dangling from his arm. He looked, too, and kind of smiled at me in the mirror, then motioned with 'his head.

I knew what he meant. I didn't like it, but what else was there to do? Jump him? Sure, go ahead and jump him.

"Come on, pal," he whispered.

We went around through a big living room, with shadowed paintings hanging on the wall. Over one of the paintings a light was lit, and the little light had been made just for the painting. It gleamed down in the darkened room, lighting up a violent picture of wild colors. It looked like maybe the artist had stood off about ten feet and socked gobs of color at his canvas with a slingshot. Any color that happened to come handy, and it didn't matter where it landed.

We went on through there, then through a little alcove with rubber plants and ferns growing out of shadowed pots, and then we were in the room where the piano was.

It was a big room, all right, with window seats all around the windows piled here and there with pillows and a couple of books. There were bookshelves up against the wall where we entered. All the rest was windows. Over there was a huge record player, open, with stacks of records piled on it, and more records were strewn around the floor, albums open, like that.

Angers walked right on into the room, toward the piano.

The little girl looked up and saw him. Then she saw me, then she looked at him again, and she quit playing.

"Don't stop," Angers said.

The little girl swallowed and I saw she was old enough to be scared. She saw the gun in his hand and swallowed again, just sitting there. She opened her mouth to say something, but nothing came out.

"Play it," Angers said. "Don't stop, little girl. Keep right on playing. I want to listen to you play."

Chapter Twelve

The house was very quiet.

"You know my mommy?" the little girl said.

"No," Angers said. "No, we don't know your mommy. Play the piano," he said. "Play."

She sat there, looking up at him. I didn't move. She had big round blue eyes and they were puzzled and frightened. She was maybe eleven years old, wearing a red and white polka-dot playsuit. She just kept on looking at Angers, and she didn't move an inch. Her mouth was a small pink pout.

"Play, little girl," Angers said. "Play that same song. The one you've been playing. Go ahead, little girl."

She squirmed over to the side of the piano bench, her bare legs squeaking on the smoothly polished wood. She slid down to the floor and, without looking at either of us, started walking rapidly for the door.

"Here," Angers said.

She kept right on walking. Her golden curls swung along her back.

Angers hurried over to her, took her shoulder. She stopped walking, but she didn't turn around. He turned her around slowly and she kept looking at the gun in his hand.

"I just want to hear you play," he said. "You've got to play for me."

"I don't want to play any more."

"Please."

"No." She broke away and started for the door again, not running, just walking rapidly.

He rushed to her side and said, "You've got to play."

My insides went all hollow.

I went over and said, "Play for him, will you? Just a little?"

She looked up at me with those round eyes. Hell, there was nothing I could do. What could I do? The poor little kid was scared silly. She wasn't crying or anything, but I don't know what held the tears back.

"Now, come on and play," Angers said in that flat voice of his.

"How did you get in?" she said.

"Never mind," Angers said. "We walked in. I want to hear you play now. What's your name, little girl?"

"Joan."

She said it without thinking, looking at him.

"That's nice," he said. "Get over to the piano."

I stood there and he looked over at me and winked. It was like a doll winking, or a robot, maybe.

He took her by the shoulder and kind of ushered her over to the piano. Her feet dragged, but he got her there and then she got up on the piano bench.

"Play, Joan," he said. "Play 'Dancing in the Dark.' "

"I don't want to." She sat there, staring at the piano keys.

"But I want you to." He leaned on the piano and laid the roll of paper down, then he laid the gun down, with his hand resting next to it. Then he stood up straight, with just his hand out by that gun.

"If—if I play for you, will you go home?"

"Yes, sure. Play the piano."

She began to play. Only it wasn't "Dancing in the Dark."

"Wait," he said. She stopped. "Play the other," he said.

She began playing "Dancing in the Dark." He just stood there and listened.

She played it fast. She went through it fine, without missing a note, only she played it much too fast. Nobody said a word and Angers just stood there, listening. Finally she finished, and looked up at him.

"Now will you go home?" she said.

"Play it again," Angers said. "Play it like you did before, a little slower. Play it right."

"I guess I played it too fast," she said.

"Yes."

"All right. I'll play it just once more. Then you'll have to go home. Mommy wouldn't like it."

Angers said nothing. He just watched her.

She swallowed again, put both hands up to pull her curls away from her neck where they were a little damp now, and she began playing again.

I went over and sat on the window seat. If her parents came home and found us here it was going to be bad. I looked at her and began to pray. Angers stood there by the piano. He hadn't moved. He was listening and nothing showed on his face, nothing. While she played, he picked up his gun and went over and got a chair and dragged it to the piano, so it was facing the little girl. Then he sat down with the gun in his hand, watching her and listening.

You could see it in her eyes, a kind of terrific fright that slowly grew back there in her head. If she'd been much older, she might have started screaming. Younger, she wouldn't have even been scared. It would have been a party. But she was just right, where it all got to her, and she missed a note.

She glanced over at him as if she'd committed a terrible crime. He didn't move a muscle. She took up where she left off and missed the same note again. Then she did it again and finally got it right and went on and her hands were beginning to tremble now.

She finished. "There," she said. "Is that how you like it?"

"Yes," he said. "That was beautiful, Joan. Don't you think it's a beautiful piece?"

She nodded, swallowed, flipped her damp curls back, and started to climb down off the bench.

"Play it again," he said.

She stood there, half off the bench, and looked at him, and the tears began to come.

"Hurry up," he said. "I want to hear it again. Just play the piano."

She worked herself back onto the bench and sat there with the tears beginning to spring out of her eyes and trickle along her cheeks. She turned and looked over at me and I looked at the floor.

"Isn't that a wonderful thing, Steve?" he said. "The way she plays that?"

"Yes. But maybe she's tired."

"I'm tired," she said. "Please, I'm tired. Mommy—"

"Play it again, Joan," he said. "You're not tired, you know you're not. Why, who could be tired? Are you tired, pal?" he said, turning to look at me.

"Yes."

"Imagination."

"I'm tired," she said. "Mommy will be home, and she—"

"Come on, Joan. Play me the piano. Play 'Dancing in the Dark,' Joan."

She glanced over at me again and I nodded. Please, little girl, I thought, play the piano until your fingers are bloody. Don't stop for anything. Not until he says so.

So she began to play again and it went on and on and on. She would stop and look at him and he would grin and she would begin again. It was pretty awful to watch. Finally it got so she was missing notes steadily, all the time. But it didn't seem to matter to him any more. Just so long as she played. He sat there watching her and once in a while he would nod his head when it sounded especially good to him. He didn't look at all tired.

The little girl kept playing and she was sagging over the keyboard now. She was crying and sobbing and playing all the notes cockeyed. You could hear her sobs ring out right along with the tune.

"Look, Ralph," I said. "Let's go. Let the poor kid stop playing." I thought, Maybe if I treat him just like a regular guy ... But I had tried that. It didn't work.

"No," he said. "Go sit down."

"But, Ralph—"

"Take it easy. I want to hear her play."

She heard our voices and stopped playing.

"Play," Angers said kindly.

She shook her head, staring down at the keyboard. She was shaking all over and you could tell she could hardly sit up on the bench.

Angers rose, lifted the gun, and slammed it down on the top of the piano. She wailed still louder.

"Play!" he shouted. "Play that piano!"

I was on my feet, moving toward him. I couldn't help it. "Hey, Ralph!" I shouted.

He turned toward me slowly, not startled, and I went right on talking, but not shouting now, talking as calmly as I could.

"What about your hospital, Ralph? There isn't much time. They're trying to stop you, and if you want to show them they're wrong, you'd better get busy on the hospital."

He walked toward me. His eyes showed nothing. Then he said, "Right, pal, we'd better get going. I want to phone a real-estate office."

The little girl sat there on the piano bench.

He went over and picked up the roll of blueprints. He looked at her.

"Thank you, Joan," he said. "It was beautiful."

She didn't look up. He motioned to me and we walked on out of the room and out of the house.

There wasn't a sound. Just the wind blowing in the pines up there.

Chapter Thirteen

We were in the side yard, walking toward the street, when a car turned in the drive and came along by the other side of the house. It stopped by the front door and the door flew open and the little girl ran down the steps screaming.

"Mommy! Mommy!"

A woman ran from the car and knelt down and the little girl was in her arms.

"Hurry up," Angers said. "Over here."

"Where?"

"The house there."

He kept nudging me along across the lawn, through bushes and trees, then across another spreading lawn. It was the house right next door to where we'd been. It was just as large a place as the other. It was dark. There were no lights at all.

I kept trying to angle my way, so I could maybe jump him and get hold of that Luger. But he wasn't taking any more chances, like back there in the car. And he was fast, alert. He always had his eye on me. Maybe I was his pal and all that, but suspicion lurked in that brain, I felt sure.

I knew that now the little girl would tell her mother everything and the place would be crawling with cops. It was a big break. I figured it was, anyway.

The only trouble was, I didn't want to die. You get like that. I was so scared I was living it that way, straight up.

We were over by this house now. 'Way back, through the trees, we saw lights come on at the other house, blink, blink, blink, as somebody walked through rooms and threw switches. Maybe they thought we were still in the house.

"It's closed up," Angers said.

"What?"

"The house, pal. It's all shuttered, see?"

He was right. Whoever owned the place was probably up North. All the windows were shuttered and the grass needed cutting, too. It was a three-storied house.

"We'll go in there," he said.

I thought about how the law might be around here as soon as those people put in an alarm. It was all right. Actually, it didn't matter, because I was sure he'd get his way.

"All right," I said. "Let's go."

He grinned at me and said, "That's better, Steve. I like to hear you talk that way. You were pulling against me for a while there, weren't you?"

"It was that poor little girl."

"I don't mean that. She's all right, anyway."

"Well, Lillian, when she—"

"Forget it, Steve. Let's just go in here. Maybe we can find some clean clothes. They've probably left lots of things in the house."

"How we going to get in?"

"Hell, I don't know."

We went over by the door and he tried it. It was locked, naturally, and we stood there a while. He was thinking, or at least it seemed that way.

"You know," he said, "she could really play that piano. It always gets me when I hear that tune. Always, pal. I can't stand it. It's like all the good things that ever happened to me are coming into my head. I remember all sorts of things when I hear that tune. And they're all good things. It kind of wrings me out. It's almost like sleeping. I feel as though I've just had a good night's sleep."

It was all right with me if he wanted to stand here on the porch. I could still see that little girl playing the piano. It was something I would always remember.

I laughed out loud.

"What's the matter, pal?"

"Nothing, just thinking." I was thinking how I was in this now, right now. I had thought once that things couldn't get any worse. It goes to show you.

He walked over across the porch, kind of looked sideways at me, waiting for me to come along, too. I went along. He looked at the windows. They were shuttered. He tried one and the shutter came open. That's the kind of luck they have. A madman's luck.

"Well," he said. "Let's see, here."

He opened the shutters all the way. They were cobwebbed. He tried the window and it was locked. So he reached out with the gun, and *clunk*, the pane shattered and tinkled onto the porch floor at our feet. It was all done in a single gesture.

"Well," he said. He reached inside and unsnapped the catch and slid the window up. It didn't stick; it went up real easy.

"Pick up the broken glass there, Steve. Toss it inside the house."

He looked at me as I hesitated. Then I picked up the glass and tossed it inside. It didn't make any noise when it hit in there. It was like throwing it into dark air and having it vanish.

"O.K.," he said. "Let's go in. Go ahead."

I went in and he came through after me, fast.

"Now, this isn't any good," he said. "We aren't going to be able to see."

"Not very well," I said, thinking that maybe this was my chance.

"Well," he said.

We stood there for a while, like that. Light from the street light lit up the room very dimly, but that was all. If I moved, he'd be able to see it.

"We've got to have a light," he said. "That's all there is to it. Now, Steve, you walk right ahead of me and try to find the kitchen."

He dropped the roll of blueprints on a chair. I watched him standing there, facing me, and I wondered just what he was thinking.

"Why do you want to find the kitchen?" I said.

"In a house like this," he told me, "they're bound to have a flashlight lying around someplace."

He knocked me in the back with the gun. It was a friendly gesture, I suppose, that was all. I moved through the room and everything was black or gray, but you could still make out shapes in here. I headed toward an arch that seemed to lead into what looked like a hall. It was real black there, all right. If I could get in there with him, maybe I'd have some sort of a chance. He couldn't see any better than I could.

We came to the arch and I felt the gun muzzle snuggle up against my ribs.

"I hate to do this, pal," he said, "but you know how it is."

I didn't say anything.

"Makes me feel foolish, pal," he said. "But you've got me jumpy, ever since back there in the car. This way I feel better and neither of us will get excited. All right, pal?"

"Sure," I said.

Chapter Fourteen

I stared at the dark. It seemed as if he would have to start things. I kind of wished he would shoot. Maybe he'd miss, or just graze me. Sure, I thought, just graze the skin—a surface wound. That's the way they do, then they whirl and smash the gun out of the guy's hand and wrestle around and dive for the gun and maybe club him over the head with it. Triumphant, that's what. Sure, I thought. Go ahead, Logan, whirl....

"You saved my life," he said. "I'll never forget that. I wish you wouldn't forget it, either. I'm going to need help and I need somebody to talk with who understands what I'm up against. They're all trying to keep me from going through with this, you know. Well, we'll do it, by God!"

"Sure."

"Go ahead," he said. "I just wanted you to remember. Let's find the kitchen."

It was a big room and there were no shutters on the windows, so light from a street lamp down the way took care of any plans I might have made. Not that I made any. But I could feel myself rebel all the time. Maybe rebellion wasn't enough. All the way down the dark hall, he'd kept that damned gun in my back and breathed against my neck. Off the kitchen was a pantry and there was a lot of drawer space in there. That's where we found the flashlight. He never missed, that guy. There were three flashlights.

"One will do," he said.

"Only one of them works," I told him after I'd tried them.

"Just flash it on when you need it. We've got to go back to the front room and close that shutter."

"All right."

"The police are sure to be around here," he said. "But they won't find us."

We went back into the front room and I waited while he went over to close the shutters on the window. He just stood there with one hand reaching out for the shutter, kind of keeping his eye on me, too.

He turned to me. "Come here, Steve, quick!"

I went up close to him.

"Out on the porch," he whispered. "Quick."

"But—"

"Get out there!" The gun came hard against my side. I climbed through the window out onto the porch and he came through behind me.

"Crouch down by the railing," he said.

I crouched down and then I began to curse inside. Somebody was coming across the lawn, slowly, coming from tree to tree. And whoever it was wore a white dress. Lillian. I went tense, and that gun of his went into my side.

"You'd like to see her get away, wouldn't you, pal?"

I said nothing.

"Just be quiet," he said.

She came along toward the side of the house, staring up at the window we'd broken. She couldn't see us crouched down in the shadow of the railing. I wondered what she was trying to do. Well, whatever it was, it was all up with her now.

She came by the side of the porch, then along the front of the railing, still looking at the window. She walked right in close, touching the railing of the porch with her hand. She got almost right up to where we were and I could see her face plain. Angers didn't move.

She stood there with one hand on the porch railing, looking at the window. We weren't eight feet away. She moved a little closer, still looking, and her face was strained, her teeth sunk into her lower lip. Once something made a noise out on the lawn behind her and she whirled as if she'd been stabbed.

Then she looked at the window again, listening. She moved another step closer and Angers stood and reached over and grabbed her arm.

She screamed. It wasn't loud. But it was pure fright. I thought she'd faint, but she didn't, and Angers just held her arm and lifted her straight up from the ground over the railing.

"Oh, God!" she said. She kept saying that. She didn't try to fight, she knew it was useless. She dragged against the railing, and he pulled her right on over, like a sack of potatoes.

All the time I'd kept an eye sharp for any opening. But he'd been just as careful not to let any opening occur. She was between us and he grinned at me, with his eyes shining a little the way they did when he got excited.

"You followed us!" he said. "Damn you, Lil!"

"Please, please! Let me go!"

"I should kill you, Lil—right now."

She sobbed hysterically, looking straight into his eyes, sobbing, trying to pull away from him. I could see him strain and grip her arm as hard as he could. She began to make little mewling noises in her throat, broken with the sobs.

"Get in the house," he said.

He gave her a hell of a push toward the window. It sent her sprawling against the window sill. She was sobbing and shaking all over. She landed on her knees, then suddenly rose up and started to run straight for the other side of the porch.

"Lillian!"

He took a quick step and nailed her hard. He held onto her and she came around like a whip, up against him. Crying, she held her head back and stared into his face.

"In the house!" he snapped.

Again he hurled her at the window. I was over there by the window now and I caught her, holding her arms.

I looked at him. He wasn't smiling now, he just stood there pumping that gun up and down like a pump handle.

"Inside," he said. His voice was flat and dead again, and the gun kept working up and down in his hand.

"Do like he says, honey," I told Lillian. "Come on, now. It's all right. Climb through the window."

She was weak and trembling, trying to say something. Then she gave up and crawled through the window.

Inside, Angers closed the shutters on the window, and we stood there. All of us were breathing hard. Lillian kept right on crying and it was worse than hearing that little girl. The sobs came up out of her from way down inside and you could tell they hurt.

"What were you trying to do, Lillian?" Angers said.

She burst into wild crying and I held her up against me. She was scared and like a little kid. She'd get to sobbing backward in a wild string and you'd wonder if she'd ever stop.

"Let her go, Steve."

I took my arms away from her and she kept crying. I never saw anybody so frightened and crushed as Lillian was right then.

"I asked you what you were trying to do," Angers said.

"Oh! Go away! Please, go away!"

"Women. They're all alike," Angers said. "I thought I could depend on Lil, here, pal. But you see? You shouldn't think about your wife, either, pal. Hell with them."

I said nothing.

"I—I followed you," Lillian said brokenly.

"Never mind," I said.

"I want him to know!" she said. "I want him to know!"

"I know without you telling me," he said.

"No," she said. "I followed you because— And then I lost you. I couldn't find you. I followed you from where the car wreck was, but I lost you, and all the time you were in that house next door." She began carrying on loudly again. "Oh, if I'd only known! I looked all over for you. Then I saw you come out of there and come over here."

"That's enough," I said. I got it all right, and I didn't want her to say any more. Likely he got it too. It didn't matter. But just her saying any more might get him wound up to where he'd blast her with that gun.

"You could have called the police, then, is that right?" Angers said. "And you were just checking here to make sure we were staying long enough so you could phone the police, right?"

She said nothing. I could feel her fright, though. It seemed to seep from her to me and the tension in the house became stronger.

"Too bad," Angers said. "You went to a lot of trouble for nothing."

He was right. Leaving the car as she had would have done no real good. She wouldn't have been able to tell the law anything of value. So she'd taken it into her own hands and tried to follow us, pin-point us. But she hadn't been able to contact the police.

She'd lost us when we went into the house next door because of that damned piano.

Now all of us were dancing in the dark....

She would have been safe if she'd stayed away. That's what got me. If she'd just stayed away and not been so bloody brave. She had to go and be a brave one.

"Anyway—anyway, two are better than one," she said.

I looked to see how he'd take that. I'd got what she meant, but he didn't say a word. You could talk about anything right to his face. Maybe he didn't do anything because there wasn't anything to do.

"Listen," he said. "I feel funny. I don't want to kill you two."

We watched him. I could feel her stiffen beside me.

"You're my pal," he said. "Aren't you? Hell," he said. "Don't make me kill you. Don't do it."

I didn't know what to say. His voice sounded as if he were holding himself down.

"Well, you're back now, Lil," he said flatly. "I still like you."

It probably wouldn't matter even if he'd seen the look of fear she shot him right then. I didn't know what to do. Maybe she thought two were better than one against Angers, but I didn't. Alone, I might have had a chance. This way, I'd have to be looking out for her. I didn't like it. It was bad enough just watching out for myself.

"Why didn't you keep going when you left the car?" I said.

"Maybe you should have, Lil. Maybe Steve's right."

"I couldn't—"

I didn't know how to manage it. I had to win his confidence back. If he'd ever really had any confidence in me. There was something about him, the way he was now. It was a little worse than usual. Everything was drawn taut. Probably because of the episode with Lillian, finding her that way. One slip was all he allowed. I'd made mine back there in the car. So had she. But you couldn't tell with this guy.

He got his roll of paper, tucked it under his arm.

"Now, let's go upstairs and find some clothes," he said.

"Sure, Ralph."

There weren't any angles. I hadn't been able to jump him because he didn't leave himself open. Even out there on the porch, he'd had that gun on me all the time. We were trapped, as trapped as you can get. And all the time I kept trying not to remember Ruby, because thinking of her drove me wild.

He waited for us to move, standing there with his roll of paper under his arm, the flashlight in one hand, the gun in the other. He was too quiet.

We went into the hall. By the stairway was a small table with a telephone on it and he told us to wait a minute. We stood by the stairs with the circle of light from his flash playing across our feet.

"I had to do it," Lillian whispered to me. She had quit sobbing, but her chin was trembling. "I just had to, Steve!"

Angers was listening at the telephone.

"It's working," he said. "I'll use that later."

Folks left their phones connected when they went away from down here. Otherwise they might not be able to get their phone back from the company. Too much demand.

Lillian and I started up the stairs. She held my hand and I wished there were something I could do for her. Angers came along behind us.

"You tried to shoot me, Ralph," she said, turning and releasing my hand.

She was getting hold of herself, but I wished she hadn't said that. Maybe she was rattled.

"Shut up about that," he said. He came up behind us and stopped. He held the light on the stairs.

"Why did you do that, Ralph?"

"I said for you to shut up about that!"

I took her arm, trying to warn her. That's what was the matter, she was so frightened she didn't know what she was doing.

"Let's get on upstairs," I said.

"You've got to have faith," he said, jamming his head close to Lillian's. "Faith in what I'm trying to do. You've got to have faith," he said. "Faith!"

"Sure," I said. I pulled at her arm.

She was staring at him, starting to back up the stairs. Then she turned around and would have run if I hadn't held to her. Her breathing was fast and shallow. I turned and went along beside her. It was pretty bad when you turned your back on him.

"We've got to get some clothes," I told her. "We fell in the drink, didn't we, Ralph?"

"Yeah, pal."

As we reached the top of the stairs, turned to walk down the hall, I heard a car out on the street.

"We'll try the closets," Angers said.

I heard another car outside on the street, then, and I heard it stop nearby. Then another car came along and stopped. I didn't say anything, but Lillian had heard, too. She touched my hand with hers. I prayed it was the police. But, maybe that was the wrong thing to pray for. If we could only warn them some way, let them know where we were. Only you never knew what he'd do.

"Empty," he said, glancing into a closet, flashing the light around on the floor.

There were no shutters on the bedroom windows up here. If he didn't notice the cars out there, he might accidentally flash that light on one of the windows. It would be all they'd need. So far he had used it only to glance inside the closet.

We went into the hall again and made a tour of the upstairs. In one closet there were plenty of clothes. Suits, dresses, and a pile of white shirts sitting on a shelf. The closet was thick with the odor of moth balls.

He made us select clothes to wear, even Lillian, and he took a suit for himself.

We were dressing when the siren moaned. I'll bet some copper cursed like hell because he'd tripped the button without meaning to. It moaned almost like the wind, but you knew right off it was a siren.

"They're here," Angers said. "It took them long enough."

Lillian was dressing right there with us. In the pale light she had a gorgeous body, all right. She had long legs and her underwear was very tight, her breasts thrusting out almost as large as Ruby's. Angers was watching her, watching her closely.

"Lil," Angers said, "I'd almost forgotten. It's a long time since last night, isn't it?"

She was pulling the dress down over her hips now. It was a stretch. The dress had looked red in the light from the flash before he'd turned it off. Now you couldn't tell what color it was. Only it fitted her very tightly. You could see that.

She glanced quickly at me, then just sort of looked at him. Then she went back to wriggling into the dress, kind of peeling it down over her hips.

"You hear me, Lil?" Angers said. "I'd almost forgotten how nice you were. It would be good if you kept reminding me. Funny I'd forget a thing like that."

She still didn't say anything.

He had on a suit again. He looked just exactly like always.

He herded us back along the hall to a front bedroom, overlooking the front lawn and the street.

They were down there, all right.

"Look," Angers said. "Look at them."

We stood by the window, watching the cops out there. I saw four or five cars, strung down the street, all with spotlights on their roofs. Two of them had their parking lights lit. They went out as we watched. You could see the men walking up and down out there, shining flashlights. They acted as if it was Christmas.

Chapter Fifteen

Angers turned away from the window.

"You might as well sit down," he said. "We can't do anything till they leave."

"Maybe they won't leave, Ralph," Lillian said. She wasn't sobbing any more now. There was that old ring to her voice, reminding me of how well she'd acted at the Grahams'.

"They'll leave," he said.

"You can't tell," she said. "Maybe they'll come in here."

"It would be a shame."

"Sure," she said. "I'll bet they come right in here."

He kind of chuckled in his throat.

"She's right," I said.

"You know why they won't?" he said. "Because I haven't finished my job yet. There's a lot to do, pal."

Lillian and I sat on a bed, where we could look out of the window. Out there the cops kept prowling around, mostly off to the left, over by the house where the little girl had been.

Angers half sat against the window sill, holding the gun on his knees. You could see the black outline of his face against the paler shadows. He had quite a jaw, too. He leaned down and set the roll of blueprints on the floor by the wall.

"I wanted to show you those," he said, tapping the paper. "But it'll have to wait a while."

Lillian and I sat there. I had a comb from my other clothes and I'd transferred the wet money to the clean pants. I wore a white shirt that was too tight and a pair of expensive gabardine pants. I didn't know what color they were. I combed the muck out of my hair as best I could, and dropped the comb on the floor.

Lillian sighed and lay back on the bed and I looked at her. She had her eyes closed. It was very quiet and peaceful in the house. From outside you could hear an occasional voice and once in a while a car hissed along up the street.

"We've had quite a day, haven't we, pal?"

"Yes."

Lillian moved on the bed. She moved until she was over against me, her leg and her hip against me, and she put her arm around me, her breast pressed tight against me as she lay there on the bed. It was good to feel her there. It was reassurance that there was still good in the world; that the whole world hadn't gone off its bat.

Angers glanced at us, then away. He began to tap the muzzle of the Luger against his knee, kind of half watching out the window, and half watching us. Lillian's breathing was slowing down now, evening out.

"I hadn't planned it this way," he said. "It makes things harder now, this way. But we've only wasted a day, pal—one day is all."

"That's right."

Lillian stirred against me and it was quiet for a time. Then *bang*—they were using the spotlights. One shone straight in the window. The room lit up like day, bright and clear, and Angers dropped fast. The spotlight passed right on by. It had been there only a brief instant. They were shining them all around the streets out there, up into the trees and at all the houses all around.

Angers chuckled a little and sat up on the window sill again.

A car started, one of the police cars, and it backed up until it was right in front of this place, then it stopped. You could see a cigarette glowing in the car. The engine was turned off and nobody got out.

The spotlights flashed around for about five minutes, then they quit that. One of the cars started up and drove away, hissing in the night.

Two cops were standing out on the sidewalk, talking. Then they went and got into a car and drove away, too.

"Here they come," Angers said.

Lillian moved against me and I heard her say, "Please."

I looked out of the window and three cops were coming across the lawn toward this house. They walked between the trees and they weren't talking. One had a flashlight, but he turned it off as they came nearer.

Angers stood up by the window.

I watched them come along through the trees. My heart started pounding. If Angers would only turn his back, let me have a chance at him. But he was too damned wise for that.

The three men halted out there and looked at the house. I reached down and squeezed Lillian, and she began to sit up. She was tense as a board, sitting there. She saw them and looked at me. Maybe we could make a noise, but that's about all you had to do. Just *think* and he was on you.

"Now, look," he said. "Both of you. I don't know what these fools are up to, but be quiet, understand? I honestly will kill you. I honestly will. I don't want to, but I promise you, I will. Everything depends on what I'm going to do."

Lillian shrank against me.

Outside the three cops came on again and you could hear their feet on the ground. They still weren't talking.

"You understand?" Angers said. He was pumping the gun again.

"I was a cop once," I said. "Up in Jacksonville."

"I never want to be a cop," he said.

Then we couldn't see them any more. They were approaching the porch and this window overlooked the porch roof. We heard them on the porch, then.

One of them spoke:

"Hell, they ain't around here. They're in Georgia by now."

"Just the same, we're going in. That's orders."

Angers moved in close by us. You could hear him breathe. It was raspy, as if he couldn't get enough air, and you could smell that gun. He was that close. My heart began going. If there were only some way to let them know! Lillian sat tight up against me and she was hot, her hands were all sweaty when she touched mine.

"Remember," Angers said. "Please remember."

"Yes, Ralph," Lillian said. "Yes, Ralph, honey, yes."

A new voice said, "I'd kind of hate to meet up with that guy, the way he shot Bud Lyttle."

"He's just a guy, like anybody else."

Their feet scraped.

"The door's locked. Here, I'll try them keys.... No good."

"Let me try. You ain't got the touch."

"Hell, they're in Georgia."

"I know it. There."

We all tensed. The door came open down there and the voices were much clearer. Their feet came into the downstairs hall.

"You figure this Logan is in with him?"

"What you mean, in with him?"

"I'd blast him, by God!"

They walked into a room and their voices changed to an indistinguishable muttering. They returned to the hall again. For a moment they stood in the hall and you could see they were using a flashlight.

"Hell, you can't tell," one said. "You can't tell anything about this. The girl wasn't with them at the house over there."

"Wasn't that hell, though?"

"Wonder where the girl is."

"They probably knocked her off."

"That Mrs. Graham says Logan wasn't with him, anything like that."

"What did she know?"

"It's plain hell."

They went down the hall toward the rear of the house. I heard them rattle the door in the kitchen.

Angers hadn't moved. He stood right in front of us, holding the gun, and

we didn't move, either. If there only were some way to let those men know.
If they came upstairs, Angers would shoot his way out. I knew he would.
He leaned down close, with his head by our faces.

"Remember," he whispered. "I meant what I said." Then he straightened
again, and stood like that.

"I was in bed," one of them said. "Right there in bed."

"They got me up, too. Whole force is on this."

"Wonder if she's nice."

"The girl?"

"Nice and dead, I reckon."

"A shame."

They laughed. The laughter echoed all through the house and for a
moment it was quiet. They were in the hall, by the foot of the stairs.

"This Graham dame, she can't talk much yet?"

"She's alive and that's all."

"Town never had anything like this."

"The Chief's got ants."

"Who wouldn't? He's responsible. Everybody looks at it that way,
anyways. Well, they ain't down here."

"They're in Georgia."

"He's a good shot with that gun, all right."

"Wonder what's the idea."

"You heard them say he's nuts."

I looked up at Angers. He didn't move. The gun didn't move from right
there by our heads. He was watching us, listening to them down there.

"What would you do if you saw him right now?"

"Orders are shoot on sight."

"What about the guy with him?"

"Come on, let's go back. Hell with this."

"We better look upstairs. Suppose they're right upstairs?"

"Orders are to shoot on sight. The Chief says to hell with this trying to
take him alive. Nobody really knows this guy Logan. I'll shoot on sight,
man, let me tell you. Fast."

"You and your fast."

"A shame. A doctor, too. Would you think it? They traced him. An eye
surgeon from Seattle. You hear about it?"

"I been out since before supper. I ain't ate yet, even."

"Doctor from Seattle. He cracked up, from what they say. Worked too
hard or something. He cracked up once before, over in Korea. He's a
veteran."

"I'm going to look around upstairs."

"He's a veteran now, all right. How about the dame?"

We heard the man beginning to come up the stairs. He came slowly and the flashlight began to brighten even the walls of this front bedroom. Angers didn't move at all. The gun just lifted a little. It was pointed straight between my eyes. Lillian was so stiff with fright I don't believe she could have moved. I wondered if this might set Angers off. He might shoot just for the hell of it. That's usually the way he did do it. It looked that way, always.

"They don't know, isn't much on her," one said as the man kept coming up the stairs. "Just she was a dancer in Seattle. Nobody ever saw her with him, so the report says. She had an act in a joint in Seattle. A dancer."

"See anything?"

"It's quiet up here."

"Go ahead, look around."

The man was at the head of the stairs. He took a couple of steps and now Angers changed. You could feel it, not even touching him—like a charge of electricity. The light swept our doorway, banged into the room and out again.

"The hell with it. Nothing up here."

Lillian began sobbing quietly and Angers reached out and touched her forehead with the muzzle of the gun. She ceased, holding her breath. She was vibrating with pent-up fear and hope.

The man pounded down the stairs. The door slammed. They scraped and clumped off the porch and pretty soon I saw them walking back across the lawn. They paused out front and Angers crouched quickly. The flashlight came on, flashing around on the house. Once the light whisked brilliantly across the window. Then it blinked off and they turned, walking over to the cars by the curb.

"That's it," Angers said. "They've done their duty. They won't be back again."

He stood there taking big breaths, blowing them out.

I felt let down. It was as if a big chunk of hope had been gnawed out of me, leaving only a writhing black despair. The despair was mixed with the fear and I knew Lillian must feel the same. Both of us had done a lot of hoping and praying during the past few moments. It had all gone to nothing. Yet, if they had found us, it would have been hell. It would have been war and Lillian and I would have been in the middle.

Maybe it was a good thing they didn't find us.

I sat there watching him, with Lillian sort of trembling inside her skin beside me.

"You heard what they said, pal?"

"Yes."

"It was mostly right, pal. Only I haven't cracked up or anything like that—not by a long shot."

Lillian made a small noise. He didn't seem to hear her.

"That was just—well, part of the plan," he said.

"I understand."

"It was a secret at first, you see?"

"Sure."

Lillian pressed close against me.

His voice went flat. "They criticized me," he said. "They criticized me for the way I went about things, my dreams." His voice became like still water, like a nest of sleeping snakes, and you could feel the mad wrath contained within that voice. "They always criticized me, even when I did big things. I'm doing a big thing now. They won't criticize me. If they do, I'll kill them. Ignorance. There's no room for it in my plans. No room."

He stood there, breathing deep and slow, and I saw something. That's what got him, it must have been. Criticism. He couldn't take it. He blew his top over it. Of course, it wasn't that alone, but that was the trigger.

God help anybody who said the wrong thing to this guy.

"They don't know the half of it, how you can dance, do they, Lil?"

She didn't answer.

"They're going away out there," he said, glancing out the window. "See?"

He was right. They were going away. Only one car remained. It was parked in front of the other house, where the little girl lived.

"Now we can get moving," he said. "We've got clean clothes, everything. I'm going to phone a real-estate man."

"Oh?"

Lillian glanced at me in the pale dark, her eyes wide.

"Sure, pal. That's right. You know a good one? It doesn't matter, though. I know right where we'll build the hospital."

Lillian sat very still, looking at him. We both watched him.

"Saw the spot when we were driving by that park down there," he told us. His eyes shone bright and flat in the dimly lit room. "A good five-block stretch, without a building on it. Across from the park. There was a 'For Sale' sign on it, too."

Right then something hit me. So far I hadn't let him see how scared I was. I'd talked along with him about things, and sometimes I'd even come back at him, differed with him. And since I hadn't thought about it, maybe the fear hadn't shown in me.

I wondered then what he would do if he ever saw how really scared I was. Suppose he saw it in my eyes?

Chapter Sixteen

All right, what was I supposed to do now? There wasn't anything to do. Go along with him until you faced the muzzle of your own Luger and felt the sock of lead and heard the roar with his pale expressionless face up there looking at you. It was a nice feeling. It was fine. And now he was going to phone a real-estate man.

"We'll go downstairs while I phone," he said.

I stood beside the bed and Lillian sat there, staring across at the window. I got her hand and pulled and she stood up.

"You have some money, haven't you, pal?"

I reminded him about the twenty-six dollars Jake Halloran had paid me for the Luger.

"Good. We'll need that."

"How you going to look at land without any dough?"

"Oh, money's no object," he said. "I've got all the money I'll ever need. My God, hundreds of thousands of dollars. Millions."

"I see. Well, in that case, it's all right, then." I stood there remembering Harvey Aldercook, and the next minute I was blabbing it out about him, about how I'd needed money and he'd owed me that two-seventy and all.

"A bum, pal. Strictly no good." He shot a burst of that crazy laughter of his at the ceiling. "Money," he said. "Money. You never saw so much money. We'll build that hospital, all right. The fund is big, pal. I drove myself getting it. I've got all the money I'll ever need."

Lillian was staring at him. She looked at me.

"What's the matter, Lil?" he said.

"You've been broke ever since I knew you," she said. "We spent all my money getting here and now I'm broke."

"Let's go downstairs," he said. "They'll send me the money," he said. "Soon as I tell them what I've been doing." He glanced out the window and we all stood there and watched the last police car gun away from the curb and hiss swiftly away down the street.

"I'd saved it," Lillian said. "I'd saved that money up, and I worked hard for it, too."

"You're a good girl," Angers said. "You understand."

"Yes," she said. "Sure. I understand." She watched the floor.

"You'll never have to work again," he said. "You'll have all the money you'll ever need, like I told you. It's my dream, and when a man realizes a dream like this— well."

"Sure," Lillian said. "Sure, I know."

He phoned a real-estate man. The guy's name was Tom Bourney. Before he called we checked on the address of this house, and Angers told him to meet us here, right away. We'd be waiting out front.

"Make it as quick as you can," Angers said. "It's something that can't wait." He hung up and looked at us with that flat, mirror-like gaze.

He picked up his roll of paper and stood there.

I stepped toward the phone. "Guess I'll just give the hospital a buzz," I said. "See how Ruby is."

"Pal."

"Won't take a minute," I said. "That guy won't be here that quick."

"That's not what I mean, pal. You know what I mean."

I had my hand on the phone. He just stood there with his damned roll of paper and the gun and looked at me. There wasn't any happiness in Lillian's face, either.

"Hell," I said. I kind of looked past his shoulder now, because I kept thinking he might see how scared I was by my eyes. I didn't want him to see that.

I said, "I've got to see how she is."

"It wouldn't be smart."

Well, we stood like that for a minute.

"We'll go outside and wait by the curb for Mr. Bourney."

We went outside.

We waited out there by the curb and I couldn't help hoping some of the cops had stuck around. They apparently hadn't. It was about ten o'clock in the evening and there were still some lights lit in the house next door, where we'd listened to the piano.

"He wanted to make it tomorrow," Angers said. "I told him to bring a flashlight."

"Ralph," Lillian said, "why couldn't we just call it off till tomorrow? We could—we could go to a hotel or something. Couldn't we, Ralph, honey?"

"No, Lil. We've really started now. Like I been telling you all along, when we found the place, we'd get at it right away."

"Yes, Ralph." She paused for a moment. It was much lighter out here and I was glad in a way. I could see Angers better. "Ralph," she said, "I'm hungry. We haven't eaten since I don't know when."

I knew she wasn't hungry.

"Sure, Lil. I could eat a bear myself. We'll get something to eat."

She glanced quickly at me. She was trying to get him someplace, anyplace, where he couldn't go waving that gun around. I felt she was wrong. He would wave it anyway. And when he got around too many people, he began shooting.

Tom Bourney finally came along and stopped. He was driving a new sedan, a glistening black. I spotted him as the jovial-salesman type immediately. He was impressed with the address and we looked fresh enough in the clean clothes.

Bourney was middle-aged, wearing a sport shirt and light-colored slacks. He smiled all the time and he smoked cigars, and he started talking right away, his round face always moving and barking around the long cigar.

"Well, well. Here we are," he said, climbing from the car. "Couldn't get here any sooner," he said. "Shall we take my car, or—"

"Yes," Angers said. "These are some friends. They'll come along."

Angers had the gun in his coat pocket now. He motioned us toward the car, ignoring Bourney. We got into the back seat and he did, too.

"Why don't you sit up front?" Bourney said.

"This is fine," Angers told him.

Bourney was plainly confounded. He hadn't been introduced, he didn't know who anybody was. He chewed his cigar, standing there, then got in behind the wheel of the car. I wondered how much he'd heard about Ralph Angers.

"So you say you want to buy some property?" He hunched around, looking at us, chewing the cigar.

"That's right," Angers said.

"Well, I have-"

"I know what I want," Angers said.

"I see. Well, that's fine, now. It's a little dark, of course. Would be better tomorrow. Sure you don't want to change your mind? I could come around early in the morning. We could go inside and get together on things here tonight. Now, I've got some listings I brought along. I suppose you want beach property?"

"No."

Lillian was in the middle, between Angers and me. I could feel her move against me. Her hip snuggled against mine and she placed her hand on mine. Angers sat there, staring at Tom Bourney.

Bourney scrunched around in the seat and looked at Lillian, his eyes flicking over her legs, and then at me, and he smiled and said, "Of course."

Lillian's skirt was up over her knees. But she was too frightened and too busy thinking to bother about it. Bourney couldn't keep his eyes off her legs. She did have nice legs and to him this was an eyeful. These rich bastards, he was thinking. Boy, I've got it made. You could see it in his eyes, above the rotating cigar. He gave Lillian's legs another quick, sticky one, then looked at Angers again.

"You plan to build, is that it?"

"Yes."

"I see. Well, now, folks, suppose we talk this over, just so's I can kind of get an eye to what you want here, what you need. I've got listings, all sorts of listings. You name it, I can handle it. If I can't get you what—"

"Look," Angers said. "Let's go."

"Sure, Mr.— Ah, well. Yes. Hadn't we better see? Now, here," he craned his neck, looking at Lillian's legs again. As he looked, she crossed them and his eyes looked startled. I saw he reacted quickly to what he saw. The cigar burned, smoldering. Smoke filled the car. He looked at Angers again. "Just exactly what are you looking for?" he said.

"There's some land for sale down by the park there," Angers said. He looked at me.

"Bayside Drive," I said. "By Coffeepot Bayou, across from the park he means."

"Oh, that!" He smoked rapidly. He blinked as he smoked and his face was eternally cheerful. He didn't dare look at Lillian's legs any more; it did too much for him. "Where the apartment buildings are? Kennely's spot, yes." He chuckled. "Well, surely, now, you don't want that."

"Yes," Angers said. "Let's just drive over there, Mr. Bourney."

"But-Well. Here, now. Well, I brought a flashlight." He held up a five-cell flashlight and grinned back at us. Then he turned around in the seat again. "Just a small lot, of course?"

"No," Angers said. "There's about five blocks, I saw. I think I want it all. I want to look at it."

"Five blocks. Yes." He stared blankly back at us. He had to believe it, because nobody smiled or anything. He had to believe it, but he couldn't. Five blocks, he was thinking. You could see it in his eyes. All that whole stretch of Kennely's, my good Lord, what a thing! He was talking himself into it. It was the biggest he'd ever had and it scared him.

"Well," he said. "Certainly. That *is* a nice spot."

"Suppose we go over there right now," Angers said. His voice had that matter-of-fact, deadly ring.

"We better go over there," I said. "It's getting late," I added.

"Yes, certainly." He paused, looked squarely at Angers. "You know, of course, what a piece of property like this will cost?"

Angers had the roll of paper between his knees. He waved his hand. "Never mind the money," he said. "Show it to us."

Bourney was all for it. He reached his hand across the back of the seat, offering Angers his hand. "Well, O.K. We will. Now, I'd like to meet you folks. I'm Tom Bourney, been in town for fifteen years. Fifteen years in real estate, and truthfully, I want to help you. What's your name?"

"This is Lillian," Angers said. "That's Steve and I'm Ralph Angers."

Tom Bourney had his hand stretched out like that. Angers hadn't moved.

I looked at the floor, then at Bourney again.

Lillian began to tremble again.

It took a long while to seep through the excitement in Tom Bourney's brain. He'd heard the name before someplace, and it wasn't attached to anything good, he knew that You could see him remembering and you could see memory lighting his eyes and you saw when he had the answer.

He bit hard on the cigar with his hand out.

"Let's go," Angers said.

I felt sure he knew he'd told the man his name and what it might mean to Bourney. Why had he done it?

Bourney turned slowly around in the seat and sat there. He took the cigar out of his mouth and dropped it from the window of the car.

"I'm going to build a hospital," Angers said. "That's why I need that stretch of land, Mr. Bourney. It will be perfect for recovering eye patients, too. A nice view of the bay. They'll be able to sit out on the porches and look at the sky and the bay. Florida. I'm going to transplant eyes, Mr. Bourney. It's going to be the greatest thing the world has ever heard of. Actual transplanting of eyes, the entire eye, Mr. Bourney."

He still hadn't started the car. He just sat there.

"Please!" Lillian said. "Please, for God's sake do like he says!"

"Let's go," Angers said.

Bourney started the car and sat there. He turned the headlights on.

"All right," I said. "You've heard, Mr. Bourney. Now, just drive us over there."

"I better drop by the office," he said. All the fine joviality was gone. His voice was meek, almost pleading. "I got to stop by the office," he said. "First."

"No, we'll go over where I said," Angers told him.

Bourney pulled away from the curb and started driving. I knew how he felt and there was nothing to do about it. Angers sat there with his hand in his pocket, on that gun. He looked straight ahead and I was afraid Lillian was going to begin crying again. I didn't want that. There was enough strain without that.

And all the time there was Ruby. I wasn't numb; it just became worse and worse all the while.

"I know what," Bourney said, driving toward town, away from the bay. "I'll run over to Kennely's place. I know right where he lives. We'll tell him about it. You see, he has that location, it's his. He should really handle it."

"Turn around," Angers said. "You're going in the wrong direction. We're wasting time. I don't want to waste any more time. You're all alike. Damned fools. It's beginning to get me down."

He was winding up like a clock.

"You're a real-estate man," Angers said. "And that's all I need. Now, turn around."

Bourney slowed the car, backed into a drive, and turned around, and we started off toward the bay. You could feel his terror.

We drew up alongside the park. The stretch of land Angers had been speaking of was right across the street. Bourney didn't move. He held to the wheel and sat there, staring straight ahead.

"Get your flashlight," Angers said. "I want to take a good look at this."

Nobody moved. Lillian tightened her grip on my hand and her hand was cold and sweaty again. She felt cold all over.

"Here," Bourney said.

He held the flashlight over the back of the seat, without turning around. "You take it. I won't get out, I'll wait here. I'll run over some of these listings, case you don't want this."

"Come on and bring the flash," Angers said. "Steve, open your door. Let's go."

I opened the door and Lillian got out after me. Angers was right behind us with the gun in his hand now.

"Come on, Mr. Bourney," he said.

Bourney didn't look up. He opened his door and climbed out with the flashlight in his hand. He looked like hell under the street lights. He was perspiring, the water was streaming from every pore in his body. He was a wreck. His face seemed to have aged in these past few moments, his eyes and mouth haggard and forlorn. He was so entirely overcome with fright he could hardly stand.

He grabbed my arm. "Please," he said. "You're a right guy. Tell him to let me go. And she—" He shrank back against the car, his eyes batting around, watching all of us. His face was as pale as Angers'.

"I've got to get home," he said. "My wife won't know where I am."

A car went swiftly by on the street and he turned wildly toward it, holding himself against his car.

"Across the street," Angers said. "Come on."

Bourney started walking around the car. He started across the street with the flashlight in one hand. We all went across the street. Angers carried his big roll of blueprints and the gun.

We stood on the sidewalk in front of the immense "For Sale" sign with Kennely's name on it.

"There you are," Bourney said. "Right there."

He wouldn't look at any of us now. He couldn't bring himself to.

"This is something," Angers said. "This looks good." He turned to me. "Steve, just look over there at the park and the bay. It's perfect."

"I'm glad."

"Yes, pal, this looks as if it might be it. Here," he said, turning to Bourney. "Shine that light. Let's go in here and look around."

Bourney seemed to shrink from going in there. He didn't actually move, but you could feel it. I felt the same way, and Lillian said, "Can I wait here, Ralph, honey?"

"No. We'll all go in there," Angers said.

It was a jungle. The grass was waist-high and trees of all kinds grew in wild jungle havoc on the property. Somebody had probably bought this many, many years ago and hung onto it, not selling. The city had sprung up all around it. Now they wanted to sell and it was really something to see. To the right it ended in a forest that pushed right up against the street across from the dark, gleaming waters of the bayou. Far down to the left, blocks distant, were large apartment buildings looming against the sky. They were closed down now, for the summer months. All around it was dark, save for the street lights, which wouldn't help in there. Nothing could be seen through the trees toward the other side of the property. It was dark, dreary, dismal, and frightening.

"We'll look it over now," Angers said. "I want to make up my mind tonight."

"I'm not going in there," Bourney said. "Snakes. I'm not going in, I tell you."

"Sure," Angers said. "Pal, take that light from the man and bring him along. We're going to look around."

I took the flash from Bourney's listless fingers.

"You want to get me in there," he said. "That's what you want."

I looked at him. Even the way things were, I didn't like him. He had no more guts than a snail and he was likely to talk himself straight into trouble. I didn't want that to happen.

"I'll—I'll tear my stockings," Lillian said.

I looked at her, trying to warn her. She should know better than to antagonize the guy. But she couldn't help it, I knew. It was getting too much for me, too.

Bourney started walking straight into the grass. We all moved along after him, me with the light. I flashed it around as best I could and I hoped Angers was seeing what he wanted. It was brighter in here than I had supposed. The moon was blossoming in the sky and everything was a cold-looking gray. But I kept the light lit just the same. Angers was close to Lillian and me and Bourney walked stolidly through the grass and into the trees. Where the trees were, there wasn't so much grass.

"Can't see much," Angers said. "Let's walk through to the other side. How wide is this?" he asked Bourney.

"I don't know."

"What's the price?" Angers asked him.

Bourney turned and looked at us. He looked as crazy as Angers sometimes did. His eyes had that crazy look, as if he was haunted. "My cigars are back in the car," he said. "I've got to have a cigar." His mouth got crafty. "I couldn't go along without a smoke."

Angers stepped up close to him, reached out, and pulled a cigar from the man's shirt pocket. He jammed it at Bourney's mouth and it stuck there. Bourney reached into his pocket, brought out a lighter, lit up. He blew smoke skyward and the crafty look was all through him. It began to shine from his eyes. We were in the middle of the property now, standing under some young oak trees that dripped a scattering of moss. All around us the crickets chirped.

"Going to build a hospital, eh?"

"That's right," Angers said. He seemed suddenly pleased.

"Good place for a hospital," Bourney said. He drew on his cigar, puffing smoke.

Lillian stepped over closer to me, watching. She glanced at me and shook her head, puzzled. I didn't like the way Bourney was acting. Lillian's hand found mine, squeezed, went away again.

"It's going to be wonderful," Angers said. "These are the blueprints." He tapped the roll of paper with the gun muzzle.

"Well, well," Bourney said. Some of the perspiration on his face was beginning to dry. "Well, well," he said. "A hospital. Think of it."

Angers looked at him.

"All you folks going to build hospitals, huh?"

I got it. He was assuming we would play along with him. He was going to humor this guy. That's what he was going to do. He'd heard Angers was batty, so he'd worked up his nerve and he was going to play along with it. I looked at him, trying to warn him, knowing how useless it was.

"Y'know, that's a smart move, building a hospital out here. Nice, eh?" He smoked. Angers watched him.

"Hadn't we better look around some more?" Lillian said.

"No," Angers said. "Just wait a minute. Mr. Bourney interests me."

Bourney sensed something.

"Go on, Mr. Bourney," Angers said. "Tell me some more about it, will you?"

Bourney shrugged. "Just I think it's a fine idea. I really do."

"They sent you, didn't they?" Angers said flatly.

"Sent me?"

"They sent you after me, didn't they? They thought you could stop me, didn't they? With your talk."

"Ralph," I said. "This is the real-estate man, remember?"

"Sure, pal. I remember a lot of things. That's what they told me back there. 'Go home, Ralph—sleep it off,' they told me. 'Take a rest, Ralph.' They didn't want me around, because they knew I was the one man who could get it done—get that hospital built. See?"

"Oh, please," Lillian said. It came past her lips, a prayer. "Ralph," she said, "let's look around."

"We are," Angers said softly.

"Maybe that's what you should do," Bourney said. "Why don't you sleep on it tonight? We could come back in the morning. You can't build a hospital—"

The gun exploded. Twice, three times it roared in the darkness. I'd had the flashlight on Bourney, turning it there inadvertently as he spoke. A slug caught him in the head, the other two in the chest, and he sat down with the cigar in his mouth, and died.

Chapter Seventeen

The echo of the shots struck the apartment buildings down there and rattled back into the night. The sound rippled out across the park and the bay and then it was quite still. The crickets had ceased. Then slowly, one by one, they picked up their chorus again.

"Let's go back to the car," Angers said. "There's no use standing around here."

Lillian was looking down at the dead man. She had both hands to her face and it was as if she couldn't bring her gaze away from down there.

The cigar smoldered in the grass.

"Bring the flashlight, pal. We might need it." He didn't look at Bourney, lying there on the grass. It made you want to do something, but there wasn't anything you could do. Unless you were anxious to be there with Bourney. The gun dangled from Angers' arm like an extra hand.

Lillian turned slowly, still staring, as if it were impossible to believe. It wasn't.

"They sent him," Angers said. "That's what they did. It was probably Dr. Bernstein. He sent him, no doubt. Bernstein always was telling me to take it easy, always telling me I had the wrong slant on the matter. He's the one who said I was crazy when I talked about transplanting the whole eye. Just because it hasn't been done successfully—because the books say no. Well, they don't know. But I do."

We started back through the grass. He was through with looking at the property. It wasn't even in his head any more.

"So Bernstein sent him. Tom Bourney." He shot some of that crazed laughter into the night. It was as if he spat it out of him. "He had me fooled, all right."

Lillian and I walked together, letting him talk.

"The things we did out there," he said. "We did things right there on the battlefield that you'd never believe possible. With nothing, nothing. We performed miracles. I did. I performed all sorts of miracles. Right in the mud there, with all the blood. And they say I can't—" He stopped.

It was becoming much worse. He hadn't acted this way before. I was beginning to understand a bit more about Angers, but what good was that?

"Pal," he said, "we've got a car now. I'll have to wire them soon for some money."

"Yes."

"They'll send me all I need."

"Sure," I said. "You'll need plenty, won't you?"

We came out onto the sidewalk. We were all covered with beggar lice and sandspurs. A car rolled by along the street and a woman's laughter trailed heady and rich in the soft winds coming across the bay full of salt and fish and freedom. We went on across the street toward the car.

"You know," he said, "I've been giving a lot of thought to what you told me about this fellow who owns the boat. What was his name? Aldercook?"

"Yes. Forget it."

"Can't forget him, pal. I've been through lots of that sort of thing, pal. I want to meet him. Bernstein was that kind of guy."

"Never mind," I said. "Forget it. It's nothing."

"I want to meet him. Now. You said he had a boat, didn't you?"

We reached the car. Lillian stepped up onto the curb and looked at me. I didn't know what to do. I hoped she was going to be able to stand up under this a little longer. She looked numb, unreceptive.

"Listen," I said, turning to Angers. "Why don't you show me the blueprints? We could go someplace and you could show them to me, tell me all about the hospital. Why don't we do that?"

He shook his head, grinning quietly. "No, pal. I want to meet your friend. Let's go."

I looked over beyond him, across the street, at the silent stretch of choking weeds and jungle over there. I wondered how long it would be before somebody found Bourney.

It might depend on the sun.

Driving to the yacht basin where the Rabbit-O was moored was like rolling along in a trance. Lillian and I were in the front seat of Bourney's car, with me driving again. It was somehow like earlier this evening. And we'd been on the same street, between the palms, with the bay and Tampa far across the waters, lighting up the night sky. Only that was long ago. It was before true consciousness; before you could understand reality and what you were really up against.

I knew it was only a matter of time before he turned the gun on us. I couldn't figure what had kept him from killing both of us long before. A whim. It would be little more than a whim when one of us finally faced the muzzle of the Lüger and saw the flame and felt the slug.

There would be no warning. There had been no warning for the others. I don't believe any of them knew what was going to happen. Except the cop. He knew. I still remembered the expression on his face; the suddenly patient return to memory because it was all up with him and he knew it. So he stood there and took his time. Remembering.

I would never forget the expression on that cop's face.

Now we were returning on the outside of the vicious circle of events that had started with Harvey Aldercook on a morning so long ago. It was a morning when I had no more to worry about than the possibility of raising some cash so I could buy food, and assure myself that Ruby would have the very best of care at the hospital while she had our baby.

What a Ruby she was! I didn't like to think about it, but I couldn't help it. I wondered if I still had her. I tried not to remember Bill Watts on the TV screen, saying I was needed at the hospital. What could it have been for? Whatever it was, the time was long past.

We turned down onto the pier by the yacht basin and I parked the car by the curb in front of the slip where the Rabbit-O was moored. A radio pounded from someplace, wild, throbbing music.

"We here already?" Angers said.

"Yes, this is it."

"Good."

Lillian stared straight ahead through the windshield. She had her hands folded in her lap and she seemed resigned now. She no longer spoke much and she seemed somehow disinterested.

I looked over toward the Rabbit-O and I didn't like what I saw and heard.

Angers was leaning against the back of the front seat, and as I turned my head to speak to him, the gun wasn't more than an inch from my face.

"Listen," I said. "They're having a party."

"Fine."

"No. It's not fine. There'll be too many people there, Ralph. Suppose we go get a room someplace, get some sleep. We all need sleep."

He said nothing. Lillian just sat there, staring straight ahead. I had hoped she would join me in trying to persuade him.

"We need rest," I said. "We don't want to go on the boat now. We could come back here first thing in the morning."

"Pal, first things first, and I want to meet him."

"But why? What the hell difference does it make?"

"He owes you some money, you said."

"Forget that."

"He owes you two hundred and seventy dollars, doesn't he?"

I turned back and looked at my hands on the steering wheel. I had tried, hadn't I? What else could I do?

We opened the wooden gate on the slip and started along the wooden pier. Lillian hadn't said a word for a long time. She just went along with it. Maybe that was a good thing; I didn't know.

Angers came along with his roll of paper under one arm, as always, and his gun in his hand.

"She's a nice-looking boat," he said.

"Yeah."

They were having a party all right. And that's where the music came from. Down there inside the Rabbit-O. Through the windows and out on the stern deck were several men and women, all in various stages of undress and alcoholism. Up on the bow in the shadows lay a man and woman close together, both holding glasses, both in swimming suits. They apparently didn't notice us as we passed toward the stern.

I caught a glimpse of Harvey Aldercook coming through the cabin with a bottle in his hand. There must have been about six couples.

On the boat on the other side of the pier a man was sitting in a rocking chair, smoking, with a dog lying at his feet. He had figured probably that he wouldn't get any sleep tonight. He looked at us, but it meant nothing. Even seeing the gun probably wouldn't have bothered him any, because this was the way to the Rabbit-O.

I didn't see anything of Spindleshanks. You couldn't tell about women. They might look like cardboard dolls and at the same time be the hottest nymph that ever backed into a mattress. But I could still remember how she'd cringed against the wheel of the Rabbit-O, frightened out of her wits because I was a nasty old man. What in hell was Harvey? That was a good question.

"Let's go aboard," Angers said. His voice right there by my ear startled me.

Just then a woman seated against the stern steps leading to the deck looked up and saw us.

"Harvey," she called. "Here's somebody new." She craned her neck, looking us over, and she saw the gun and called, "Bandits, Harvey. I mean pirates. They're going to board the ship."

She stood up. She was the only girl aboard who was wearing a skirt. It was some skirt. Every color there was had been splashed on a very thin cloth, which she then fastened to her naked body. She wore a handkerchief of the same material around her breasts and she was a redhead.

"What?" Harvey Aldercook said. He stepped through the cabin doorway with a glass in his hand. He looked up and saw us and the glass dropped from his hand and shattered at his feet.

He knew.

"No," Harvey said. "No."

"Jump aboard," Angers said. He gave Lillian a push and she landed on the gunwale. She leaped and went to her knees on the deck, by Aldercook. He stared at her, kind of shrinking back into the cabin doorway.

"Go on, pal," Angers said.

"It's them," Harvey said. "It's them!"

"Who, Harvey? Who d'you mean?" the redhead said. Two men came up behind Harvey and looked over his shoulder.

We went down onto the deck and Angers leaned against the stern of the boat by the bait wells that never got used and looked at them.

"Tell those folks up front to come back here. That man and woman up front—on the bow," Angers said. He said it to Harvey Aldercook.

Aldercook looked exactly as he had this morning. In the same pants and sweat shirt, with the yachting cap.

"Wilma," he called. "Wilma and Jack—come on back here."

"Ah, go take a leap," a man said from up there.

"Hurry up," he said. "Something's happened."

"Something's happened up here, too."

"Get him back here," Angers said. "And turn off that radio." He turned to me. "That is him, isn't it, pal?"

"Yes," I said. "That's right."

Aldercook hadn't moved from the cabin doorway. He turned his head and said, "Somebody shut that damned radio off." Then he looked at Angers again. It was as if he were mesmerized.

Angers stood leaning there against the stern by the bait wells with the gun in his hand. Somebody shut the radio off and it was very still. Jack and Wilma came around and jumped down into the stern.

"What the hell is this?" Jack said.

Wilma just grinned behind smeared make-up, her blonde hair tousled. She was a little crocked.

"Now," Angers said. "Everybody get inside there."

Somebody laughed. First a man laughed from inside the cabin there, then a woman began laughing. They both laughed. It was very funny and Harvey stood in the cabin doorway watching us. He didn't know what to do or say.

I didn't enjoy it. Maybe I should have, but I didn't.

Jack and Wilma caught the fact that there was something in the wind, but they didn't know who we were. Neither did the redhead, but she knew something was up, too. All three tried to get by Harvey into the cabin. The rest of them inside were by the door, trying to see what was going on. The man and woman kept on talking and laughing.

"Get inside," Angers said quietly.

"Steve," Harvey said. "What do you want?"

I didn't say anything. Just then I heard her squeal. It was Spindleshanks. She was peering through the screened window looking aft from the cabin. She said, "It's that Logan!" She whirled from the window and started frantically telling everybody who we were. Harvey and she must have spent a nice day, following us around by radio. Reading the newspapers about how I was probably dead must have been a pleasure. He wasn't happy, now, though.

The place in there got very quiet all of a sudden. Lillian pushed by Aldercook and went into the cabin. Angers didn't move.

"I wanted to meet you," he said to Harvey. "Go on inside," he told him. He stepped toward Harvey. Harvey faded back into the cabin.

There were six couples, as I'd thought. The redhead was nearest the door, sitting on a couch. Two men were very drunk, but conscious of what was going on, and they were sorry they were drunk. One stood over by the wheel housing, the other by the companionway leading into the foreward cabin where the bunks were.

Everybody was quiet and nobody spoke. But they looked plenty.

Two men sat with their women in a small booth, a kind of breakfast nook. They avoided our eyes. Harvey faded on back until he was in the middle of the main cabin. The rest of the women, with Jack, were on the couch, stacked together in a welter of flesh. Lillian went over and sat on the arm of the couch and stared at the floor. Spindleshanks was beside her and one of the women began to cry.

"You know who we are, don't you?" Angers said, looking around.

I sat down on the edge of one of the benches in the breakfast nook and looked up at him. He stood in the cabin doorway with his roll of paper and the damned gun. Well, he couldn't shoot them all. If he started shooting now, somebody would get him, because the shells would run out. He wouldn't have a chance to reload. My God, I hoped he wouldn't start to shoot.

"You owe my friend some money," Angers said to Harvey.

"I—I do? Do I?" Harvey began smiling all over. "Well, now, is that it?" he said.

"That's not it," I said. "But for God's sake, use your head."

"He just stands there," one of the women whispered.

"He's crazy," another whispered. "He's going to kill us."

The one that was crying began wailing. She was a large woman, very lush and sexy-looking, dressed in a tight white two-piece bathing suit. She had an enormous quantity of jet-black hair. Her breasts swelled and she wailed and it looked very silly, somehow. She had her eyes wide open, wailing.

For the first time, just then, I noticed Harvey's nose. It wasn't bandaged, he probably couldn't stand marring his beauty with a bandage, and there were no bruises that showed. But his nose wasn't right. It was a little off center, and I remembered how it had felt against my knee. He was running around with a broken nose, without any bandage, for the sake of a party.

"My friend here," Angers said, "wants two hundred and seventy dollars. That's what you owe him, isn't it?"

"Sure, sure," Harvey said.

"Come up here," Angers said. "Come here."

Aldercook walked slowly up to Angers and Angers stood there looking at him.

"Why didn't you pay Steve what you owed him?" Angers said.

"Why …" Harvey tried to keep his voice level. It didn't look as if anything was going to happen to him. This guy Angers wasn't so bad, after all. A little pale, maybe, that's all. Maybe most of these stories were the bunk. Who really knew? I could see that's how his mind was working. He couldn't help it because he was born like that.

"Tell me about it," Angers said. "I want to know. You see, Steve saved my life today, and he's my pal. We're buddies and buddies stick together. I want to know why you didn't pay him the money you owed him."

A woman laughed. It was Wilma. It wasn't funny laughter, it was the tense laughter of nervous release. She sat there very tight and stiff and sober-looking now, and the laughter simply burst out of her face. It was the same kind of laughter that erupted from Angers once in a while, only not quite so mad.

"Tell me," he said.

She did it again. He looked over at her and she looked at him and she laughed right in his face. It was pretty bad. She was trying to control herself but it didn't work. She kept looking at him and laughing. She roared with it. It rocked her and the other woman kept on crying while she sat there looking at Angers, trying with all her might not to laugh.

"It's real funny, isn't it?" Angers said.

I felt Lillian's eyes on me. Her eyes smiled a little at me, wrinkling up at their corners. And I knew something. She had given up. All the way.

Harvey wasn't as scared as he had been because Angers seemed so calm.

"I think this money business should be between Steve and me," Harvey said.

"Do you?"

"Yes. Why are you here?"

"I wanted to meet you. I want that money. I want you to give it to Steve, so your friends can see. I want your friends to see what kind of a man you are."

That got him a little. He didn't like it and it scared him just a little.

He took out his wallet and counted out two hundred and seventy dollars from a wad of greenbacks that swelled the wallet so much it didn't close right. That's the kind of guy he was. He laid the money on the little table in front of me and the two men and the two girls looked at it. Everybody watched Harvey now.

"There," Harvey said. "There's the money."

"It's not enough," Angers said.

Harvey looked at him.

"It's not enough for the kind of job he did," Angers said. He turned to me, holding the gun. "Is it, Steve?"

I didn't answer him. I just sat there. I could feel all the tension and I looked up at the cabin window and the man who had been sitting in the rocking chair was standing up there on the wooden pier. He was trying very hard to act nonchalant, as if he were just out walking his dog. Only it wasn't that. He stood up there kind of watching us through the cabin window. Then I got it. He was watching the street out there, too.

I began to perspire.

The man took two steps toward the street, watching, then two steps back again, still watching. He was very nervous, trying not to show it. He was a big man, dressed in shorts, smoking a pipe. Every time he took a step, the dog took a couple and sat down. The dog was a cocker.

The woman who had been crying was sniffling now.

"How much money have you there?" Angers said.

Harvey looked at his wallet, just held it in his hand and looked at it.

"Take it out and count it," Angers said.

One of the men in the booth where I was saw the man up on the pier. He looked away immediately, then glanced at me. I nodded my head slightly.

I had a friend. It felt great. It was a fine sensation. The best in a long while. This bird in the booth knew what was going on, he'd got it straight, and he wasn't brave and he wasn't a dope, either. He was my friend. I could depend on him if anything happened.

So what good did it do?

Harvey counted the money in the wallet and said, "There's two hundred and fourteen dollars here."

"Put it with the other and we'll call it all right," Angers said.

Harvey did as Angers said. He looked at me sitting there and there was no expression on his face. He was scared all over again now.

"See, pal?" Angers said.

I didn't say anything.

"Take the money, pal," Angers said. "There's four hundred and eighty-four dollars there. I figure that's about right for a job of this kind, don't you?"

I didn't want to take the money. Harvey watched me. He didn't want to look at Angers any more. Only Angers wasn't through with him.

"That's the kind of friend you have," he told the people in the cabin. "Isn't he a nice guy, though?"

Harvey stood there with the empty wallet in his hand and swallowed. He looked around at them all and smiled a sickly smile and nobody smiled back. Then he had to look at Angers again, he had to, standing there with the wallet in his hand.

"Now," Angers said, "I want you to get a piece of paper and a pencil and write out on it that you paid Steve that money for the work you had him do. And I want you to sign it with your name."

"This is foolish," Harvey said.

"Is it?"

The man in the booth, my friend, pushed a pad of paper across the table, took a pencil from the pocket of his sport shirt, and laid it by the pad.

"Go ahead, Harve," he said. "Do like the man says."

"Sure, sure," Harvey said. He wrote fast on the paper and signed his name. Then he laid the pad down and tore off the top sheet and put it with the money. "There," he said, looking at me. "But you couldn't do it alone, could you? I threw you off the boat and now you've got to get a friend." He pushed the money and the note over to me.

I felt sorry for the guy. He couldn't help getting his oar in.

"Feel of your nose," I said. "How did you cover up the swelling?"

"Pick up the money, pal," Angers said.

I took the money and the note and shoved it all into my pants pocket in a wad. As I did that, I glanced up at the pier. The man out there was still watching us and watching the street out there. I was positive he had called the law. He'd heard what was going on and the cops could be here any minute. I prayed for that, but at the same time I didn't know whether it was the right thing.

If they came now and started shooting it would be plain mayhem.

"Lillian," Angers said. "Come here."

Lillian got up from the arm of the couch and went over by Angers. She acted as if she were in a dream. Everybody watched her cross the cabin. Harvey just stood there, staring at Angers, and I saw my friend look up at the pier again.

Then everything went sour inside me, because Angers saw him look, too. And the guy out there saw it happening. He saw Angers turn his head and stare out the cabin window at him and he froze. Oh, it was grand. The guy out there froze solid and the cabin lights shone on his guilty face.

You could almost see it come into Angers. The understanding of what was going on. I was glad it wasn't me Angers had noticed.

"Well," he said. "Pal, we're leaving now."

Harvey began to tremble. His throat and chin were fleshy, bloated, and the flesh trembled.

The woman who had been sniffling fainted. She just collapsed, and spread back on the couch, and fell over against Wilma. Wilma began laughing again. It was a kind of snicker, from the side of her mouth. She tried to keep her mouth closed, but it wouldn't work. The woman who had fainted finally sprawled down into Wilma's lap, out cold. Wilma kept on snickering.

"Look," the man in the booth by me said. "Why don't we all have a drink on it?"

He was going to be brave. He had to. I suppose he felt it was the only thing to do. He was the one man in the whole room who understood the score. You could tell it in his face and now he was going to be brave.

"Harve," he said, "why don't you fix these folks a drink?"

"We have to go," Angers said, looking at the man.

I stood up and looked at the man, too. "Forget it," I said.

He understood, all right, but something inside him kept egging him along. "Hell," he said, "we could make this a real party. We could take the boat out, couldn't we, Harve?"

I knew then that he'd been drinking a lot, this guy, and maybe that accounted for the way he was acting.

"Come on, pal," Angers said. "We're leaving."

"Sure."

We'd only been here a few minutes and the guy who was trying to detain us knew that if we'd stay a little while longer, the cops would be here. I knew that, too. But he didn't understand Angers. He hadn't seen Angers work with that Luger.

I didn't dare look out the cabin window now. I didn't know whether the man was still out there with his dog or not.

Angers pulled the cabin door open and motioned us outside. Nobody said a word. It had been a bad time so far and I was drenched with perspiration.

The guy in the booth knew Angers was wise and Angers kept looking at him as he closed the cabin door. It was a screen door, and everybody sat inside watching us. You could feel the breeze outside.

"Lillian," Angers said, "I want you to go back in there."

She looked at him. Her eyes were numb. She didn't speak.

"Go on," he said.

She walked back into the cabin.

"All right, pal. Up on the pier. Go ahead now."

I went up the steps and jumped onto the pier. The man was getting aboard his boat with his dog in his arms. Angers came up behind me.

"Out to the car, pal," he said. "Hurry up."

As we went past the Rabbit-O, I glanced down into the cabin, and they were all sitting there, just as we'd left them. Harvey and Lillian were standing in the middle of the cabin. Their eyes followed us along the pier.

"Run," Angers said behind me. "We haven't much time, pal, and this can't be botched now."

We went past the guy with his dog and Angers didn't even look at him. On the street there was no sign of the police.

As we reached the stretch of grass by the curb, Angers grabbed my arm.

"We may run into some trouble, pal. Stick by me, will you?"

I looked at him. I didn't say anything. I couldn't. After all, he believed in all the things he was doing and he at least half believed in me.

Down there in the cabin it had meant a lot, momentarily, to know that I had a friend in the crowd who understood what was going on. Well, I got to thinking how Angers must be with his mucked-up mind and everything.

"What about Lil?" I said.

"To hell with Lil," he said. "Get in the car."

I got in beneath the wheel of the car and Angers slammed his door and turned to look at me. He set the roll of paper on the floor between his knees and sat there with the gun in his fist.

"I think somebody called the police," he said. "I just feel it. I saw something."

I didn't say anything. I tried to stall as long as I could. I didn't start the car. Maybe we were both wrong.

"You've got to stick with me, pal," he said.

"Sure."

"Start the car, then. We've got to get out of here."

I stepped on the gas and knew the fellow on the boat next to the Rabbit-O had missed his chance. He should have fixed this car. He hadn't. It ran fine.

"Turn around right here," Angers said.

I thought of Lillian back there with them and what she would do now. She was out of it, anyway. She was safe.

"I didn't like letting Lil go," Angers said. "But what could I do? Anything could happen and I don't want her hurt."

I glanced at him.

Somebody yelled nearby. It was the man with the dog. He was running out on the wooden pier toward the slip gate as I made a U turn. He ran out into the street, waving his arms and yelling as loud as he could. The dog bounded along beside him.

"I was right," Angers said.

Up at the head of the pier, a police car turned off the intersecting street and started down toward us, moving slowly. The man was in the street, yelling and pointing at us.

"Step on it," Angers said. "They've seen us."

I heard a shot and saw it was Angers with the Luger. He was leaning out of the window and he had fired just once at the man back there. I didn't know whether he'd hit him or not. I couldn't see back there.

The police car kept coming and I saw fire leap from the window and heard the sound of another shot. Then we were past them and they were turning. Another police car came around the corner up there.

"Turn to the right," Angers said. "And drive as fast as you can, pal."

He didn't have to tell me. I didn't want to get it, not yet. Not while there was still a chance. I was in the middle and I knew it and I didn't like it.

"We've got to get away from them," he said. "We've got to, Steve. You hear?"

"I'm doing all I can."

We went around the corner fast and the sirens were beginning now. It was a sound I'd been waiting for a long time. Now that I heard them, really close, I didn't want to hear them. I knew Lillian was listening back there. I wondered what she thought.

I began to drive, let me tell you.

Chapter Eighteen

I did not want it to end this way.

It wouldn't be right if they got me, too. Because they would, I could feel it. But that wasn't the only reason for the way I felt. It wasn't sudden, either; it had been coming on me for a while now and I knew it was the right thing. Two of us were against all of them and I knew that's the way it was going to be. But all the time I knew how wrong that was.

It was wrong for him. He was trying to accomplish something he believed in. He had an aim, a deep-seated one, and to him it was as right as the sun in the morning. Maybe you can't grasp that, understand it. But it was how I believed.

He was doing something he thought was right.

And I wanted to see Ruby. God, how I wanted that! Things had changed, blurred. I wanted to see her just once more—alive, happy.

I don't know. I'd been going along with this guy, wanting to get him if I could, wanting to get away from him, and I hadn't been understanding it right, either. Sure. But he hadn't killed me. Had he? Well, I'd be happy if he could get away from them. I knew that now. Maybe he'd taught me something I couldn't put into words; I don't know.

I settled down to driving as I'd never driven before. It wasn't wild; it was determined effort to get away. I'd flash a glance at him and he'd be sitting there, watching me, kind of nodding, with the gun on his knee.

He half believed in me, as I say, and it was hell knowing that. Maybe he believed in me all the way. I was his pal. And you could never explain it to him now. There was no straightening this out.

They were after both of us.

"You're doing fine, Steve," he said between the wails of the sirens not far behind us. "Just don't get rattled. You got nerve, pal."

"Thanks. We're going to need it."

We came down past the Vinoy Yacht Basin and I wheeled her left around in front of the Vinoy Hotel sitting up against the paler night sky like a huge black monster without eyes, wearing a top hat. We headed straight for town.

They came along back there, three of them, three cars, all with their sirens moaning and wailing, and it was fine.

Nobody but Lillian and I would ever really know how it was. We were the only ones, and how could you explain it? It came on you slowly.

If you can't feel it, you can't, but there was a sadness there. It kept coming up on me, getting into my mouth, like the taste of bright metal, dry and cold....

Stop lights didn't mean anything, and probably the whole town knew about it by now. We came whispering up the street from the bay side, passing through a residential section, and you could see the people on the lawns, flashing by like white-faced posts with stiff arms.

I took another left, then the first right into an alley beyond a store front. We went through that alley bouncing on the bricks and sliding a little in wet places and 'way ahead you could see it was a dead end, but a driveway turned right, so I took that and boomed along rutted shell and out into a street again.

We were on one of the main streets, heading west, and I opened her up, right down the middle of the street, with cars peeling off to the right and left as we came along.

"You're never going to be able to build the hospital in this town," I said, not looking at him. "You know that, don't you?"

"Yes. I know that now."

"What are you going to do?"

"I don't know, Steve, but I'm going to build the hospital."

I drove a while, getting through some thick traffic that was trying just as hard to keep out of the way. Behind us the wail of sirens began getting loud again. That alley had flipped them for a moment and I knew I could lose them. If I drove her right and used my head and didn't lose my nerve and didn't get rattled. Then I could lose them.

We weren't going awfully fast.

"They'd get us outside town," I said.

"I know it."

"You don't want them to get us, do you, Ralph?"

"No. I'm just thinking about Lillian."

You can say what you want about cases like this. They've got feelings. It's just they're cockeyed on one thing and killing is a blind means. Or maybe like when you brush that fly off your arm next time. Remember it.

Well, it's perspective. It's seeing things one way or seeing them another. I knew. It's believing. It's believing so hard in one thing that you become blind except in one direction. And it doesn't matter whether the direction is good or bad, because it's what you're blind to that really matters.

It's a funny thing, but that's the way it works. Try it and see.

Only he was affected by criticism, too.

Only what would have happened if Ralph Angers had been allowed from the very beginning to build his hospital and attempt to satisfy himself about transplanting the human eye?

We came onto Ninth Street and I turned left into traffic and went along the middle of the street. It was a good bet, because of the traffic. It would slow us, maybe, but it would slow them still more.

"Steve," Angers said, "I'm counting on you. I can't drive, you know. Never learned. I was always too busy. Even during the war."

"We can't head into the country," I said. "They'd get us sure, so we've got to lose them here in town."

He didn't say anything.

"I know the town pretty good," I told him.

"I can't help thinking about Lillian," he said.

"She'll be all right."

"I know it."

"Then don't worry."

We both saw the police car on the corner up ahead. It was nosing out into the street from a cross street, only some cars were in the way because of a stop signal. I went right on by and you could see them looking at us.

They couldn't shoot, either, because of the other cars and the people on the street.

"I'm not worrying," he said. "I'm thinking about your eye, too, Steve."

"Never mind that."

I was driving carefully and easily. If you get in a sweat, things don't go so well. Bourney's car was swell and for an instant I saw him back there, in my mind, lying on the grass with his cigar.

"I want you to know something," Angers said.

I wheeled right, off Ninth, and the sirens got faint because of the buildings. I knew they were back there and that they'd seen where we turned. I took it sharp into an alley, then right into another alley, then left again, and we were on a dirt road right in the middle of town, bouncing all over the place, downhill. I opened her up and we stuck in the ruts fine going down through there and the sirens were very faint now and I heard them going on up the street. They had missed the alley.

We came out of the dirt road going uphill, and over a bridge by some big trees, and the car lights swirled on the trees among the leaves and it looked peaceful, like driving on a summer's night in the country.

Then we came out onto a main street again, bounding up off the dirt onto the pavement. A police car went by, going like hell, and they saw us.

I slammed the car out of there with the sound of the police car's screaming tires, and as we went off away, I saw them coming around in a wild U turn that took them over the curb and across a funeral parlor's front lawn and under a canopy by the sidewalk. Their siren started.

I went left off the street and we were in a residential section again. I really rode it now, hanging on, and letting Bourney's car do whatever it could.

"Steve?"

"Sure, sure."

"Tell you something."

I shot a glance at him and he hadn't moved. He was still sitting like that, with the gun on his knee, as if he were dreaming. Sure, I was afraid of him. Right now he might shoot me, just like that.

"What?"

"That eye of yours."

"Forget the eye!"

"No, Steve. If something isn't done about that eye of yours, you know what's going to happen?"

I didn't answer. I was too busy with the wheel on this brick street. The street had been laid perhaps twenty-five years before and the bricks were loose and it was pocked with potholes and it was bad. The car drummed like a machine gun, the wheel going in a tight mad staccato.

"You'll go blind in one eye," Angers said. "I'm not kidding you, pal.

That's the way it is. I know. Maybe both eyes. Sympathetic reaction."

I heard him but it didn't touch me. Not then, anyway. I didn't feel sympathetic, so I kept quiet, and he didn't say any more, either. Not about that.

"I haven't forgotten," he said.

"All right."

"I want you to know, pal," he said. "I'll never forget, and when things were a little tight today— Well, you know how it is, pal. Everything depends on what I'm doing. It's important. Only I want you to know I haven't forgotten how you saved my life, pal. There wouldn't have been any hospital if you hadn't come along."

Now he had the hospital all built.

"I'd like to make you my first patient," he said.

I wanted to tell him to shut it off. It was getting to me. Everything was getting to me, from every angle, angles he couldn't or wouldn't see.

Ruby, Ruby, I thought. What a Ruby you are!

I was crying, sitting there behind that wheel, crying and driving like hell. Because it was getting to me from every angle about everything and it was all cockeyed and mixed up with wanting to reach Ruby, and this guy believing what he believed....

The police car wasn't closing in like it should. Then I heard why. Up there ahead of us someplace the sirens were converging and we were cut off. They had a radio and they used it.

"We're going to stop," I said.

"We'll have to, won't we, pal?"

"Yes. Right up ahead there. We'll run for it."

I glanced over at him and he was loading the clip for the Luger, slipping the gleaming brass shells in, *tick, tick, tick.*

I thought of wrecking the car, trusting luck to pull me out of it. But I wanted to live too much. I couldn't do it, and by the time I had her slowed down, he went *snickety-smack* with the slide and was waiting, with the Luger all ready.

We were in a fine section of town. For maybe a mile square there was nothing but scrap heaps, junk yards, factories old and new, demolished and in process of building, railroad yards stringing through everything.

I drove the car up a long cement ramp into a huge empty barn made of sheet metal. From the ceiling of the barn hung a single electric light bulb. Yellow light from the bulb didn't reach the distant walls and barely touched the floor.

"Let's go, pal," Angers said.

We climbed out of the car and stood there a moment. He had his big roll of blueprints that I'd never seen. They were under his arm again. He looked almost as he'd been this morning except that his beard had grown. That was all.

You could hear the sirens, plain.

We started walking toward the back of the barn, where a pale rectangle of light showed there was a door. We came out onto some railroad tracks and started running across toward what looked like a black tunnel.

Chapter Nineteen

There was no tunnel. It was a board fence and its shadow was deceiving. We came along that to where it ended, and turned behind it into a junk yard. In the moonlight were the bodies of old cars stacked ten and fifteen high, like layers of steel cake. It was a morgue for old cars that were waiting to be buried.

"Let's go on through," Angers said.

Back there the sirens came into the barn and you could hear men running. I looked at him and he was watching me. All around us, now, hovered the dark hulks of buildings. Fences and girders and smokestacks spouting sputtering embers into the night.

"We've got to hide," he said. "We've got to make it, pal." His voice was flat and even and all this time there had never been the slightest expression on that face.

A single siren moaned up to the left, then ceased, and two car doors slammed.

"They're coming after us," I said.

"Yes."

"They'll surround the place. But it's a big place."

He didn't say anything. He touched my arm and we started walking through the yard, down aisles between the stacked cars. It was very quiet, and far off to the left, coming from somewhere you couldn't see, was the sudden hiss and white glare of a welding torch. It flared and hissed and steel clanged and banged. Shadows stood out in stark black shapes. The white glare shot up fanlike into the darkness, cutting it just like metal. A brilliant shower of bright white sparks arced up and over onto the stacked cars.

We went down along the dirt yard, walking through puddles of water and through a gate in a board fence.

We were in an alley. Over across the way was an immense building, girders sticking up, corrugated iron sides riffling the shadows as the torch flared.

Two men were working in there, making steel ladders. They wore what looked like diving suits and helmets with glass facepieces, not just the helmets themselves. A furnace was roaring in there. A man shoveled coal into the open furnace door from a wheelbarrow. The man was stripped to the waist and he looked red and you could see the sweat from where we stood.

"We've got to keep moving," Angers said.

We crossed the dirt floor of the alley and moved on down past the shed where the welders were. We passed a long row of single-storied open-fronted garages, with wrecked cars standing out front. Inside were more wrecked cars and it was all brightly lit in there, with men working on them, or talking.

Yet it was quiet. We kept on moving and pretty soon we came to a lumber company.

"Let's go in here," Angers said.

We turned into a passage that led between two buildings. A truck was parked there with its lights on.

Somebody ran hard back there someplace and stopped and a flashlight cut the night and somebody shouted. We went up over a pile of lumber and Angers dropped his roll of blueprints. He looked down at them, then at me.

Then he jumped off the lumber and grabbed the blueprints. He scrambled back up. I had waited for him.

We came down off that pile, dropping into the dirt. It was darker in here. You could smell the sweet, clean, fresh, good smell of the green-cut lumber. It was all around. It seemed endless. Pile upon pile of boards and planks stretched and faded as far as you could see.

"Thing to do," Angers said, "get on through to the other side and find a car."

"Sure," I said.

"We've got to get a car. I'll have to leave this town, pal, that's all there is to it. It's a shame, because I wanted to build here."

"There's lots of nice towns."

"How far do you think this place runs? Not the lumber, pal, the whole place?"

"About a mile."

He looked at me.

"We better run for a while," he said. "Come on, pal."

We started running, jogging along down between the tiers of stacked lumber. Occasionally we'd pass a dangling light bulb, shedding its glare on the freshly cut planks.

There was an alley between the lumber and down there was a door, with a red light by it. It led outside, and you could see the sky again.

Angers sat on a small pile of boards, leaned the roll of blueprints against his leg, and looked at me. His eyes were bloodshot and glassy. They weren't seeing anything, only the things inside his head. He might talk with you and agree with you on things, or disagree, even carry on a conversation, but he was only seeing what was in his head. I knew nothing really affected him then, and I knew how lonely it was.

And I saw how he hadn't ever talked much, too. It had only been about one thing. The hospital.

It was all very well, feeling sad and all that. But the way he looked at me now, I wanted to run—run like hell.

He sat there with the gun resting on his knee. He stared at the gun for a while and the only sound was our breathing.

Then they came at us from both directions. I saw their uniforms and they were running at us, down the tiers of lumber.

"Come on, pal," Angers said. "We've got to push."

I was ahead of him, making for the door with the red light by it. We went out into the night, running, and found we were in the shed with the welders. There was a cement floor and every step rang out like a drumbeat.

"Keep straight through," he said.

There were only three men in the building. They stood watching us. One of the guys in a diving suit with a torch in his hand yelled something, but I couldn't make it out.

We went right on across that endless cement floor.

Behind us there was a shot and the slug slammed into sheet steel and glanced off and clanged against another sheet of steel.

Angers stopped and turned. A cop was running across the cement floor at us and Angers lifted the gun and fired and the cop dropped. He was some shot. The other three men in the building dropped and another gun banged by the door from where the lumber was.

We turned and ran.

We went on down an alley and past some lighted store fronts advertising auto parts, used, and down another alley.

Then we were running on soft earth by pine trees, and to our left were the railroad tracks. They were about a block wide, with switches lit up green and red and freight cars parked on the tracks in places.

The road we were on had just been cut from woods; the tree stumps still stood in some places.

I heard a car and looked behind us and a spotlight began probing around back there. It was a cruiser, running right up the road behind us.

Angers looked back and fired three times, then turned and ran. I was a little behind him now. He could sure run. He turned, looked back at me, his face all white in the dark. His face looked slick.

"Come on, Steve! We've got to run!"

"Sure." I came up to him and we slogged along. Up ahead there was a street. There was a hump in the road where it crossed the railroad tracks. I saw a car coming along the street.

Angers ran over onto the tracks, kind of looking at the car, and then there were two cars.

"Steve, we'll run over there to the other side," he called back. "Hurry up, Steve—pal!"

He kept calling to me, but I couldn't run any faster. Up ahead, the railroad tracks vanished into darkness between some big warehouses that sat right up against the road.

"There they come!" he shouted.

He was almost to the street and two of the cars were coming along toward the tracks. They were police cars, all right. You could tell from the spotlights on the roofs. But they hadn't seen him, or they'd have used the lights.

The other car that had been behind us was still coming along, and it hadn't seen us, either. The spotlight was turned off now.

I crossed on the tracks, running toward Angers. I was dazed. I didn't know why I was running. I was tired, and as I ran I kept staggering.

I quit running. I just stood there watching. I could feel everything go up tight inside me and stay that way, like steel and iron and wire, and then it began coming loose, a strand at a time.

Angers was at the crossing. Then the lights by the crossing began blinking red. You could hear it coming, like a big wind blasting someplace, only you didn't know where it was coming from.

"Steve," he called. "Hurry up, pal!"

I ran stumbling along the tracks toward him. I crossed over onto the other side when I reached the street and he turned to look at me. I couldn't speak. I wanted to but I couldn't do it, not for anything.

Then they put the spotlights on him and he just stood there with the roll of paper in one hand and the gun in the other. He looked straight into the spotlights and shot that crazy wild bursting laughter at them. He set his head back and shot that laughter into the sky. It was all bright there with him standing in the middle with the spotlights on him, like that, laughing. Laughing like all hell, he was.

The warning lights kept flashing.

And you heard it coming. I wanted to run out there and grab him, push him—something, anything. But I couldn't. I couldn't move. I couldn't even speak. And he turned with the spotlights on him all the time and looked at me with his face all shiny with sweat, then he looked back at the cars and laughed again.

"Come on, pal," he said. He said it flat and even, just like always.

They began shooting at him. He shot back, facing those spotlights, not even crouched down. He just stood straight and fired at them.

Well, they missed and I took a step onto the tracks. I guess they were out of the cars along the side of the road. Then I jumped back off the tracks and she burst out from between the warehouses like a one-eyed monster.

The train crashed straight out toward us with the big train spotlight weaving back and forth and the horn blatted so loud I couldn't hear.

It rushed right on by and he was gone.

I stood there and waited while the rest of the train went by, with the brakes squealing, steel on steel, and finally it was all past and slowing up there in the yards.

He was there, all right. The roll of blueprints was all cut on the tracks and I took one look at him and turned away.

He was still holding the Luger.

They called my name out there.

"Logan?"

I just waited. I stood there by what was left of Ralph Angers. Then they came up onto the tracks and stood with me in the bright white glare of their spotlights. One of them reached down and picked up the Luger. He stood there looking at it and said, "Just think."

At the police station, they talked with me for a while, and I told them what I knew. As I talked with them I was still out there at that railroad crossing in my mind's eye. It was something I would never be able to forget. They were probably picking up what was left of him out there now.

He'd been exactly what he claimed. Reports from Dr. Bernstein at the hospital in Seattle had come in, and Ralph Angers was a top surgeon, all right. He had a breakdown in Korea because he'd worked too hard, and the same thing had happened weeks before in Seattle. There had been a hospital fund, too, and Bernstein was coming here from Seattle to pick up the body because Angers had no family. Everything Ralph Angers told me had been the truth. All except the building of the hospital. He'd stolen the blueprints, met Lillian someplace, and then gone off on the beginning of the end.

I told the police about Harvey Aldercook and gave them what money Angers had taken from him. All but the two hundred and seventy dollars. I figured that was mine.

They got a laugh out of that.

I figured that since Angers had been right about everything else, he might just be right about my eye, too. So I planned to ask this Dr. Bernstein what he thought, when he showed up the next day.

Lillian was at the station, and when they released me, they let her go, too. We walked over to the hospital together. I was scared, let me tell you. I didn't know whether I even wanted to go to the hospital. So much had happened that I was sick.

"Don't worry," Lillian said. And we walked along and she said, "I'll be leaving tomorrow, Steve. I'm going home."

I told her that was good and we walked along and there wasn't anything to say. Finally we shook hands in front of the hospital and I gave her fifty dollars and she kissed me and went away.

At the desk I asked one of the Gray Ladies what room Ruby Logan was in. She told me, and then I asked her about Betty Graham and she said Mrs. Graham was getting along just fine.

Well, I felt a little better.

Ruby was in a white bed and she looked up at me and she kept spinning and smiling and spinning through all the tears in my eyes.

"We'll call him Steve, like you," she said. He was some boy, all right. She had him there in bed with her.

"Like hell," I said. "I won't stand for any Juniors in this family."

"Yes, we will, hon. I like that name."

And she kept on spinning through the tears and then the nurse came in and took young Steve away. I didn't care, right then.

"Gosh, hon, I was scared," she said. "I was awful sick and you didn't come for so long."

"I'm here now, Ruby."

"Sure, hon."

Well, she'd had to go through a Caesarean operation and they'd had a time because she was a little anemic, or something like that. They told me that can cause trouble. Imagine, Ruby anemic!

She kept looking at me like that and I took her hand and knelt beside the bed. I didn't think about anything, kneeling there. I just held her hand. It was good, I'll tell you.

THE END

GIL BREWER BIBLIOGRAPHY
(1922-1983)

NOVELS:

Love Me and Die (1951; w/Day
  Keene, published as by Day
  Keene)
Satan is a Woman (1951)
So Rich, So Dead (1951)
13 French Street (1951)
Flight to Darkness (1952)
Hell's Our Destination (1953)
A Killer is Loose (1954)
Some Must Die (1954)
77 Rue Paradis (1954)
The Squeeze (1955)
The Red Scarf (1955)
—And the Girl Screamed (1956)
The Angry Dream (1957;
  reprinted as The Girl from
  Hateville, 1958)
The Brat (1957)
Little Tramp (1958)
The Bitch (1958)
Wild (1958)
The Vengeful Virgin (1958)
Sugar (1959)
Wild to Possess (1959)
Angel (1960)
Nude on Thin Ice (1960)
Backwoods Teaser (1960)
The Three-Way Split (1960)
Play it Hard (1960)
Appointment in Hell (1961)
A Taste for Sin (1961)
Memory of Passion (1962)
The Hungry One (1966)
The Tease (1967)
Sin for Me (1967)
It Takes a Thief #1: The Devil in
  Davos (1969)

It Takes a Thief #2:
  Mediterranean Caper (1969)
It Takes a Thief #3: Appointment
  in Cairo (1970)
A Devil for O'Shaugnessy (2008)
Redheads Die Quickly (2012;
  stories)
The Erotics (2015)
Gun the Dame Down (2015)
Angry Arnold (2015)

As Harry Arvay
Eleven Bullets for Mohammed
  (1975)
Operation Kuwait (1975)
The Moscow Intercept (1975)
The Piraeus Plot (1975)
Togo Commando (1976)

As Mark Bailey
Mouth Magic (1972)

As Al Conroy
Soldato #3: Strangle Hold! (1973)
Soldato #4: Murder Mission!
  (1973)

As Hal Ellson
Blood on the Ivy (1970)

As Elaine Evans
Shadowland (1970)
A Dark and Deadly Love (1972)
Black Autumn (1973)
Wintershade (1974)

As Luke Morgann
More Than a Handful (1972)
Ladies in Heat (1972)

Gamecock (1972)
Tongue Tricks! (1972)

As Ellery Queen
The Campus Murders (1969)
The Japanese Golden Dozen
  (1978; rewrites by Brewer)

UNPUBLISHED NOVELS:

House of the Potato
  (autobiographical novel, late
  1940s)
Firebase Seattle (Executioner
  novel, 1975)
The Paper Coffin (spy novel,
  1970s)

STORIES:

With This Gun— (*Detective Tales*,
  Mar 1951)
It's Always Too Late (*Detective
  Fiction*, Apr 1951)
Final Appearance (*Detective Tales*,
  Oct 1951; *Invincible Detective
  Magazine*, Feb 1952)
Moonshine (*Manhunt*, Mar 1955;
  Giant Manhunt #6, #7, 1955)
I Saw Her Die (*Manhunt*, Oct
  1955; *Giant Manhunt* #8, 195?)
Teen-Age Casanova (*Justice*, Oct
  1955)
Red Scarf (*Mercury Mystery
  Book-Magazine*, Nov 1955)
Die, Darling, Die (*Justice*, Jan
  1956)
They'll Find Us (*Accused
  Detective Story Magazine*, Jan
  1956)

Fog (*Manhunt*, Feb 1956)
The Gesture (*The Saint Detective
  Magazine*, Mar 1956)
Home (*Accused Detective Story
  Magazine*, Mar 1956)
Come Across (*Manhunt*, Apr
  1956; *Giant Manhunt* #8, 195?)
Goodbye, Jeannie (*Accused
  Detective Story Magazine*, May
  1956)
Matinee (*Manhunt*, Oct 1956;
  Giant Manhunt #9, 195?)
The Tormentors (*Manhunt*, Nov
  1956; *Giant Manhunt* #10,
  1957)
The Axe Is Ready (*Trapped
  Detective Story Magazine*, Dec
  1956)
Renegade (*Blazing Guns Western
  Story Magazine*, Dec 1956)
On a Sunday Afternoon
  (*Manhunt*, Jan 1957; *Giant
  Manhunt* #10, 1957)
Kill Crazy (*Posse*, Apr 1957)
Prowler! (*Manhunt*, May 1957;
  Giant Manhunt #11, 1957)
Stop Off (*Man's Life*, May 1957)
I'll Be in the Bedroom (*Trapped
  Detective Story Magazine*, June
  1957)
Bothered (*Manhunt*, July 1957;
  Giant Manhunt #11, 1957)
Old Timers (*Murder*, July 1957)
That Damned Piper (*Pursued*, July
  1957)
The Glass Eye (*Guilty Detective
  Story Magazine*, Sept 1957)
The Price of Pride (*Triple Western
  Sum*, 1957)
Meet Me in the Dark (*Manhunt*,
  Feb 1958; *Giant Manhunt* #12,
  #13, 1958)

Death of a Prowler (*Trapped Detective Story Magazine*, Apr 1958)

Getaway Money (*Guilty Detective Story Magazine*, Nov 1958)

Redheads Die Quickly (*Mystery Tales*, Apr 1959)

This Petty Pace (*Mystery Tales*, June 1959)

Harlot House (*Mystery Tales*, Aug 1959)

Cop (*Mike Shayne Mystery Magazine*, July 1965)

Goodbye, Now (*Alfred Hitchcock's Mystery Magazine*, July 1968)

Sympathy (*Mike Shayne Mystery Magazine*, June 1969)

The Mountain Kid (*Zane Grey Western Magazine*, Oct 1969)

Swing with Me (*Caper*, Oct 1969)

Trick (*Alfred Hitchcock's Mystery Magazine*, Nov 1969)

Pawnee (*Zane Grey Western Magazine*, Dec 1969)

Small Bite (*Alfred Hitchcock's Mystery Magazine*, Feb 1970)

Token (*Mike Shayne Mystery Magazine*, June 1972)

Peccadillo (*Mike Shayne Mystery Magazine*, May 1973)

I Apologize (*Mike Shayne Mystery Magazine*, Feb 1974)

Investment (*Mike Shayne Mystery Magazine*, Mar 1974)

Blue Moon (*Mike Shayne Mystery Magazine*, Apr 1974)

Mother (*Mike Shayne Mystery Magazine*, July 1974)

Deadly Little Green Eyes (*Mike Shayne Mystery Magazine*, Feb 1975)

Cave in the Rain (*Ed McBain's 87th Precinct Mystery Magazine*, Apr 1975)

Love-Lark (*Don Pendleton's The Executioner Mystery Magazine*, Apr 1975)

The Gentle Touch (*Don Pendleton's The Executioner Mystery Magazine*, May 1975)

A Waking Dream (*Ed McBain's 87th Precinct Mystery Magazine*, May 1975)

Live Bait (*Don Pendleton's The Executioner Mystery Magazine*, June 1975)

Upriver (*Ed McBain's 87th Precinct Mystery Magazine*, June 1975)

The Getaway (*Mystery Monthly*, June 1976)

The Thinking Child (*Mystery Monthly*, Sept 1976)

Swamp Tale (*Mystery Monthly*, Dec 1976)

Hit (*Alfred Hitchcock's Mystery Magazine*, June 1977)

Family (*Alfred Hitchcock's Mystery Magazine*, Mar 1978)

The Closed Room (*Alfred Hitchcock's Mystery Magazine*, Apr 1979)

Fool's Gold (*Alfred Hitchcock's Mortal Errors*, ed. Cathleen Jordan, 1983; *Alfred Hitchcock's Anthology #17*, 1984)

Sweet Amy (*Needle*, Fall 2011)

As Jim Beard

Brother Bill (*Don Pendleton's The Executioner Mystery Magazine*, Apr 1975)

As Clinton L. Brewer
A Good Ship Dies (*Adventure*, Dec 1959)

As Roy Carroll [house name]
Shot (*Manhunt*, Feb 1956)

As Eric Fitzgerald
The Screamer (*The Pursuit Detective Story Magazine*, Sept 1955)
Death Comes Last (*Hunted Detective Story Magazine*, Oct 1955)
Sauce for the Goose (*The Pursuit Detective Story Magazine*, Jan 1956)
The Black Suitcase (*Hunted Detective Story Magazine*, Feb 1956)
Home-Again Blues (*The Pursuit Detective Story Magazine*, Mar 1956)
Alligator (*Hunted Detective Story Magazine*, Apr 1956)
Cut Bait (*The Pursuit Detective Story Magazine*, May 1956)
Return to Yesterday (*The Pursuit Detective Story Magazine*, July 1956)

As John Harding
Spaghetti (*Don Pendleton's The Executioner Mystery Magazine*, Apr 1975)

As Bailey Morgan
Dig That Crazy Corpse (*The Pursuit Detective Story Magazine*, Mar 1955)
Sudden Justice (*Hunted Detective Story Magazine*, Apr 1955)
My Lady Is a Tramp (*The Pursuit Detective Story Magazine*, May 1955)
Gigolo (*The Pursuit Detective Story Magazine*, July 1955)
Death in Bloom (*The Pursuit Detective Story Magazine*, Sept 1955)
Hammer (*Hunted Detective Story Magazine*, Oct 1955)
Speak No Evil (*The Pursuit Detective Story Magazine*, Nov 1955)
Don't Do That (*Hunted Detective Story Magazine*, Dec 1955)
Wife Sitter (*The Pursuit Detective Story Magazine*, July 1956)
Cold Rain (*The Pursuit Detective Story Magazine*, Sept 1956)
Whiskey (*The Pursuit Detective Story Magazine*, Nov 1956)

From the Master of Obsessive Noir....

Gil Brewer

Wild to Possess / A Taste for Sin
1-933586-10-9 $19.95
"Permeated with sweaty
desperation."
—James Reasoner, *Rough Edges*

A Devil for O'Shaugnessy /
The Three-Way Split
1-933586-20-6 $14.95
"Brewer's insights into the
psychology of sexual enthrallment
and obsession still resonate."
—David Rachels, *Paul D. Brazil Blog*

Nude on Thin Ice /
Memory of Passion
1-933586-53-2 $19.95
"His entire livelihood came from
writing works in which lurid
narratives were rendered in a
punchy, unadorned prose style."
— Chris Morgan,
Los Angeles Review of Books

The Erotics / Gun the Dame
Down / Angry Arnold
1-933586-88-5 $20.95
"Showcases the impressive
storytelling talents of Gil Brewer, a
true master of the noir mystery
genre... strongly recommended."
—*Midwest Book Review*

Flight to Darkness /
77 Rue Paradis
978-1-944520-58-8 $19.95
"Murder, madness, swamps, gators,
a savagely beautiful woman... it
doesn't get much better than this
for noir fans... crazed and
breakneck."
—James Reasoner, Rough Edges

"Brewer is a skilled craftsman and he builds suspense slowly
and deliberately, leading the reader down an unavoidable
path of doom."—Ron Fortier, *Pulp Fiction Reviews*

Stark House Press, 1315 H Street, Eureka, CA 95501
707-498-3135   www.StarkHousePress.com
Retail customers: freight-free, payment accepted by check or paypal via website. Wholesale: 40%, freight-free on
10 mixed copies or more, returns accepted. All books available direct from publisher or Baker & Taylor Books.

Made in the USA
Coppell, TX
20 November 2021

66105869R00134